IF NOT NOW, WHEN?

Primo Levi

Translated
from the Italian by
William Weaver
Introduction by
Irving Howe

SUMMIT BOOKS
NEW YORK

This novel is a work of fiction. Names, characters, places and incidents are either the product of the author's imagination or are used fictitiously. Any resemblance to actual events or locales or persons, living or dead, is entirely coincidental.

ORIGINALLY PUBLISHED IN ITALIAN AS *SE NON ORA, QUANDO?* BY
GIULIO EINAUDI EDITORE
COPYRIGHT © 1982 BY GIULIO EINAUDI EDITORE, S.P.A., TORINO
TRANSLATION COPYRIGHT © 1985 BY SIMON & SCHUSTER, INC.
INTRODUCTION COPYRIGHT © 1985 BY IRVING HOWE
ALL RIGHTS RESERVED
INCLUDING THE RIGHT OF REPRODUCTION
IN WHOLE OR IN PART IN ANY FORM
PUBLISHED BY SUMMIT BOOKS
A DIVISION OF SIMON & SCHUSTER, INC.
SIMON & SCHUSTER BUILDING
1230 AVENUE OF THE AMERICAS
NEW YORK, NEW YORK 10020
THE PUBLISHER GRATEFULLY ACKNOWLEDGES THE GENEROUS
SUPPORT OF THE ITALIAN CULTURAL INSTITUTE
FOR THE TRANSLATION OF THIS BOOK.
MANUFACTURED IN THE UNITED STATES OF AMERICA
1   3   5   7   9   10   8   6   4   2

LIBRARY OF CONGRESS CATALOGING IN PUBLICATION DATA

LEVI, PRIMO.
IF NOT NOW, WHEN?

TRANSLATION OF: SE NON ORA, QUANDO?
BIBLIOGRAPHY: P.
1. WORLD WAR, 1939-1945—FICTION.   2. JEWS—ITALY—
HISTORY—20TH CENTURY—FICTION.   I. TITLE.
PQ4872. E8s413   1985   853'.914   85-2526
ISBN: 0-671-49336-1

Introduction

Primo Levi: An Appreciation

THERE ARE WRITERS, a few of them, who stir an immediate personal response. You need only read a few of their pages and you know right off that an unspoken, subterranean kinship will blossom. Usually it's not the writers' opinions or subjects that really grip you, it's the tone of voice, perhaps a lilt of wry sincerity or a murmur of reflectiveness.

For me, the Italian-Jewish memoirist and novelist Primo Levi is such a writer. I stand at some distance from his culture and even more from his experience—he is a survivor of Auschwitz—yet when I read his books I feel a sense of exhilarating closeness. I want to start holding imaginary conversations, as if Primo Levi and I were friends who have known each other for years.

In his native Italy Primo Levi has a considerable reputation, but here in America his books have still not reached a sufficiently large public. There are the familiar reasons: delays in translation, a recent shift in American taste to a narrow self-involvement that cuts out a good many foreign writers. But there's another and more complex reason. Levi is associated with Holocaust literature, and some people feel they have taken in as much of this writing as they need to or can bear. Others, more justifiably, are dismayed by the vulgarizations to which public discourse on the Holocaust has recently been subjected and therefore prefer to keep away from writings on this theme.

Real as all these barriers are, we should find ways of dismantling or evading them, for Levi is a writer of integrity, seriousness, and charm.

He is also a writer molded and marked by our century. He knows—can it really be a matter for dispute?—that he has lived through the most terrible decades in the history of mankind. Writers burdened with this awareness cannot pretend to "understand" Auschwitz and the Gulag. But they know, especially those who are survivors of the concentration camps, that they must live with an experience that has scarred them forever. Repeatedly and often compulsively, they return to their subject—even as, I feel certain, they wince at the shoddy rhetoric it evokes from publicists and politicians. The writers of whom I speak have no choice: they are captives of history, they write from their need.

So somber a fate could hardly have been anticipated for the young Primo Levi, born in 1919 to a cultivated middle-class Jewish family in Turin. The Italian Jewish community is the oldest in Europe and has behind it notable religious and literary traditions. By the time, however, that Levi entered adolescence, the Jews were being increasingly assimilated into Italian society, often into the professional and intellectual classes. Some Italian Jews kept a fragile tie to their past, a filament of memory with Jewish traditions and learning, if not with Judaism as a religion. At least some Jewish families held on to fragments of the Hebrew language and its linked rituals and customs. At the age of thirteen Primo Levi went through the bar mitzvah ceremony, but this didn't really signify a strong attachment to Jewishness. Thinking back in later years to the time of his youth, he would speak of being Jewish as "a cheerful little anomaly" occasionally disturbing his relations with gentile friends. In those years Italy seemed free of the racial anti-Semitism that was poisoning European society.

The young Levi studied to be a chemist. But for a "sudden" blow—which now, with the easy wisdom of retrospect, we can see was not so "sudden"—he might have continued along the conventional path of professional life. In the late 1930s Mussolini, in his nasty clownish style, began to imitate the anti-Semitic brutalities of his partner Hitler. Quite unprepared by his family or milieu for the kind of persecutions that Jews over the centuries had come to take for granted, the young Levi found himself "cut" by haughty or shamefaced professors. Only one teacher of low rank took him on as a doctoral student, with the curt, memorable sentence: "Follow me." In 1941 Levi received his doctorate, but because of the racial laws could not find work as a chemist. He took odd jobs in a varnish factory, a nickel mine.*

Levi soon drifted over to Milan, the intellectual capital of Italy, and only there did he begin to acquire a bit of political awareness. He learned about isolated clusters of Italian anti-Fascists who had not "bent their backs." He heard stories about such intrepid (and, it's worth noting, Jewish) libertarians as the Rosselli brothers, murdered by Mussolini's thugs, and Carlo Levi, sentenced to internal exile. The bulk of the Italian Jewish community had kept a wary distance from politics, with a small minority

---

*I draw these facts, necessary for understanding Levi's career as a writer, from his memoir, "Beyond Survival," translated into English in *Prooftexts* No. 4, 1984, and from a lovely little book by the historian H. Stuart Hughes, *Prisoners of Hope*, in which he discusses twentieth-century Italian Jewish writers.

attaching itself opportunistically to the Fascists and another small minority joining the opposition, much of it scattered in exile. But now, during the war years, a new and substantial resistance movement came into being and "Jewish participation," writes Levi, "was actually fairly considerable."

In September 1943 he joined a unit of partisans in the hills of Piedmont. Inexperienced, the group soon suffered betrayal by an informer. Levi was arrested in December. At the Fascist interrogation, he admitted to being a Jew, "partly out of fatigue, but partly out of a sudden surge . . . of haughty pride." In February 1944 the Italian Fascists handed him over to the German Nazis for deportation to Auschwitz:

> The railroad convoy that took us to the Lager contained 650 persons; of these 525 were immediately put to death; 29 women were interned at Birkenau; 96 men, myself among them, were sent to Monowitz-Auschwitz, a *Nebenlager* belonging to IG Farbenindustrie. Of these only about twenty of the men and women returned to their homes. I survived imprisonment by a fortunate chain of circumstances; by never falling ill; by the help of an Italian brick-layer [who brought Levi food]; by being able to work two months as a chemist in an IG Farbenindustrie laboratory. I was liberated thanks to the rapid advance of the Red Army in January 1945.

It was during his months in Auschwitz that Levi's mature consciousness was formed, that humane sensibility, at once modest and resolute, one encounters in his books. Auschwitz would be "the fundamental experience of my life . . . I knew that if I survived, I would have to tell the story." Many survivors have also wanted "to tell the story," and some of them suffered even more than Levi did, but very few would be able to write with the reflective depth that he has.

One reason is that in the hell of Auschwitz he formed friendships with prisoners, east European Jews, who passed on to him bits of knowledge about Yiddish culture—its spiritual and moral resources—which helped Levi to gain new personal strength. Some of these Jews from Poland and Russia were humane even in this most inhumane of places, some were twisted psychically and morally by their ordeals. But all had stories to tell. All opened up to Levi the values of a Jewishness he had never before encountered. Auschwitz became for him "a brutal confirmation of my condition as a Jew: a condemnation, a relapse, a reliving of Biblical stories of exile and migra-tion. It was a tragic return . . . "

After the war, back in Italy, he heard from a friend re-ports about a Yiddish-speaking partisan unit that had survived the fighting in eastern Europe and somehow had ended up in Milan. This story, together with the stories he had heard in Auschwitz, seems to have lodged itself deeply in his mind, though it was not until many years later, after publishing several other books, that he would come back to the Yiddish partisans. In 1982 he published a novel based on their experiences, with the title *If Not Now, When?**—the book, in English translation, that you now hold in your hands. A great success in Italy, *If Not Now, When?* should be read, first of all as a tribute to those east European Jews who tried to offer some resistance to the Nazis. It is a gesture of solidarity and, in a quiet way, identification.

The immediate occasion for this novel, Levi has writ-ten, was a noisy controversy—and probably a fruitless one too—that has been raging for several decades about the behavior of the Jews during the Holocaust:

Did [the Jews] really allow themselves to be led to the slaugh-ter without resistance? . . . In my opinion, this discussion is unhistorical and polluted by prejudices. As a former partisan and deportee, I know very well that there are some political and psychological conditions in which resistance is possible,

---

*Levi's title is taken from a famous passage of Rabbi Hillel: "If I am not for myself, who will be for me? If I am for myself alone, what am I? If not now, when?" (*Sayings of the Fathers*)

and others in which it is not. It was not my intention to enter the controversy. But it seemed to me to carry a sufficient narrative charge so that I could draw [from it] a story worthy of being read ... Beyond that I wanted to do homage to those Jews, whether few or many, who in the unequal struggle had found their dignity and freedom anew.

Once liberated from Auschwitz in early 1945, Levi still could not return to his home. Because of bureaucratic confusion, he had to spend eight months in a bizarre journey through Poland and Russia before finally arriving in Turin. This journey would also become part of his "fundamental experience," indeed, the matter of what is probably his best book.

Back home, Levi began to make notes, and then a coherent account out of his notes, about the Auschwitz experience. He knew, or in the course of writing learned, that with materials so dreadful in nature, so without historical precedent and therefore so resistant to conceptual grasp, the writer needs most of all to keep a strict discipline of exactitude in recall and description. It is *his* recollection, and he must be there, in the remembrance, as the one who saw and suffered; but precisely the terribleness of his story requires an austere self-effacement as well. How difficult and at times impossible this discipline can be, anyone who has read Holocaust memoirs and fictions can testify. It requires an emotional restraint and a steadiness of creative purpose that can seem almost indecent to demand from survivors. Yet if such memoirs are to constitute more than a howl of rage or pain, there is no other way to write them.

Speaking about Levi's first book, the recollection of Auschwitz entitled *If This Is a Man* (1947), H. Stuart Hughes finds its point of distinction in Levi's "equanimity, punctuated by an occasional note of quiet humor." That is right, but I would also speak about a quality in Levi's work that might be called moral poise. I mean by this an act of complete reckoning with the past, insofar as there can be a complete reckoning with such a past. I mean a strength of remembrance that leads Levi into despair and then at least partly beyond it, so that he does not flinch from anything, neither shame nor degradation, that actually happened at Auschwitz, yet refuses in his writing to indulge in those outbursts of self-pity, sometimes sliding into self-aggrandizement, which understandably mar a fair number of Holocaust memoirs and fictions.

Close to the finely woven surface of *If This Is a Man* there hover all the terrible questions that the Holocaust has forced upon us, questions about the nature of man and the absence of God, or, if you prefer, the failure of man and the search for God. But Levi is sufficiently shrewd a writer to avoid a head-on collision with his theme—even when writing about the Holocaust, a writer needs a little shrewdness. Perhaps later; perhaps future generations will be able to "make sense" of it all; but not now.

For "we became aware," as Levi writes, "that our language lacks words to express this offense, the demolition of a man." Every writer of sensibility who has ventured to approach the Holocaust has been afflicted with this problem: "our language lacks words." If there is a solution it lies in the kind of muted tactfulness that Levi shows in his work. He recognizes that there are some things that can be said and some that cannot. Employing a prose of refined simplicity, he seldom presses for large "meanings" or a rhetoric of "transcendence," since he knows how treacherous these can be, how sadly they can betray the limits of our thought and imagination when we try to confront the Holocaust.

I would cite here a passage from T. S. Eliot: "Great simplicity is only won by an intense moment or by years of intelligent effort, or both. It represents one of the most arduous conquests of the human spirit: the triumph of feeling and thought over the natural sins of language."

Exactly what Eliot meant by that astounding phrase, "the natural sins of language," I cannot say with assurance, but that it applies to a fair portion of Holocaust writing, both memoir and fiction, strikes me as true. A "natural sin" of such writing can be a mistaken effort—

sincere or grandiose—to whip language into doing more
than it can possibly do, more than thought and imagination and prayer can do. Or it may signify our inclination
to grow wanton over our deepest griefs, learning comfortably to exploit them. Or, worst of all, to employ the Holocaust as "evidence" for ready-made ideological and
pietistic doctrines. To warn against "the natural sins of
language" in Holocaust writings is to say that writers
must curb, resist, even deny some part of their spontaneous outcry. Not everything that "comes out" of the heart
is true or good; it must be sifted and tempered. Our language lacks words to express this offense, "the demolition
of a man," and the words we do have—so badly abused
and degraded in public declamation—can easily betray.

One reason we are tempted to succumb to such "natural sins" is that anyone thinking or writing about the Holocaust must finally come up against a wall of blank
incomprehension: how could it be? If we fall back on intellectual shorthand, we call this the problem of radical
evil, a phrase that strongly implies the impossibility of
coping with the problem. Finally, we cannot "understand" the Holocaust, we can only live with it, in a state of
numb agitation. And it is Levi's tacit acceptance of this
view that makes him so fine a writer. A feeling of guilt, he
remarks, suffuses modern consciousness, guilt that such a
crime as the Holocaust "should have been introduced irrevocably into the world." The key word here is *irrevocably*,
with its implication that after the Holocaust human consciousness cannot quite be the same as it was before. But
exactly what this might mean, exactly how consciousness
might be transformed, it is extremely hard to say. Nor
does Levi try to. "It is foolish," he writes, "to think that
human justice can eradicate" the crimes of Auschwitz.
Foolish, also, to think that any theorizing can find a point
either of rest or satisfaction in trying to grasp it. With
some subjects writers need a pledge of stringent omission.

Toward those, however, with whom he shared suffering
and death, Levi is invariably generous. He writes not so
much to record the horrors, though there is no shortage of

them in *If This Is a Man,* but to salvage memories of human beings refusing, if only through helpless symbolic gestures, to cease being human. There is a stirring passage in *If This Is a Man:* Levi recalls a day when he and a few other prisoners were put to work scraping an underground gasoline tank. They worked in almost total darkness, and the work was very hard. Then, from some inner fold of memory, Levi began telling young French prisoners about Dante's great poem, reciting the lines

> Think of your breed; for brutish ignorance
> Your mettle was not made; you were made men
> To follow after knowledge and excellence.

Coming "like the blast of a trumpet, like the voice of God," these lines flood the hearts of the prisoners, so that "for a moment I forget who I am and where I am" and the wretched might suppose they are still human beings.

Quietly, without any overbearing pressure, Levi tells of another incident, also concerning human salvage. A week after arriving in the camp, Levi grew demoralized and began to neglect himself and his body. A prisoner named Steinlauf sternly

> administers me a complete lesson. . . . This was the sense, not forgotten then or later: that precisely because the Lager was a great machine to reduce us to beasts, we must not become beasts . . . and that to survive we must force ourselves to save at least the skeleton, the scaffolding, the form of civilization. . . .

A few weeks later Steinlauf was swept away in one of the "selections" of "the great machine." Levi clung to his words.

If one can detect traces of a "Jewish" spirit or tone in Levi's first book, then the next one, published in Italy in 1963 and as *The Reawakening* in the United States,*

---

*In England, published as *The Truce.*

seems rather more "Italian." Something of what we like to suppose as essentially Italian—a gaiety of voice, a fine free pleasure in the things of this world—breaks through in *The Reawakening,* even as its figures still bear the stigmata of the camps. The book, a memoir of Levi's wanderings through eastern Europe after being released from Auschwitz, moves with a strong, even lyrical, narrative thrust. It is filled with vibrant sketches of former prisoners and stray soldiers, mostly young, who marvel at their own survival. In their rags and amid hunger, they are overwhelmed with a guilty joy at being free to savor the commonplace sensations of existence. The book itself also radiates that guilty joy, as its narrator yields to the pleasure of being able to smile at misadventures that still carry pain but, in representing a return to the realm of the human, can be endured, even accepted.

Wandering across Poland and Russia, Levi and his companions enact a curious version of picaresque adventure. Outwardly, along the skin of narrative, *The Reawakening* appears to follow the traditional pattern of picaresque: a series of more-or-less comic episodes loosely strung together with a central narrator-observer who does not so much act on his own as "receive" the actions of others. But in basic spirit the book is antipicaresque. Between the external form of the narrative and its inner vibrations of memory there is a strong nervous tension—quite as between the first hesitant taste of freedom and the overpowering image of the camps. To sustain this tension throughout the narrative is a remarkable feat of literary craft.

Levi has a special gift for the vignette, and in this book it reaches an easy fruition. He moves from figure to figure, each of whom enacts a sort of ritual return to life by yielding to the delights of free sensation, even the sensation of that bewilderment and pain that is one's own, not imposed. For Cesare, a young roughneck from Trastevere, the plebeian neighborhood of Rome, this means using all the tricks of street huckstering that he remembers, as he now charms and swindles the residents of a ruined Polish city:

> The art of the charlatan is not so widespread as I thought: the Polish public seemed to be unaware of it, and was fascinated. Moreover, Cesare was also a first-class mimic; he waved the shirt [which he wanted to sell] in the sun, holding it tightly by the collar (under the collar there was a hole but Cesare held the shirt in his hand at the very place of the hole), and he declaimed its praises with torrential eloquence, with new and senseless additional digressions, suddenly addressing one or another member of the public with obscene nicknames which he invented on the spot. He stopped abruptly (he knew by instinct the oratorical value of pauses), kissed the shirt with affection and then began again, with a resolute yet desolate voice, as if it tore his heart to part with it, and he was only doing it for love of his neighbor: "You, Big Belly," he said, "how much will you give me for this little *koshoola* of mine?"

A darker note is struck toward the end of *The Reawakening,* as if the narrator, once separated from the companions of his journey, must again be overcome by the pain of his memories:

> I reached Turin on 19 October [1945]. . . . My house was still standing, all my family was alive, no one was expecting me. I was swollen, bearded and in rags, and had difficulty in making myself recognized. I found my friends full of life, the warmth of secure meals, the solidity of daily work . . . I found a large clean bed, which in the evening (a moment of terror) yielded softly under my weight. But only after many months did I lose the habit of walking with my glance fixed to the ground, as if searching for something to eat or to pocket hastily or to sell for bread; and a dream full of horror has still not ceased to visit me, at sometimes frequent, sometimes longer intervals.

Soon after *The Reawakening* appeared in English translation, a British critic, John Gross, wrote some thoughtful comments upon reading it:

We are all predisposed to praise books by concentration camp survivors; and indeed no record of that most terrible of experiences can be without value. Under the circumstances, it usually seems tactless to raise questions of literary merit. . . . Yet the sad fact is that the quality of the writing *does* count, however harrowing the subject, and that much of [Holocaust] literature . . . is effective only at the level of poignant documentary. To have been a witness, and a survivor, and a born writer was a rare combination.

Now, on the face of it Gross is surely right: "the quality of the writing *does* count." Yet even while nodding agreement, we are likely to notice within ourselves a decided inner resistance. Before so intolerable a subject, may not the whole apparatus of literary criticism, with all its nice discriminations and categories, seem incongruous, even trivial? A Yiddish poet, Aron Tsaitlin, wrote shortly after the Holocaust, "The Almighty Himself . . . would maintain a deep silence. For even an outcry is now a lie, even tears are mere literature, even prayers are false." In this context the phrase *mere literature* seems crushing. Yet we also know that it has proved impossible for most writers to remain silent. Nor did Tsaitlin himself, even as he excoriated his need to "cry out."

I am inclined to think that there is no easy answer, perhaps no answer at all, to this problem. The more sensitive writers on Holocaust themes have apparently felt that their subject cannot be met full face or head-on. Before the unspeakable, a muteness, a numbed refusal, comes upon one. If approached at all, the Holocaust must be taken on a tangent, with extreme wariness, through oblique symbols, strategies of indirection, and circuitous narratives. Yet the irony is this: no sooner do we speak about ways of approaching this subject than we return to a fundamental concern of literary criticism, thereby perhaps acknowledging that John Gross was right, after all, in what he wrote about Levi's work.

Several of Levi's books, including some collections of short stories, have not been translated into English, and

one can only hope they soon will be. Here I need only add
a few words about *If Not Now, When?*, a book that presents
no major impediments to a direct encounter.

If Not Now, When? is a curious work of fiction. Levi
stakes everything on his capacity to imagine experiences
that by their very nature must be alien to him. And it is
because these experiences—the ordeals of the east European Jews—are not known to him firsthand that he
chooses to take the risk of rendering them. Since he has
had "to reconstruct an era, a scenario, and a language
[Yiddish]" which he "knew only spottily" the result cannot quite have the sensuous immediacy and abundance of
many episodes in *The Reawakening*.

Yet it's in *If Not Now, When?* that certain of Levi's
strongest literary gifts reach full play. All along he had
shown a large and "natural" gift for narrative movement,
although his early books, by their very nature, could not
bring that gift to full development. But *If Not Now, When?*
speeds along with an accumulating energy, even suspense,
its treatment of the struggle undertaken by the powerless
Jewish partisans resembling somewhat an adventure
story. True, a strange kind of adventure, with pitifully few
possibilities for external action. It's rather an adventure in
which a few desperate acts and small deeds must be taken
as tokens of a large spiritual intention. What these partisans do has little military significance, it is closer to gesture than achievement; but through their raids and
escapades they are trying to establish that a pacific people
can master the use of arms without, perhaps, abandoning
its deep repugnance at having to take up arms. These ill-
trained fighters making themselves learn how to kill retain
the hope that they may avoid becoming killers.

Quite the strongest part of the novel is, I think, the one
in which two stragglers, Mendel and Leonid, stumble
upon the "republic of the marshes," an encampment of
Jews who have fled the Nazi terror of the cities and are
now huddling together in a precarious community. Levi's
evocation of life in this little oasis is simply brilliant, start-
ing with his physical description of the place and pro-

ceeding to sharply etched portrayals of the figures who have here found a moment or two of rest. This little settlement comes to seem emblematic of the Jewish situation during these years—a moment of breath before asphyxiation, a wish to hold together even though everyone knows this to be impossible. It is like the soul's last cry for air and sun.

Later, the novel changes course, and Levi presents an often fierce and exciting story of partisan activities: their relations with Russian and Polish guerrilla fighters, their occasional encounters with the Germans, and their inner crises and transformations. Reading this portion of Levi's book, I found myself responding to it less as a depiction of events supposedly happening than as an effort by this writer from Turin to thrust himself into the situation of the east European Jews, indeed, to become one with them. It's as if the novel here turned into a kind of exemplary fable, a story mediated through the desires of a writer who has yielded himself utterly to unseen brothers and sisters in martyrdom.

And I felt about Primo Levi: he is a friend, this writer who creates for us a miniature universe of moral striving and reflectiveness, filtered through ordeals of memory, reinforced by resources of imagination. I kept hearing the voice of a man struggling to retrieve the sense of what it means in the twentieth century to be, or become, a *mensh*. How would you say that in Italian?

Irving Howe

IF NOT NOW, WHEN?

1

July

1943

"In my village there weren't many clocks. One on the church steeple, but it had stopped years and years ago, maybe during the Revolution. I never saw it working, and my father said he hadn't either. Not even the bell ringer had a clock."

"So how was he able to ring the bells at the right time?"

"He would listen to the time on the radio, and he would judge by the sun and the moon. For that matter, he didn't ring every hour, only the important ones. Two years before the war began, the bell rope broke. It snapped near the top; the stairs were rotten; the bell ringer was an old man, and he was afraid to climb up there and put in a new rope. So after that he announced the time by shooting a hunting rifle into the air; one shot, or two or three or four. That went on till the Germans came. They took his gun away from him, and the village was left without any time."

"Did he shoot the gun at night, too, this bell ringer of yours?"

"No, but he hadn't rung the bells at night, either. Everybody slept at night, so there was no need to listen to the hours. The only one who really cared was the rabbi: he had to know the correct time so he could tell when the Sabbath began and ended. But he didn't need the bells: he had a grandfather clock and an alarm clock. When they agreed, he would be in a good humor. When they didn't agree, you could tell right away, because he would turn quarrelsome and hit the children's fingers with his ruler. When I was older, he called me to make the two clocks run together. Yes, I was a watchmender, with a certificate and all. That's why the recruiting office people put me in the artillery. I had just the right chest measurement, not an extra centimeter. At home, I had my workshop: small, but fully equipped. I didn't mend just clocks and watches; I was good at fixing almost anything, even radios and tractors, provided nothing too serious was wrong with them. I was the kolkhoz mechanic, and I liked my job. I would fix clocks privately, in my spare time. There weren't very many; but everybody had a shotgun, and I could fix guns, too. If you want to know the name of the village, the name is Strelka, like God knows how many other villages. Was Strelka, I should say, because that one doesn't exist any more. Half the villagers are scattered through the countryside and the forest, and the other half are in a pit, and they're not crowded, because a lot of villagers had already died before. In a pit, yes; and they had to dig it themselves, the Jews of Strelka. But there are Christians in the pit as well, and now there isn't much difference between the two any more. And I must tell you that the man here speaking to you, me, Mendel the watchmender, who repaired the kolkhoz tractors, had a wife and she's in the pit, too; and I consider myself lucky that we didn't have any children. I must tell you also that, time and again, I used to curse the village that's gone now, because it was a village of ducks and goats, and there was the church and the synagogue, but there was no movie theater; and when I think of it now it seems like the garden of Eden, and I'd cut off a hand if that would make time run backwards and everything could be the way it was before."

Leonid listened, not daring to interrupt. He had taken off his boots and unwound the rags from his feet, and had put boots and rags in the sun to dry. He rolled two cigarettes, one for himself and one for Mendel, then he dug the matches from his pocket, but they were damp, and he had to strike three before the fourth one caught. Mendel observed him calmly: he was of medium height, his limbs more wiry than sturdy; he had straight black hair, a tanned oval face, not unpleasant though smudged with beard, a short, straight nose, and a pair of intense dark eyes, slightly protruding, from which Mendel could not remove his gaze. Uneasy, staring, then shifting, those eyes were filled with demand. A creditor's eyes, Mendel thought, or the eyes of a man who feels he's owed something. But who doesn't feel owed something?

Mendel asked him, "What made you stop here, specifically?"

"Just chance. I saw a barn. And then because of your face."

"What makes my face any different from others?"

"That's it: there's nothing different about it." The boy ventured an embarrassed laugh. "It's a face like lots of others; it inspires trust. You're not a Muscovite, but if you were to walk around Moscow, foreigners would stop you and ask directions."

"And they'd be making a big mistake. If I were all that good at finding my way, I wouldn't have stayed here. Mind you, I can't offer you much, for your belly or for your morale. My name's Mendel, and Mendel is short for Menachem, which means 'consoler,' but I've never consoled anybody."

They smoked for a few minutes in silence. Mendel had taken a knife from his pocket, picked up a bowl from the ground. He spat on it at intervals, and sharpened the blade against it. From time to time he checked the edge, testing it with his thumbnail. When he was satisfied, he began to cut his other nails, handling the knife as if it were a saw. When he had pared all ten, Leonid offered him another cigarette. Mendel refused.

"No, thanks. I shouldn't smoke, really; but when I find tobacco, I smoke. What can a man do, when he's forced to live like a wolf?"

"Why shouldn't you smoke?"

"Because of my lungs. Or my bronchia, I can't say. As if smoking or not smoking mattered any when the whole world is collapsing around you. Sure, give me that cigarette. I've been here since autumn, and this is maybe the third time I've had anything to smoke. There's a village, four kilometers from here; it's called Valuets. It's surrounded by woods, and the peasants are good people; but they don't have any tobacco, and not even any salt. For a hundred grams of salt, they'll give you a dozen eggs, or a whole chicken."

Leonid was silent for a few moments, as if making up his mind, then he stood up and, barefoot as he was, went into the barn, came out with his knapsack and started rummaging inside it. "Here," he then said curtly, showing Mendel two packets of coarse salt. "Twenty chickens, if you're right about the price."

Mendel held out his hand, grabbed the packets, and weighed them on his palm, with an approving look. "Where does this come from?"

"From far away. When it was summer, and the army-issue bellyband was no use to me any more—that's where this comes from. Trade never dies, not even where grass and human beings die. There are places where they have salt, others where they have tobacco, and others where they don't have anything. I come from far away, too. For six months I've been living from day to day, and walking without knowing where I want to go; I walk to keep walking. I walk because I'm walking."

"So you come from Moscow?" Mendel asked.

"I come from Moscow and a hundred other places. I come from a school, where I learned to be a bookkeeper, and then promptly forgot it all. I come from the Lubyanka, because when I was sixteen I stole, and they locked me up for eight months. It was a watch I stole, so you see we're practically colleagues. I come from Vladimir, from the paratroop school, because when you're a bookkeeper they send you to be a paratrooper. I come from Laptevo, near Smolensk, where they parachuted me into the midst of the Germans. And I come from the *Lager* of Smolensk, because I escaped. I escaped in January, and since then I've done nothing but walk. Forgive me, colleague, but I'm tired, my feet hurt, I'm hot, and I'd like to sleep. But first I'd like to know where we are."

"I told you: we're near Valuets: it's a village three days' walk from Bryansk. A quiet place. The railroad's thirty kilometers away, the woods are thick, and the roads are full of mud, or dust, or snow, according to the season. The Germans don't like places like this; they only turn up to confiscate the livestock, and not all that often. Come, we'll go bathe."

Leonid stood up and started to put his boots back on, but Mendel stopped him. "No, not at the river. You have to be careful; and for that matter, it's far off. Here, behind the barn." He showed Leonid the little installation: a plank booth, a corrugated metal tank on the roof, where the water warmed in the sun, a little stove for the winter, made of fire-hardened clay. There was even a showerhead, which Mendel had made by jabbing holes in a tomato can, connecting it then with the tank by a length of metal pipe. "All made with my own hands. Didn't cost a ruble, and with no help from anybody."

"Do the people in the village know you're here?"

"They know, and they don't know. I go to the village as little as possible, and each time I arrive there from a different direction. I fix their machines, keep my mouth shut, accept payment in bread and eggs, and I leave. I leave at night; I don't think anyone's ever followed me. Go ahead, strip. I don't have any soap, not at present anyway: you have to make do with ashes. In that jar there, mixed with sand from the river. It's better than nothing, and they say it kills lice better than the medicated soap they give you in the army. By the way—"

"No, I don't have any. Don't worry. For months now I've been traveling alone."

"Go ahead and undress and give me your shirt. No need to take offense. You may well have slept in some haystack or barn, and they're a patient race: they know how to wait. Like us, in other words, making all proper distinction between man and louse."

Mendel examined the shirt with an expert eye , seam by seam. "Yes, it's kosher: no two ways about that. I would have welcomed you all the same; but without lice, I welcome you more gladly. You take the first shower. I had one this morning already."

He took a closer look at his guest's thin body. "How come you're not circumcised?"

Leonid avoided the question: "And how did you catch on that I'm a Jew, too?"

"A dozen rivers can't wash away the Yiddish accent," Mendel said, quoting. "In any case: welcome. Because I'm tired of being alone. Stay on, if you like: even if you are a Muscovite and are educated and have run off from God knows where and once stole a watch and don't want to tell me your story. You're my guest. It's lucky you found me. I should have made four doors for my house, too: one for each wall, the way Abraham did."

"Why four doors?"

"So wayfarers wouldn't have trouble finding the entrance."

"Where did you learn these stories?"

"That's in the Talmud or somewhere in the Midrashim."

"So you're educated, too! You see?"

"When I was little, I studied with that rabbi I mentioned. But now he's in the pit, too, and I've forgotten almost everything. I remember only the proverbs and the fairy tales."

Leonid was silent a moment, then said: "I didn't say I don't want to tell you my story. I only said I'm tired and sleepy." He yawned and went towards the shower stall.

At four in the morning it was already day, but the two men didn't wake for another two or three hours. During the night the sky had clouded over, and it was drizzling; from the west came long gusts of wind, like waves of the sea, heralded from the distance by the rustle of leaves and the creak of boughs. The men rose fresh and rested. Mendel didn't have much left to hide:

"Sure, I'm missing, too, a straggler, but not a deserter. Missing since July of 'forty-two. One of the hundred thousand, two hundred thousand missing. Is there anything to be ashamed of, in being missing? And can the missing perhaps be counted? If they could, they wouldn't be missing. You count the living and the dead: the missing are neither alive nor dead, and they can't be counted. They're like ghosts.

"I don't know if they teach you paratroopers how to jump. Us, they taught everything: all the big guns and all the little guns of the Red Army, first with drawings and photographs, and it was like being back in school, and then from life: some of those monsters were really scary. Well, when they sent me to the front with my company, everything was different, and you couldn't understand any of it. No two pieces were the same. There were some Russian pieces from the First World War, some German and Austrian ones, even some that came from Turkey; and you can imagine the confusion they all caused when it came to ammunition. It was exactly a year ago: my gun was set up in the hills, halfway between Kursk and Kharkov. I was the crew chief, even if I was a Jew and a watchmender; and the piece didn't come from the First World War, but the second; and it wasn't Russian, but German.

Yes, it was a Nazi one-fifty-twenty-seven that had been left behind there, God knows why, maybe because it had broken down, since October of 'forty-one, when the Germans made their big advance. A thing like that, you know, once it's in place, it's hard to move. They assigned me to it at the last moment, when the ground had already started shaking, on all sides, and the smoke hid the sun, and it took courage not only to shoot straight but just to stay there. And how can you shoot straight if nobody gives you the firing data, and you can't ask anybody because the telephone's out, and anyway who would you ask, since everything's chaos again, and the sky is so black you can't tell if it's day or night anymore, and the earth is blowing up all around, and you feel like a landslide's about to bury you, but nobody tells you where it'll come from, and then you don't even know what direction to run off in?

"The three crew members ran off, and maybe they were right, I couldn't say, because that was the last I saw of them. Not me. Not that I wanted to be taken prisoner, but our rule is that an artilleryman mustn't leave his piece to the enemy. So instead of running away, I stayed in my position, trying to figure out the best way to sabotage that piece. Of course, wrecking a thing is easier than mending it, but to wreck a cannon so it can never be fixed again takes intelligence because each piece has its weak point. In other words, the idea of running away didn't appeal to me. Not that I'm a hero, it never crossed my mind to be a hero, but you know how it is: a Jew in the midst of the Russians has to be twice as brave as they are, otherwise they immediately say he's a coward. And I was thinking that if I didn't manage to sabotage the piece the Germans would turn it around again and fire on us with it.

"Luckily they settled the question themselves. While I was fiddling with it, my head full of sabotage and my legs eager to carry me away, a German grenade landed, stuck in the soft earth just under the mount, and exploded. The piece gave a jump, then fell on its side, and I don't think anybody will ever set it upright again. I also think that it was the piece that actually saved my skin, because it shielded me from all the grenade fragments. Just one, I don't know how, grazed me here—you see?—on the forehead and scalp. The wound bled a lot, but I didn't faint, and afterwards it healed on its own.

"Then I started walking—"

"In what direction?" Leonid interrupted.

Irritated, Mendel replied: "What do you mean, what direction? I tried to catch up with our men. And you're not a court-martial, you know. I told you: the sky was all black with smoke, and there was no way of getting your bearings. And war, most of all, is a big confusion, on the field and in people's heads: half the time you can't even figure out who's won and who's lost. The generals decide that afterwards, and the people who write history books. That's how it was, all confused, and I was confused, too; the shelling continued, night came. I was half deaf and covered with blood, and I thought my wound was more serious than it really was.

"I started walking, and I thought I was going in the right direction, namely away from the front and towards our rear lines. In fact, as I walked on, the racket gradually lessened. I walked all night. At first I saw other soldiers walking, then nobody. Every now and then I would hear the whistle of a grenade coming, and I would flatten on the ground, in a furrow, behind a rock. At the front you learn fast, you spot a furrow where a civilian would see only a field flat as a frozen lake. The sun was beginning to rise, and I heard a new sound growing, and the earth began to shake again. I couldn't figure out what it was: it was a vibration, a steady rumble. I looked around for a place to hide, but there were only mown fields or untilled land, without a hedge, without a wall. And instead of shelter I saw a thing I had never seen, though I'd been in the war for a year. Parallel to where I was walking there was a railroad—I hadn't noticed it before—and on the track, what seemed at first a line of barges was moving along, like on rivers. Then I realized I had taken the wrong direction; I was on the German side, and that was a German armored train. It was heading for the front, and instead of a line of cars, it looked to me like a line of mountains; and this will seem strange to you, or stupid, or even a blasphemy, because I don't know how you feel about these things, but I was reminded of the blessing my grandfather used to say when he heard thunder, 'thy strength and thy might fill the world.' Eh, these things are beyond understanding: because the Germans made that armored train, but God made the Germans: and why did he make them? Or why did he allow Satan to make them? For our sins? And what if a man doesn't have any sins? Or a woman? And what sins did my wife have? Or must a woman like my wife die perhaps and lie in a pit with a hundred other women, and with children, for the sins of somebody else, maybe for the sins of the very same Germans who machine-gunned them at the edge of the pit?

"I'm sorry. I got carried away. But, you see, it's almost a year that I've been brooding on these things, and I can't make sense of them. It's almost a year since I spoke with a human being, because it's best for a straggler not to talk: he can talk only with another straggler."

It had stopped drizzling, and a faint aroma of mushrooms and moss rose from the unsown earth. The music of peace could be heard in the raindrops falling from leaf to leaf and from the leaves to the ground, as if there were no war, as if the war had never been. All of a sudden, over the music of the raindrops, a different sound was heard: a human voice, a sweet, childish voice, the voice of a little girl singing. They hid behind a bush, and saw her: she was lazily driving a little herd of goats ahead of her, she was thin and barefoot, bundled in an army tunic that came down to her knees. She had a kerchief tied under her chin, and her little face was wan and fine, tanned by the sun. She sang sadly, in the artificial, nasal tone peasants have, and she was coming idly towards them, not guiding her goats, but following them.

The two soldiers exchanged a look: there was no choice, they couldn't leave their hiding place without the girl's seeing them; and she would see them anyway, because she was coming straight towards them. Mendel stood up and Leonid imitated him; the girl stopped short, more dumb-founded than frightened, then she started running, passed her goats, collected them, and pushed them back towards the village. She hadn't said a word.

Mendel was silent for an instant or two. "That's it. No choice. That's what living like wolves means. Too bad it had to happen when you've just come. But it's worse now, because there are two of us. For months it didn't happen. Then comes a little girl, and that's that. Maybe she was frightened, seeing us, though we're no danger for her. But she's a danger for us, because she's a child and she'll talk. And if we threatened her and told her to keep quiet, she'd talk all the more. She'll talk and say she saw us, and the Germans of the garrison will come looking for us: in an hour, or a day, or in ten days. But they'll come. And if the Germans don't come, or before the Germans come, the peasants will come, or bandits. Too bad, colleague. You arrived at the wrong moment. Here, lend me a hand. We're moving. I'm sorry about leaving everything I fixed here. It's all to do over again, from the beginning. Thank God it's summer."

It wasn't a great move; all of Mendel's belongings, including his food supplies, could fit nicely into his army knapsack. But when the baggage was ready, Leonid realized that Mendel was hesitating before setting out. He seemed to dawdle, as if torn between two choices.

"What's wrong? Have you forgotten something?"

Mendel didn't answer: he had sat down on a log and was scratching his head. Then he stood up, decisively, slipped his short entrenching tool from his pack, and said to Leonid: "Come with me. No, we'll leave the packs here; they're heavy. We'll collect them afterwards."

They went into the woods, first along a well-marked path, then into the thickets. Mendel seemed to get his bearings from signs known only to him, and he spoke as he walked, without turning around, without making sure whether or not Leonid was following him or listening to him.

"You see, having no choice is an advantage. I have no choice: I have to trust you. And anyway I'm fed up with living alone. I've told you my story, and you don't want to tell me yours. No matter, you must have your own good reasons. You escaped from a *Lager:* I can understand why you don't feel like talking. For the Germans you're an escaped prisoner, in addition to being a Russian and a Jew. For the Russians you're a deserter, and you're also suspect, you could be a spy. Maybe you are. You don't have a spy's face, but if all spies did, they wouldn't be able to be spies any more. I don't have any choice. I have to trust you, so I must tell you: over there you see a big oak tree, the farthest one, and beside the oak there's a birch that's been hollowed out by lightning, and among the roots of the birch there's a submachine gun and a pistol. It's no miracle: I put them there myself. A soldier who lets himself be disarmed is a coward, but a soldier who carries arms on him behind the German lines is a fool. Here we are: you dig, you're younger. And excuse me for saying 'coward,' it wasn't intended for you: I understand, all right, what it means to land with a parachute behind the enemy lines."

Leonid dug in silence for a few minutes and the weapons emerged, wrapped in some oil-soaked tent cloth.

"Shall we wait here until nightfall?" Leonid asked.

"Better not. Otherwise there's a risk somebody will come and take our packs."

They went back to the barn and Mendel dismantled the gun so it would fit into the knapsack. They waited for night, sleeping. Then they set out, heading west.

After three hours' walking, they stopped for a break.

"Tired, eh, Muscovite?" Mendel asked. Leonid denied this, but without conviction.

"It's not that I'm tired. I'm just not used to your pace. On our training course, we went on marches, and they also explained to us how to survive in the woods, how you tell directions, the moss on the tree trunks, the polestar, and how to dig a hideout. But it was all theory, the instructors were Muscovites themselves. And I'm not used to walking away from roads."

"Well, you'll learn here. I wasn't born in the midst of the woods, either; but I learned. The only wood in the history of Israel is the Earthly Paradise, and you know how that ended up. Then nothing for another six thousand years. Ah yes, when a war's on, everything's different, we have to resign ourselves to being different, too, and maybe it won't do us any harm. In the summer, the wood is a friend, too; it has leaves to hide you, and it even provides you with something to eat."

They resumed their way, still heading west. It was Moscow's order, which they both knew: stragglers caught behind the enemy line must avoid capture, penetrating the territory occupied by the Germans and remaining hidden. The two walked for a long time, first in the faint glow of the stars, and after midnight, by the moon. The ground was firm and, at the same time, soft; it didn't echo their footsteps, and didn't hinder their progress. The wind had dropped, not a leaf stirred; and the silence was total, broken only at intervals by a rustle of wings or the sad cry of some distant nocturnal bird. Towards dawn the air became cool, steeped in the damp respiration of the sleeping forest. They forded two streams, crossed a third thanks to a providential and inexplicable little footbridge: throughout the whole night it was the only human sign they came upon.

They found another as soon as day broke. A milky fog had risen, low, almost sticky: in some places it barely came to their knees, but it was so dense that it hid the terrain, and the two men felt as if they were wading through a swamp. Elsewhere, it was over their heads and impeded their orientation. Leonid stumbled over a fallen branch;

he picked it up and was amazed to see it had been chopped off neatly, as if by a hatchet blow. A little later they realized that the ground was covered with shreds of bark and bits of leaves and wood: above their heads, the forest seemed brutally pruned, boughs and treetops beheaded as if by the sweep of a gigantic scythe. The farther they advanced, the closer the level of the pruning came to the ground; they saw saplings lopped off at half their height, metal shards and wreckage, and then it: the beast come from the sky. It was a German fighter-bomber, a twin-engine Heinkel, lying on one side in the midst of the tortured trees. It had lost its wings, but not its landing gear; and the blades of the two propellers were bent and twisted as if they were made of wax. On the rudder was painted the swastika, proud and horrible, and beside it, one below the other, eight stencilled forms that Leonid could easily interpret: three French pursuit planes, a British reconnaissance plane, and four Soviet troop carriers: the adversaries the German had shot down before crashing himself. The crash must have occurred several months previously, because grass had already begun to grow in the furrows he had plowed in the dirt, and the underbrush was sprouting again.

"Our lucky star," Mendel said. "What could make a better camp? For a few days at least. Before, it was master of the sky, and now we're its masters." It wasn't hard to force open the door of the fuselage; the two men climbed in and, with lighthearted curiosity, devoted themselves to taking inventory. There was a felt toy dog, greasy and limp, to which someone had applied a little collar of dark fur: a mascot, which obviously hadn't worked. A little bunch of fake flowers. Four or five snapshots, the usual snapshots soldiers of every country carry on them: a man and a woman in a park, a man and a woman at a village fair. A little German-Russian dictionary. "I wonder why he took it along on a flight," Mendel said.

"Maybe he foresaw what was going to happen to him," Leonid answered. "The parachute's gone. Maybe he jumped and is somewhere around here, missing like us. The dictionary must have come in handy." But they examined it more closely and saw that the little book had been printed not in Germany but in Leningrad. Strange.

As their inventory proceeded, this plane became stranger and stranger. Two of the photographs showed a slim young man in Luftwaffe uniform, with a short, plump girl wearing dark braids; the other three, on the contrary, showed a young man in civilian clothes, thickset and muscular, and his girl was different: she was also a brunette, but with short hair and a snub nose. In one of these three, the young man was wearing a shirt with an embroidered geometric pattern, and in the background you could see a square and an arabesqued building with terraces and arched windows: it certainly didn't look like a German setting.

The radio had been removed, and there were no bombs in the bomb bay. But they found three loaves of stale rye bread, a number of full bottles, and a pamphlet in Byelorussian, which urged the male citizens of White Russia to enlist in the German-organized police force, and the women to present themselves at the offices of the Todt Organization: they would earn good wages working for the Great Reich, enemy of bolshevism and sincere friend of all Russians. There was a fairly recent issue of *New Byelorussia,* the newspaper the Germans printed, in Byelorussian, in Minsk; it was dated Saturday, 26 June 1943, and it listed the hours of masses in the cathedral and included also a series of decrees regarding the dismemberment of the kolkhozes and the division of land among the peasants. In the plane, too, there was a chessboard, the work of rough, patient hands, fashioned from a broad strip of birch bark. The black squares had been made by removing the white strip on the surface of the bark. There was also a pair of boots, which Mendel and Leonid both turned over in their hands, unable to figure out what the material was. No, it wasn't leather; the occupant of the plane had cut away the fake-leather upholstery of the seats and had sewn these boots, in big stitches, with fine electric wire found in the wreckage. A good job, Mendel said appreciatively; but now what were they to do, since their proposed lodging was already taken?

"We'll hide and wait for him. We'll see what he looks like, and then we'll decide."

The tenant arrived towards evening, with cautious tread. It was the muscular little man of the snapshots. He was wearing army trousers, a sheepskin jacket, and the black-and-white-checked cap of the Uzbeks. A bag was slung over his sturdy shoulder, and he took a live rabbit from it. With a sidelong chop of his hand on the animal's neck, he killed it, then he gutted it and began to skin it, whistling. Mendel and Leonid, too close, didn't dare speak, for fear of being overheard. Leonid, who had slipped off his knapsack, opened it slightly and pointed to the packets of salt. Mendel caught on immediately and, in reply, pointed to the gun. They could introduce themselves.

The Uzbek, seeing them stand up from the bushes, betrayed no surprise. He set down rabbit and knife and welcomed the strangers with suspicious formality. He wasn't as young as he had looked in the snapshots; he must have been about forty. He had a beautiful bass voice, soft and polite; but he spoke Russian haltingly, with mistakes and with irritating slowness. He didn't hesitate over the choice of words but would arrest his speech at every sentence, without tension or impatience, as if he had lost interest in what he had been saying and considered it superfluous to reach the conclusion; then, unexpectedly, he would resume speaking. Peiami, his name was: Peiami Nazimovich. Pause. A strange name, to be sure, but his country was also strange. Strange for the Russians, as the Russians were strange for the Uzbeks. A long pause, which threatened never to end. Missing? Yes, of course, he was also missing, a soldier of the Red Army. Missing for more than a year, almost two. No, not always here in the plane: moving about, from one peasant izba to another, working a bit on the kolkhozes, occasionally joining up with some band of deserters, or staying with some girl. The girl in the picture? No, that was his wife, far, endlessly far away, three thousand kilometers, beyond the front, beyond the Caspian, beyond the sea of Aral.

Room in the plane? They could see for themselves. No, there wasn't much room. For a night, if they squeezed a bit; perhaps even for two, out of politeness, hospitality. But the three of them would be uncomfortable. Leonid spoke rapidly in Yiddish to Mendel: they could settle the question quickly, without wasting any time. No, Mendel answered, not moving his head or changing the expression on his face; he didn't feel up to killing the man, and if they drove him away, he might report them. And anyway, a crashed plane was not an ideal or a definitive solution. "I've done too much killing already. I won't shoot a man for a place in a plane that won't fly."

"Would you kill a man if the plane did fly? If it would take you home?"

"What home?" Mendel asked. Leonid didn't answer.

The Uzbek hadn't understood the dialogue, but he had recognized the harsh music of their Yiddish.

"Jews, are you? It's all the same to me: Jews, Russians, Turks, Germans." Pause. "One eats as much as another when he's alive, and one stinks as much as the other when he's dead. There were Jews in my village, too, good at business, less good at making war. Me either, for that matter. What reason would we have to make war among ourselves?"

The rabbit was now skinned. The Uzbek put the skin aside, cut up the animal with his bayonet, leaning on a stump, and started roasting it on a piece of metal from the plane's body, which he had bent into the shape of a pan. He had put no fat or salt on it.

"Are you going to eat it all?" Leonid asked.

"It's a skinny rabbit."

"Could you use some salt?"

"I could."

"Here's the salt," Leonid said, taking one packet from his knapsack. "Salt for rabbit: a fair trade all around."

They negotiated a long time as to how much salt half a rabbit should cost. Peiami, though he remained calm, was a tireless bargainer, always ready to adduce more arguments: trading entertained him, like a game, and excited him, like a tournament. He pointed out the fact that, even without salt, rabbit is nourishing, whereas salt without rabbit is not nourishing. And his rabbit was lean, and therefore of high quality, because rabbit fat is bad for the kidneys. And though he was out of salt at the moment, salt was cheap in the area, there was plenty of it, the Russians dropped it by parachute to the outlaw bands. The pair of them shouldn't take advantage of his temporary lack; if they were heading for Gomel, they'd find salt in every izba, at disastrously low prices. And finally, simply out of cultural interest and a natural curiosity about other people's customs, he enquired, "Do you eat rabbit? The Jews in Samarkand won't eat it: for them it's like pork."

"We're special Jews," Leonid said, "hungry Jews."

"I'm a special Uzbek, too."

Once the deal was closed, apples emerged from a hiding place, and slices of roast turnips, some cheese, and wild strawberries. The three dined, bound by that superficial friendship born of bargaining; at the end, Peiami went into the plane to get the vodka. It was samogon, he explained: wild vodka, homemade, distilled by the peasants, much stronger than the government kind. Peiami informed them that he was a special Uzbek because, though a Moslem, he was very fond of vodka; and also because, though the Uzbeks are a fighting race, he didn't have any desire to fight in the war:

"If nobody comes after me, I'm going to stay here trapping rabbits till the war ends. If the Germans come, I'll go with the Germans. If the Russians come, I'll go with the Russians. If the partisans come, I'll go with the partisans."

Mendel would have liked to know more about the partisans and the bands that the Russians dropped the salt for. He tried in vain to dig more information out of the Uzbek: by now the man had drunk too much, or else he considered it imprudent to talk about the subject, or else he really didn't know anything more. For that matter, the samogon was really powerful, almost a narcotic. Mendel and Leonid, who weren't great drinkers and who hadn't drunk any hard liquor for quite a while, stretched out in the cabin of the plane and fell asleep before dusk. The Uzbek stayed outside longer; he cleaned up the implements (namely, his unorthodox pan), first with sand and then with water, he smoked his pipe, he drank some more, and finally he also went to bed, pushing aside the two Jews, who didn't wake up. At eleven, towards the west, the sky still had a faint glow.

At three in the morning it was already day: the light entered abundantly not only through the two windows, but also through the rips in the metal body, shattered by the impact of the plane against trees and ground. Mendel was achingly awake: his head hurt and his throat was parched. All because of the samogon, he thought; but it wasn't only the samogon. He couldn't get his mind off the remark the Uzbek had made about the bands hidden in the woods. Not that it was entirely news to him: he had heard talk about them, and often. In the villages he had seen the German bilingual signs, posted on the huts, offering money to anyone reporting bandits and threatening punishment for anyone helping them. He had also seen, more than once, the horrible hanged bodies, boys and girls, heads brutally dislocated by the yank of the rope, the eyes glassy, the hands tied behind their backs; and around their necks they wore signs, written in Russian, "I have come back to my village" or other mocking words. He knew all this, and he knew also that a soldier of the Red Army—such as he was, and was proud of being—if he is missing must go underground and continue to fight. And at the same time he was tired of fighting: tired, empty, bereft of wife, village, friends. He no longer felt in his heart the vigor of the young man and soldier, but only weariness, emptiness, and a yearning for a white, serene nothingness, like a winter snowfall. He had experienced thirst for revenge, he hadn't slaked it, and the thirst had slowly died away until it was gone. He was tired of the war and of life, and instead of the soldier's red blood, he felt flowing in his veins the pale blood of the breed he knew he descended from, tailors, merchants, innkeepers, village fiddlers, meek and prolific patriarchs, and mystical rabbis. He was tired, too, of walking and hiding, tired of being Mendel: what Mendel? Who is Mendel son of Nachman? Mendel Nachmanovich, as was written, Russian-style, on the roster of his platoon; or Mendel ben Nachman, as, in his day in 1915, the rabbi with the two clocks had written in the registry of Strelka?

And yet he felt he couldn't go on living as he had. Something in the Uzbek's words and actions had made him suspect that the man knew more than he wanted to let on about the partisans in the woods. Something the Uzbek knew, and Mendel, deep in his heart, in an ill-explored corner of his heart, felt a thrust, a prod, like a coiled spring: something had to be done, to be done at once, on that very day whose light had torn him from his samogon sleep. He must learn from the Uzbek where they were and who they were, these bands, and he had to decide. He had to choose, and the choice was hard; on the one hand there was his thousand-year-old weariness, his fear, his horror of the weapons that he had buried all the same and then brought along with him; on the other side, there was not much. There was the little coiled spring, which *Pravda* perhaps would call his "sense of honor and duty," but which would perhaps be more appropriately described as a dumb need for decency. He mentioned none of this to Leonid, who had waked up in the meanwhile. He waited till the Uzbek woke, then asked him some specific questions.

The answers were not so specific. Bands, yes: there were some, or there had been: partisans, or outlaws, he couldn't say, nobody could really say. Armed, to be sure, but armed against whom? Ghostly bands, cloudlike bands: here today, blowing up the railroad track, and forty kilometers away tomorrow, looting the silos of a kolkhoz. And the faces were never the same. Russian faces, Ukrainian, Polish; Mongols, who had come from no telling where; Jews, too, yes, some; and women, and a kaleidoscope of uniforms: Soviets dressed as Germans, in police uniforms; Soviets in tatters, still with their Red Army tunics; even some German deserters. . . . How many? Who knows? Fifty here, three hundred there, groups that formed and broke up: alliances, quarrels, sometimes even shooting.

Mendel insisted: Peiami knew something, then. Well, he knew and he didn't know, Peiami answered; these were things that everybody knew. He had had only one contact, months ago, with a band of fairly decent people. At Nivnoye, in the midst of the marshes, on the White Russian border. A business deal: he had sold the plane's radio, and in his opinion it had been a good deal, because the radio was smashed to pieces, and he certainly didn't think those people were capable of fixing it. They had paid him well, with two cheeses and four boxes of aspirin, because it was still winter then, and he suffered from rheumatism. He had made a second trip, afterwards, in April, and he had taken the dead German's parachute with him. Oh yes, when he arrived, the German was still here, dead for God knows how long, already half-eaten by crows and rats. It had been a nasty job, cleaning up a bit and tidying the interior of the plane. He had taken away the parachute, but at Nivnoye he had found a different bunch of people, different faces, different chiefs, and they hadn't stood on ceremony. They took the parachute away from him and paid him in rubles. A real swindle: what use did he have for rubles? And from that parachute they could make at least twenty shirts. In other words, a disastrous deal, not to mention the trip itself: it was a good three or four days' walk from here to Nivnoye. No, he hadn't gone back there again; also because they had told him they were about to move on, God knows where: they themselves didn't know, or didn't want to say. They were the ones who had given him the German dictionary: they had a whole bundle of them. Obviously, Moscow had printed up a lot.

There, that was everything he knew about the bands, except, naturally, the salt business. They had no salt: it was dropped for them by parachute. And not only salt. That was why they had set such a low value on the German's parachute, even if it was made of the finest stuff. In other words, going into business is always a risk, but it becomes a serious risk when you don't know the market conditions; and what kind of market is a forest, where you don't even know if you have neighbors, or what kind of people they are, or what they need?

"Anyway, you two are my guests. I don't imagine you want to start walking on right away. Stop off here, make your plans, and leave tomorrow, more comfortably. Unless you have some reason to be in a hurry. You can share my day: you'll get some rest, and for one day I won't be alone."

He took them for a walk around the wood, along barely marked trails, to check his traps; but there were no rabbits. There was a weasel, half-strangled by the noose, but still alive; indeed, so alive that it was hard to defend yourself against its frantic snapping. The Uzbek slipped off his trousers, folded them double, stuck his hands into them as if putting on gloves, and freed the animal, which then quickly darted off through the undergrowth, as supple as a snake. "If a man is really hungry, he could eat one of those animals, too," Peiami said, in a melancholy tone. "In my village we didn't have such troubles. Even the poorest could get his fill of cheese, seven days a week. We never knew hunger, not even in the worst years, when in the city they were eating rats. But here it's different, it's not easy to stave off hunger; according to the season you can find mushrooms, frogs, snails, migratory birds; but not all seasons are good. You can go to the villages, of course, but not empty-handed; and you have to be very careful, because they're quick to shoot, without asking questions."

About a hundred meters from the plane, he showed them the German's grave. Peiami had done a good job, a hole more than a meter deep; no stones, because there were none to be found here, but a cover of branches, a pile of packed earth, and even a cross with the man's name on it: Baptist Kipp. The Uzbek had discovered it on the army tag.

"Why all this trouble to bury an infidel? And a German at that," Leonid asked.

"So he won't come back," the Uzbek answered, "and because the days are long and you have to fill them one way or another. I like playing chess, and I'm pretty good. In my village nobody could beat me. Well, here I made some chessmen, carving them out of wood, and I made that chessboard with birch bark. But playing against yourself is no fun. I invent problems, but it's like making love alone."

Mendel said that he also liked to play: there were many hours of daylight left, why didn't they have a game? The Uzbek accepted, but when they got back to the plane, he expressed a wish that the two of them, Mendel and Leonid, should play the first game. Why? A host's courtesy, Peiami said; but it was really clear that he wanted to have some idea of how his two prospective opponents played. He was one of those who play to win.

The white men fell to Leonid, and the pieces really were white and still redolent of fresh wood. The black men were actually of various dark shades: charred, smoked. Both sets were fairly unsteady, because the board was not really flat, but uneven, undulating, full of bumps. Leonid made a queen's pawn opening, but it was soon obvious that he didn't know the opening, and he was in trouble, with a pawn down, and the others poorly developed. He muttered something about the game, and Mendel answered him, also in a subdued tone, but in Yiddish: "You keep an eye on him; you can never tell. The gun and the pistol are in the plane. Check." It was a tricky check, with the white king awkwardly trapped behind his pawns. Leonid sacrificed a bishop in a hopeless attempt at defense, and Mendel announced a mate in three. Leonid put down his king in sign of surrender and tribute to the victor but Mendel said: "No, let's play it out." Leonid understood: Peiami had to be satisfied. There was no danger of his going off, he was following the game with professional attention, that sanguinary attention of bullfight fans: it was best not to rob him of the spectacle of the coup de grace. The coup de grace came. And the Uzbek challenged Leonid, who accepted reluctantly.

The Uzbek opened aggressively, with the queen's bishop's pawn; his eyes, the sclera so white it had a bluish tinge, were even more aggressive. He played with showy grotesque gestures, advancing his shoulder and arm with each move, as if the piece he shifted weighed a dozen kilos. He would slam it down on the board as if to drive it in, or he would twist it, pressing it, as if it were a screw. Leonid was immediately at a disadvantage, both because of this pantomime and because of his opponent's obvious superiority. It was clear that Peiami simply wanted to get him out of the way as quickly as possible, in order to pit himself against Mendel. The Uzbek moved with insolent rapidity, not pausing to ponder his moves and displaying a rude impatience at Leonid's hesitations. He mated Leonid in less than ten minutes.

"Now you and me," he said at once to Mendel, with a tone so determined that Mendel felt both amused and uneasy. Mendel, too, played to win this time as if the stake were a mountain of gold or security for life or eternal happiness. He sensed vaguely that he was playing not only for himself, but also as the champion of something or someone. He opened cautiously, paying attention, forcing himself not to allow the other man's behavior to unsettle him. For that matter, the Uzbek soon gave up his jarring gesticulation and also concentrated on the board. Mendel was meditative; Peiami, on the other hand, tended to a bold, flashy game: behind his every move, Mendel couldn't really understand if there was a hidden, thought-out plan or a desire to amaze or the imaginative boldness of an adventurer. After about twenty moves, neither man had suffered losses, the situation was even, the board was frightfully confused, and Mendel realized he was having fun. He deliberately lost a tempo, simply to induce the Uzbek to reveal his intentions, and he saw the other man grow nervous: now the Uzbek was the one who hesitated before moving, looking into Mendel's eyes as if to read a secret there. The Uzbek made a move immediately revealed as disastrous, he asked to take it back, and Mendel agreed. Then the man stood up, shook himself like a dog emerging from the water, and without a word went off towards the plane. Mendel signaled to Leonid, who understood and followed Peiami, stepping into the cabin behind him. But the Uzbek wasn't thinking about weapons; he had only gone to get the samogon.

All three drank as the sky was beginning already to grow dark, and the cool westerly wind was rising. Mendel felt odd, outside time and place. That game, concentrated and serious, was linked in his memory with times and places intensely different: with his father, who had taught him the rules, had easily beaten him for two years, then had beaten him with difficulty for another two, and then had accepted his own defeats comfortably; with his friends, Jews and Russians, who at the chessboard had been trained with him in cleverness and patience; with the peaceful warmth of his lost home.

Probably the Uzbek had drunk too much. When he sat down again at the board, he unleashed an endless series of exchanges, from which a simplified situation emerged: him, with a pawn down, Mendel holding the long diagonal and safely castled. The Uzbek drank again, perfected his own catastrophe with an absurd attempt at counterattack, then admitted defeat, declaring that he wanted a return game: he had been weak, he knew that you mustn't drink when you're playing, and he had succumbed to his vice like a child. Now it was dark, but he wanted a return game. Tomorrow morning. First thing. At daybreak. He said good night, stumbled up the rickety ladder to the cabin, and five minutes later he was already snoring.

The other two men were silent for a few moments. Over the rustling of the boughs, stirred by the breeze, less familiar sounds were heard: the hum of insects or little animals, a creaking, a distant chorus of frogs.

Mendel said: "He's not the traveling companion we need, is he?"

"We don't need any traveling companions," Leonid said, still grouchy after his defeat.

"That remains to be seen. In any case, it's time for us to move on, before the night gets any darker."

They waited until the Uzbek's snoring had become regular, then they collected their knapsacks from the cabin and started off. As a precaution, they headed south first, then made an abrupt turn towards the northwest: but the ground was dry and held no footprints.

2

July–August

1943

On the basis of the vague information extracted from the Uzbek, Mendel wanted to go to Nivnoye. Leonid didn't want to go anyplace, or rather, he didn't know where he wanted to go, and didn't even know if he wanted to go someplace or do something. Not that he rejected Mendel's proposals or rebelled against his decisions; but he exercised a subtle, passive abrasion against every active thrust: like dust in a watch, Mendel thought to himself. He's got dust in him, even though he's young. It's stupid to say the young are strong. You understand many things better at thirty than at twenty, and you can also bear them better. For that matter, he, Mendel, if they were to ask him his age, and he decided to answer sincerely, what could he say? Twenty-eight, according to his papers, a bit older when it came to his joints, his lungs, and heart; and on his back, a mountain of years, more than Noah and Methuselah. Yes, more than they, since Methuselah begot Lamech at the ripe old age of one hundred eighty-seven, and Noah was five hundred when he brought Shem, Ham, and Japheth into the world, six hundred when he built the ark, and a little older when he got drunk for the first time; and according to the two-clock rabbi, on that same occasion he was thinking of begetting a fourth son, but then that nasty business with Ham occurred. No, he, Mendel the watchmender, roaming about the woods, was older than they. He no longer wanted to beget sons or plant vines or build arks, not even if the Lord commanded it; but so far it didn't seem that the Lord had bothered much about saving him and his family. Perhaps because he wasn't as just a man as Noah.

Leonid's silences oppressed him. Instinctively, he liked Leonid, who seemed one of those men you can trust; but this passivity was irksome. When a watch is dusty, that's a sign it's very old, or else the case has come loose; and then you have to take it completely apart and clean it, piece by piece, with light gasoline. Leonid wasn't old; so it was his case that had some crevices in it. What kind of gasoline would be needed to clean Leonid's works?

He had tried several times to make Leonid talk. He had got some shreds from him, bits of a mosaic, to be reassembled patiently, like a puzzle, afterwards, the way you fit certain children's games together. The German *Lager,* of course: it can't have been pleasant, but he had been there only a short time and had kept his health; indeed, he had been lucky—why wouldn't he admit it? If they had realized they had a Jewish paratrooper in their midst, things would have ended differently for him. To be lucky is a good thing, a guarantee for the future; to deny your own luck is blasphemy. The stolen watch, prison: Lord God, he had sinned, he had expiated. If all sinners only had the good fortune to expiate, to square their accounts. There must have been something else inside Leonid, an inner scar, a bruise, perhaps a painful aura around a human face, a portrait: Mendel thought of those big oval photographs of the last century, the solemn image of an ancestor in the center of a vague, gray halo. It was his family:

Mendel was convinced of that, not on the basis of Leonid's answers, brief and impatient, but on the basis of his silences. Yes, the mosaic to be pieced together was composed to a large extent of blank bits: evasive replies, or outright refusals, even insolent. It would take patience, little by little the picture would come clear. Now Mendel was a patient man. Night after night along their way, frustrated by the rejections, the wrathful, frantic parries of his traveling companion, he examined himself; beyond any doubt, he, Mendel, was not a man of many virtues, but he did possess patience. Well, if a man has patience, let him use it.

To reach the Nivnoye marshes, the three days the Uzbek mentioned were not enough. It took Mendel and Leonid six: six nights, rather, because they preferred to stop during the day. They crossed roads and deserted trails, a railroad (it must have been the Gomel-Bryansk line, Mendel figured), clearings, various limpid and shallow streams, a relief for their thirst and their tired feet. They skirted villages and farms: this forced them to make long detours, but were they in any hurry, after all?

In this way, moving only under cover of darkness and avoiding inhabited places, they encountered few people, shepherds, peasants in the fields, belated wayfarers, who paid no attention to them. One encounter, however, they were unable to avoid. The fourth day, at the first light of dawn, as they were following a wagon track, they had to pass along a trench cut through a rise in the ground; from the other end of the trench a little cart was advancing, driven by a middle-aged man and drawn by an old, tired horse. On his arm the carter wore the blue band of the Ukrainian auxiliary militia. Mendel asked him, "What are you carrying?"

"Flour, as you can see."

"Where are you taking it?"

"To the Germans. To the quartermaster stores at Mglin."

"Climb down and clear out. Yes, clear out. Start walking."

The Ukrainian shrugged; such mishaps must not have been new for him. "What am I supposed to say?"

"Whatever you like. Say some bandits stopped you."

The Ukrainian went off. On the cart there were six sacks of flour and a bundle of freshly mown hay. Mendel had put away the pistol; he looked puzzled.

"Now what do you plan to do?" Leonid asked.

"I don't know. I don't know what we'll do, but what I wanted to do was right. I wanted to take a stand, like when you burn a bridge behind you, and you don't know if it's right or wrong, but after you've decided, the bridge is gone and you no longer have choices: you can't turn back. Come on, help me unhitch the horse, and we'll see how many sacks he can carry."

"Why don't we keep the cart, too?"

"Because now they'll start looking for us, and we have to stay away from roads."

The horse didn't promise to be much help. He kept his head and ears down, and on his withers he had oozing sores covered with gnats and horseflies. With some lengths of rope they found in the cart, they managed to tie two of the sacks on him; more wouldn't have been sensible. Above the sacks, which hung awkwardly over the scrawny ribs of the animal, they fixed the bundle of hay.

"What about the cart? And the other sacks?"

"We'll hide them, as best we can."

It wasn't easy, but they finally succeeded, even before it was broad day: the cart in a ditch full of brambles, and the sacks under the cart. Then they set off again, abandoning the road and pulling the horse behind them, lazy and restive and, what's more, clumsy because of the badly loaded sacks, which kept getting caught in the lowest branches. They walked in silence for a long time, then Leonid said, "I don't know what I want, but I know I don't know it. You don't know what you want, either, but you think you know."

Mendel, who was walking ahead and tugging the horse by its halter, didn't turn and didn't answer; but a little later Leonid attacked him again. "There was no movie theater in your village. Weren't there even any horses?"

"There were, but I never had to deal with them. I had a different trade."

"I also had a different trade, but a horse like this can't carry a load this way, or can't carry it for long. Anybody could see that."

There was little to rebut; and for that matter there was too much light for them to proceed. They stopped in a thicket by a stream, watered the horse, tied him to a tree, gave him the hay to eat, and went to sleep. When they woke, in midafternoon, the hay was finished, the horse had cropped the few bushes he could reach, and was yanking at the rope, to stretch farther; he must have been really hungry. Too bad the sacks contained flour and not oats. They tried putting a bit of flour in front of him, but the animal got his muzzle all pasty right up to his eyes, and then began to cough as if he were about to strangle; they had to wash his lips and nostrils in the stream. Then they set off again. They could sniff a new smell in the air, fresh and sweetish: the marshes were obviously not far off.

Half a day's walk from Nivnoye they came upon an old peasant woman and decided to strike up a conversation. The horse? The woman studied it with an expert eye. "Eh, poor creature. He's not worth much, that's for sure; he's old, tired, hungry, and he looks sick to me, too. The flour's another matter, but I can't make you an offer, because I don't have anything to offer."

She was no fool. She examined the pair again closely; then, as if answering a tacit question, she added, "Don't be afraid. There are lots like you around here. Too many, perhaps, but the Germans are few and not very dangerous. As for the horse and the flour, like I said, I have nothing to offer you; but I can talk with the village elder, if you want."

Mendel was in a hurry to get rid of the animal; it was little or no use to them; indeed, its mere presence seemed to excite Leonid's ill temper, his critical spirit, and his desire to quarrel. Mendel conferred with him briefly. No, no go-betweens: obviously the woman would try to cut herself in on the deal, for some amount, great or small. But both men were chary of entering the village.

"All right," Mendel said, "try to make an appointment for us with this elder, halfway, in some secluded place. Is that possible?" It was possible, the woman said.

The elder arrived promptly, at sunset, in a hut the woman had pointed out. He was around sixty, a man of few words, stocky, white-haired. Yes, he, or rather the village, was solvent: they had eggs, lard, salt, and honey; but the horse wasn't worth much.

"There isn't just the horse," Mendel said. "There's also a cart and six sacks of flour: two here and another four hidden not far away, along with the cart."

"This business isn't clear," the elder said. "I can see the horse and the two sacks; but what's the value of a cart and four sacks of flour hidden in the woods, God knows where? I don't even know if they really exist. What's the value of a treasure on the moon?"

Leonid took one step forward and spoke up harshly: "They're worth as much as our word and our faces are worth, and if you don't—"

The elder looked at him, maintaining his calm. Mendel put his hand on Leonid's shoulder and intervened:

"Reasonable men can always reach an understanding. Look, the stuff is near the road, sooner or later somebody will find it and carry it off free, and that will be a shame for us and for you. And if it starts raining again, the flour won't last long. And we are just passing through, we're in a hurry to be on our way."

The elder had small, sly eyes. He trained them on the horse, the sacks, and on Mendel, in succession; then he said, "It's a bad thing to have to go slow when you're in a hurry. If you keep the horse, you'll have to go slow, at his pace. If you sell him and don't sell the two sacks, with a hundred pounds each to carry, you won't go fast or far: at best you'll go and trade with somebody else. You don't have much choice."

Mendel caught a look of Leonid's, rapid but charged with malicious joy: it was his revenge for the defeat at chess. The old man's logic was strong, and Mendel would have been wiser not to mention their hurry. He could only concede.

"Very well, old man. Let's get down to business. How much will you offer for what you see? For two sacks of flour and the horse?"

The old man scratched his head, shifting his cap over his brow. "Hm, the horse—we needn't mention him. He's not worth anything, not even as meat for slaughter. Maybe the hide, if it's tanned properly. As for the flour, there's no knowing where it comes from: you didn't tell me that. You could tell me, and I could believe you or not; a trader has the right to tell lies. It could be Russian or German, bought or stolen. I don't want to know anything about it, and in exchange I offer you eight kilos of lard and a plait of tobacco leaves. Take it or leave it. It's stuff that doesn't weigh much, and you can carry it easily."

"Make it ten," Mendel said.

"Ten kilos, but then no tobacco."

"Ten kilos, and the tobacco for the horse's hide."

"Nine kilos and the tobacco," the old man said.

"All right. And how much will you offer for the goods that can't be seen? Two quintals of flour and the cart?"

The old man pushed his cap even lower. "I won't offer anything. Goods you can't see might as well not exist. If it's there, we'll find it even if you don't tell us where it is; and even if you do tell, and tell the truth, maybe we'll go there and not find anything. There are lots of people roaming in the woods; and not only people, also foxes, rats, crows. You said so yourself: somebody else might find it. If I made you an offer, they'd laugh at me in the village."

Mendel had an idea. "I'll make you a proposal: information for information, goods you can't see in exchange for other goods you can't see. We'll tell you where the cart is and you tell us . . . what I mean is, along our way we heard some rumors, about how in Nivnoye, or near Nivnoye, or in the marshes, there are certain people, or there were . . ."

The old man pushed the visor of his cap up again and looked Mendel straight in the eye: something he hadn't done till that moment. Mendel insisted: "It's a good deal, isn't it? It doesn't cost you anything; it's as if we were giving you the cart and the flour; because they really do exist, we're not swindling you, I give you a soldier's word."

To the surprise of Mendel and Leonid, the elder relaxed and became almost talkative. Yes, there was a group, or had been: a band. Fifty men, maybe even a hundred, some local and some not. Some, maybe half a dozen, were boys from his own village: better to go underground than to end up in Germany, right? Yes, armed. And smart, too; a bit too smart sometimes. But they had left a few days ago, with their weapons, their belongings, and a few animals. It was better for everyone, their leaving. Where had they headed? No, that he didn't know for sure; he hadn't seen anything. But some people had seen them go, and they seemed to be marching in the direction of Gomel or Zhlobin. If the two of them were to take the path for Zhurbin, that was a short cut, and maybe they could catch up. He went off, came back half an hour later with the lard, the tobacco, and scales, so that the two men could be sure the weight was correct. When they had checked, Mendel explained precisely where the cart was hidden. Unexpectedly, the old man took a dozen hard-boiled eggs from his sack. This, he said, was an extra, a present he was giving them, because they were likable people; and it was also a compensation, because it would have been his hospitable duty to offer them a place to sleep, but the village council had objected. He led them to the path and took his leave, pulling after him the horse with the two sacks.

"If he hadn't recognized us as Jews, tonight we would have slept in a bed," Leonid grumbled.

"Maybe, but even if he had made the offer, I'm not sure we would have been wise to accept. We know nothing of this village, what people live there, how they think, whether they're only afraid, or whether they're working for the Germans. I can't be sure, it's just an impression, but I would have trusted the old woman more than this elder: he didn't seem so much a friend as a half-friend. He was in a hurry to get rid of us; that's why he gave us the eggs and showed us the way. For that matter, we've made a decision now, haven't we?"

"What decision?" Leonid asked, with hostility.

"To catch up with the band, no?"

"That's a decision you've made. You didn't ask me anything."

"There was no need to ask. We've been talking about it for days, and you've kept quiet."

"Well, now I'm not keeping quiet. If you want to go with that band, you can go by yourself. I've had my fill of war. You have the weapons, and I have the lard: that suits me. I'll go back to the village, and I'll find a bed, and not just for one night."

Mendel turned and stopped abruptly. He wasn't prepared to face wrath, still less a weak man's wrath, and in Leonid he sensed a weak man. Nor was he prepared for the hurricane of words that Leonid, so silent till then, unleashed in his face:

"Enough! Enough of this! I found you in the woods, but I didn't marry you. I thought you were fed up, the same as I am: I was mistaken. All right. But I've had enough, I'm not taking another step. You go into the marshes: you were afraid to sleep in that village, and now you want to take me along with some people, and you don't even know what language they speak, or if they want us with them, or where they come from or where they're going. I come from Moscow, but I have strong arms, and a good head, too; I won't starve to death. I'd rather go and work in a kolkhoz, or in the Germans' factories. I'm not taking another step and I'm not firing another shot. Never again. It isn't right, it isn't right for a man to. . . . And besides, you

don't know what you want, either. I told you: you think
you know, but you don't. You play the hero, but you want
what I want: a house, a bed, a woman, a life that has some
meaning, a family, a village that's your village. You want
to go with the partisans, you think you want to, but you
don't know what you want or what you're doing; I realized that after the horse business. You tell lies to yourself.
You're a man like me. You're a nebbish, a loser, a meshuggener." Leonid slowly bent over and sat down on the
ground, as if he had drained his soul and no longer had
the strength to stand on his feet.

Mendel had remained standing, more curious and surprised than enraged. He realized he had been expecting
this outburst for some time. He gave Leonid a few moments to calm down a little, then he sat beside him. He
touched his shoulder, but the boy jerked away as if a searing iron had grazed him. A nebbish is a man of scant
worth, helpless, useless, to be pitied, almost a nonman;
and meshuggener means crazy, but Mendel didn't feel in-
sulted or, still less, like returning the insult. He was wondering, instead, why Leonid, whose mother tongue was
Russian, had used Yiddish, which he spoke with difficulty, on this occasion. But Yiddish, as everyone knows, is
an immense reservoir of picturesque, ridiculous, or blood-
thirsty insolence, and each insult has its own nuance: that
could be an explanation. A Jew punches you on the nose
and then cries for help, he thought; but he didn't utter the
saying aloud. Instead, in a voice so calm it surprised even
him, he said: "Of course, it wasn't an easy choice for me
either; but I believe it's the best. A man has to weigh his
choices carefully." And he added meaningfully, "And also
his words." Leonid didn't answer.

By now it was almost dark; Mendel would have preferred to walk at night, but the path was difficult and
poorly indicated. He suggested camping on the spot, since
it was a warm evening and the night would be short;
Leonid agreed with a nod. They wrapped themselves in
their blankets, and Mendel was already almost asleep

when Leonid, as if continuing a speech long begun, suddenly started saying:

"My father was Jewish, but not a believer. He worked for the railroad, and he was accepted into the party. He fought in the 1920 war against the Whites. And then he brought me into the world, and then they sent him to prison, and after that to the Solovki Islands, and he never came back. That's the way it is. He had already been in the czar's prisons, before I was born, but he came back from that. They sent him to Solovki because they said he was sabotaging the railroad: it was his fault the trains didn't run. There you are."

Having said this, Leonid rolled on to his other side, turning his back to Mendel, as if the subject were closed. Mendel thought this was an odd way of apologizing, but then he promptly came to the conclusion that it was, nevertheless, an apology. He let a few minutes pass, then he shyly asked Leonid, "What about your mother?" Leonid grunted. "Leave me alone now. Please, just leave me alone. That's enough for now." He was silent and didn't move again, but Mendel was well aware that he wasn't sleeping, only pretending. But to insist he continue would have been pointless, or rather, harmful; like picking a mushroom that has barely sprouted. You prevent it from growing, and you take nothing home with you.

They walked for two weeks, sometimes during the day, sometimes at night, in the rain and in the sunshine. Leonid talked no more, either to tell of himself or to dissent; he grimly accepted Mendel's decisions, like an indifferent servant. They encountered a few people, a burned village, more and more abundant signs of the band that was on the move ahead of them: ashes of campfires at the side of the trail, prints in the dried mud, traces of meals, a fragment of a pot, a rag. These people took few precautions against being noticed. At one of their stops Mendel and Leonid actually saw a tree riddled with bullets: someone must have engaged in target practice; perhaps they had held a contest. The two men were rarely obliged to ask directions from the local people: yes, they had gone by, headed in this or that direction. Stragglers, or deserters, or partisans or bandits, according to the point of view; anyway, in everyone's opinion, people who went on their way without causing too much trouble or demanding too much from the peasants.

The pair overtook them one evening: they sighted them and heard them almost at the same time. Mendel and Leonid were at the top of a hill: they saw the lazy bends of a big river, no doubt the Dnepr, and near the shore, three or four kilometers away, a fire glowed. The pair began their descent, and they heard shots, ragged fire from rifles and pistols. They saw red flashes, followed by the duller explosions of hand grenades. A battle? Against whom? And then why the fire? Or a quarrel, a brawl between two factions? But during the break in the shooting they could make out the sound of an accordion and cries and jolly calls: it wasn't a battle, it was a party.

They approached cautiously. There were no sentries, nobody stopped them. Around the fire were about thirty bearded men, some young, some older, dressed in many different ways, visibly armed. The accordion was giving out a lively song, some clapped their hands to the rhythm, others, with all their weapons on them, were dancing furiously, spinning on their heels, standing, or crouching. Somebody must have seen the strangers; a thickened but thunderous voice shouted, absurdly, "Are you Germans?"

"We're Russians," the two answered.

"Come, then. Eat, drink, and dance! The war's over!" As an exclamation point there came a long submachine-gun volley, rattled off against a sky reddened by fire and smoke. The same voice, suddenly wrathful and addressed in the opposite direction, went on: "Styoooooopka, you idiot son of a crow, bring some bottles and messtins. Can't you see we have guests?"

It was now dark, but the camp could be discerned, quite makeshift, focusing around three centers: the fire, where there was a noisy stir of celebrating men; a big tent, in front of which two horses were dozing, tied to two pegs; and, more distant, a group of three or four young men silently busy at something.

The man with the thunderous voice came towards the two, a bottle of vodka in his hand. He was a young, blond giant, his hair cropped short, a curly beard covering half his chest. He had a handsome oval face with regular, but strongly marked, features; and he was so drunk he could hardly stand up. There was no sign of rank on his Red Army uniform.

"Your health!" he said, gulping from the bottle. "Health to you, whoever you may be." Then he handed the vodka to the pair, who drank and returned the toast. "Styopka, you lazy fool, where's that soup?" Then he went on, giving them a radiant, innocent smile: "You have to forgive him, he may have had a bit too much to drink, but he's a fine comrade. Brave, too, considering he's a cook. But quick, no. He's not very quick. Oh, here he is. Let's hope the soup hasn't turned cold along the way. Eat now, then we'll hear the rest of the news, if there is any."

Contrary to the giant's opinion, Styopka seemed neither very slow nor very foolish. "No, Venjamin Ivanovich, it's downright impossible. They've all had a try at it, one after the other; but the signal's too weak. You can't make out anything: all you can hear is static."

"They're a bunch of no-goods, the devil take them! Today, of all days, they had to wreck it! Now I ask you: the war ends, any minute now Stalin will come on and tell us all to go home, and these sons of bitches put the radio on the blink. . . . What? You haven't heard anything? The Americans have landed in Italy, we've recaptured Kursk, and Mussolini's in jail. In jail, yes, like a bird in a cage. The king put him in jail. Come on, comrades, another drink! To peace!"

Leonid drank; Mendel pretended to drink, and then they followed Venjamin to the radio. "It's the Uzbek's radio!" Mendel said to Leonid, reading the metal plate on the machine in the light of the lanterns. "But, obviously, with batteries like these, it couldn't last very long." Mendel managed to stand between Venjamin, who continued pouring out curses and vain threats, and the three boys charged with receiving. There was then a muddled technical argument for several minutes, often interrupted by Venjamin's outrages and those of other bearded men who had come to stick their noses in and speak their minds. "I know very little about radios, but these men know nothing at all," Mendel muttered to Leonid. In the end there was a suggestion to replace the electrolyte of the batteries with water and salt. Venjamin immediately espoused the idea, summoned Styopka, issued confused orders. The water and salt arrived, the operation was performed among intent faces, in an atmosphere of religious expectation, and the batteries were again connected; but the radio emitted only some stupid pop music for a few seconds and then fell definitively silent. Venjamin became ill-humored and blamed everyone. He spoke to Leonid, as if seeing him for the first time: "You two, where did you pop up from? Russians? You don't look like Russians to me; but we won't bother about that today, even if you did break our radio, because today's a holiday."

Mendel said to Leonid: "We'll think about this tomorrow, when he's sober again; but things don't look so promising to me."

They were awakened the next morning by the peaceful sounds of the camp. The horses were grazing on the bank of the river, naked men were washing or wriggling in the shallow water; others were mending their clothes or doing their laundry; and still others were stretched out in the sun. And nobody seemed to pay any attention to the pair of strangers. Most of the men were Russians, but you could hear shouts and singing also in languages Mendel couldn't identify. Late in the morning Styopka came looking for them.

"Would you like to help me? There's a sick man in the tent there; he's groaning and he has a fever, and I don't know what to do. Would you two come with me?"

"But we're not doctors," Leonid protested.

"I'm not a doctor either, or even a nurse, but I'm the oldest in the band; and besides I lost my weapons when we attacked the Klintsy station, so they make me do a bit of everything, but they don't send me out to fight anymore. I even act as guide, because I know these parts well, better than anybody, better than Venya himself. I was a guide before, in 1918, for the Red partisans, just around here, and there's not a path or a ford or a road I haven't traveled over dozens of times. Well, now they also give me the sick to take care of, and you two must help me. He has a fever; and his belly's as hard as a board."

Mendel said, "I don't understand why you keep insisting. I don't know any more about this than anyone else."

Styopka looked embarrassed. "It's because . . . they say that you people, for centuries and centuries, have been good at—"

"We people are no different from you people. Our doctors are as good as yours, but no better and no worse, and a Jew that isn't a doctor and treats a sick man risks killing him the same as a Christian. All I can tell you is that I'm an artilleryman, and I've seen all too many people with their belly split open, after a bombardment, and anybody with an open belly mustn't drink. But that's another story."

Leonid spoke up. "Your chief looks like a smart man to me: why don't you let him handle it? There must be a town, a village somewhere near. Take the sick man there; he'll surely be better off there than here in the camp, and you'll find a doctor somehow."

Styopka shrugged. "Venjamin Ivanovich is smart about other things. He's brave as a devil, he knows lots of tricks and invents more all the time. He can make people respect him, even fear him; he never loses confidence, and he's strong as a bear. But he's only good for fighting. And besides, he likes to drink, and when he drinks, his mood changes every minute."

To satisfy Styopka, they followed him to the sick man's

pallet. The man was a Tatar, a deserter from the German police, whose uniform he was still wearing. To Mendel, he didn't seem seriously ill: his belly was indeed a bit taut, but it didn't hurt when it was touched, and his fever couldn't have been very high. He was well nourished: Mendel tried to reassure Styopka; he advised giving the patient no food for a day, and no medicines.

"No danger of that," Styopka said, "we don't have any medicines. We had a bit of aspirin, but we've run out."

As they emerged from the tent, they ran into Venjamin. He was unrecognizable: no longer the easygoing host, drunk on vodka and victory, or the overgrown child pouting over the broken radio. He was a fearsome human specimen, a young warrior of prompt and precise movements, intelligent face, and intense but inscrutable gaze. An eagle, Mendel thought to himself; we must be on our guard.

"Come with me," Venjamin said, with calm authority. He took them off to a corner of the tent, and asked them who they were, where they came from, and where they were going. He spoke in the soft, confident voice of a man who knows he will be obeyed.

"I'm an artilleryman, and he's a paratrooper. We're stragglers, missing, and we met by chance, in the Bryansk woods. We heard about this band, we looked for you, and we caught up with you."

"Who told you about us?"

"The Uzbek who sold you the radio."

"Why did you follow us?"

Mendel hesitated for a moment. "Because we'd like to join the band."

"Are you armed?"

"Yes. A submachine gun, a German pistol, and some ammunition."

Without changing his tone, Venjamin addressed Leonid: "And you? Why don't you say anything?"

Embarrassed, Leonid replied that he let Mendel do the talking, because he was older and the weapons belonged to him.

"The weapons don't belong to him," Venjamin said. "They belong to everybody; weapons belong to those who know how to use them." He was silent for a moment, as if expecting a reaction; but Leonid and Mendel also remained silent. Then he went on: "Why do you want to join us? Answer separately. You?"

Leonid, caught off guard, was tongue-tied. He felt as if he had been demoted to schoolroom questioning or, worse, to the humiliating interrogation he had undergone when they arrested him and imprisoned him in the Lubyanka. He murmured something about a soldier's duty and his wish to be not just a straggler.

"You were a prisoner of the Germans," Venjamin said.

"How do you know that?" Mendel intervened, surprised.

"I'll ask the questions. But you can see it on his face. And what about you, artilleryman? Why do you want to come with us?"

Mendel felt he was being weighed, as if on scales; and he felt irritated at being weighed. He answered: "Because I've been a missing person for a year. Because I'm tired of living like a wolf. Because I have a score of my own to settle. Because I believe our war is just."

Venjamin's voice sank still lower. "You found us yesterday on a strange day, good and bad. A good day, because the news you heard is true, the radio repeated it twice: Mussolini has fallen. But that doesn't mean the war will end soon. Last night we yelled it into one another's ears, each of us convinced the others, and we were all ready to be convinced, because hope's contagious as cholera. Last night we were on vacation. But we know the Germans. During the night I thought it over, and I believe the war will last a long time still. And yesterday was a bad day because the radio broke down. Worse than you might think: a band without a radio is a bunch of orphans, deaf and dumb. Without the radio we don't know where the front is, and in Moscow they don't know where we are, and we can't call on planes to drop things. Everything comes through the radio: medicine, grain, weapons, even vodka. With the radio comes news, courage, too. And since you can't live without grain, and when it's lacking, you have to take it from peasants; so a band without a radio becomes a band of bandits. It's good for you to know these things, and give them some thought before deciding. And it's good for you to know something else, too. Eight months ago there were a hundred of us, and now there are less than forty. In our war no two days are ever alike: we're poor a bit and rich a bit, full one day and hungry the next. And this isn't a war for anybody with weak nerves. We come from far away and we're going far away, and the weak are dead or have dropped out. Think it over. And before giving you an answer, I'll think it over, too."

A metallic clang was heard. Noonday soup was ready, and Styopka had sounded assembly, striking a stone against a length of railroad track hanging from a bough. They all lined up at the pot, Venya too, and Mendel and Leonid; and Styopka distributed the food. Nearly everybody had finished eating, and many were already lying in the sun and smoking, when a voice came from the shore, a yell: "Tree trunks coming!" And, in fact, they were arriving, floating slowly on the current: heavy trunks, stripped of branches, scattered, a few at a time. Venjamin went to the water and became alert. He asked Styopka, "Where are they coming from?"

"As a rule they come from the Smolensk dock, three hundred kilometers upstream. They've always done it like this. It costs less than shipping them by rail. They go down to the Ukraine, and they're used as supports in the mines."

"They've always done it like this, but now the mines are working for the Germans," Venjamin said, scratching his chin. At that moment, at a bend of the river, something bigger appeared: it was a convoy of rafts, tied in a line, maybe ten of them, appearing one after the other from behind a tongue of wooded land. "We have to grab them," Venjamin said.

"It's not a job I've ever done, but I've seen others do it," Styopka said. "Farther down, a kilometer from here, there's a stagnant branch. If we hurry, we'll get there in time. But we need some poles."

In a moment Venya was master of the situation. He left ten men to guard the camp, sent another ten with hatchets to chop down and strip some saplings, and he promptly hurried along the shore with those who were left, including Leonid and Mendel. They reached the stagnant water before the timber did, and a little later the ten men arrived with the saplings; but the convoy was already in sight. "Hurry! Who's the best swimmer? You, Volodya!" But Volodya, either because there was a real impediment or because he had little desire, couldn't get his boots off in time. He was huddled on the ground, all twisted, his face flushed by the strain; and Venya lost patience. "Good-for-nothing! Idler! Come, give me that pole." In a moment he was barefoot and naked. Wading a bit and swimming a bit, with one hand, he crossed the stagnant water; and when he had reached the green point that separated the two branches of the river, the convoy of rafts was already going by. He was heard cursing, then seen sinking again into the stream. Other men followed him with other poles. He swam rapidly towards the rafts, missed the first ones, and managed to climb on to the last, which he immediatelly maneuvered with his pole, directing it towards the grassy point, where it ran aground in the mire. But it was soon apparent that the raft wouldn't stay there long: the other rafts, idly drawn on by the current, tugged at its anchorage; and one man couldn't hold it fast. Out of breath, Venya shouted to the men to climb on to the rafts, one to each, and each was to thrust his pole hard into the muddy bed. They managed to move the convoy away from the shore, struggle across the current, come around the point, and triumphantly push the timber into the still water of the stagnant branch of the river. "That's good," Venjamin said, getting dressed. "Now we'll see. Maybe we'll put them ashore and set fire to them. Just so long as they don't get to the mines. Now back to the camp."

On the brief march back, Mendel fell in beside him and

congratulated him. "I know, I know that for the Germans it doesn't represent serious harm," Venjamin replied. "But for men like these, there's nothing worse than idleness. And nothing better than an example. Dry yourselves, you two, and then meet me in the tent."

In the tent, Venjamin came straight to the point. "I've thought it over, and it's not easy. You see, in our way, we're specialized. We know this area, we're trained. Having you with us would be a responsibility. I'm sure you're good fighters; but we're not fighters so much as rear-guard men, spoilers, saboteurs. Each of us has his tasks, and you can't learn them in a few days. And besides—"

"You didn't talk like this earlier, this morning," Mendel said.

Venya lowered his eyes. "No, I didn't talk like this. Look, I don't have anything against you people. I've had Jewish friends since I was a child and I had others as my companions at Voronezh, at training camp, and I know you're men like everybody else, neither better nor worse, or rather maybe a bit more—"

"That's enough for me," Leonid said. "If you don't want us, we'll go, and it'll be best for everybody. We're not going to get down on our knees to—"

Mendel interrupted him: "But I still want to hear what happened between this morning and now."

"Nothing. Nothing happened. No specific thing. I just overheard people talking, and—"

"We're soldiers, you and I. We wear the same uniform, and I want you to tell me who spoke and what was said."

"I won't tell you who spoke. It was more than one. For myself, I would accept you; but I can't prevent my men from talking, and I don't know if you would be sufficiently protected. Here there are people with different ideas, and quick to act."

Mendel insisted. He wanted to know, word for word, what the others had said, and Venjamin repeated it to him, with the expression of a man spitting out a morsel of spoiled food: "They say they don't like Jews much, and Jews that are armed even less."

Leonid spoke up. "We're leaving, and you can tell those men of yours that in Warsaw, last April, armed Jews held out against the Germans longer than the Red Army did in 'forty-one. And they weren't even properly armed, and they were hungry, and they were fighting in the midst of the dead, and they had no allies."

"How do you know these things?" Venjamin asked.

"Warsaw isn't all that far away, and news spreads even without a radio."

Venjamin stepped out of the tent, spoke in a low voice to Styopka and Volodya, then came back inside and said, "I should take away your weapons, but I won't. You've seen who we are and where we are; I shouldn't let you leave, but I will. One day with us wasn't much, but maybe what you've seen will be of use to you. Move on, keep your eyes open, and go to Novoselki."

"Why Novoselki? Where's Novoselki?"

"In the bend of the Ptich, a hundred and twenty kilometers to the west, in the midst of the Polessia marshes. It seems there's a village of armed Jews there, men and women. The foresters told us about it: those men go everywhere and know everything; they're our telegraph and our newspaper. Maybe there your weapons will be of use to you. You can't stay with us."

Mendel and Leonid took their leave, crossed the Dnepr on a raft made of four logs tied together, and resumed their way.

They walked for ten days. The weather had turned bad; it rained often, sometimes in sudden downpours, sometimes in a fine, penetrating drizzle that was like a mist; the paths were muddy, and the woods gave off a pungent aroma of mushrooms that already heralded autumn. Provisions were beginning to grow scarce; the two had to stop at night at isolated farms and dig up potatoes and beets. In the woods there were blueberries and strawberries in abundance, but after two or three hours' picking, hunger increased instead of diminishing: hunger and Leonid's irritation.

"This stuff is good for schoolboys on holiday. It stimulates your stomach without filling it."

Mendel was brooding on the news they had learned in Venjamin's camp. What significance could it have? Told like that, without any comment, without a general evaluation, the news was as irritating as the blueberries, and left the mind similarly hungry. Mussolini in prison, and the king back in power. What is a king? A kind of czar, bigoted and corrupt, a thing of the past, a fairy-tale character with braid, plumes, and ornamental dagger, arrogant and base. But this Italian king must be an ally, a friend, since he had had Mussolini imprisoned. Too bad there was no longer the kaiser in Germany, otherwise the war might really have ended, as Venjamin had said, in his drunkenness. The news that Fascism had fallen in Italy was certainly good, but what importance could it have? It was hard to get an idea: in the articles in *Pravda,* Fascist Italy had been described, according to the time, as a dangerous and untrustworthy adversary, or as a contemptible jackal in the shadow of the German beast. To be sure, the Italian soldiers on the Don hadn't lasted long, poorly equipped and poorly armed and with no will to fight; everybody knew that. Maybe they had had their fill of Mussolini, and the king had followed the wishes of the people; but in Germany there was no king, there was only Hitler. Better not to harbor any illusions.

If a king is a fairy-tale character, a king of Italy is doubly fictional, because Italy itself is a fairy tale. It was impossible to form a concrete idea of it. How can you condense into the same, single image Vesuvius and gondolas, Pompeii and Fiat, La Scala opera and the caricatures of Mussolini in *Krokodil,* that kind of highwayman with a hyena's jaw, wearing a fez with a tassel, displaying a capitalist's belly, and holding a knife in his hand? Mendel would have given a fortune for a radio, but it was only a figure of speech: they had nothing left to barter except the gun and the pistol, and it was wiser to hang on to those.

He wondered if there were Jews in Italy. If so, they must be strange Jews: how can you imagine a Jew in a gondola or at the top of Vesuvius? But there must actually be some, there are Jews even in India and China, and they aren't necessarily bad off. Maybe the Zionists of Kiev and Kharkov were right when they preached that the Jews are well off only in the land of Israel, and they should all leave Italy, Russia, India, and China and settle there to raise oranges, learn Hebrew, and dance the hora all in a ring.

Perhaps because he was tired, or because of the dampness, the scar beneath Mendel's hair had begun to itch. Leonid's boots had come unsewn, and his feet slithered in the water and the mud. Behind him, Mendel felt Leonid's negative presence, the weight of his silence; they hampered Mendel's progress more than the mud. This was no longer just mud after rain, the fertile mud that comes from heaven and must be accepted in its season. Gradually, as they advanced westward, they encountered more and more a different, permanent mud, master of the area, which came from the ground and not from the sky. The wood had thinned out, they came upon vast clearings, but with no sign of human labor. The earth was no longer black or clayey, but of a cadaverous pallor. Though moist, it was thin, sandy, and it seemed to lack water from its very womb. Yet it wasn't sterile: it nourished canebrakes, succulent plants that Mendel had never seen, and vast beds of sticky-leaved shrubs, sprawling on the ground and as if bored by the sky. The two men sank into the terrain, or the rotten leaves, up to their ankles. Leonid took off his now-useless boots, and soon Mendel imitated him: his boots were still serviceable, but it was a shame to wear them out.

On the seventh day of walking it became a problem to find a patch of dry ground where they could spend the night, even though the rain had stopped. On the eighth day it became hard also to maintain their direction; they had no compass, the sky was rarely clear, and the path was broken more and more often by shallow ponds, which still obliged them to make exhausting detours. The water was clear, unmoving, smelling of peat, with thick, round leaves floating on it, fleshy flowers, and an occasional bird's nest. They looked for eggs in vain: there were no eggs, only bits of shell and soaked feathers. But they found frogs, plenty of them: adult frogs the size of a hand, tadpoles, and slimy garlands of frogs' eggs. They caught several adults easily, roasted them on sticks, and ate them. Leonid ate with the ferine greed of a hungry nineteen-year-old; Mendel, amazed to discover in himself a trace of the ancestral repulsion for forbidden meats.

"Like in Egypt, in the time of Moses," Mendel said, just to make conversation. "But I never understood how they could be a plague: the Egyptians could have eaten them, like we're doing."

"Frogs were a plague?" Leonid asked, chewing.

"The second plague: *Dom, Tzefardea'; tzefardea'* are frogs."

"What was the first?"

"*Dom.* Blood," Mendel answered.

"We've had blood," Leonid said, pensively. "And the others? Which are the ones that come afterwards?"

To assist his memory, Mendel began to chant the jingle that is recited at Passover to amuse children: "*dom, tzefardea', kinim, 'aroiv . . .*" Then he translated into Russian: blood, frogs, lice, beasts, scabies, pestilence, hail, locusts. . . . But he broke off, before finishing the list, to ask Leonid: "But you . . . when you were a child, didn't you ever keep Passover?"

He immediately regretted the question. Though Leonid didn't stop eating, he looked away, and his eyes became grim and blank. After a few moments, with apparent incoherence, he said:

"When they sent my father to Solovki, my mother didn't wait for him. She didn't wait long. She put me in an orphanage and went to live with another man, and never bothered about me any more. He was a railroad man, too, and he always spoke in a whisper. Maybe he was also afraid of ending up on the islands; he was afraid of everything. As far as I know, they're still together. And now I've had enough. Enough walking towards God knows where. Enough of blood and frogs, and I want to stop, and I want to die."

Mendel didn't answer; he realized his companion wasn't one of those men who can be healed with words; perhaps nobody with a story like his behind him could be healed with words. And yet Mendel felt in his debt: guilty towards him, at fault, as if he were seeing a man drown in shallow water and, since the man doesn't call for help, allowing him to drown. To help Leonid you had to understand him, and to understand him, he would have to talk, and he talked only like this: a few words, then silence, his eyes avoiding Mendel's. He was ready to wound and ready to be wounded. What if Mendel tried to force his hand? That could be dangerous: like when you stick a screw awkwardly into a nut and you feel resistance. If you force it with the screwdriver, you strip the threads and you have to throw the screw away. But if you have patience and you start over again from the beginning, you can turn it without effort, and in the end it holds fast. It takes patience, even in someone who doesn't have any. Especially for someone who doesn't have any. Who has lost it. Who has never had it. For one who never had the time and the clay to build it for himself. Mendel was about to answer: If you really want to die, you'll have plenty of opportunities. But, on the contrary, he said, "Let's get some sleep. Tonight at least we have full bellies."

By the ninth day of their walking the path had virtually disappeared: it could be identified at intervals, on the sandbars that wound among the marshes, as they became more and more broad, flowing one into the other. The wood had dwindled to isolated patches, and the horizon surrounding them had never been so vast throughout their journey. Vast and sad, steeped in the intense, funereal odor of the canebrakes. On the still water the round clouds were sharply mirrored: white, motionless in the sky. At the slippery footsteps of the two men, an occasional duck flapped off into the canes, but Mendel chose not to shoot, reluctant to waste bullets and to signal their presence. A wooden building loomed up. When they reached it, they saw it was a watermill, abandoned and half-ruined; the wheel's rusted blade dipped into the murky water, which proceeded, in ramifications, through the marshes. It had to be the Ptich. Novoselki couldn't be far away.

On the other side of the river the terrain was firmer; in the distance they could make out a slight rise, covered with dark trees, oaks or alders. Mendel put his boots back on; Leonid remained barefoot, with only some rags wrapped around his feet to protect them against the thorns. After half an hour's walking, he cried, "Hey! Look here!" Mendel turned and saw him holding a doll in his hand: a poor little pink doll, naked, one leg missing. Mendel held it to his nose and caught an odor of childhood, the pathetic odor of camphor, of celluloid—for a moment, evoked with brutal violence—his sisters, their little friend who was to become his wife, Strelka, the pit. He remained silent, gulped, then said to Leonid in a soft voice, "You don't find these things in the woods."

To the right of the track there was a clearing, and in the clearing they saw a man. He was tall, thin, pale, with narrow shoulders; when he became aware of them, he tried awkwardly to run off or to hide. They called to him, and he let them approach. He was dressed in rags and wore on his feet a pair of sandals made from old tires; he had a bunch of grass in his hand. He didn't look like a peasant. They asked him, "Is the village of the Jews here?"

"There's no village here," the man answered.

"But aren't you a Jew?"

"I'm a refugee," he said, but his accent gave him away.

Leonid showed him the doll. "What about this? Where did it come from?"

The man's gaze shifted slightly: someone was approaching, behind Leonid. It was a little girl, dark and tiny; she took the doll from his hands, saying very gravely, "It's mine. You were very smart to find it."

3

August–November

1943

It wasn't exactly a village: it was a "republic of the marshes," the man explained to Mendel, not without pride. It was rather an encampment, a haven, a fortress; and the two of them would be welcome, because hands capable of working were scarce, and men able to handle weapons were even scarcer. His name was Adam. As night was about to fall, he collected the children, who were hunting grasses at the edge of the clearing; and he invited Mendel and Leonid to follow him. The children, boys and girls, numbered about a dozen, between the ages of five and twelve; and each had gathered a little bundle of grasses, separated into several bunches. "Here everybody has to make himself useful, even the children. There are herbs for curing diseases, others are good to eat, cooked or raw. Grasses, berries roots: we've taught the children to identify them. Eh, we don't teach them much else here."

They started on their way. The children looked at the two soldiers with distrustful curiosity. They didn't ask the men any questions, and they didn't talk among themselves, either. They were shy, wild little animals, with restless eyes; without Adam's giving them any order, they spontaneously formed a line, two by two, and set off towards the rise, following a trail that they seemed to know well. They, too, were wearing sandals cut from tires; their clothes were old army uniforms, tattered and ill-fitting. The little girl who had recovered her doll held it tight against her chest as if to protect it, but she didn't speak to it or even look at it: she looked to either side, with the uneasy, darting glances of a bird.

Adam, on the contrary, had a great desire to talk and to listen. He was fifty-five years old, he was the oldest of the camp, and therefore he was charged with minding the children: yes, there were women, but not many, and they were suited for heavier tasks; one of them was his daughter. Before answering their other questions, he wanted to know the story of the two newcomers: Mendel was glad to satisfy him, and in detail, but Leonid managed it in a few words. He, Adam, came from far away: he had been a textile worker in Minsk, active in the Bund, the Jewish labor organization, since he was sixteen. He had been in time to get a taste of the czar's prisons, which still hadn't saved him from going to the front in the First World War. But a Bundist is a Menshevik, and as a Menshevik he had been tried and again imprisoned in 1930: it hadn't been nice, they had put him in freezing cells and in others that were torrid and airless, they wanted him to confess that he had been bribed by foreigners. He held out through two interrogations, then slashed his wrists. They sewed him up again so he could confess: for two weeks they didn't allow him an hour's sleep, and then he confessed everything the judges wanted. He spent another couple of years in prison and three more in a camp, at Vologda, halfway between Moscow and Arkhangelsk: that was better than a prison, he worked in a kolkhoz, which was where he had learned what grasses are good to eat. There are a lot more than city people know, and so even from confinement some good can come. In the summer, grasses are important, they contain some nourishment, even if you eat them without seasoning. Of course, winter is another matter: it was best not to think about winter.

After his confinement was over, they had sent him home, but the war came and the Germans reached Minsk in a few days. Well, Adam felt a weight on his conscience, because he, and other old men like him, had known the Germans in the other war, and had tried to reassure everybody: the Germans were good soldiers, but civilized people, why hide or run away? At most, they would give the land back to the peasants. Instead, in Minsk, *those* Germans had done a thing that he couldn't tell about. He couldn't and wouldn't and shouldn't. "It's the first rule of our republic. If we kept on telling one another what we've seen, we'd go crazy, and instead we all have to be sane, children included. Besides the different grasses, we teach them to tell lies, because we have enemies on all sides, not only the Germans."

While he was talking like this, they had arrived at the camp. Actually, it would have been difficult to define it with a single word, because it was something Mendel had never seen and couldn't have imagined possible. In any case, it was much more a refuge than a fortress. On the hillock they had glimpsed from the distance, and which didn't rise more than twenty meters or so above the plain, there was an old monastery, hidden among the thick trees. It consisted of a brick construction forming three sides of an open quadrangle, two stories aboveground. At the two corners, two squat towers rose, one supporting what remained of a bell chamber. The other, half-destroyed then reconstructed in wood, must have been used as a lookout post. Not far away, opposite the open side of the quadrangle, there was the monastery barn, a building of roughly stripped logs, with a wide wagon entrance and some tiny windows.

The monastery was not so much hidden by the trees as besieged by them. Of its three wings, only one was intact; the other two bore signs of destruction, ancient and recent. The roof, originally of tiles, had collapsed in several places, and had been haphazardly patched up with straw and reeds; the outside walls also displayed big gaps through which you could see the rooms inside, filled with rubble. Everything must have been abandoned dozens of years before, perhaps even at the time of the civil war, because alders, oaks and willows had grown against the walls, and some even inside, sending roots down into the piles of detritus and seeking the light through gaps in the roof.

It was almost dark by now. Adam had the two men wait outside in the courtyard invaded by trampled weeds; he returned a little later and led them into a big room, its floor covered with straw and sunflower stalks, where many people were already waiting, some seated, some lying down. The children also arrived, and in the semidarkness a grass soup was distributed to all. There were no lights; two women prepared the children for sleep; Adam came back and cautioned the newcomers not to strike any matches. Mendel and Leonid felt guarded and protected. They were tired: only for a few minutes were they aware of the murmuring of their neighbors, then they fell into the unawareness of sleep.

Mendel woke in the morning with the happy-uneasy impression of being in another world and another period: perhaps in the midst of the desert, on the march for forty years towards the promised land, perhaps inside the walls of Jerusalem besieged by the Romans, or perhaps in Noah's ark. In the big room, besides the two of them, only two men and a woman had remained, all three middle-aged, and apparently ill: they spoke neither Russian nor Yiddish, but some Polish dialect. Children, perhaps the same as the previous evening, peered in at the door, curious but silent. A girl entered, small and thin, with a submachine gun slung over her shoulder; she saw the two strangers and went out at once, asking no questions. A subdued bustle could be heard all around, as of mice in an attic: brief calls, a hammering, the creak of a well chain, the hoarse cry of a rooster. The air that came through the open windows, bringing the damp breath of the marsh and the wood, dragged other, sharper and unfamiliar smells, of spices, singed fur, of cramped rooms, poverty.

A little later Adam came and asked them to follow him: Dov, the chief, was waiting for them. He was awaiting them at headquarters, Adam specified proudly, which meant a little room with paneled walls of fir planks, half-occupied by a built-in stove, at the heart of a big shed that had been the outbuilding of the monastery. On the stove and beside it were three pallets, and near the door there was a table of rough planks nailed together: there was nothing else. Even the chair on which Dov sat looked solid but crude, the work of expert hands with little help from tools. Dov was middle-aged, short, but with strong bones and broad shoulders: without actually being hump-backed, he was bent and carried his head down, as if he were wearing a burden; so he looked up at his interlocutors from below, as if above the rims of nonexistent eye-glasses. His hair, which must once have been blond, was almost white, but still thick: he wore it carefully combed, parted straight down the middle. His hands were big and strong; when he spoke, he kept them motionless, hanging from his forearms, and he looked at them from time to time as if they weren't his. He had a square face, steady eyes, honest features, worn and vigorous; he was slow of speech. He had the two men sit down on the pallet nearest the stove, and spoke these words:

"I would have received you in any case, but it's good luck that you're soldiers: we already have too many people who've come here looking for protection. They come even from far away, seeking safety. They aren't mistaken, this is the safest place a Jew can find within a radius of a thousand kilometers, but that doesn't mean the place is safe. It isn't, not at all: we are weak, poorly armed, we are in no

condition to defend ourselves against a serious attack.
There are also too many of us: actually, we don't even
know how many of us there are at any given moment.
Every day there are people who come and people who
leave. Today there must be about fifty of us, not all Jews:
there are also two or three families of Polish peasants. The
Ukrainian nationalists stole their provisions and livestock
and burned their houses, they were terrified, and so they
came here. The Jews come from the ghettos, or have
escaped from the German labor camps. Each of them has
a terrible story behind him: there are old people, women,
children, sick. Only about a dozen young people know
how to handle weapons.

"What weapons do you have?" Mendel asked.

"Very few. A dozen hand grenades, a few pistols and
submachine guns. A heavy machine gun with ammunition for five minutes' fire. Luckily for us, the Germans
have rarely been seen around here so far; their best troops
have been recalled to the front, which is hundreds of kilometers away. In these parts there are only a few garrisons
scattered here and there, for requisitioning provisions and
labor and guarding the roads and railway. The Ukrainians
are the most dangerous; the Germans have organized and
armed them, and they indoctrinate them: as if there were
any need for that! The Ukrainians have always considered
Poles and Jews their natural enemies.

"The best protection the camp has is the marshes. They
go on and on for dozens of kilometers in every direction,
and to cross them, you have to know them well: in some
the water comes up to your knees, but in others it's over a
man's head, and there are few fords and they're hard to
find. The Germans don't like them because you can't have
a blitzkrieg in marshes: even tanks get stuck, and the
heavier they are the worse it is."

"But the water must freeze during the winter."

"Winter is a time of terror. In winter the woods and the
marshes become our enemies, the worst enemies of people
in hiding. The trees shed their leaves, and it's like being

naked: reconnaissance planes can see everything that happens. The marshes freeze, and they're not a barrier any longer. You can read footprints on the snow. And your only protection against the cold is a fire, but any fire makes smoke, and smoke can be seen far off.

"And I still haven't mentioned food. For food, too, we have no certitude. Some we get from the peasants, obtained politely—or otherwise—but the villages are poor and far away, and the Germans and the bandits are already quick to strip them. We get some things from the partisans, but in the winter they have the same problems we have; still they sometimes receive supplies by parachute drops, and then we get something too. And, finally, some food comes from the woods: grasses and herbs, frogs, carp, mushrooms, berries, but only in summer. In winter, nothing. In winter only terror and hunger."

"Isn't there some way to establish better contacts with the partisans?"

"So far our contacts have been irregular. For that matter, what is more irregular than the *partizanka?* I was with them, until winter before last: then they declared me unfit, because for them I was an old man, and besides I was wounded and couldn't run any more. The local bands are like drops of mercury: they come together, they break apart, they join up again: they are destroyed and new ones are formed. The biggest and most stable have radios and keep in contact with the Great Land . . ."

"What's the Great Land?"

"We call it that, too: it's the Soviet territory beyond the front, the part not occupied by the Nazis. The radio is like blood: thanks to the radio they receive orders, reinforcements, instructors, arms, provisions. Not only by parachute: when it's possible, planes from the Great Land come down in the partisan zone, unload men and goods, take away the sick and the wounded. For this, on the contrary, things go better in winter, because for planes you need an airfield, or at least a stretch of flat, open land; but land like that can be seen clearly from the air, and the

Germans, as soon as they see it, they promptly drop bombs to make it unusable. But in the winter any lake or marsh or river will do, provided the ice is thick enough.

"But you mustn't imagine a regular service. Not all the drops and the landings end happily, and not all the bands are prepared to share their things with us. Many partisan leaders consider us useless mouths because we don't fight. For that very reason we have to prove ourselves useful, and we can do this in various ways. First of all, anyone able to walk and shoot must consider himself a partisan, contribute to the defense; and if the partisans ask for him, he has to go with them. Practically speaking, between the bands and the monastery there is a constant exchange, and the monastery itself, until the Germans discover it, is not a bad refuge for tired or wounded partisans, too. But there are other things that can be done, and we do them. We mend their clothes, do their laundry, tan hides with oak bark and make boots from the hides: yes, the smell you smell comes from the tanning vats. And with birch bark we make pitch so the boot leather will remain soft and waterproof. Do you have a trade?" he asked, addressing Mendel.

"I'm a watchmender by trade, but I also worked as mechanic in a kolkhoz."

"Good. We'll find work for you right away. What about you, Muscovite?"

"I studied to be a bookkeeper."

"That's a bit less useful, for us." Dov laughed. "I'd like to keep accounts, but it's impossible. We can't even count the people who come and go. Here we get Jews who have miracuously escaped the SS massacres; peasants come seeking protection; and dubious people we have to watch out for. They could even be spies, but what can we do? There's nothing to do but trust their faces, the way I trust yours now: we don't have a secret service. Many arrive, others leave, or die. The young leave, with my permission or without: they prefer to join up with the partisans properly, rather than vegetate in this republic in hunger and fear. The old and the sick die, but young and healthy people also die, of despair. Despair is worse than disease: it attacks you during the days of waiting, when no news comes and no contacts, or when they announce German troop movements or movements of Ukrainian and Hungarian mercenaries: waiting is as fatal as dysentery. There are only two defenses against despair: working and fighting; but they're not always enough. There's also a third, which is telling one another lies: we all fall into that. Well, that's the end of my speech; it's good you've come here armed, but if you'd brought a radio transmitter it would have been better still. So it goes, you can't have everything, not even in Novoselki.

They immediately became part of the guards' roster; this was the most important service of the community, and the two old towers of the monastery served well for the purpose. As a rule, every able-bodied refugee had to put in twelve hours of work, then eight of rest, and four on guard duty, divided into two shifts of two hours each; this led to complications, but Dov kept a precise schedule and insisted that it be respected. That same night Mendel stood guard with the slim girl he had glimpsed in the dormitory, each to a tower; he learned that her name was Line, but little more. As the shift ended, he asked her, "I have a rip in my trousers. Could you please mend it for me?" Line answered curtly, "I'll give you a needle and thread, and you can fend for yourself. I don't have time." She raised her lantern and looked Mendel in the face, with an almost insolent attention: "Where did you get that scar?" Mendel answered, "At the front," and Line didn't pursue the matter, but went off to sleep. Leonid, on the other hand, found himself paired with Ber, a bespectacled boy, still almost a child, and also of few words.

The work in the tannery, to which both newcomers were assigned, proceeded in the midst of disgusting fumes, in a silence broken only by the splashing of the vats and by brief murmurs. With closed faces, men and women scraped the hides to eliminate flesh and fur: they were hides of rabbit, dog, cat, goat. Nothing was wasted, the fleshy residue of the freshest hides was carefully saved, for use as fertilizer. Other workers boiled the bark of trees or stretched the hides on wooden frames.

They soon adapted themselves to this sort of life and to the obsessive, paradoxical order, which each one seemed to maintain with effort and stubbornness, every minute. There were no community meals: at midday and in the evening all lined up at the pots in the kitchen, then each one huddled in some corner to consume in silence what he had received: mostly a thin soup of herbs with a few scraps of potato, rarely a bit of meat or cheese, a spoonful of blueberries, a glass of milk.

Adam, perhaps because he was the oldest, was the only one who hadn't forgotten the pleasure of storytelling:

"Dov? He's a man who never has to be coaxed. It's a good thing he's here to settle the quarrels. He's seen life, Dov has, and he comes from afar. He comes from a remote village on the plateau of central Siberia, I can never remember the name: his grandfather, a Nihilist, was deported there, back in the days of the czars, and his father was born there, and so was he. When the war broke out, he was mobilized and sent to the air corps. He was taken prisoner right away, in July of 'forty-one; the Germans put him in a *Lager* that was barely a hectare of land surrounded by barbed wire, and nothing inside, not a barracks or a shed; only ten thousand exhausted soldiers, wounded, crazed with hunger and thirst. In the confusion they didn't realize he was a Jew, so they didn't kill him. A few days later, they loaded him and a thousand others on to a train. He realized that the planks on the floor of his car were rotten, he kicked them loose; and dropped from the speeding train. Only him. The other eighty in the car didn't have the nerve. He broke a leg, but he managed all the same to get away from the railroad line and reach the house of some peasants who kept him for months without reporting him, and they even set his leg. As soon as he could walk he went with the partisans, but last winter he was wounded in the knee, and since then he's been lame. The partisans helped him, and he settled here with a handful of other Jews. He's a hardheaded Siberian; in a few months he and the others transformed this monastery, which was just a pile of rubble, into a place where you can live."

All through August, in the republic of the marshes nothing worthy of note occurred. From Ozarichi nine stragglers from the Red Army arrived; on their own initiative they had burned and looted a German depot. They brought two mules loaded with sacks of potatoes, four Italian rifles, and twenty hand grenades; and news that was worth all the rest put together: the Russians had recaptured Kharkov. Among the citizens of Novoselki there was an immediate, impassioned argument: how far away was Kharkov? Some said five hundred, some six hundred, some eight hundred kilometers. These last accused the first of being dreamers; and the first considered the last defeatists, or rather, traitors.

The Ozarichi men had also dragged with them a doctor, and for Novoselki a doctor would have been very valuable; but this one, a Jewish captain of about forty, was very sick. He had a fever; during the last stages he had barely managed to drag himself along, and from time to time they had loaded him on the mule. The moment he reached the monastery he had to go to bed because he couldn't stand up any more; purplish spots had appeared on his face, and he could speak only with difficulty; just with his lips, as if his tongue were paralyzed. He made his own diagnosis: he said he had spotted fever, that he was about to die, and that he wanted only to die in peace and not infect anybody else. Dov asked him how he could be treated, and he answered that there was no treatment: he asked for a bit of water, then didn't speak again. They had him lie down on the ground, outside the building, and they covered him with a blanket. The next morning he was dead. He was buried with every precaution against contact; Ber, the youth with the eyeglasses, a student of a rabbinical college, came to say Kaddish over the grave. What to do to avoid contagion? Or was typhus fever carried perhaps only by lice? Nobody knew. To make doubly sure, Dov had them burn every object the dead man had touched, including the precious blanket.

September came, and the first rainfalls, the first leaves began to turn yellow. Mendel realized that something was changing in Leonid. At the beginning of their stay in Novoselki, he hadn't departed from his usual behavior, consisting of long, frowning silences and outbursts of anger addressed solely to him, as if Mendel had been the one to sign the pact with the Germans and had unleashed the war and spread terror through the country. As if Mendel had sent him to the paratroops and had flung him in the midst of the marshes. But now Leonid sought out Mendel less and less frequently, or rather, he seemed to avoid meeting him, and when he couldn't avoid it, he took care not to look Mendel in the eye. One day Mendel no longer saw him around the tanning vats; Mendel was told that Leonid couldn't stand the smell and had asked Dov to transfer him to the room where Line and two other girls distilled birchwood to make tar. Another day Dov complained to Mendel because his friend hadn't shown up for work, and this was a serious breach, which Dov couldn't understand. Mendel replied that he wasn't responsible for what Leonid did or didn't do, but as he said this he felt something like an itch around his heart, because he had realized that the words that had come from his mouth were the ones that Cain had said when the Lord asked him about Abel. What nonsense! Was Leonid his brother? Not a brother, he was just another poor wretch like himself, and like everybody else, someone collected along the road. Of course Mendel wasn't his keeper, and still less had he shed Leonid's blood. He hadn't killed him in the field. And yet the itch persisted: maybe this is really how it is, maybe each of us is Cain to some Abel, and slays him in the field without knowing it, through the things he does to him, the things he says to him, and the things he should say to him and doesn't.

Mendel told Dov that Leonid had had a difficult life, but Dov answered him with a single syllable, looking into his eyes: "*Nu?*" In Novoselki this wasn't any excuse. Who didn't have a difficult life behind him? There were no excuses for *partisanshchina*, Dov said sharply. What was *partisanshchina?* Partisan anarchy, Dov explained: lack of discipline. A serious danger. To live outside the law didn't mean not having any law. To escape the Fascists' killing it was necessary to accept a discipline even more severe than the one imposed by the Fascists: more severe but more just, because it was voluntary. Anyone unable to accept it is free to leave. Mendel and Leonid should think it over. In fact, they should think it over immediately, because there was a job for them to do: an urgent, important job, and not even all that dangerous. Orders had come to sabotage a railroad. Well, this was just the right job for them, to win citizenship in the republic; for that matter, this was the partisan custom, to ask newcomers to do a job as a test, as when you enter a factory.

The day after, Dov also summoned Leonid and went into details:

"The Brest-Rovno-Kiev line has been blown up, the line that supplied the German front in the south Ukraine. From now on, all the war traffic will go by way of Brest-Gomel. This line runs south of Novoselki, about thirty kilometers away: it's a single track. It has to be put out of commission as soon as possible. This is the job you're to do. Any ideas?"

"Do you have explosive?" Mendel asked.

"We have some, but very little and not suited for this. We extracted it from a few shells that dropped into the swamp and didn't explode."

Leonid interrupted him, giving Mendel an insolent glance: "Excuse me, Chief. For jobs like this, explosive is more a hindrance than a help. Sabotaging railroads is a job I know: during parachute training they explained all the methods to us. A big wrench is much better, more sure, makes no noise, and leaves no trace."

"On your course," Mendel asked, irritated, "did they also give you practical training, or just theory?"

"I'll assume the responsibility for this job. You, for once, mind your own business."

"All right," Mendel said, underlining his words, "I have nothing against that. I'm better at mending things than at blowing them up."

Dov listened, as if he were amused by this bickering. "Just a moment," he said. "It would be a good idea to combine the sabotage of the tracks with the derailing of a train: a broken bit of track can be repaired in a few hours, but an overturned train, besides being a dead loss, blocks the line for several days. But the Germans know this, too: for a while now, if a train is important, they've been sending a scout car ahead of it."

There was a brief technical discussion between Dov and Leonid, which then hatched the definitive plan. It would be unwise to sabotage the line in the stretch near Koptsevichi, the point directly south of Novoselki: it would put the Gestapo on the trail of the hideout. Better to go farther on, near Zhitkovichi, fifty kilometers to the west, where the line crosses a bridge over a canal: there, that would be the ideal point.

"Get ready," Dov said. "You leave in two hours. You'll have a guide who knows the area. Take no weapons. Work out together how to sabotage the line; if you have learned some tricks, Leonid, so much the better. And remember: no quarrels during the mission. They're preparing the wrenches at the forge: two of them, the right size."

A guide like this was something Mendel could gladly have done without, but there was no question that he really did know the area, and especially the fords. His name was Karlis; he was a Latvian, twenty-two years old; he was tall, thin, blond, and he moved with silent agility. How did someone born so far away know so well the marshes of

Polessia? He had got to know them under the Germans, Karlis said, speaking Russian rather badly. In his village they preferred the Germans to the Russians, and he preferred them, too, or had, at least at the beginning. He had gone over to their side, and they had taught him how to hunt partisans. Yes, right here, in this country: he had been here almost a year, and he knew the zone inch by inch. But he wasn't a fool, after Stalingrad he realized that the Germans would lose the war, so he deserted a second time. He gave the two of them a half smile, seeking consensus. Always better to be on the winning side, wasn't that right? But now he had to be careful not to fall into the hands either of Hitler or of Stalin. Was that why he had taken refuge at Novoselki? Leonid asked. Yes, of course: he, personally, had nothing against the Jews.

"We have to be careful, too," Mendel whispered to Leonid, "this one has the *Dom Israel* on his hands, the blood of Israel."

Karlis smiled his crooked smile again. "It's no good your speaking Yiddish. I understand it, and I understand German, too."

"So you think the Jews of Novoselki will be the winners?" Mendel asked.

"I didn't say that," the Latvian answered. "Careful, the water gets deep here. We'll stay more to the right."

They emerged from the marshes at dawn, and went on for a few hours through meadows and untilled land. They rested until early afternoon, and reached the railroad late in the night. According to Karlis, they should follow it westward for eight or ten kilometers before crossing the canal; it was best not to walk on the track, but to keep a few hundred meters away, parallel to it, without losing sight of it. There was a moon: it made their walking easier, but if there hadn't been one, they would have felt safer. They were tired by now; still, Leonid forced the pace and tended to take the lead. The Latvian, on the other hand, managed to remain last; this irritated Mendel, who at a certain point said to him sharply, "You! Walk on. I'll be last."

Leonid sighted the bridge at sunrise. It wasn't the best hour to start work, but there wasn't a living soul to be seen, and the bridge, only a few meters long for that matter, wasn't guarded. Leonid was obviously eager to take charge of the mission: he gave orders in a low, but excited, nervous voice. With Mendel's help he loosened the plates at the rail joints, just at the head of the bridge, and then he undid all the bolts that connected the ties to the tracks. The wood was rotten and the bolts came out easily. Karlis listlessly offered to help, but then he contented himself with keeping watch, to see nobody came near. When the two tracks were free, Leonid didn't move them, but tied them crosswise with a rope about thirty meters long, the longest there was in Novoselki, unfortunately. The free part of the rope was buried under loose earth and brush. Done, Leonid said proudly, now all we have to do is wait for the train. Let the scout car go by, and then, right in front of the locomotive, we pull the rope and shift the rails. Not too soon: otherwise, the engineer would notice something was wrong.

They spent the day sleeping, in turns. Towards evening, in the silence of the countryside, the sound of the train was heard. All three men grabbed the end of the rope and lay down among the bushes, so as not to be seen. There was no scout. The train consisted of about thirty closed freight cars, and it was advancing rapidly. But once in sight of the bridge, it began to slow down. Mendel suddenly felt an intense desire to pray, but he repressed it, because none of the prayers of his childhood was suited to the situation, and he wasn't even sure that the Holy One, blessed be He, had any jurisdiction over railroads. The train was proceeding slowly; it came to the disconnected stretch. "Now!" Leonid ordered. The three men leaped to their feet and yanked on the rope, and the rope obeyed their frantic efforts: but not much, not more than the breadth of a hand.

The locomotive shrieked as the brakes were abruptly applied, and sparks flew from the wheels. The driver must have seen something and tried to reverse the locomotive, but too late. The bogey wheels ran off the tracks onto the gravel of the embankment, locomotive and cars advanced another ten meters out of inertia in a deafening racket and a cloud of dust, then everything stopped. Only the cowcatcher of the locomotive was on the bridge, and it was tilted slightly; it must have touched the parapet, and from some broken pipe a jet of steam emerged with an earsplitting hiss, so loud that the three men couldn't exchange a word. Pale as a corpse, Leonid motioned to the others to follow him to the first car: perhaps in search of loot. Insane! Human figures could be seen running up and down alongside the train. Mendel took over: with Karlis's help, he dragged Leonid towards the nearest wood. They looked one another in the face, panting: a half derailment, a half success. The locomotive broken down, but not destroyed; the line interrupted, but capable of being repaired in a few days; the bridge and the cars almost intact. Leonid cursed himself, he should have foreseen that the train would slow down at the bridge. If he had sabotaged the track a kilometer farther down, the damage would have been ten times greater.

The men of the escort, no more than half a dozen, were busy with the locomotive, giving no thought to those responsible for the breakdown. The three waited, hiding, until it was dark, then they set off, in no hurry, on the way home. Leonid seemed dejected, and Mendel tried to cheer him up: it wasn't his fault, they didn't have the means; and anyway the train had somehow been stopped. Leonid was silent for a long time, turning his back; then he said, "You don't understand: it was a present."

"A present. Who for?"

"For Line, the girl with the gun, yes, the one who's on guard duty with you. She's my woman, since the other night. The train was a present for her."

Mendel wanted to laugh and to cry. He was about to tell Leonid that Novoselki wasn't the place for a romance, but then he checked himself. They walked on in silence; halfway through the night they realized that Karlis had lagged behind, and they stopped to wait for him. An hour went by and Karlis didn't reappear: he had gone. The two resumed their way in the darkness that grew thicker all the time.

When they reached the camp, they made their report, and Dov listened to them without commenting or passing judgment: he knew how these ventures went. Karlis's flight was too bad, but it couldn't have been foreseen or avoided; and for that matter, it wasn't the first case of the kind. Novoselki wasn't a *Lager,* anybody who wanted to leave, left. Would he talk? The police reward was attractive, ten rubles a head for every Jew reported: the Germans are a generous nation. But on the other hand, with the Germans Karlis also had some accounts to settle, and besides he had always been well treated at the monastery, and, finally, he had other ways to earn his bread. In any case, there was no help for it: they would just have to be on the lookout, especially these first few days, and if there was an attack, they would defend themselves.

No attack came. Instead, towards the middle of September, brought by Dov's mysterious informers, came the news that Italy had surrendered, and this put the camp in an uproar. War news, invariably triumphant, was a basic feature of Novoselki. Not a week went by without the Allies landing in Greece or Hitler being assassinated or the Americans wiping out the Japanese with a miraculous new weapon. Every announcement then circulated breathlessly and became embellished, enriched with details, and for days was a defense against anguish: the few who refused to believe were regarded with contempt. Then the news faded, was forgotten, and left no trace, so the next piece of news was accepted without reservations.

But this time it was different; the announcement of the capitulation was confirmed by two sources; it came from Radio Moscow and it had been personally certified by Dov, who as a rule was skeptical. The comments were frenzied; nobody talked about anything else. So the Axis forces had been halved. So the war would be over in a month, two at most. It was impossible that the Allies wouldn't exploit the situation: hadn't they already landed in Italy? For their armies Italy would be only a way station, in three days they would reach the border and would strike right into the heart of Germany. What border? Europe's geography was passionately reconstructed, through scholastic, legendary recollections. Pavel, the only citizen of the marshes who had actually been in Italy, sat like an oracle in the center of a continually renewed circle.

Pavel Yurevich Levinski set great store by his patronymic, and less by his too-revealing surname: he was a Jewish Russian, not a Russian Jew. At the age of thirty-five he had a varied career behind him: he had been a weight-lifter, an amateur actor, then a professional one, then a singer, and even, for a few months, an announcer with Radio Leningrad. He liked to play cards and dice, he liked wine, and when required he could curse like a Cossack. In the wan community of Novoselki he stood out because of his athletic appearance: nobody could understand where, on those starvation rations, Pavel could get nourishment for his muscles. He was of medium height, compact, sanguine. His beard, which he kept close-cropped, grew up to his eyes, and it sprouted so fast that a few hours after his razor had been over it, a bluish-black shadow already spread on his face. His hair and eyebrows were black and bushy. He had a real Russian's voice, deep, soft, and resonant, but when he had finished speaking or singing, he shut his mouth tight as a steel trap. His face had accentuated features, like hills and valleys; his cheekbones stood out, the little channel between nose and upper lip was deep; and the junction of that channel with the lip was marked by two fleshy bumps. His teeth were strong and spaced, and he had a hypnotist's eyes. With those eyes and with his stubby, heavy hands, he could make the aches disappear from your joints and back, and sometimes, for a few hours, he could dispel even hunger and fear. He had little inclination towards discipline, but at the monastery he enjoyed a tacit impunity.

His listeners besieged him with questions about Italy.

"Of course, I was there. Some years ago, with the famous tour of the Moscow Jewish Theater. I was Jeremiah, the prophet of calamities: I came on stage with a yoke on my back, to prophesy the deportation of the Jews to Babylon, and I would low like an ox. I had a purple wig, and I was stuffed to make me look even bigger, and the soles of my shoes were built up, because a prophet has to be tall. We played in Hebrew and in Yiddish; the Italians, in Milan, Venice, Rome, and Naples, didn't understand a word, and they applauded like lunatics."

"So you've really seen Italy with your own eyes?" Ber, the rabbinical student, asked.

"Of course. From the train. All of Italy is as long as from Leningrad to Kiev; in one day you can go from the Alps to Sicily. Now that the Italian Army's given up, the Allies will reach the German border in a flash. For that matter, even before they surrendered, the Italians were never really convinced Fascists: in fact, Mussolini himself brought the Moscow Theater there to Rome, and the Italian soldiers in the Ukraine didn't put up any fight. Italy's a beautiful country, with sea and lakes and mountains, all green and in flower. The people are friendly and polite, and well dressed, though they're thieves a bit: I mean, it's a strange country, very different from Russia."

But the borders? Where would the Allies get to? Here it was obvious that Pavel Yurevich's notions weren't clear, he vaguely remembered Tarvisio, but he didn't know if there was Germany on the other side, or Yugoslavia, or Hungary. Still, he remembered a black-eyed girl he had spent the night with in Milan; this episode, however, was of no interest to his listeners.

October went by, the cold began to be felt, and the collective spirit began to wilt. Contradictory news arrived: the Russians had recaptured Smolensk, but the Germans hadn't caved in. There was fighting in Italy, but not at the border, not in the Alps; there was talk of Allied landings in places they had never heard of. Was it possible that the English and the Americans, with all their oil and their gold, weren't able to give the Germans the knockout blow? And the Holy One, blessed be He, why was he hiding behind the gray clouds of Polessia instead of succoring His people? "You have chosen us among the nations": why us, exactly? Why do the wicked prosper, why are the helpless slaughtered, why are there hunger, mass graves, typhus, and SS flamethrowers into holes crammed with terrified children? And why must Hungarians, Poles, Ukrainians, Lithuanians, Tatars rob and murder the Jews, tear the last weapons from their hands, instead of joining with them against the common enemy?

And then winter came, friend and ally of the Russian armies, cruel enemy for those confined in Novoselki. The Siberian wind had already spread a veil of transparent ice over the black face of the marshes: soon they would harden and would support the weight of the hunters of men. The traces of footsteps in the snow would be legible from the air or even on the ground, as the scrolls of Scripture are legible. There was no lack of wood, but every fireplace was an informer; the columns of smoke rising from the monastery chimneys would have been visible dozens of kilometers away, pointing like an extended forefinger towards the ground: "the victims of the sacrifice are here." Dov gave orders that during the day all citizens exempt from labor should be gathered into a single room and should sleep at night in the same dormitory. Only one fire was to be lighted; the pipe from the fireplace had to be redirected so that it ended amidst the boughs of a big oak that grew against the wall. In this way the soot would settle on the branches instead of blackening the snow all around. Would all this do any good? Would it be enough? Maybe yes, and maybe no, but it was important for all to be doing something for the common cause; all should have the sensation that something was being decided and done. Tanners and cobblers set to making boots of every size, using all the skins the peasants were prepared to sell, even skins of cats and dogs: crude, barbaric boots sewn with string, the fur on the inside. And not only for local consumption: Dov sent a delegation to Rovnoye, a village of Ukrainian Baptists, despised and persecuted by both Germans and Russians; they had good relations with the Jews.

The envoys returned from Rovnoye a few days later, with a fair load of goods and with a message for Dov. It was signed by Gedaleh, the legendary leader, the one who had headed the revolt in the Kossovo ghetto, and whose life had been saved by a violin. Dov, who by now considered Mendel his lieutenant, read him the message and discussed it with him. It raised two issues: first, Gedaleh informed Dov that in the now-decimated ghetto of Soligorsk the Germans had posted a decree of "amnesty," written in their cynically euphemistic jargon: the *Umsiedlungen,* the forced transfers (they called them transfers!) were indefinitely suspended; Jews hiding in the area, and especially artisans, were invited to return to the ghetto, they would not be punished for their flight, and would be given ration cards. Dov, with winter coming on, should act as he thought best.

In the second place, Gedaleh invited Dov to a hunting party. A hunt for hunters: it was a unique opportunity. Count Daraganov, once the great landowner, had returned to his lands in the wake of the Germans, and was offering them a great hunting party in his estate on the shores of lake Chervonoye, one day's march from Novoselki. There would be a dozen high officers of the Wehrmacht there; the information was sure, it came from a Ukrainian who collaborated with the partisans and had been chosen as a beater. The band to which Gedaleh temporarily belonged was strong and well organized, made up mostly of volunteers from the winter of 'forty-one, namely, the aristocracy of Soviet partisans. Gedaleh thought that Jewish participation in the hunt would be welcomed and opportune, and perhaps also rewarded with weapons or something.

On the first issue, Dov thought to delay his decision a bit; on the second, his choice was immediate. It was important to show the Russians that the Jews also knew how to fight and wanted to. Mendel offered himself as a volunteer: he was a soldier, he knew how to shoot. Dov thought it over a few moments; no, neither Mendel nor Leonid, precisely because they were trained fighters. The action Gedaleh proposed was important as propaganda, it was a trick on the Germans, but from a military standpoint it didn't mean much and was dangerous. Partisan logic was ruthless, it prescribed that the best men be saved for serious operations, for sabotage, assault, and defense. Dov would send Ber and Vadim, two hopeless *nebbishes*, precisely because they were hopeless. "Do you think I have dirty hands? I do. Like anybody who has to make choices."

Ber, the bespectacled boy who stood guard with Leonid, and Vadim set out self-confidently; Vadim, a thoughtless youth, talkative and absentminded, actually displayed a lighthearted pride: "We'll fill their bellies full of holes, we'll pierce all their medals!" They had one pistol and a pair of hand grenades apiece. Vadim returned alone, two days later, ashen and exhausted, with a bullet hole in his shoulder, to narrate the enterprise. It hadn't been a game; it had been a slaughter, a mess. Everybody was shooting at everybody else, bullets were flying in every direction. The Russian partisans began, they were well hidden among the bushes; with one round they killed four of the German officers, colonels or generals, no one knew for sure. Then they saw the Ukrainian auxiliaries come out into the open, shooting at the partisans, and shooting into the air, and also among themselves. One of them, before Vadim's very eyes, killed a German officer with the butt of the rifle. Ber died at once, God knows who killed him; maybe it was an accident. He was standing up, looking around; his eyesight was poor. Vadim tossed his grenades at the Germans, who instead of scattering had gathered together, in a group; one grenade had exploded, the other not.

Dov sent Vadim off to get some rest, but the boy

couldn't rest. He had violent coughing fits and spat up a bloody froth. During the night he developed a fever and became unconscious; in the morning he was dead. Dead: why? The boy was twenty-two, Mendel said to Dov, and he couldn't suppress a reproachful accent. "We may come to envy him, for the way he died," Dov answered.

Vadim was buried at the foot of an alder, in the midst of a sudden snowstorm. On his grave Dov had a cross planted, because Vadim was a converted Jew; and since nobody knew the Russian Orthodox prayers, Dov said Kaddish himself. "It's better than nothing," he said to Mendel. "It's not for the dead man, but for the living, who believe in it." The sky was so dark that the snow, on the ground and whirling in the air, looked gray.

Dov sent a messenger to Rovnoye, to seek out Gedaleh and his band and ask immediately for reinforcements; but the messenger came back without an answer. He hadn't found anybody; but he had seen the peasants of Rovnoye, men and women, collected in the square, with their hands bound. He had seen an SS squad, pointing their weapons, forcing them all to climb into a wagon. He had seen men of the auxiliary militia, Ukrainians or Lithuanians, taking armfuls of shovels from a shed and loading them into the wagon, and he had seen the wagon go off towards the gulley to the south of the village, followed by the SS, laughing and smoking. This is what he had to tell.

There wasn't a soul in Novoselki, or in all the occupied territory, who didn't know the meaning of shovels. Dov said to Mendel that he regretted having sent Ber off like that, unprepared.

"If the mission had gone well, with a distinct victory, I would have been right to risk two men. Instead, it went fairly badly, and now I'm wrong. Ber, even dead, is a Jew: anybody can tell that. I was wrong to pick him. The Gestapo will surely examine his corpse. Our share in the hunt may have made Gedaleh's Russians revise their opinion of us, but it will also prompt the Germans' reprisal. The flight of Karlis, the shovels of Rovnoye, Ber: these are three threatening signals. The Germans won't be so long in locating us. Our miraculous impunity is over."

And so the old people of the camp must have thought also; Dov had spoken to them of the "amnesty" promised by the Germans. They wanted to return to Soligorsk: they asked to leave, to be taken back to the ghetto. They would rather cling to the Nazis' promises than face the snow and certain death at Novoselki. They were artisans, in the ghetto they would work, and in Soligorsk there were their houses, and near the houses, the cemetery. They preferred servitude and the scant bread of the enemy: how could you say they were wrong? Mendel was reminded of a terrible voice, three thousand years old, the protest addressed to Moses by the Jews pursued by the Pharaoh's chariots: "Because there were no graves in Egypt, hast thou taken us away to die in the wilderness? It had been better for us to serve the Egyptians, than that we should die in the wilderness." The Lord our God, the King of the World, had divided the waters of the Red Sea, and the chariots had been engulfed. Who would divide the waters before the Jews of Novoselki? Who would feed them on quails and manna? No manna descended from the black sky, but only pitiless snow.

Let each choose his own destiny. Dov had three sledges fitted up to take to Soligorsk the twenty-seven citizens who had no military duties and had chosen the way of the ghetto; these included all the children. Adam preferred to stay. The mules, brought by the men from Ozarichi, were only two: one of them had to pull two sledges. The people set out, dumb, exchanging no farewells, bundled in rags, straw, blankets, obeying the poor hope of a few weeks more of life granted in this way.

Immediately hidden from sight by the curtain of snow, they vanish from this story.

Dov had them dig three bunkers or rather three dens, in the naked earth, which despite the cold was not yet frozen. They were about two hundred meters from the monastery, in the direction from which the Germans were expected to arrive, from half-destroyed Rovnoye, where there was an outpost. Each den could hold two men, and it was hidden by brush, which is quickly covered with snow. "We can use shovels, too," he said; and sent another team to dig a square hole, two meters deep, across the biggest track that led from Rovnoye to the monastery. He had it covered with frail planks, and over these he had them put brush up to the level of the snow on the surrounding terrain; after another night of steady snowfall you could hardly see any break in the level. On the track, and on the trap that had thus been prepared, he made two men go back and forth several times, pulling after them two shovels weighted with stones, to imitate recent wagon tracks. He passed out weapons to all, and had the heavy machine gun set up on the intact tower.

The hunters of men arrived two days later. There were more than fifty of them; somebody must have overestimated the strength of the defenders. The clatter of half-tracks was heard before anything could be seen through the veil of snow, still falling heavily. A light half-track led the column, following the trail that Dov had prepared. It advanced slowly, reached the trap, swayed on the edge, and fell in, shattering the planks with a splitting sound. Dov climbed up on the tower, where Mendel was all ready with the machine gun. Dov restrained him: "Save bullets. Only shoot if you see somebody trying to get out of the hole." But nobody came out; the vehicle had perhaps overturned.

Behind the light half-track, a heavy vehicle was coming, and behind that, men on foot were fanning out over the trail and among the trees. The heavy tracked vehicle went around the hole and opened fire; at the same instant Mendel began firing in brief spurts, gripped by the fever of battle. He saw some Germans fall, and at the same time he heard two violent explosions beneath him. two anti-tank rockets had hit the roof of the monastery, which caved in and caught fire. More bullets shattered the walls of the building in several places. In the midst of the smoke and noise Dov shouted into his ear: "Empty the gun now. Don't hold back. We're fighting for three lines in the history books." Dov also fired downwards, with one of the Italian rifles. All of a sudden Mendel saw him sway; he fell back, but stood erect again immediately afterwards. At the same time, Mendel heard other shots, of light weapons, coming from the bunkers: obeying Dov's orders, the bunker fighters were firing on the Germans from behind. Taken by surprise, the Germans broke up, turning their back on the monastery: Mendel rushed down the steps with Dov amidst the rubble and flames. He saw people moving, and he shouted at them to follow him; they came out into the open on the opposite side of the building, among the trees: "in safety," he thought, absurdly. On the other side, the fighting had resumed. He heard the crash of grenades and orders shouted through a loudspeaker; he saw men and women come through the gaps with their arms raised. He saw the manhunters search them, laughing, and question them and line them up against the wall. But what happened in the courtyard of the Novoselki monstery will not be told here: this story is not being told in order to describe massacres.

They counted themselves. They were eleven: Mendel himself, Dov, Leonid, Line, Pavel, Adam, another woman whose name Mendel didn't know, and four of the men from Ozarichi. Adam was bleeding from a wound in the upper thigh, too close to the groin for it to be possible to apply a tourniquet; he stretched out on the snow and died in silence. Dov wasn't wounded, just dazed. His temple was bruised, perhaps by a ricocheting bullet or a stone flung by the explosions. The Germans stayed on till nightfall to blow up what was left of the monastery; they didn't pursue the trail of the fugitives, which the snow had already blurred: they went off, carrying their dead with them and the machine gun.

4

November 1943–
January 1944

They had few weapons, little ammunition, and nothing to eat. They were stunned and listless, overcome by that leaden passivity that follows action, and constricts the spirit and the limbs. The war would last forever; death, pursuit, escape would never end, the snow would never stop falling, day would never break. The red stain around Adam's body would never be erased, they would never see peace again, the mild and happy season, the works of man. The woman whose name Mendel didn't know, her face frank and sweet, her body solid, a peasant's, sat on the snow and wept quietly. Mendel learned that her name was Sissl and she was Adam's daughter.

The first to recover was Pavel. "*Nu*, we're alive, and the Germans have gone. We can't stay out here all night. Let's go into the cellars; they can't have blown up all of them." Dov also got a grip on himself; of course, under the monastery there was a network of tunnels, several hundred meters of them. There were some provisions, and in any case the area could serve as a temporary shelter. There were two trapdoors, but the larger was covered by an impressive pile of rubble. The smaller, in the kitchen floor, was almost clear. They all groped their way down the ladder, found some straw and wood, and made a fire. They also found faggots of fir branches; in the light of makeshift torches they saw that the store of potatoes and corn was intact, and so was the ammunition store. They held council.

"We can stay here for a few days, to rest and eat; then we'll see," Pavel said, but Dov and Mendel disagreed. Dov said, "The Germans have set up a garrison at Rovnoye, and some of their men were killed here. They're bound to come back; they never leave things half-done. And we no longer have a heavy weapon; there are only a few of us, and we're tired, and we can't live in a cellar like this. We'll die either of the cold or the smoke."

"We must join up with Gedaleh," Mendel said. "Where is Gedaleh?"

"I don't know," Dov answered. "The last I heard, he was in a well-organized band of veteran partisans; he was second-in-command. And being experts, they won't leave any traces, and it'll be hard to find them."

"But they'll have informers in Rovnoye; they'll hear about the German attack on the monastery, and they'll send somebody to see what happened," said Line, who had been silent till then. Mendel turned to look at her, in the unsteady light of the torches. She was sitting on the ground beside Leonid, small and slight, her eyes dark, her black hair cropped short, her nails gnawed like a schoolgirl's. She had spoken in a low but firm voice. Not an easy woman to interpret, he thought: not simple, not straightforward. For Leonid, an unlikely companion; they could draw strength one from the other, or destroy themselves reciprocally. Then he looked at Sissl and felt suddenly the dumb weight of loneliness: woe to the man alone. If he had had a woman beside him, any woman, the way would have been different for him too.

Pavel agreed with Line's observation, and added, "If they send somebody, they'll do it fast."

The next morning, in fact, they heard a dog bark. Pavel climbed up into the open, and through the breaches in the wall he saw Oleg, the old forester, wandering among the ruins of the monastery. He was a man to be trusted; he had already proved that on other occasions, exploiting his rounds of inspection to maintain contacts among the bands and to transmit information. Yes, he had been sent by Ulybin, the chief of Gedaleh's band: they were passing the winter in a camp near Turov, seventy kilometers to the west. Ulybin would accept trained people, in good shape, but nobody else; it wouldn't be hard to reach him.

"Take the forest trails and stay clear of the roads. It's harder, but you don't risk running into the patrols."

They followed the forester's advice, but it was a painful march. The snow was deep and soft; the leader would sink in up to his knees. Sometimes they encountered pockets of snow piled up by the wind, and then they sank to their hips; they took turns in the lead position, but even this way they risked covering no more than two or three kilometers an hour, also because they were weighed down by the provisions and munitions they had found in the cellar, and because Dov was forced to stop often.

It had let up snowing, but the sky was still low and threatening, so opaque that it wasn't possible to get bearings. At evening, to west and east there was the same gray, spent light. They tried to maintain the direction indicated by Oleg, studying the moss on the tree trunks, but the woods were made up mostly of birches, and moss wouldn't grow on their white bark. For that matter, the trees were thinning out; rolling open spaces alternated with flat areas more and more extensive, obviously frozen ponds or lakes. None of them knew the area particularly well, and soon they ended up trusting Pavel. Pavel made a show of strength and confidence. He was solicitous of Dov, exhausted by the long march with his wounded knee and still weak from the blow he had received during the German attack. Pavel helped him walk, supported him, assumed a good part of his load; at the same time he tended to take Dov's place in making decisions and giving orders: "This way. Right, Dov?"

Pavel insisted he could sense north, without knowing how, just as a dowser senses water. The others evinced distrust and even impatience, but in fact, the few times they came upon an oak, the moss was on the side Pavel had predicted: however approximate, the direction Pavel chose was the right one. In addition to their fatigue, they also suffered thirst. They were all sufficiently familiar with the Russian winter to know that eating snow is useless and dangerous: long before it quenches thirst it irritates the mouth and makes the tongue swell. For thirst you need water, not snow or ice; but to get water you need a fire, and for a fire you need wood. They found wood fairly often, abandoned by the peasants in piles, but Pavel wouldn't let them touch it; or rather, he expressed in the form of a command an exchange of opinions that had taken place among Mendel and Dov and himself.

"No fires during the day, Dov says. Hold out, bear with your thirst. You don't die of thirst in a day. Smoke in the daytime can be seen a long way off. We'll make a fire at night; fire can also be seen a long way off, but we'll build a screen around it, with snow; or with our bodies, so we'll also warm ourselves a bit. But I think we'll find a shelter before long. In country like this, we ought to find some izba."

Whether it was intuition, second sight, or some fakir's trick, Pavel had clearly guessed right. Towards evening, on the desolate plain they saw a rise; from the snow the tips of a fence emerged, black and shining with tar, and the roof of a hut. They dug the snow away in front of the door, and they all went inside, pressing into the scant space. Inside there was nothing, except the terra-cotta stove and a zinc bucket; under the snow, against the rear of the hut, there was a good supply of wood. They managed to bake potatoes in the embers of the stove and melt snow in the bucket. They lighted a fire near the hut, in a hole dug in the snow, and boiled corn in their messtins; they achieved an unpleasant, tasteless mush, which nevertheless warmed them and allayed their hunger and thirst. Then they stretched out to sleep, the men on the floor, the two women on the bunk above the stove. They all fell asleep in a few instants, except for Dov, whose knee had begun to hurt from the old wound, and whose battered bones aches. He moaned in a doze; and turned constantly, seeking a position that wouldn't sharpen his pain.

Halfway through the night Mendel also woke, with a start: not a sound was to be heard, but a soft shaft of intense light came through the little window; it was shifting from one corner of the izba to another, as if to explore. Mendel went to the window: the shaft of light framed him for a moment and then went out. When he had recovered from his dazzlement, in the glare of the snow he could make out three human forms: three men in white jumpsuits, on skis, armed. One of them was carrying an automatic rifle to whose barrel a flashlight was tied; at that moment barrel and light were turned towards the snow. The three were murmuring among themselves, but inside the izba no sound could be perceived. Then the shaft of light again came through the window, a pistol shot was heard, and a voice shouted in Russian:

"Don't move, or we'll shoot. Put your hands on your head. One of you come out with his hands up and unarmed." Then the same voice repeated the instructions in bad German. Dov turned towards the door, but Pavel was ahead of him. Before Dov was fully on his feet, Pavel had already opened the door and stepped outside, his arms raised.

"Who are you? Where have you come from and where are you going?"

"We're soldiers, partisans, and Jews. We don't come from around here. We come from Novoselki."

"I asked you where you're going."

Pavel hesitated; Mendel came out with his hands raised and stood beside him.

"Comrade, there were fifty of us and now ten of us are

alive. We fought, and our camp was destroyed. We're lost and tired, but we're able-bodied; we're looking for a group that will take us. We want to continue our war, which is yours, too."

The man dressed in white answered, "We'll see how able-bodied you are. We can't feed any useless mouths; with us only those who fight, eat. This is our territory, and you've been lucky. We saw your women over the stove, so we didn't shoot. As a rule we don't act like this. If you shoot on sight you don't make any mistakes." The man laughed curtly and added, "Hardly ever!" Mendel's heart swelled.

Dawn was breaking. Two of the men took off their skis and came into the izba; the third, the one who had spoken, remained outside with his gun aimed. He was tall, very young, and wore a short black beard; and all three, their clothes padded under the camouflage, gave the impression of being fat, contradicting the agility of their movements. The two, gripping their pistols, ordered them all not to move, and with rapid, expert gestures, they searched everyone, even the two women, with some joking remark of apology. They asked each his or her name and home, they stacked the weapons and ammunition they had found in one corner, then went out again and gave their chief a short report, which could not be heard inside. The bearded young man lowered his weapon, took off his skis, came in and sat on the ground, in a familiar way.

"For us, you're not dangerous. My name's Piotr. Who's your chief?"

Dov said, "As you can see, we're not a complete band. We're the survivors of a camp of families; with us there were also old people, children, transients. I was their elder, or their chief, if you want to call me that. I fought with Manuil 'Arrow' and with Uncle Vanka, and I was wounded at Bobruysk last February. I was in the air force. With Uncle Vanka there was also Gedaleh; he and I were friends. Do you know Gedaleh?"

Piotr dug a short pipe from his pocket and lighted it.

"For us, you're not dangerous, but you could become a danger. You have white hair, chief. You were a partisan; don't you know that nobody asks partisans questions?"

Dov was silent, humiliated: yes, in wartime, you grow old fast. He remained with his head bowed, looking at his big hands hanging limp from his wrists, and massaging his knee from time to time.

Piotr continued: "But we'll see you're not abandoned, whether you're fighters or not. At least for a while. What may happen later, we don't know, neither our leaders nor anybody. Our time runs like hares run, fast and zigzag. Anybody who makes a plan for tomorrow and then carries it out, is good; anybody who makes plans for next week is crazy. Or a spy for the Germans."

He smoked calmly for a few more minutes, then he said, "Our camp isn't far, we could get there before tomorrow evening. Keep your weapons, but unloaded; the ammunition, I'm sorry, but we'll take that. For now. Later, when we get to know one another, we'll see."

They set off, the three men on skis in the lead, the others behind. The snow was deep and floury, and the weight of the three wasn't enough to pack down the path; the ten who were on foot advanced painfully, sinking in at every step and slowing progress. The slowest was Dov; he didn't complain, but he was visibly in trouble. Piotr gave him his ski poles, which still weren't much help: he was gasping, pale, beaded with sweat, and he had to stop frequently. Piotr, at the head of the line, turned now and then to look, and he was uneasy: this was open country, without trees or cover; frozen marshes alternated with slightly rolling bleak expanses, and from the top of these, looking back, you could see their trail, deep as a crevasse and straight as a meridian. At the end of the trail, there they were, thirteen ants: if a German plane were to arrive, they were doomed. Luckily the sky was still cloudy, but it wouldn't stay that way long. Piotr sniffed the air like a bloodhound: a faint wind was blowing from the north; in the long run it would shift the snow and wipe out the trail, but the sky would clear first. He was in a hurry to reach the camp.

He moved off the track and let the others pass. When Dov was at his side, he said, "You're tired, Uncle. No offense meant. Come here, stand on my skis and hold on to me; it'll be less of an effort." Dov obeyed without speaking, and the new couple resumed the lead position. It was an advantage for everyone: under the double weight the snow was packed harder, and those on foot hardly sank at all now. Line, the lightest of all, was wearing a pair of outsize army boots, and she skimmed over the snow as though she were wearing snowshoes; Leonid kept within reach of her. They walked till night, then camped in a bivouac Piotr knew and continued their march the next morning. They came within sight of the camp sooner than they had foreseen; in midafternoon, under a bright sun, unnaturally warm. "Within sight," that is, for those who knew where and how the camp was located. Piotr pointed out to them, towards the southwest, a vast stretch of forest that, like a horizon drawn with a fine brush, separated the white of the snow from the blue of the winter sky. There, somewhere among those trees, was the camp of Ulybin's band; they would reach it at night, but not by a straight line. This was an experience they had learned at their cost: never leave tracks that are too legible in clear weather, without wind. They had to make a detour; they would take the right direction once they were under the cover of the trees.

To the former citizens of the marshes, it seemed a dream. Novoselki had represented precarious safety and had been an intelligent makeshift: the camp they were entering was a professional job, consolidated by the experience of three years. Mendel and Leonid could compare the sound organization of Ulybin's band with the bold and capricious enterprises of the wandering band of Venjamin.

In the thick of the forest, barely visible to an eye not alert, they found a group of three wooden barracks, almost completely buried, arranged to form an equilateral triangle. In the center of the triangle, just as hard to spot, were the kitchen and the well. The hearth whose smoke was scattered through the thick branches had not been a Novoselki invention: the same thing had been done here; when the time is ripe certain discoveries blossom in various places, and there are circumstances in which a problem has only one solution.

In Novoselki Dov had joked about Leonid's profession: he didn't need a bookkeeper. At Turov they found one, or rather they found a quartermaster in full operation. He was at the same time the NKVD representative and the political commissar, and he dealt with the newcomers efficiently and briskly. Name, patronymic; corps for the soldiers; age, profession, registration of documents (but very few of them had any documents); then to bed, the rest would be handled in the morning. Yes, to bed: inside each barracks there was a stove and planking covered with clean straw, and the air was dry and warm, even though the floor was almost two meters below the level of the ground. Mendel fell asleep in a whirl of confused impressions: he felt exhausted, disoriented, and at the same time protected, less a father and more a son, more secure and less free, at home and in barracks; but sleep came immediately, like a charitable blow on the head.

The next morning, the camp offered the refugees a hot bath, no less, in a vat set up in the kitchen area, the women properly separated from the men. Delousing followed, or rather an invitation to a conscientious self-examination, and then distribution of linen, rough and not new, but clean. Finally, some splendid kasha, nourishing and hot, eaten with real spoons from real aluminum plates, and followed by abundant sweet tea. It looked like a calm day, and the air was unusually mild for this season: in the places exposed to the sun the snow showed signs of melting, which aroused a certain uneasiness. "The freeze is all right with us," Mendel was told by Piotr, who was doing the honors as host. "With the thaw, if we're not careful, the barracks become flooded, and we drown in the mud." Proudly, he showed them the electrical system. A talented mechanic had adapted the conical coupling of an old mill to the gearbox of a German tank: a blindfolded horse walked in a slow circle, and a system of gears worked a dynamo that charged a group of batteries. The batteries, if everything was going well, produced electric light and power for the radio transmitter. "Last autumn we put four Hungarian prisoners in the horse's place for a week."

"And did you kill them afterwards?" Mendel asked.

"We only kill the Germans, and not always them. We're not like them; we don't enjoy killing. While they were still blindfolded, we took the Hungarians to the other side of the river and turned them loose, to go where they pleased. They were a bit dizzy."

Piotr warned them not to try to leave the camp, or rather, not to move away from the buildings for more than thirty meters. "All around us, the woods are mined. There are mines buried under three fingers of earth, and there are paired mines, connected with a taut string under the snow. We've done a good job: slowly, night after night, we cleared a whole German minefield, we saved the mines, and we buried them here. We didn't lose a single man, and since then the Germans have left us in peace. But we don't leave them in peace so much."

Piotr seemed attracted, his curiosity aroused, by the group of ten he had found in the izba and had nearly killed; he was particularly friendly with Mendel. He showed him a little project, an idea conceived and carried out by Mikhail, the radio operator, all on his own. In one corner of his barrack there was a venerable, pedal-operated press, with a little supply of letters, in Cyrillic and Latin type. Mikhail was no printer, but he had managed. He had composed a bilingual manifesto, on two facing pages, like the ones with which the Germans had flooded all the cities and villages of occupied Russia. The German text was copied from the original German posters: it promised the restoration of private property and the reopening of the churches, it invited young people to enroll in the Labor Organization, and threatened serious punishments for partisans and saboteurs. The facing Russian text was not a translation of the German, but instead its opposite. It said:

> Young Soviets! Don't believe the Germans, who have invaded our country and are massacring our people. Don't work for them; if you go to Germany you will be starved and beaten, and they will brand you like animals. When you come back (if you do come back!) you'll have to face Socialist justice. Not a man, not a kilo of grain, not a word of information must go to Hitler's killers! Come with us. Join the Partisan Army!

In both versions there were various spelling mistakes, but they weren't the fault of the radio operator: in the boxes of type there was a scarcity of *a*'s and *e*'s, so he had used the letters that seemed possible to him. He had printed several hundred copies, which had been distributed and posted in places as far away as Baranovichi, Rovno, and Minsk.

There were a number of small arms to repair and grease: at Turov Mendel found his job at once. In the hours when he was free of his duties, Piotr was constantly at his side.

"Are all ten of you Jews?"

"No, only six: me, the two women, the boy who's always with the young girl, the old man you carried on your skis, and Pavel Yurevich, the strongest of the lot. The other four are stragglers, who joined us just before the Germans destroyed our camp."

"Why do the Germans want to kill all you people?"

"It's hard to explain," Mendel answered. "You have to understand the Germans, and I've never managed that. The Germans think a Jew is worth less than a Russian, and a Russian less than an Englishman, and that a German is worth most of all; they think, too, that when one man is worth more than another man, he has a right to do what he likes with the other, make a slave of him or even kill him. Maybe not all of them are convinced, but this is what they're taught in school, and this is what their propaganda says."

"I believe a Russian's worth more than a Chinaman," Piotr said, pensively. "But if China didn't do Russia any harm, it would never occur to me to kill all the Chinese."

Mendel said, "On the contrary, I believe it doesn't make much sense to say that one man is worth more than another. One man can be stronger than another but less wise. Or more educated but not so brave. Or more generous but also more stupid. So his value depends on what you want from him; a man can be very good at his job, and worthless if you set him to do some other job."

"It's just like you say," Piotr said, all radiant. "I was the treasurer of the Komsomol, but I was absentminded, I got the figures all wrong, and everybody laughed at me and said I was good for nothing. Then the war came, I volunteered right away, and ever since then I think I'm worth more. It's odd: I don't like killing, but I do like shooting, so it happens that even killing doesn't affect me much anymore. At the beginning it was different: I was reluctant, and I also had a stupid idea. I thought that the Germans, instead of having a skin like ours, were sheathed in steel, and that bullets would ricochet. Not any more; I've killed quite a few Germans, and I've seen they're as soft as we are, maybe more. And you, Jew: how many Germans have you killed?"

"I don't know," Mendel answered. "I was in the artillery, you know. It's not like having a rifle. You set up the piece, you aim, you fire, and you can't see a thing. When all goes well, you see the incoming rounds five or ten kilometers away. Who knows how many men have died at my hand? Maybe a thousand, maybe not even one. Your orders come by field telephone or radio, through earphones: left three, drop one, you obey, and that's the end of it. It's like bomber planes; or when you pour acid into an anthill to kill the ants: a hundred thousand ants die, and you don't feel anything, you aren't even aware of it. But in my village the Germans made the Jews dig a pit, then they lined them up along the edge, and they shot them all, even the children, and also a lot of Christians who had hidden Jews, and among those they shot was my wife. And after that I think that killing is bad, but killing the Germans is something we can't avoid. From a distance or close by; your way or ours. Because killing is the only language they understand, the only argument that convinces them. If I shoot at a German, he is forced to admit that I, a Jew, am worth more than he is: that's his logic, you understand, not mine. They only understand force. Naturally, convincing a man who's just about dead isn't much use, but in the long run his companions will also come to understand something. The Germans began to understand only after Stalingrad. So that's why it's important for there to be Jewish partisans, and Jews in the Red Army. It's important, but it's also horrible; only by killing a German can I manage to persuade the other Germans that I'm a man. And yet we have a law that says: 'Thou shalt not kill.' "

"But you're strange people, all the same. Strange. Shooting is one thing and reasoning is another. If a man reasons too much, in the end he can't shoot straight, and you people always reason too much. Maybe that's why the Germans kill you. Look, take me for example: I've been in the Komsomol since I was a little boy, I'd give my life for Stalin the way my father did, I believe in Christ the Redeemer of the world the way my mother believes, I like vodka, I like girls, I also like shooting, and I live well here in the plains hunting the Fascists, and I don't stop and think about it so much. If one of my ideas doesn't agree with another, I don't give a damn.' "

Mendel was listening with his ears and with half of his brain while with the other half and with his hands he was using some kerosene to clean the rust from the screws and springs of an automatic rifle he had dismantled. He took advantage of this moment of intimacy to ask Piotr something that was troubling him and Dov.

"What's happened to your second-in-command?

Wasn't Gedaleh here with you, Gedaleh Skidler, a Jew, half-Russian and half-Pole, who fought at Kossovo? A tall man, with a beak nose and a wide mouth?"

Piotr didn't answer at once; he looked up and scratched his beard, as if to recall to mind memories vanished years before. Then he said, "Yes, yes, Gedaleh, of course. But he was never second-in-command; just now and then he gave orders, when Ulybin was away. He's on a mission, Gedaleh. He'll be back. Yes, in a week, or maybe two, or maybe even three. Or it could be that he's been transferred; in the *partinsanka* you can never be sure about anything."

This Piotr is better at skiing than at telling lies, Mendel said to himself. Then, laughing, he asked, "Was he one of those men who reason too much?"

"It's not that he reasoned too much. No, not that at all: that wasn't what was wrong with him. But he was strange, too. I told you: you Jews are really all a bit strange, one way or another, no offense. This Gedaleh could shoot almost as well as me, I don't know who taught him; but he made up poems, and he always carried a violin around with him."

"Did he make up songs and play them on the violin?"

"No, the poems were one thing and the violin another. He played it in the evening; he had it on him in August, when the Germans made the big roundup operation in the Luninets area. We managed to slip through the net, but a sniper shot at him; the bullet went right through the violin, and so it lost its strength and didn't hurt him. He mended the holes with pine resin and adhesive tape from the infirmary, and ever since he's always carried the violin on him. He said it sounded even better than before, and he actually pinned a bronze medal on it that we had found on a dead Hungarian. You see, he was a strange character, all right."

"If we were all alike, it would be a boring world. We have a special blessing, to address to God when we see somebody different from the others: a dwarf, a giant, a black man, a man covered with warts. We say: Blessed be Thou, Lord God, king of the Universe, who hast varied the aspect of Thy creatures. If we praise Him for warts, we have all the more reason to praise him for a partisan who plays the violin."

"You're right, but you make me angry, all the same. Gedaleh was like that, too. He always had to have his say, and he didn't get along with Ulybin, or with Maksim, either. Maksim is the quartermaster, the scribe, that is, the one who keeps the accounts and comes from the NKVD. They sent him here from Moscow, by parachute, so he would maintain discipline: as if discipline was the most important thing. For that matter, I don't get on all that well with Maksim myself."

Mendel wanted to strike while the iron was hot. "So what happened between Gedaleh and the chief?"

"Well, there was a quarrel, at the beginning of winter. They hadn't been getting on for quite a while, Ulybin and Gedaleh. No, not because of the violin; there were more serious reasons. Gedaleh wanted to go around the woods and marshes and collect a band of Jewish partisans. But Ulybin said the orders from Moscow were different; Jewish fighters were to be accepted, a few at a time, into the Russian units. The break came when Gedaleh wrote a letter and sent it to Novoselki without Ulybin's permission; I don't know what was in that letter, and I couldn't tell you, either, which of the two was right. The fact is that Ulybin was angry, he shouted so loud you could hear him all over the camp, and he was hammering his fists on the table."

"What was he shouting?"

"I couldn't make it out clearly," Piotr answered, turning bright red.

"What was he shouting?" Mendel insisted.

"He was shouting that in his unit he didn't want to hear poets mentioned again."

"He surely didn't use the word 'poets,' " Mendel said.

"No. He didn't say 'poets.' " Piotr was silent a moment, then added, "But tell me: is it true that it was your people who crucified Jesus?"

*   *   *

In the Turov camp the refugees from Novoselki found safety and a certain material well-being, but they felt ill at ease. The four from Ozarichi were regularly taken on; the other six, including the two women, were assigned various tasks in the service unit. A few days after their arrival, Ulybin received them with detached politeness, but after that he wasn't seen again.

The temperature had gradually descended; towards mid-January it was fifteen below zero, and by the end of the month it was thirty below. Little patrols of skiers set out from the camp, on supply expeditions, or for harassing actions and sabotage, of which Mendel received fragmentary news from Piotr.

One day Ulybin sent someone to ask if any of their number spoke German. All six Jews spoke it, more or less correctly, with a more or less pronounced Yiddish accent. Why this question? What was it all about? Ulybin, through Maksim, informed them that he wanted to see the man with the best accent. Not the women; for this business they wouldn't do.

That evening, in the well-heated barracks, a special meal was distributed. Shortly after sunset a sledge had arrived at the camp, unloaded a crate, and then gone off again at once; at supper, the quartermaster gave each one a peculiarly shaped can. Mendel turned it over in his hands, puzzled: it was heavy, it had no label, and the soldered lid was smaller than the outer diameter of the can. He saw the others using the tip of a knife to make two holes in the ring-shaped space around the lid: one little and one big. Into the big hole they poured a bit of water, then sealed it with a pellet of bread. More and more curious, he imitated them, and he felt the tin grow so warm that it scorched his hand, while from the still-open hole came the familiar smell of acetylene. Like the others, he held a lighted match to it, and soon the table was surrounded by a bright wreath as in a fairy tale. Inside the can there was meat and peas; in the lining there was carbide, which, reacting with the water, heated the contents.

As the blizzard whistled outside, in the tremulous light of the flames, Pavel put on a show. He made a pretense of comic indignation:

"What? Have you forgotten me? Or were you pretending not to know? Obviously, of course, why, *ganz bestimmt!* I speak German like a German, if I want to; better than Hitler, who's an Austrian. I can speak it with a Hamburg accent, or a Stuttgart accent, or Berlin, whatever the customer wants. Or with no accent, like the radio. I can also speak Russian with a German accent, or German with a Russian accent. Tell the commander that. Tell him I was an actor and I've been all over the world. And I've also been a radio announcer, and on the radio I also did some comic skits; by the way, have you heard the one about the Jew who ate herrings' heads?"

He told the story in Russian enlivened with ridiculous Yiddish inflections, then he told another, and yet another, drawing on the endless supply of Jewish self-mockery, surreal and subtle, the proper counterweight to Jewish ritual, equally surreal and subtle: perhaps the most refined fruit of the civilization that, through the centuries, has been distilled from the moonstruck world of Ashkenazic Judaism. His companions smiled, embarrassed: the Russians were clutching their bellies and exploding in thunderous laughter. They gave him loud slaps on his sturdy back, urging him to keep on, and Pavel could ask for nothing better: how many years had it been since he had an audience?

" . . . and the story of the *yeshiva bucherim,* the rabbinical college students, who were enrolled in the army. Do you know that one? It was in the days of the czars, and there were many rabbinical schools then, from Lithuania to the Ukraine. It took at least seven years to become a rabbi, and almost all the students were poor; but even those who weren't poor were thin and pale, because a *yeshiva bucher* must eat only bread seasoned with salt, drink only water, and sleep on the benches of the school, so that even today we say: The poor 'nebbish, he's as thin as a *yeshiva bucher.*' Well, in one rabbinical school the recruiting officers suddenly appear, and all the students are drafted into the infantry. A month goes by, and the instructors notice that all these boys have an infallible aim: they all become first-rate marksmen. Why? I can't tell you the reason, because the story doesn't say. Maybe studying the Talmud gives you sharp eyesight. The war comes, and the regiment of Talmudists goes to the front, right to the front line. They're in the trench, with their rifles aimed, and the enemy starts to advance. The officer shouts, 'Fire!' Nothing happens, nobody fires. The officer again shouts, 'Fire!', and again nobody obeys; by now the enemy is only a stone's throw away. 'Fire,' I said, you ugly bastards! Why don't you shoot?' the officer yells . . ."

Pavel broke off: Ulybin had come in and sat down at the table, and at once the excited murmuring of the listeners had stopped. Ulybin was about thirty, of medium height, muscular and dark: he had an oval face, impassive, always freshly shaven.

"Well, why don't you go on? Let's hear the ending," Ulybin said.

Pavel resumed, with less confidence and less gusto, "Then one of the students says: 'Can't you see, Captain, sir? They aren't cardboard outlines, they're men, like us. If we shoot, we might hurt them.' "

The partisans around the table ventured some hesitant little laughs, looking from Pavel to Ulybin. Ulybin said, "I didn't hear the beginning. Who were those men who didn't want to shoot?"

Pavel gave him a fairly sketchy summary of the beginning of the joke, and Ulybin asked, in an icy voice, "And you here, what would all of you do?"

There was a brief silence, then Mendel's soft voice was heard: "We're not *yeshiva bucherim.*"

Ulybin didn't answer, but a little later he asked Pavel, "Are you the one who speaks German?"

"Yes."

"Tomorrow you'll come with me. Is there any kind of an electrician in your bunch?"

Mendel raised his hand. "In my village I used to fix radios."

"Good. You'll come, too."

Ulybin had Mendel and Pavel woken at four the following morning, still the heart of the night. While they ate a quick snack, he explained the purpose of the expedition. One of the partisans, on patrol through the woods, had seen that the Germans had run up a telephone line between the village of Turov and Zhitkovichi station: they hadn't erected poles, but had simply nailed the wire to the trees. The partisan climbed a tree and cut the wire, then came back to the camp, proud of his initiative. And Ulybin told him he was a jackass: telephonic communications should not be interrupted, but intercepted. At the Turov camp there was a field telephone, never used. Was it possible to repair the line and hook themselves up to it so they could hear what the Germans were saying to one another? Yes, Mendel answered, it was possible, provided there was a receiver. They had to set off at once, Ulybin said, before the Germans realized the line was interrupted and got suspicious.

Four of them went off: Ulybin, Mendel, Pavel, and Fedya, the boy who had found the line and cut it. Fedya wasn't yet seventeen, he was born right in Turov, less than an hour's walk from the camp, and he had known these woods since he came here bird-nesting as a child. He darted on his skis, silent and sure as a lynx in the darkness, stopping every now and then to wait for the other three. Ulybin managed fairly well; Mendel struggled along with an effort, as he was practically untrained and hampered by the bindings that were too loose; Pavel was on skis for the first time in his life, he was sweating despite the intense cold, he fell down often and cursed in a whisper. Ulybin was impatient; it would have been prudent to repair the line before daybreak. Good thing that, according to Fedya, the place wasn't far away.

They reached it after an hour's march. Mendel had

brought a few meters of wire with him; he took off his skis, and climbing onto Pavel's shoulders, in a few minutes he reconnected the two ends of wire that were dangling in the snow; but to perform this operation he had to take off his gloves, and he could feel his fingers rapidly turned numb from the chill. He had to stop and rub his hands at length with snow, while Ulybin peered at the sky, beginning to grow light, and stamped his feet because of the cold and his impatience. Then Mendel connected the overhead wire to one of the wires of the receiver, he came down, drove a stake into the ground and connected the other wire to it. Ulybin tore the receiver from his hand and held it to his ear.

"What can you hear?" Mendel asked in a whisper.

"Nothing. Just static."

"That's all right," Mendel whispered. "It's a sign that the contacts are working."

Ulybin handed the receiver to Pavel. "You listen, since you understand German. If you hear any talk, give me a sign." Then he asked Mendel. "If we talk among ourselves, can they hear us?"

"Not if we don't talk too loud, and we cover the microphone with a glove. But if necessary, we can disconnect the contact at the stake: it's a matter of a moment."

"Good. We'll wait till daybreak, then we'll go. We'll come back here tomorrow evening. If you're cold, Pavel, I'll relieve you."

In fact, all four took turns; when one of them felt cold he went off to clap his hands and stamp his feet far from the receiver. Around seven, Fedya started nodding his head brightly and handed the receiver to Pavel. Ulybin drew the boy off to one side.

"What did you hear?"

"I heard a German calling 'Turov, Turov'; but nobody was answering from Turov." At that same moment, Pavel waved his gloved hand and nodded his head, yes, several times: somebody had answered. He listened for a few minutes, then said, "They've finished. Too bad!"

"What were they saying?" Ulybin asked.

"Nothing important, but I was enjoying myself. There was one German complaining he hadn't slept because of stomach cramps, and he was asking another German if he had a certain medicine. The one with the cramps is named Hermann, and the other, Sigi. Sigi didn't have the medicine, he was yawning, he sounded annoyed, and he hung up. I was about to tell him we have the right medicine for him: would he have heard me?"

"We're not here to make jokes," Ulybin said. Then he added that, in spite of the risk, he had decided they would stay there a few more hours: it was too good an opportunity.

In fact, a little later they intercepted a more interesting conversation. This time it was Sigi, from the Turov post, calling Hermann, to announce that he had tried several times to make contact with the Medvedka garrison, but from Medvedka there was no answer. Hermann, still in pain, answered that maybe the four men in Medvedka had all gone out for a stroll, and Sigi wasn't to worry. But Sigi insisted on clarifying the matter: he had heard talk of *Banditen* in the area. Hermann, of higher rank, or perhaps only older, had given him some advice: to take one of his men, dress him up as a woodman, with ropes and an axe, and send him from Turov to Medvedka to see for himself what was happening.

"How far is Medvedka?" Ulybin asked Fedya.

"Maybe six or seven kilometers from here."

"And how far is it from Turov to Medvedka?"

"About twice that."

"How big is Medvedka?"

"Medvedka isn't a village: it's just a collective farm. About thirty peasants used to work there, but now I believe it's abandoned."

"You two go," Ulybin said to Fedya and Mendel, "and bring me the woodman alive. We'll wait for you here, or nearby."

Mendel and Fedya came back around noon, bringing

the prisoner with them, unharmed but terrified; they had bound his hands behind his back with telephone wire. They found Ulybin quivering with impatience. Sigi had called Hermann again; he was uneasy, the woodman hadn't come back yet. Hermann had grumbled something about the snow and the woods, then he had told Sigi to send another man, dressed as a peasant, by the path along the river. For verisimilitude, he should take two hens with him. Ulybin told Mendel and Fedya they were to set off at once for the bend of the river and wait for the peasant there.

This time the waiting was longer: the two men, with the second prisoner and the two hens, arrived only at sunset. The two prisoners weren't German, but Ukrainians from the auxiliary police, and it wasn't hard to make them talk. At Turov there were only seven or eight Germans, territorials, no longer young, with little desire to leave the village and none to get involved with the partisans. At Zhitkovichi the situation was different; in October somebody had sabotaged the railroad lines not far from the town, a freight train had been derailed, damaging a bridge, and afterwards there had been a more substantial and more mettlesome garrison that kept the station and the train tracks under surveillance. There was a platoon of the Wehrmacht with a little arsenal and about twenty Ukrainian and Lithuanian auxiliaries. There was also a depot of food supplies and forage, and a Gestapo office.

Before setting off for the camp, Ulybin decided to send the Germans a message. He gave instructions to Pavel, who replied, "Leave it to me," then went to the receiver, calling Turov and Zhitkovichi at intervals until a voice answered. Then Pavel said, "This is Colonel Graf Heinrich von Neudeck und Langenau speaking, the commanding officer of the Third Regiment of the Thirteenth Division of the Red Army, Internal Front and Occupied Zones department. I want to speak with the ranking officer of the garrison." Pavel was overjoyed with his role. Stuck in the snow up to his knees, in the now-dark wood, swept by a freezing wind, the absurd telephone receiver in his hand, its wires draped from the thicket of snow-laden boughs, he produced an authoritarian, resonant German, martial and guttural, with rich *r*'s and *ch*'s that reechoed at the base of his throat; mentally he praised himself: bravo Pavel Yurevich, dammit, you're more Prussian than a Prussian!

A frightened and puzzled voice answered him, asking for an explanation: it came from the garrison of David-Gorodok.

"No explanations," Pavel answered, in a thunderous voice. "No questions. We will attack your station tomorrow with five hundred men: we give you four hours to evacuate, you and your bootlicking traitors. Not one must remain: we will hang everyone we find in the place. Over and out." At a sign from Ulybin, Mendel tore away the connections, and the four men with the two prisoners set off for the camp. Even the grim Ulybin, so sparing of words and especially of praise, couldn't suppress a dry, crooked smile, which didn't extend to his eyes, but curled his lips, pale from the cold. Not addressing anyone in particular, as if he had been thinking aloud, he said: "Good. Tonight they'll have something to talk about at Gestapo HQ. They'll telephone Berlin to find out who this deserter Graf is."

Mendel asked Pavel: "Was the colonel your idea?"

"No, the colonel was Ulybin's invention, but I added the Graf on my own. And didn't I find a nice name for him?"

"Very nice. How did it go again?"

"Eh, you expect me to remember? If you like, I'll find you another."

Ulybin, paying no attention to the presence of the prisoners, said, "We won't attack David-Gorodok with five hundred men. We'll attack Zhitkovichi with fifty men. I don't believe the Germans swallowed the story, but just in case, they'll send reinforcements from Zhitkovichi to David-Gorodok, and we'll encounter less resistance."

It was night by now; from his pack Ulybin took a flashlight and strapped it to the barrel of his gun, but didn't turn it on. They marched on, Fedya in the lead on his skis, then the two Ukrainians, and after them, in order, Pavel, Mendel, and Ulybin. As they were passing through a thick patch of forest, the Ukrainian dressed as a woodman suddenly darted from the trail, attempting to escape to the left, struggling in the deep snow, and trying to take cover behind the trees. Ulybin turned on the flashlight, trained the narrow cone of light on the fugitive, and fired a single shot. The Ukrainian bent forward, took a few more steps, then fell on his hands; in that position, on all fours like an animal, he advanced several meters, digging a blood-stained trench in the snow, then he stopped. The others overtook him: he was wounded in a tibia, the bullet had apparently pierced his leg, shattering the bone.

Ulybin handed the gun to Mendel, without saying a word.

"You want me to—?" Mendel stammered.

"Go ahead, *yeshiva bucher,*" Ulybin said. "He can't walk, and if they find him, he'll tell what he's seen. A spy never changes; he stays a spy."

Mendel felt a bitter saliva fill his mouth. He stepped back two paces, aimed carefully, and fired. "Let's go," Ulybin said. "The foxes will take care of him." Then he turned again to Mendel, illuminating him with the flashlight. "Is it the first time? Don't think about it. It gets easy afterwards."

5

January–May

1944

The Zhitkovichi attack never came off. The camp radio, which for many weeks had given only information about German movements and news from the front, the evening that Ulybin's group came back began to transmit repeatedly the coded phrase that meant "keep listening." There was an argument between Ulybin and Maksim, and the latter's opinion prevailed, since he was considered the representative of the government and the party in the band: take no initiative, wait, maybe orders would arrive for some special operation.

Ulybin shut himself up in isolation. He was rarely seen, and then only to hand out comments and reproaches. To the cook because the kasha was too salty: did he think salt came down free from heaven, plentiful as snow? To the radio operator because his notes were illegible. To Pavel because he ate too much and talked too much. The two women, who had been relegated to the kitchen, he regarded with suspicion; whether through shyness or contempt, he never addressed a word to them except for strict questions of duty.

Towards Dov, Ulybin displayed the grouchy respect due to old people over whom one has superior authority, a respect that easily turns into irritation and rudeness. Dov hadn't really recovered from the strain of the last march. His wounded knee hurt relentlessly; at night it kept him from sleeping, and during the day it made his movements awkward. At Novoselki, in an enclosed community, on the defensive, his scant physical efficiency could be tolerated because his experience made up for it. In the Turov camp, composed entirely of young people, Dov knew he was a burden and had no illusions about it. He tried to make himself useful in the kitchen, cleaning, doing little maintenance chores: nobody rejected him, but he felt superfluous. He became taciturn, and since everybody knew how contagious sadness and disheartenment are, very few spoke to him. Pavel, who had achieved a certain popularity thanks to the interception business, treated him with noisy and polite cordiality: of course, the cold and the damp make your bones ache, it happens even in Moscow, so obviously here, in the midst of the marshes and in these buildings, half under the snow, it's bound to be worse. But spring would come soon, and with spring, who knows? maybe peace would come, too: it seemed the Russians had crossed the Dnepr, and they were fighting somewhere around Krivo Rog. . . .

Dov felt at ease only with Mendel and with Sissl. Mendel tried to cheer him up, but with instinctive discretion he avoided any reference to his handicap and his fatigue; he tried to distract Dov, asking him for advice, for comments on the progress of the war, as if Dov could know more than was broadcast over the radio. Still more restful for Dov was the presence of Sissl. Calm in her speech and her movements, Sissl would sit down beside him while, with her deft hands, big as a man's, she was peeling potatoes or patching trousers and jackets already desperately patched. They would be silent for a long time, savoring that relaxed and natural silence born from reciprocal trust: when you share deep experiences you don't feel any need to talk. Mendel also liked to stay and look at the face of Sissl intent on her work, under the warm light of the undernourished electric bulb. That face contradicted the woman's sturdy, mature body, and it testified to a complicated mixture of bloodlines. Sissl had pale skin, smooth blond hair that she wore parted straight down the middle and gathered in a knot at her nape. Her eyebrows were also blond; her eyes slanted, joined to her nose by a slight Mongol fold, but they had the gray color of the Baltic peoples. Her mouth was broad and soft; she had high cheekbones, her chin and jaw were nobly drawn, but strong. No longer young, Sissl emanated security and tranquillity, but not gaiety, all around her, as if her broad shoulders could have served as shield against any adverse event.

She never spoke of her father. She made Dov tell stories of hunting in the forest, the sly tricks of the lynx, the strategy of the wolf pack, the ambushes of the Siberian tiger. In Dov's village, Mutoraj on the Tunguska, three thousand kilometers away, winter lasted nine months, and beyond the depth of a meter, the ground never thawed, but Dov spoke of the place with homesickness. Back there, anyone who wasn't a hunter wasn't a man. Mutoraj was like no other village in the world. In 1908, when he was ten, a star had fallen eighty kilometers away, or a meteor, or a comet; scientists had come from all over the world, but hadn't cleared up the mystery. He remembered that day well: the sky was serene, but there had been an explosion like a hundred thunderbolts, and the forest had caught fire, with so much smoke that it darkened the sun. There was an enormous crater, and for a radius of sixty kilometers all the trees were burned or had been felled. It was summer, and the fire died out right at the gates of the village.

Mendel, Pavel, Leonid, Line, and the Ozarichi men

took part in the training hikes, the marksmanship exercises, and the foraging expeditions to the surrounding farms and villages. For the most part these took place without friction or resistance on the part of the peasants: supplying provisions to the partisans was a taxation in kind, imposed at first, and by now taken for granted. The peasants, even those least pleased with collectivization, realized by now which was the winning side; moreover, Ulybin's partisans defended them against the roundups of the Germans, starved for manpower for their labor camps.

From one of these expeditions Pavel returned on horseback, with a braggart manner, his fur cap twisted sideways. It wasn't a saddlehorse, but a workhorse, old and stately; Pavel said he had found it lost in the woods and starving to death, but nobody believed him: the animal wasn't all that skinny. Pavel considered it his by right, became fond of it, and the horse became fond of him; when called, it came running like a dog, at its heavy, breathless trot. Pavel had never ridden in his life, and for that matter the horse's withers were so broad that a rider was forced to sit in an unnatural position, but in Pavel's off-duty hours you could often see him practicing equitation around the barracks. Ulybin said that Pavel's horse should take turns with the other, driving the dynamo. Pavel objected, and several partisans sided with him; and Ulybin, who displayed an inexplicable partiality towards Pavel, let it go.

The commander was less indulgent towards Leonid. He didn't approve of the relationship with Line, which for that matter inspired comments and jokes from everyone, kindly or malicious, according to the circumstances. Leonid had clung to the girl with the frantic tension of a shipwrecked man who has discovered a floating plank. He seemed to want to enfold her in a total embrace that would shield her from all other human contacts and isolate her from the world. He no longer spoke with anyone, not even Mendel.

One day Ulybin stopped Mendel. "I don't have anything against women, and this is none of my business; but I'm afraid that friend of yours is going to get himself in trouble and may make trouble for others, too. Steady couples are all right in peacetime; here it's different. Here there are two women and fifty men."

Mendel was about to give him the same answer he had given Dov in September at Novoselki, namely that he wasn't responsible for Leonid's actions; but he sensed that Ulybin was made of sterner stuff than Dov. He restrained himself and vaguely replied that he would speak to Leonid, but he knew he was lying. He wouldn't dare say anything to Leonid; when he thought of the younger man's relations with Line, Mendel felt a knot of conflicting feelings which, ever since they had been in Turov, he had tried in vain to untangle.

He felt envy: on this point he had no doubt, and in fact, he was a bit ashamed. It was an envy tinged with jealousy, of Leonid's nineteen years, of this sudden and innate love that reminded Mendel painfully of his own, of six years ago (or sixty, or six hundred?), the love that had flung him into the arms of Rivke like an arrow hitting the target: Rivke! Envy also of the good luck that had brought Leonid within the field of force that Line radiated: a boy like him could have fallen into any trap, but Line, to him, didn't seem a trap-woman. What could Line have found in Leonid? Mendel wondered. Perhaps only a shipwrecked boy: there are women born to rescue, and perhaps Line was one of these. I'm a rescuer, too, Mendel thought, a consoler. A fine profession, consoling the afflicted in the midst of the snow, the mud, and with weapons at the ready. Or perhaps it's something else: Line isn't looking for a shipwrecked man to save, but on the contrary, she is looking for a humiliated man she can humiliate still further, to climb on him the way you climb up on a platform, to stand a bit higher and see farther. There are people like that; they harm others without realizing it. Leonid should be careful. I envy him, but I'm also afraid for him.

The days of truce followed one another at Turov, and Mendel and Sissl became lovers. There was no need of words, it was natural and due, as in the Earthly Paradise, and at once hasty and uncomfortable. There was the sun, and all the men were outside beating blankets and oiling weapons. Mendel went to find Sissl in the kitchen and said to her, "Will you come with me?", and Sissl stood up and said, "I'll come." Mendel took her into the woodshed, which served also as a stable for the two horses, and there they went up the steps to the hayloft. It was cold, they half undressed, and Mendel was dazed by the female smell of Sissl and the glow of her skin. Sissl opened like a flower, docile and warm; and Mendel felt in his loins exploding the power and desire that had been dumb for years. He sank into her, but without abandoning himself; on the contrary, all cautious and alert: he wanted to enjoy everything, lose nothing, engrave it all inside himself. Sissl received him, trembling slightly, her eyes closed as if she were dreaming, and it was immediately over: voices and footsteps could be heard nearby, Mendel and Sissl broke from their embrace, brushed off the wisps of hay, and dressed again.

After that they didn't have many other opportunities to meet. They managed to maintain discretion, but not secrecy; the partisans spoke to Mendel of Sissl, saying, "your woman," and Mendel felt pleased. In Sissl he found peace and refreshment, but he wasn't sure he loved her, because there were too many burdens on his soul, because he felt somehow cauterized, and because Line's presence troubled him. With Line, Mendel couldn't escape the impression of a rare and precious human substance, but upset and upsetting. Sissl was like a palm tree in the sun; Line was a tangled ivy, nocturnal. She must have been only a few years older than Leonid, but the privation she had suffered in the ghetto had erased the youthfulness from her face, whose skin seemed dull and tired, marked by precocious wrinkles. She had big, widely spaced eyes in ashen sockets, a little, small nose, and fine, cameolike fea-

tures that gave her an expression at once sad and determined. She moved with rapid security, at times in
brusque jerks.

Line had insisted to Ulybin that she should be allowed
to participate in the training: she was a partisan, not a refugee. At Novoselki Mendel had admired her skill in handling weapons, and during the march through the snow
her endurance was at least the equal of Lèonid's. This is
not a gift of nature, Mendel thought: it's a store of courage
and strength that has to be renewed each day; we should
all act like her. This girl knows how to want something;
maybe she doesn't always know what she wants, but when
she does know, she achieves it. He envied Leonid; and at
the same time was worried about him: the boy seemed to
have been hitched up by Line, and the rope was too taut.
A taut rope can snap: and then what?

Line spoke little, and never idly: few, pondered, unem-
phatic words, said in a low, slightly hoarse voice, her eyes
trained steadily on the interlocutor's face. Her ways were
different from those of other women, Jews or not, that
Mendel had encountered in the past. She showed no reticence or false modesty, she didn't playact or have whims;
but when she talked to someone, she moved her face close
to his, as if to observe his reactions intently; often she
would place her strong little hand, with its gnawed nails,
on the shoulder or arm of the person facing her. Was she
aware of the feminine charge in this gesture of hers? Mendel felt it deeply and was not surprised that Leonid followed Line like a dog following his master. It was an effect
of long abstinence perhaps, but Mendel, when he observed Line, was reminded of Rahab, the harlot of Jericho, and the other temptresses of the Talmudic legend. He
had found tales of them in an old book belonging to his
teacher the rabbi: a forbidden book, but Mendel knew
where it was hidden and had furtively leafed through it
several times, with a thirteen-year-old's curiosity, when
the rabbi would fall asleep on sultry afternoons in his
chair with its tall back. Michal, who fascinated all who

saw her; Jael, the fatal partisan of her time, who had driven a nail through the temple of the enemy general, but who seduced all men with the mere sound of her voice. Abigail, the sensible queen, who seduced anyone who thought of her. But Rahab was superior to them all; a man who simply uttered her name spilled his seed immediately.

No, the name of Line did not have this power. Everyone at Novoselki knew the story of Line and her name, which isn't Russian or Yiddish or Hebrew. Line's parents, both Russian Jews and students of philosophy, had brought her into the world without giving the matter much thought, in the blazing years of the Revolution and the civil war. Her father had joined up as a volunteer and had vanished in Volhynia, fighting the Poles. Her mother had found work in a weaving mill. Previously she had taken part in the October Revolution because she had seen in it her own liberation, as a Jew and as a woman; she had made speeches in squares, in the soviets. She was an admirer and follower of Emmeline Pankhurst, the proper, indomitable English lady who in 1918 had won for English women the right to vote. And, a few months later, the young Russian mother had been happy to bear a little girl, because she could give her the name Emmeline, which everybody then, from day school on, had abbreviated to Line. But neither had Line's maternal grandmother, Anna Kaminskaya, been a woman confined to kitchen, children, and church. She was born in 1858, on the same day, month, and year as Mrs. Pankhurst; she had run away from home to study economics in Zurich, and then had come back to Russia to preach the renunciation of earthly possessions, rejection of matrimony, equality for all who work: Christians or Jews, men or women. This had got her sent to Omsk, where Line's mother had been born. In the tiny room where Line and her mother lived, in Chernigov, as Line recalled, on the wall behind the stove there hung a framed photograph of Mrs. Pankhurst that her mother had clipped from a magazine. It showed the arrest, in

1914, of the tiny revolutionary in her long skirt and her hat with her ostrich plume; she was suspended in midair, a yard above the London pavement glistening with rain, dignified and impassive in the clutch of a British policeman who pressed her slender back against his own gigantic belly.

At Chernigov, then in Kiev, where she had gone to study to be a schoolteacher, Line had frequented Zionist groups and also the local Komsomol: she saw no contradiction between Soviet communism and the agrarian collectivism preached by the Zionists. But after 1932, Zionist organizations had led a more and more precarious existence, until they were officially disbanded. To the Jews who wanted a land of their own, where they could organize themselves and live according to their traditions, Stalin had offered a bleak territory in Eastern Siberia: Birobidzhan. Take it or leave it. Anyone who wanted to live as a Jew should go to Siberia; if anyone refused Siberia, that meant he preferred to be Russian. There was no third way. But if a Jew wanted to be Russian, what can, what should he do, if the Russians deny him access to the university, and call him *zhid*, and turn the pogromists on him, and form an alliance with Hitler? He can't do anything—especially if he's a woman. Line remained in Chernigov, and the Germans came and sealed the Jews in the ghetto. In the ghetto she found again some Zionist friends from Kiev; with them, and this time with the help of Soviet partisans, she bought weapons—few, inadequate—and learned how to use them. Line wasn't inclined to theories; in the ghetto she had suffered hunger, cold, exhaustion; but she felt her many souls blend together. The woman, the Jew, the Zionist, and the Communist had been fused into a single Line, who had a single enemy.

At the end of February came the radio message they had been expecting for so long, and it caused an uproar in the camp. Near David-Gorodok, on the Stviga marshes, frozen for four months, the Germans had set up a field for night drops from planes: a simple field of snow, marked out by three fires at the points of an extended triangle; the fires, mere piles of branches, were lighted when the radio transmitted a certain signal. Ulybin's unit was charged with preparing a similar terrain, not far from the Turov camp and ten kilometers from the German camp: Ulybin was to decide where. At the signal, one squad should light the fires of the fake field; another would distract the Germans and put out the fires of the real field. On the uniform plain, the German aircraft would have no reference points but the fires of the partisans' field, and they would drop their parachutes there. They were expecting drops of food, winter clothing, and light weapons.

Ulybin sent two skiers, at night, to take the measurements and note the orientation of the German triangle. They came back a little later: everything was just as the radio had said. The field was already laid out, with the three piles of wood at its points, oriented from west to east; a country road ran alongside it, which had been made passable by sending a snowplow over it. On the road there were old and recent hoofprints of horses, wagon tracks, and tire marks. Between the road and the field there was a wooden shack, small, with a smoking chimney: it couldn't hold more than ten or twelve men. It was likely that the goods to be dropped were meant not only for the David-Gorodok garrison, but for all the German garrisons scattered over Polessia and in the Pripet marshes: in those areas the partisans' presence was being felt, and the air route was not only quicker but also safer.

It wasn't hard to find ground similar to the Germans' field: it would have been hard to find a place any different. Ulybin selected a great pond about twenty minutes' march from the camp, also parallel to a road, and he had them build a little plank hut in a position corresponding to that of the Germans: it was unthinkable that the Germans would make daytime drops, but they might send a reconnaissance plane to photograph the terrain. Then, as they were waiting for the German radio signal, Ulybin chose two squads. The first, charged with harassing the Germans and putting out the fires on their field, comprised nine men, among them Leonid, Piotr, and Pavel. The second, which was to light the fires of the fake field, was made up of six men, including Mendel. All the others were to remain ready. When the job was done, they informed the partisan command by radio.

The cold weather held. Towards the fifth of March it snowed again, a dry, fine snow, in scattered, intermittent flurries; between snows, the sky remained clouded, hazy. For the drops the Germans would surely wait until the sky was completely clear. Nevertheless, one morning they heard the sound of a plane: it came and went, not high but invisible above the clouds, as though it were seeking a place to land. It seemed too low to carry out a drop, and besides there had been no warning message from the radio. Ulybin gave orders to set up the heavy machine gun, now mounted on a sledge; they unbolted it and, held by hand, aimed it at the sky. The plane continued to come and go, but the sound was growing weaker. The partisans came out of the barracks to look at the sky, luminous but impenetrable; at intervals they could glimpse the sun, haloed; then it immediately vanished.

"Everybody inside, you stupid do-nothings!" Ulybin shouted. "If it comes down below the clouds it'll strafe us all." In fact, all of a sudden, the plane appeared, barely above the tops of the trees: it was heading straight for them. The two men supporting the gun turned to aim at it, but they heard various voices shouting: "It's one of ours! Don't shoot!" And, in fact, it was a little pursuit plane that bore beneath its wings the emblems of the Soviet air force; it swooped over the barracks, and an arm could be seen, waving a greeting. All the men on the ground waved their arms wildly, to point out the direction of the field for the drops; the plane headed in that direction and vanished beyond the screen of the trees.

"Will it manage to land?"

"It has skis underneath, not landing gear; if it finds the right direction, it'll make it."

"Come on, let's follow it." But Ulybin asserted his authority: only he, Maksim, and two others slipped on their skis and went off, first following the curious zigzag route that avoided the minefields, then straight, with the long, agile stride of cross-country skiers.

They returned an hour later, and not alone. With them were a lieutenant and a captain of the Red Army, young, clean-shaven, smiling, sheathed in splendid quilted jumpsuits, and wearing boots of shining leather. They cordially greeted everyone, but promptly withdrew with Ulybin into the little room set up as headquarters. They conferred for several hours; every now and then, Ulybin would send for bread, cheese, and vodka.

In the camp, the arrival of the two unexpected messengers was discussed at length, with pleasure, hope, distrust, and a hint of irritation. What were they bringing from the Great Land? Information, beyond any doubt, new plans, orders. And why had they come so suddenly, unannounced by radio? It's like the army, another man answered: they make inspections without warning, otherwise they're not inspections. "They do themselves proud, the gents of the Great Land," a third man said, "I bet they spent last night in their beds, with pillows and sheets, and maybe even their wife. I wonder if, besides propaganda, they also brought some shaving cream!" Because the partisans of all places and all times have much in common: they respect the central authorities, but they would gladly do without them. As for the shaving cream, this item headed the list of the camp's private jokes. In Turov, they were advised against growing beards; in other bands it was explicitly forbidden, because a bearded young man was too easily recognized as a partisan. Nevertheless, despite the prohibitions and the danger, many of the men of the woods and the marshes wore thick beards. The beard had become a symbol of the *partisanshchina,* of the freedom of the forest, of bravado without regulations, of the do-

minion of independence over discipline. More or less consciously, the beard's length was considered proportional to
a partisan's seniority, like an aristocratic title or a hierar-
chical rank. "Moscow doesn't want us to grow beards, but
they don't send us razors or soap. What are we supposed
to shave with? Axes? Bayonets? No soap, no shave: we'll
keep our beards."

"All stuff that won't harm anybody," Piotr came to announce, after he had been ordered to assort the material
brought by the two officers. "No arms or ammunition,
only printed matter and salve for scabies. No, there's no
shaving cream, either. Not even laundry soap." On his
own initiative, he went to take the news to the two women
who were busy at the laundry. "You have to be patient,
ladies. Stick to ashes and soda, the way our grannies did.
The important thing is to kill the lice; but anyway, the
war's about to end."

The two officers left that same evening. Already dressed
again in their flying suits, as they were looking out of the
little window with a great show of patience, they saw Ulybin go off with Dov and speak to him in a low voice. Then
they saw Dov stuff his few belongings into a knapsack. He
said good-bye soberly to all; his eyes became moist only
when he took leave of Sissl, with a quick embrace. He
went limping off with the two messengers and with a partisan who had the fever, and he disappeared with them in
the livid light of dusk. Piotr said, "You mustn't worry.
They'll take them to hospital, in the Great Land: they'll
be better off there than here, and they'll be cured." Mendel slapped him on the shoulder, without replying.

After that visit, Ulybin became even more silent and ir-
ritable. As if to reduce contacts to a minimum, he chose
from the partisans a kind of lieutenant, Zachar, tall and
thin as a pole and even more silent than Ulybin himself.
Zachar served as command-bearer in one direction, and as
complaint-bearer in the other, and as buffer in both. He
wasn't very young, almost illiterate, a Cossack from the
Kuban and a sheep breeder by profession. Zachar was an

instinctive diplomat; he promptly proved skillful in sooth-
ing disagreements, allaying frustrations, and maintaining
discipline and esprit de corps. A rumor had spread that
Ulybin was beginning to get drunk in the headquarters
room; Zachar denied it, but the coming and going of bottles, empty and full, was hard to conceal.

The fake field was ready, they all were ready, but the
order to go into action didn't come. The whole month of
March went by in almost total inaction, which proved
harmful for all, not only for the commander, who no
longer had anything to command. Hunger made itself
felt: not the lacerating hunger Leonid and others had
known in the German *Lagers* behind the lines, but a nos-
talgia hunger, a stubborn yearning for fresh vegetables,
for bread right from the oven, perhaps simple food, but
chosen according to the whim of the moment. Homesickness also made itself felt, heavy for all of them, a torment
for the group of Jews. For the Russians, a longing for
home was a not unreasonable hope, even probable: a
yearning to go back, a call. For the Jews, the regret for
their houses was not a hope but a despair, buried till then
under more urgent and serious sorrows, but latent always.
Their homes no longer existed: they had been swept away,
burned by the war or by slaughter, bloodied by the squads
of hunters of men; tomb houses, of which it was best not to
think, houses of ashes. Why go on living, why fight? For
what house, what country, what future?

Fedya's house, on the contrary, was too close. Fedya was
seventeen years old on 30 March, and Ulybin gave him
permission to spend his birthday at home, in the village of
Turov; and he didn't come back. When three days had
gone by, Ulybin had Zachar tell the others that Fedya was
a deserter: two men were to go and find him and bring
him back to the band. They had no trouble finding him:
he was at home, he hadn't the remotest idea that a three-
day absence in a period of inactivity was such a serious
matter. But that wasn't the worst of it: Fedya confessed
publicly that at home he had got drunk with other boys,

and that in his drunkenness he had talked. What about?
About the barracks even? Also about the fake airfield? His
face ashen, Fedya said he didn't know now, he didn't remember, but probably not, he hadn't talked about secret
things, no he absolutely hadn't talked about them.

Ulybin had Fedya locked up in the woodshed. He sent
Zachar to take him food and tea, but at dawn they all saw
Zachar going to the woodshed barefoot, and they all
heard the pistol shot. Sissl and Line had the job of un-
dressing the boy's body to recover the clothes and the
boots; Pavel and Leonid were assigned to digging the
grave in the ground soaked with water of the thaw. Why
Pavel and Leonid particularly?

A few days later, Mendel realized that Sissl was upset.
He questioned her: no, it wasn't because of the Fedya
business. Zachar had taken her aside and said to her:
"Comrade, you must watch out. If you become pregnant,
it means trouble; this isn't a hospital, and planes from the
Great Land don't arrive here every day. Tell your man
this." Zachar had said the same thing also to Line, but
Line had just shrugged. Also in this period, there was an
order of the day pinned to the board, written in pencil in a
fine hand and signed by Ulybin: soon the thaw would
begin, it was urgent to dig a gutter channel around the
barracks to prevent them from being flooded. This job was
important and took absolute precedence, so the roster of
the two squads, made up a month ago, for the action of
the airfields, had now been changed. Leonid and Mendel
were no longer a part of it; they were to put down their
guns and take up picks and shovels. Not Pavel. Pavel remained part of the first squad, the one that was to put out
the German fires. Mendel, Leonid, and four other men
began their job of digging. The snow and the ground froze
during the night, and melted into a sticky, reddish mud
during the warmest hours of the day. As if their curiosity
had been aroused, big crows lighted on the branches of
the firs to observe the work; more and more numerous, the
birds crammed one against the other; all of a sudden their

weight would bend the bough, and then all would take flight, flapping and cawing, until they went to perch on another bough.

The order came when nobody was expecting it anymore: intercepted signals of the German radio indicated the drop was imminent. It must have been an important drop, because the alert had been repeated several times. Finally, on April 12th, the definitive announcement came: the drop was scheduled for that night. The two squads left immediately; Pavel, just in case, charged Leonid with caring for his horse, which for some reason or other he had baptized Drozhd, Thrush.

The rest of the camp got ready for the night; there were no special orders, but they all were listening carefully, in particular Michail, the radio operator, and Mendel, who took turns with him so he could get some rest for a few hours. Reception was terrible, interrupted by buzzing and static; the few messages he managed to intercept were excited and repeated several times, but almost undecipherable, though both Michail and Mendel understood German fairly well.

At two in the morning a hum of engines was heard, and everybody was on his feet. The sky was clear, with no moon; the hum grew more and more intense, marked by throbbing, as when several instrument strings vibrate together, though not perfectly tuned. It certainly wasn't a single plane; there were two at least, perhaps three. They flew over, invisible, north of the barracks, then the hum died away until it was gone.

An hour later one of the partisans of the second squad arrived, breathless. Everything had gone wonderfully: fires lit at the right moment, four planes, thirty parachutes, or forty or even more, many right on the field, others among the trees, some caught in the branches. Send reinforcements at once, and a sledge, there was a lot of stuff. They all wanted to go, but Ulybin couldn't be swayed. He went himself, with Maksim and Zachar; he didn't even want the messenger who had brought the news to return to the place. For the first time in his career as a partisan horse, Thrush made himself useful: Ulybin had him hitched up to a sledge that set off over the snow, made compact by the thaw and covered with a fragile crust of nighttime ice.

In the meanwhile the first squad had also come back, all of them, though one man was wounded in the arm. The action had gone well on the whole, as Piotr and Pavel told it. They had hidden near the shed, heard the hum of the planes, and seen three Germans come out with cans of gasoline to pour on the piles of wood. They had killed the men before they could light the fires, and at the same time one partisan, who had climbed on the roof of the shed, dropped a hand grenade down the chimney. Some of the Germans must have died, but others came out of the shattered hut and opened fire. One partisan was wounded and one German was killed; another two or three had managed to start a truck, but they had also been killed as they were going away. In the shack, besides sidearms and some tinned food, they hadn't found anything interesting. There was a radio, but the explosion had destroyed it. They had stationed themselves at the sides of the road, because they thought some vehicle ought to arrive from the city to collect the dropped goods, but by midmorning they hadn't seen anything, so they came back.

The sledge returned loaded, even though the messenger must have exaggerated: there were no more than twenty packages dropped. Ulybin wouldn't let anyone touch them. He had them all piled up in his room and opened them himself, with the help of Zachar; he allowed the others to inventory their contents only after he had seen them. There was a bit of everything, like in a charity raffle: valuable things and useless, mysterious, ridiculous stuff. Luxuries such as Mendel and his friends had never seen: eggs of ersatz chocolate because Easter was coming, some other big chocolates in the shape of lambs, beetles, and mice. Cigars and cigarettes, schnapps and brandy in tins: perhaps a packaging specially conceived by German technicians to resist impact with the ground? Terra-cotta braziers, apparently meant to warm the feet of sentries. A box full of medals for bravery and other assorted decorations, along with the respective citations. There were bundles of newspapers and magazines, a pack of portraits of the Führer, a packet of private correspondence for the various garrisons of the zone, and another of official correspondence that Ulybin had them set aside. Two chests were full of ammunition for the Wehrmacht's *Maschinenpistole,* another two contained loaders for a kind of machine gun that nobody could identify. In one crate there was a typewriter with various stationery supplies. Other crates contained six devices, all alike, but nobody at Turov had seen one or could figure out its use: a flattened disk the size of a frying pan and equipped with a long handle, dismantled in segments. "This stuff is for you, watchmender," Ulybin said to Mendel. "Study it and tell us what it's good for."

That evening Ulybin allowed the event to be celebrated with moderate revelry. Then he went off with Pavel to examine the documents that had been found: they weren't in code, it wasn't sensational stuff, only detailed lists, bills in numerous copies, quartermaster's accounts. Ulybin soon wearied and had Pavel translate some of the personal letters, which were more interesting; they were written in terms that were supposed to sound coded, allusive, but they were so naive that even an alien reader like Pavel could figure them out easily: it was obvious the bad weather of which all the fathers and mothers complained was the carpet bombing of the Allied planes, and drought meant the shortages. It was involuntary defeatist propaganda: Ulybin told Pavel to translate certain passages publicly.

Pavel was reading, in Russian, but with an assumed, overdone German accent that made them all laugh. And then from the sky, in waves, came the same musical hum of the night before.

"Quick!" Ulybin shouted. "Second squad, get skis on and hurry and light the fires: they're making us a present of a second drop!" The six men of the squad rushed out, and Ulybin looked at his watch: if they hurried, in a quarter of an hour they could reach the place before the planes tired of looking for the field in the darkness. They were looking, all right: the noise of the engines would come closer, then move away; at a certain moment the squadron flew right over the barracks, then went off again. Exactly twenty minutes by Ulybin's watch had passed when they heard a salvo of explosions. Everybody went outside, not understanding: the roars were too distant and too deep to be caused by the minefield around the barracks. They could see the flames, to the northeast: after every flame they could hear the explosion with a six-second delay. there could be no doubt: these were bombs falling on the faked landing field. The Germans had caught on and were taking their revenge.

The squad came back: only four men. In halting words, the leader reported. They had made it in record time, just as the planes were flying over their heads. They lighted the first of the piles, and bombs started raining down at once: big ones, at least two hundred kilos. If the ice had been thick, as in January, maybe it would have resisted; but it was softened by the thaw, the bombs pierced it and exploded below, flinging slabs of ice into the air. The two missing men vanished, swallowed up by the marsh: no use going to look for them.

For the men of Turov a difficult period began. The thaw had started, and it was worse than winter. Ulybin sent some men to check the condition of the fake field: it was out of commission, no plane could land there, and, worse, it would be impossible to ask for drops. The deep winter ice had been ripped by the explosions: it formed again during the night, but so thin that it wouldn't even have carried the weight of a man. On the other marshes it had held better, because the snow had shielded it from the direct rays of the sun, but the snow itself had been altered by the thaw and the wind: it had been transformed into a hard, corrugated crust, on which a normal plane, even if fitted out with skis, couldn't have landed without turning over.

Ulybin had to order a radio blackout, because the rerouted drop trick seemed to have reactivated the German air force. All through the winter its activity had been minimal, and apparently random. Now, on the contrary, it was unusual for a clear day to go by without their seeing a reconnaissance plane scouring the area: and there were many clear days. The luxury provisions of the drop hadn't lasted long, and flour, lard, and canned goods were beginning to dwindle. Ulybin set up rationing, and everyone's morale sank: hunger, the haunting specter of the previous winters, was about to return, as if time had moved back to the terrible months of the beginning of the partisan war, when everything, food, weapons, shelter, plans for action, the courage to fight and to live, were the fruit of a few men's desperate initiative. Now the men insisted on resuming the foraging expeditions to the villages; they much preferred the effort and the risk to hunger, but Ulybin wouldn't hear of it. There was still too much snow; it was already hard to understand how the reconnaissance had failed to spot the barracks. Obviously, the Germans were looking for them. The buildings were well camouflaged and might still elude the search, but the Germans would infallibly notice a fresh track.

What was to be done? Wait, let time go by: the only possible solution, and yet a terrible solution. Wait for the snow to melt, because on bare ground, even if it's muddy, tracks are less noticeable. Wait till the reconnaissance planes went hunting elsewhere. Wait in silence for the news from the radio: the Germans had evacuated Odessa, but Odessa was far away. The radio blackout was as painful as a mutilation, as if a human being were gagged at the moment he wants to cry for help: together with hunger, it had created around the Turov barracks a besieged mood. Those men were not new to privations, toil, discomfort,

and danger, but their cloistered isolation found them unprepared: accustomed to space, to the precarious freedom
of forest animals, they suffered the debilitating anguish of
the trap and the cage.

Ulybin went on drinking: the fact was acknowledged
and criticized, by all of them except Zachar, in whispers,
and not always in whispers. He drank in solitude, but he
hadn't lost his lucidity or his gruff authority. Mendel
asked him to explain why Dov's departure had been so
hasty, and Ulybin answered, "Fighters, when they're
wounded or sick, are treated, as far as possible. Your
friend will be treated, too; but that's all I can tell you.
Maybe at the end of the war you'll find out something
about him, but the fate of individuals has no importance."

Ulybin was too intelligent, and too much an expert in
partisan life, not to realize that something had to be done:
tracks were dangerous, but anguish even more so. A single
track that set out from the barracks would lead the Germans to the barracks for sure, but if the track were only to
cross the little wood that concealed the barracks, the locating of the camp would not be immediate. Reluctantly,
Ulybin then authorized not one, but two foraging expeditions, which would set out on the same night in opposite
directions, towards different villages.

The squads had been gone only a short while, and
there were barely the first signs of dawn, when they heard
a new noise, alarming for the Jews, reassuring and unmis-
takable for the Turov veterans. It sounded like the crack-
ling of a motorcycle; it was faint, distant, but it was
approaching. It increased in volume, but slowed down,
like an impeded gramophone record. It sneezed a few
times and was silent. Ulybin's men were immediately all
on their feet: "A P-two! It's landed there, in the clearing!
Let's go and see!"

"Maybe there was no need to send the squads out,"
Piotr said.

"What's a P-two?" Mendel asked.

"P-twos are partisan planes. They're made of wood,

they fly slowly, but they can take off and land anywhere. They fly at night, without lights; they drop grenades on the Germans and bring supplies." A little later the pilot came into the barracks, squat and shapeless in his flying suit of reversed lamb's skin. He took it off, removed the goggles from his forehead, and they saw it was a girl, short, chubby, with a broad, calm face and a homey manner. Her hair was parted evenly and gathered at her nape in two short braids tied with black string. The two men who had gone to meet her were carrying two bags, as if they were returning from the market. The partisans pressed around her, hugged her and kissed her on her round cheeks hardened by the cold. "Polina! Good for Polina! Welcome, sweetheart. We see you again finally! What have you brought us?"

The girl, who didn't look over twenty, fended them off, laughing, with the shy grace of peasant girls. "That's enough of that, Comrades! They sent me to see what's going on here, and why your radio is silent. Let go of me now; I have to leave right away. I don't suppose there's a drop of vodka here? Where's the commander?" She went off privately with Ulybin, into the little headquarters room.

"It's Polina. Polina Michailovna," Piotr said, proud and happy. "It's Polina Gelman, of the Women's Regiment. Didn't you know? They're all women, the P-two pilots. All fine girls, but Polina's the best of them all. She comes from Gomel, her father was a rabbi and her grandfather a cobbler. She's flown more than seven hundred missions already, but she's visited us here only once before, six months ago. She stayed a few days and we made friends, but this time obviously she's in a hurry. Too bad."

Polina said good-bye and went off in her fragile plane. She had brought food and medicines, and some bad news. There were troops on the move, and armored vehicles; in various villages around Turov they were assembling units of German and Ukrainian corps, specialized in fighting the partisans. They were preparing a concentrated dragnet action, with forces enormously superior to the Turov camp's defense possibilities; there were no other bands in the area. For some reason, the Germans had overestimated the partisan forces; or perhaps it was a large-scale operation, in all the area of the Pripet marshes or in all of Polessia. The Soligorsk ghetto, where the old and ill of Novoselki had sought salvation, had been surrounded and all its inhabitants shot; the Soligorsk garrison had been joined by an SS unit expert in digging out people in hiding, with trained dogs. Many of the Turov men knew these dogs and were more afraid of them than of tanks. In other words, the camp had to be evacuated.

Ulybin summoned Mendel and asked him if he had figured out what those machines were, the ones found in the stuff from the drop.

"They're mine detectors," Mendel answered. "Or rather, metal detectors. They indicate where metallic objects are buried."

"So if the Germans are equipped with these gadgets, they would discover our minefields?"

"Of course they would. They'd find them. Maybe not right away, but they'd find them."

Ulybin gave him a grim look. "I'll have the barracks mined all the same, whether or not the Germans have those detectors of yours. They'll find the buried ones, but not the mines we'll hide in here. I'll show you: we'll blow some of them up, those bastards."

Mendel was frightened. It was clear that the chief had drunk even a bit more than usual; but the man's tone frightened him. "What are you saying, Osip Ivanovich? Why are you talking to me like this? Did I invent the mine detectors? Did I give them to the Germans?"

"I don't give a damn who invented them. The fact is, we're leaving. You don't want us to stay here and wait for the tanks and get ourselves all slaughtered?"

Mendel came out, aghast. But a little later Ulybin sent for him again. "Do they work? Those gadgets?"

"Yes, they work."

"Take Dimitri and Vladimir and show them how to use them."

"You want to mine the barracks with the mines buried around here?"

"You're smart. You guessed right. Those are the only mines we have."

"Look, this isn't a job for kids. Experts are more afraid of mines than beginners are. And besides, the longer they've been underground, the more dangerous they are."

"Feel important, don't you? That's enough. Go do what I said. I'm in command here, and I don't like complaints. You people are all alike. All good at arguing, and all half-German: Rosenfeld, Mandelstamm. . . . And you? What's your name? Dajcher, no? Mendel Nachmanovich Dajcher: even your name's German."

Mendel gave his lesson as diligently as he could. He sent the two boys to get their orders from Ulybin, and he withdrew, filled with bitterness. Once, on Yom Kippur, the Day of Atonement, the Jews used to take a goat, the priest would press his hands on its head, list all the sins committed by the people, and impose them on the animal: he and he alone was guilty. Then, laden with sins he hadn't committed, the goat was sent into the desert. This is how the gentiles think, too; they also have a lamb that takes away the sins of the world. But not I, I don't believe that. If I've sinned, I bear the burden of my sins, but only those, and I have more than enough. I don't bear the sins of anybody else. I wasn't the one who sent out the squad to be bombed. I didn't shoot Fedya while he was asleep. If we have to go into the desert, we'll go, but without bearing on our head the sins we haven't committed. And if Dimitri and Vladimir make the mines explode in their hands, must I be responsible, I, Mendel the watchmender?

On the contrary, the two boys did a good job: eight of the buried mines were defused and set in various parts of the barracks. At the end of April spring had burst out, heralded by three days of warm, dry wind. The snow on the branches of the trees melted in a constant rain, which relaxed its rhythm only at night; the snow on the ground also melted rapidly, and promptly from the soaked earth, among the prone blades of yellowish grass, soaked by the long frost, the first flowers sprouted, shy and absurd. The German reconnaissance flights became more and more frequent, and one of the planes, perhaps by chance, or perhaps made suspicious by some movement, briefly strafed the barracks, causing no victims or damage. Ulybin ordered them to prepare for abandoning the camp. The sledges, useless now, were burned; there were no wagons and no time to get any. For transporting the stores there were only the two horses and the men's backs: a caravan of porters, not a movement of fighting men. Many protested; they would have preferred to stay in the camp and face the Germans, but Ulybin silenced them: staying there was impossible, and anyway the evacuation of the camp had been ordered over the radio. The radio had also indicated the best direction for slipping through the circle of the antipartisan forces: towards the southwest, following the Stviga upstream, but without abandoning the stretch of marshes. With the thaw, and with their labyrinth of isthmuses, straits, and fords, they had once again become friendly territory.

The partisans were supposed to leave during the night of May 2, but that evening the sentries gave the alarm: they had heard sounds to the north, human voices and the barking of dogs. Many men grabbed their weapons, uncertain whether they should prepare to hold out or hasten their retreat, but Ulybin spoke up: "Stay where you are, all of you, stupid fools! Get on with the preparations. Tie up the sacks, nail the crates shut. Were you born yesterday? The Germans' dogs don't bark. If they did, what kind of war dogs would they be?"

He turned to the sentries. "Be on guard, but don't shoot. They're likely to be friends: they sent the dogs ahead to find the trail among the mines."

In fact, the dogs arrived first: there were only two, not

war dogs but humble farm dogs, excited and confused. They barked nervously, now at the barracks, now at the unknown men who still delayed in following them. Proud of the duty done, the dogs were uneasy at these new human presences; they alternately wagged their tails and snarled or did both at once even; they darted back and forth, dancing, their forepaws rigid, and they barked breathlessly, gulping air at intervals with a convulsed rattle. Then two cows were seen arriving, driven forward by some tattered youths: they were careful to see that the two animals kept to the trails made by the dogs.

Finally came the main body of the band, about thirty men and women, armed and unarmed, tired, ragged, and bold. In their midst was a man with an aquiline nose and a tanned face: over his shoulder he carried an automatic rifle and a violin. At the end of the group there was Dov. Mendel said to himself: Blessed be He who raises the dead.

All was turmoil: everybody was asking questions, and nobody was answering them. Finally the voice of Ulybin prevailed, and that of the other man, who was Gedaleh. Everyone was to be silent and await orders; Ulybin and Gedaleh withdrew into the headquarters cubbyhole. Many of the Turov men recalled the quarrel between the two at the beginning of winter: now what would happen, in this new encounter? Would they be reconciled, in the face of the imminent threat? Would they come to an agreement?

While everyone awaited the outcome of the meeting, the newcomers asked for shelter in the now-emptied barracks; some sat on the ground, others stretched out and promptly fell asleep, and others asked for tobacco or for hot water to wash their feet. They asked with the humility of the needy, but with the dignity of those who know they are entitled: they were not beggars or vagabonds, they were the Jewish band collected by Gedaleh, made up of survivors from the communities of Polessia, Volhynia, and Byelorussia; a wretched aristocracy, the strongest, the smartest, the luckiest. But some came from still farther away, along roads covered with blood: they had escaped the pogroms of the Lithuanian vandals, who would kill a Jew to rob a sheet, and the flamethrowers of the *Einsatz-kommandos,* the common graves of Kovno and of Riga. Among them were the few who had eluded the massacre of Ruzhany: they had lived for months in holes dug in the wood, like wolves, and like wolves they hunted silently, in a pack. There were the peasant Jews of Blizna, their hands hardened by the hoe and the axe. There were the workers from the sawmills and textile factories of Slonim, who even before the Hitler barbarism had gone on strike against their Polish masters and had known repression and prison.

Each of them, man or woman, had a different story behind him, but searing and heavy as molten lead; if the war and three terrible winters had left them the time and breath, each should have mourned a hundred dead. They were tired, poor, and dirty, but not defeated: children of merchants, tailors, rabbis, and cantors; they had armed themselves with weapons taken from the Germans, they had earned the right to wear those tattered uniforms, without chevrons, and they had tasted several times the bitter food of killing.

The Russians of Turov looked at them uneasily, as happens when the unexpected occurs. In those haggard but determined faces they didn't recognize the *zhid* of their tradition, the alien in the house who speaks Russian to swindle others but thinks in his own strange language, who doesn't know Christ but instead follows his own incomprehensible and ridiculous precepts, armed only by his cleverness, rich and cowardly. The world had been turned upside down: these Jews were allies and armed, like the English, like the Americans, and like Hitler three years ago, when he had been an ally. The ideas you are taught are simple and the world is complicated. Allies, and so comrades, perforce. The Turov men would have to accept them, shake their hands, drink vodka with them.

Some of the men ventured an embarrassed smile, a shy approach to the disheveled women, bundled in ill-fitting army clothing, their faces gray with fatigue and dust. Uprooting a prejudice is as painful as extracting a nerve.

The wall of incomprehension has two sides, like all walls, and incomprehension produces awkwardness, uneasiness, and hostility; but Gedaleh's Jews, at that moment, didn't feel awkward or hostile. On the contrary, they were lighthearted: in the *partisanka* adventure, different every day, in the frozen steppe, in snow and mud, they had found a new freedom, unknown to their fathers and grandfathers, a contact with friends and enemies, with nature and with action, which intoxicated them like the wine of Purim, when it's the custom to abandon usual sobriety and drink until you can't tell a blessing from a curse. They were lighthearted and fierce, like animals whose cage has been opened, like slaves who have risen up in vengeance. And they have savored it, savored vengeance, though at a high price: on various occasions, in acts of sabotage, assassinations, rear-guard conflicts; but even recently, a few days previously, and not far away. That had been their big moment. By themselves, they had attacked the garrison of Lyuban, eighty kilometers to the north, where the German and Ukrainian troops assigned to the dragnet were collecting; in the village there was also a little ghetto of artisans. The Germans had been driven from Lyuban: they weren't made of iron, they were mortal, and when they realized they were defeated they ran off in confusion, even from the Jews. Some of them abandoned their weapons and dived into the river, swollen by the thaw: it was a sight to make you rejoice, an image to carry to your grave: the Jews told the Russians about it with haunted faces. Yes, the blond, green men of the Wehrmacht fled from them, plunging into the water, trying to scramble up on the slabs of ice borne by the current; and the Jews went on shooting, and saw the Germans' bodies sink or float towards the river mouth on their catafalques of ice. The triumph was short-lived, of course:

triumphs are always short-lived and, as it is written, the Jew's joy ends in fright. They retired to the woods, taking with them those Jews from the Lyuban ghetto who seemed capable of fighting; but the Germans then came back and killed everyone left in the ghetto. Their war was like that: a war where you don't look back to take account, a war of a thousand Germans against one Jew and of a thousand dead Jews against one dead German. They were lighthearted because they were without a tomorrow and didn't bother about tomorrow, and because they had seen the supermen struggling in the icy water like frogs: a present no one could take from them.

They also brought more useful news. The roundup had already begun, and they had been driven from their camp, which for that matter was a poor camp of dens, makeshift, naturally not comparable to this Turov camp. But it wasn't true that the roundup was a big operation: there were no tanks and no heavy artillery, and a German prisoner they had questioned had confirmed the fact that the weakest point of the encirclement must be the very place that Ulybin thought: to the southwest, along the Stviga.

Dov was well, hardly limping now, but more bent than ever. His hair, again neatly combed, was thinner and whiter. Sissl asked him if he wanted something to eat, and he answered, laughing: "A sick man you ask, a well man you give." But he was more eager to talk than to eat. A group of listeners, Jews and Russians, collected around him: not many men returned from the Great Land into partisan territory.

"How long have they been talking, those two? An hour? That's a good sign: the more they talk, the more they agree; and it also means that the Germans are still far away, or have changed their route. Of course, I was treated—what did you think—in the Kiev hospital. It doesn't have a roof any more, or rather it doesn't have a roof yet: they're rebuilding it. And you know who's doing the work? The German prisoners, the ones who surrendered at Stalingrad.

"There was no roof, there was no food, no anesthetic, but there were the women doctors, and they operated on me right away: they took something out of my knee, a bone, and they showed it to me. In the cellar, they operated on me, by acetylene light, and then they put me in a ward, an endless ward, more than a hundred beds on each side, with living, dying, and dead in them. It's not nice, being in the hospital, but that ward really brought me luck: and where's there's luck even a bull will calve. There was a visitor, somebody important, from the Politburo, a Ukrainian: short, fat, bald, he looked like a peasant, but he had medals all over his chest. In the midst of that confusion of orderlies coming and going, he stopped right at my bed. He asked me who I was, where I came from, and where I had been wounded; he had the radio people following him, and he improvised this speech saying that everybody, Russians and Georgians and Yakuts and Jews, we are all the children of the great mother Russian, and all arguments have to stop . . ."

Piotr's voice was heard: "If he was a Ukrainian and a big shot, you might have told him to clean up his own house! They're rabble, those Ukrainians: when the Germans came, the Ukrainians opened their doors and offered them bread and salt. Their separatists are worse than the Germans." Other voices made Piotr shut up and urged Dov to go on.

"And he asked me where I wanted to be sent, once I was healed. I answered that my home is too far away, and I had partisan friends, and I would like to go back to them. Well, the minute they said I was cured, he got busy. Maybe he wanted to set an example. He found Gedaleh and his band and he had me parachuted near their camp, along with a crate containing four submachine guns, as his personal gift. Jumping with a parachute is kind of scary, but I landed in the mud and wasn't hurt at all."

Dov would have had many things still to tell about what he had seen and heard during his convalescence in the Great Land; but the headquarters door opened, Gedaleh and Ulybin came out, and everybody fell silent.

6

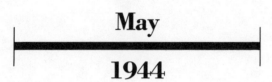

May

1944

Ulybin spoke first, in an official tone:

"My information and the information this comrade has brought coincide perfectly. These Germans come from the Polish border and not in great force. They're sending the best troops to the front, and when they come back, they're not the best troops any more. The Italians and the Hungarians have abandoned them; they don't trust the Czechs and the White Poles now. They want to surround these marshes and then tighten the circle little by little; the weakest link in the ring is to the south, towards Rechitsa and the Ukrainian border. We'll try to slip through, then we'll proceed separately: if we united the two bands, there'd be nothing gained and we'd be too visible. In any case, Comrade Gedaleh's unit has been officially recognized and supported by Moscow . . ."

"Lots of recognition and not much support!" someone interrupted, in Yiddish.

"Shut up, Jozek!" Gedaleh said sharply.

". . . and can move independently. The Jews in our camp can make their choice: either stay with us, force the circle, and head east to reach the front or . . . "

". . . or come with us," Gedaleh interjected. "We have different orders. We're in no hurry to go home. If we get through, we'll head west, to free the prisoners, harass the German rear lines, and settle some scores. Anybody who wants to come with us stand over here. Each person can keep his personal weapons, whatever he had when he arrived from Novoselki."

The barrack was overcrowded, and the sorting out was noisy and disorderly. Mendel, Sissl, Line, and Leonid chose Gedaleh's side without hesitation; around Pavel, on the contrary, a knot had formed, arguing. Pavel also wanted to come with Gedaleh, but he was attached to his horse; if Ulybin was going to keep it, then he would stay, too. Gedaleh didn't understand and asked for an explanation. Above the confusion Pavel's deep voice was heard:

"I'm useful to you because I speak German, but my horse doesn't. What will you do with him?"

Not laughing, Ulybin made a grimace hard to decipher, then said, "All right, take horse and master." But he was less agreeable when he saw that Piotr had also gone over to Gedaleh's side.

"What are you doing with them? What's come over you? Why are you on that side?"

"They all come from far away," Piotr said. "None of them knows the area. After half an hour's march they'd all be drowned."

"Nonsense. None of them asked you to be their guide. They manage well on their own. Mind what you do: you don't want to end up like Fedya."

"He asked me to be their guide," Piotr said, pointing to Dov; but he was obviously improvising. Then he added, "And this isn't deserting, Comrade Commander. This is a band, and that is a band." Still, as he was talking, he left Gedaleh's group and went back towards Ulybin, with the face of a punished child.

They had delayed too long. It was night by now, time to

leave. Ulybin had them activate the mines hidden in the barracks, and he assembled everyone outside, in the yard. They had orders not to speak, but an excited murmuring could be heard, a sound of discordant voices, like an orchestra tuning up before the overture. Discordant, but an alert ear would have caught a tune, repeated in different keys by Russians and Jews: Piotr, the bold and pure Piotr, had lost his head over the eyes of a foreign woman, like Styenka Razin. Whether they were the gray eyes of Sissl or the brown eyes of Line, on this point the versions diverged. Gossip is a force of nature; it makes many discomforts bearable, and it prospers even in the midst of marshes, war, and thawing snow.

They walked all night, in Indian file, seeing no signs of Germans. They stopped at dawn to rest in an abandoned shed, near the Polish border. Towards noon the lookouts saw some German troops passing on the high road; they all took up defensive positions, but the convoy went on, not bothering to check the shed. They resumed their march at night, and in a heath the two squads separated: Ulybin and his group bore left to reenter Soviet territory, and Gedaleh's band proceeded towards Rechitsa, across untilled fields. Gedaleh reassured them: "The worst is over. One more night's march, and we'll be outside."

But Mendel and his friends had felt safer before, in the Turov camp, where they didn't suffer hunger or cold, and each sensed over his head a roof of solid beams and an authority: Ulybin himself or the messengers that came from the sky or a more distant power. These Gedalists (as they called themselves) were foolhardy people, strays and poor. Jozek, Gedaleh's lieutenant, rolled a cigarette of straw in a scrap of newspaper, asked Leonid for a match, split it in two lengthwise, lighted up with one half, and put the other in his pocket. The two cows, he said, were war prizes; they had been captured a few days ago, during the attack on Lyuban, "because in war you have to think of goods, too." The animals were thin and contrary. Wherever they found a clump of grass they would stop, obstinately, to crop it, resisting any tugs, slowing down the march. Where there were still patches of snow in the shade of the trees, they plowed it with their hooves, searching for lichens. "The first chance we get, we'll sell them," Jozek said, in a practical tone.

Jozek was not Russian, but a Pole from Bialystok, a counterfeiter by profession. He told his story to Mendel during the first stop after the separation, not before; he wasn't sure how the Russians would have taken it.

"It's a good profession, but not easy. I began as a boy, in nineteen twenty-eight: I was an apprentice lithographer, and I made counterfeit stamps. The Polish police, in those days, had other things on their mind, so it wasn't very dangerous, but I didn't earn much, either. In nineteen thirty-seven I began with documents; I was very good at passports. Then the war came, the Russians arrived in Bialystok, and in 'forty-one, the Germans. I had to go into hiding, but I was making good money: there was a demand for documents, especially ration cards for the Poles and Aryan identity cards for the Jews.

"I could have gone on easily till the end of the war, but a rival turned me in because I wasn't charging enough. I was in jail for three weeks; obviously my own documents were also faked: I was a Christian for two generations. But they made me strip, realized I was a Jew, and sent me to a *Lager,* Sachsenhausen, to break stones."

Jozek broke off and lighted another cigarette with the half match he had saved. He was blondish, frail, medium height, a long vulpine face and green eyes almost without lashes, which he kept always half-closed, as if to sharpen his vision. The group had stopped in a clearing; Jozek was stretched out on the grass, moist with dew, smoking and enjoying himself as he smoked and told his story. Many gathered around him to listen: they already knew the story, but they liked to hear it repeated. Others slept. Leonid had gone off with Line, and Sissl was listening, but to one side: she had produced a needle and thread and was darning a stocking in the vague dawn light.

"It's a strange world," Jozek resumed. "One Jew dies, but another Jew, a counterfeiter, is saved. At the end of 'forty-two, they put up a notice in the *Lager:* the Germans were looking for printers and lithographers. I presented myself, and they sent me to a little shed towards the end of the *Lager,* and there, I thought I was dreaming. There was a shop, much better equipped than mine had been, and a group of prisoners, Poles, Czechs, Germans, and Jews, producing counterfeit dollars and pounds, and even documents for spies. Modesty aside, I was the best, and they gave me all the delicate jobs; but I soon realized that this was tricky work, and it was clear that none of us would leave there alive. Then I devoted myself to collecting gold, which is never wanting in the *Lagers,* and to fabricating a transfer order for myself."

"Why not an order of release?" Mendel asked.

"Obviously you don't know what a *Lager* is. Nobody's ever heard of a Jew being released, especially a Jew like me. I made myself a transfer order to the *Lager* of Brest-Litovsk, because if a Pole is going to escape, he's better off in Poland: a regulation order, on SS paper, with stamps and signatures, made out for Jozef Treistman, number six-seven-seven-oh-three *Funktionshälting,* functionary prisoner. It was a big risk, but not having any choice is also a choice. They put me on a train with two guards, two old soldiers from the Territorials. I bribed them with the gold; they asked for nothing better. I ran off before we got to Brest, I lived underground for two weeks, then I found Gedaleh."

As the days passed and he got to know Gedaleh better, Mendel felt nothing was more natural than that Ulybin and he shouldn't have found an agreement. Beyond the age-old division between Russians and Jews, it would have been hard to find two men more different: the only quality they had in common was courage, and this wasn't strange, because a commander without courage doesn't last long. But even their courages were different: Ulybin's courage was stubborn and dull, a duty courage that seemed the fruit of study and discipline rather than a natural gift. His every decision and his every order arrived as if coming to earth from heaven, charged with authority and tacit menace; often the orders were reasonable, because Ulybin was a shrewd man, but even when they weren't they sounded peremptory, and it was hard not to obey them. Gedaleh's courage was extempore and varied; it didn't spring from a school but from a temperament that chafed at bonds and was hardly inclined to study the future; where Ulybin calculated, Gedaleh flung himself as if into a game. In him, Mendel recognized, well fused as in a precious alloy, heterogeneous metals: the logic and the bold imagination of Talmudists, the sensitivity of musicians and children, the comic power of strolling players, the vitality absorbed from the Russian earth.

Gedaleh was tall and thin, broad-shouldered, but with slight limbs and a thin chest. His nose was arched and jutting like a prow, his forehead low under the border of black hair, his cheeks hollowed and furrowed by wrinkles in the skin tanned by the wind and the sun, his mouth broad and full of teeth. His movements were quick, but he walked with an awkwardness that seemed deliberate, like a circus clown's. He spoke in a loud, resonant voice even when it wasn't necessary, as if his chest acted as a sounding box; he laughed often, even at inopportune moments.

Mendel and Leonid, accustomed to the hierarchy of the Red Army, were bewildered and alarmed by the Gedalists' behavior. Decisions were made haphazardly, in noisy assemblies; at other times they all heedlessly accepted foolhardy notions of Gedaleh, Jozek, or others; and at still other times quarrels sprang up, but were quickly settled. It didn't seem that, within the band, there were permanent tensions or disagreements. The members declared themselves Zionists, but of varying tendencies, with all the nuances that can find a place between Jewish nationalism, Marxist orthodoxy, religious orthodoxy, Anarchist egalitarianism, and Tolstoyan return to the earth, which will redeem you if you redeem it. Gedaleh also declared himself a Zionist. For several days Mendel tried to figure out what faction he belonged to, but in the end he gave up the attempt: Gedaleh followed different ideas at the same time, or no idea, and he often changed his mind. To be sure, he was more inclined to action than to theory, and his goals were simple: survive, do the maximum damage to the Germans, and go to Palestine.

Gedaleh was curious to the point of indiscretion. He didn't ask the newcomers for any vital statistics, and didn't even put them officially on the roster; but he wanted to know each one's story, and he listened to it with the innocent attention of a child. He seemed to feel friendliness towards all, appreciate the virtues of all, ignore their weaknesses. "*L'khayim,*" he said to Pavel, after hearing his story. "To life. Welcome among us, may your back be blessed. We need backs like yours. You're a Jewish bison, a rare animal; we'll hold you dear. Maybe you'd rather not be one, but if you're born a Jew, you remain a Jew, and if you're born a bison, you remain a bison. Blessed be he who enters."

It was the first peaceful rest that the band allowed itself after having got through the encirclement. They had spent the night in the barn of an abandoned farmhouse, they had found clear water in the well, the air was light and scented, all their faces were relaxed, and Gedaleh was enjoying himself.

Leonid compressed his story into the space of two or three minutes, but Gedaleh didn't take offense and didn't make any further enquiry. He simply said, "You're very young. That's an illness that's soon healed, even without medicines, but it can be dangerous all the same. As long as you have it, take care."

Leonid looked at him, dazed and suspicious. "What do you mean?"

"Don't take me literally. I have prophet's blood in me, too, like every son of Israel, and now and again I like to play prophet."

With Line and Sissl he abandoned his prophesies and

assumed operetta manners. He called them "my noble ladies," but he wanted to know their ages, if they were still virgins, and who their men had been. Sissl answered with intimidation; Line with reserved pride, and both showed impatience to put an end to the questioning. Gedaleh didn't insist and turned to Mendel. He listened carefully to the story and said to him, "You're not playacting. You've remained a watchmender; and you haven't dressed in peacock feathers, or a hawk's either. Welcome to you, too; you'll be useful to us because you're prudent. You'll serve as counterweight. With us here prudence has been somewhat forgotten. We have a poor memory, except for one thing."

"What's that?" Mendel asked.

Gedaleh solemnly put his forefinger beside his nose.

" 'Remember what Amalek did to you on the way, after you had come out of Egypt. He attacked you while you were on the road, he killed all the weak, the sick, the weary, who were straggling behind; he had no fear of God. And so, when your God grants you peace from your enemies, you will extinguish even the memory of Amalek: don't forget it.' Yes: this is what we don't forget. I quoted from memory, but not irrelevantly, this time."

By mid-May Gedaleh's band was encamped on the shores of the Gorin, white with lilies-of-the-valley and eager daisies. Men and women, naked or almost, joyously washed themselves in the slow water of the river. With two armed companions, Jozek had set off for Rechitsa with the two cows and Pavel's horse; at Rechitsa, near the Ukrainian border, there was a market. He came back a few hours later; he had bartered the cows for bread, cheese, lard, salted meat, soap: the rest was in German occupation marks. Thrush advanced, glorious and sweating beneath the load. It seemed almost that the war was over; anyway, winter was over. In the town Jozek had found no sign of Germans; if there were any there, they were keeping out of sight. He had not been required to give explanations or to bargain; the peasants had long since learned that with partisans (of whatever color) it was best not to be curious or greedy.

On his return, Jozek saw a good half of the band lined up in silence along the river; Gedaleh was sitting on a log, his feet in the water, the violin in midair; and Izu, one of the men from Blizna, hairy as a bear and completely naked, was wading slowly, step by step, towards a rock in the midst of the current. They were all watching him, and he signaled all of them to stand still and not talk. When he was at the foot of the rock, he sank in completely, but still with extreme slowness; the water thrashed for a moment, and Izu surfaced, clutching in his hands a big, wriggling fish. He bit it behind the head, and the fish went limp: it was two handspans long, its bronze scales glittered in the sun.

"What have you caught, Izu?" Gedaleh asked.

"I thought it was a trout, but it's a sazan!" Izu replied proudly, climbing up the bank. "That's strange, in such shallow water." He crouched beside a flat stone, gutted the fish, washed it in the stream, slashed its back with his knife, and began peeling the flesh from its sides and eating it.

"What? Aren't you going to have it cooked?"

"Cooked fish has no vitamins," Izu answered, chewing.

"But it has more taste. And besides, it also has more phosphorus, and phosphorus makes you smart. Obviously in Blizna all of you eat fish raw."

Gedaleh hailed Jozek from a distance, waving his hand. "Good for you, Jozek; we're all set for a week now." Then he resumed playing his violin: he had stripped to the waist, and there was an ecstatic expression on his face, whether because of the music or the footbath wasn't clear; but Bella gave him no peace. Of the three women who had arrived at Turov with the band, Bella seemed the one closest to Gedaleh, considering herself his legitimate and definitive woman, though it seemed Gedaleh was of a different mind or else wasn't bothering to settle the matter. With some others, Bella was setting up an army tent, but she kept interrupting her work, and interrupting Gedaleh, shouting into his ear as if he were deaf. Gedaleh answered her patiently, resumed playing, and again Bella would interrupt him with her complaints:

"Lay off that fiddle, and come lend us a hand here!"

"Hang it on the willows, Gedaleh!" Dov shouted, from a distance.

"We're not in Jerusalem yet, but we're out of Babylon," Gedaleh answered and resumed playing. Bella was a thin little blond with a long, cross face. She looked to be about forty, whereas Gedaleh couldn't be over thirty; she often handed out reproaches and criticisms, and gave orders that nobody obeyed, but didn't seem to mind. Gedaleh treated her with a tenderness slightly tinged with irony.

In the late morning, the sentries sighted a man, alone, who shouted from the distance, "Don't shoot!," and they let him approach, and it was Piotr.

Gedaleh received him with no show of amazement: "Good man, you were right to join us. Sit down; we'll be eating soon."

"Comrade Commander," Piotr said. "All I have is a revolver; I left the submachine gun with Ulybin's men."

"It would have been better if you had brought it, but no matter."

"You see, I know I was wrong, but I had a quarrel with Ulybin. He was too hard, not just with me but with everybody. And one evening we had a serious argument . . . a political argument."

"And you both spoke of the Gedalists, am I right?"

"How did you guess?"

Gedaleh didn't answer, but asked a question of his own: "Won't he send anyone after you? Look, we don't want any trouble with Ulybin."

"He won't send for me. He was the one who kicked me out. He told me to put down the gun and go. He told me to come to you."

"He must have been angry when he said that. Or drunk. Maybe he'll have second thoughts."

"He was angry, but not drunk," Piotr said. "And anyway, they're four or five days' march away by now. And I'm not a deserter. I didn't come with your people out of fear; I came to fight with you."

That evening, for no specific reason, in Gedaleh's camp they had a celebration: perhaps because it had been their first day out of the marshes and out of danger, and the first day of real spring; perhaps because Piotr's arrival had cheered everybody; or perhaps only because, in the midst of the other provisions loaded onto Thrush's withers, Jozek had also brought back a keg of Polish vodka. They lighted a fire between two sand dunes; and they all sat in a circle around it; Dov said to Gedaleh that this was a bit risky, and then Gedaleh put out the fire, but the glow of the coals warmed their spirits all the same.

The first to perform was Pavel. Nobody had called him, but he stood up proudly near the coals, took a piece of charcoal and drew a mustache above his upper lip, pulled a clump of wet hair down on his forehead, saluted them all with his arm outstretched at eye level, and began to rant. First he spoke in German, with mounting anger: his speech was improvised, the tone counted more than the content, but they all laughed when they heard him address the German soldiers, urging them to fight to the last man and calling them, in turn, heroes of the Great Reich, bastards, flying hunters, defenders of our blood and our land, and assholes. By degrees, his fury became more searing, until it choked his words in a canine snarl, broken by fits of convulsive coughing. All of a sudden, as if an abscess had burst, he dropped German and went on in Yiddish, and they were all writhing with laughter: it was extraordinary to hear Hitler, in the full flood of his delirium, speaking the pariahs' language to urge somebody to slaughter somebody else, and it wasn't clear whether the Germans should slaughter the Jews, or vice versa. They applauded him frantically, insisted on an encore, and Pavel, with dignity, instead of repeating his number (which, he explained, he had created in 1937 in a Warsaw cabaret), sang "O sole mio," in a language nobody understood, though he insisted it was Italian.

Then Mottel the Throat-Cutter came on stage. Mottel was a little character with short legs and very long arms, agile as a monkey. He grabbed three, then four, then five firebrands, and whirled them around, above his head, under his legs; against the background of the purple sky he drew a maze of glowing parabolas, never repeating himself. He was applauded, he bowed his thanks to the four cardinal points, and withdrew at once, imitating the lurching gait of an orang. Why Throat-Cutter? They explained to Mendel that Mottel was not just anybody. He came from Minsk, he was thirty-seven, and he was a throat-cutter twice over. In the first half of his career, he had been a respectable throat-cutter: for four years he had been the *shokhet,* the kosher butcher, of the community. He had passed the prescribed examination, possessed a license, and was considered an expert in the art of keeping his knife sharp and of severing with a single blow the animal's trachea, esophagus, and carotid arteries. But then (because of a woman, the rumor went) he had gone to the bad: he had abandoned his wife and home, gotten involved with the local underworld, and though never forgetting his previous profession and his theoretical training, he had become skilled also at cutting purses and climbing balconies. He had retained the ritual knife, long, with a blunt tip; but still, as emblem of his new proclivities, he had broken the end obliquely, forming a sharp point. Thus altered, the knife lent itself also to other uses.

"A woman! Let's have a woman!" somebody shouted, in a voice hoarse with vodka. Bella came forward, combing her straw-colored hair; but Pavel, staggering like a bear, jostled her with his hip, sending her back into the circle of spectators as he resumed his place. He hadn't yet finished, and there was no telling whether he was drunk or only pretending. This time he was a Hassidic rabbi; drunk, naturally, who rattled off the Sabbath prayers in feigned Hebrew, though actually in a whorehouse Russian. He prayed breathlessly, at dizzying speed, because (he explained in an aside) between one picket and the next the piglet mustn't pass: between one sacred word and the next no profane thought must find a way. This time the applause was more restrained.

Bella hadn't given up. She went to the coals, raised her left hand in a graceful gesture, put her right hand on her heart, and began to sing a song, "Yes, I'll Go Far Away"; but she didn't get very far, because after a few words her voice turned shrill and she burst out sobbing. Gedaleh came, took her by the hand, and led her away.

Dov's name was being shouted from many directions. "Step up, Siberian," Piotr said to him. "And tell us what you saw in the Great Land." Pavel, who had assumed the role of master of ceremonies, seconded him. "And now, it's my great pleasure to present to you Dov Yavor, the wisest of us all, the oldest and most beloved. Come along, Dov: everybody wants to see you and listen to you." The moon had risen, almost full, and it shone on Dov's white hair, as he reluctantly came towards the center of the arena. He laughed shyly, and said, "What do you want from me? I can't sing or dance, and what I saw in Kiev I've already told you, too many times."

"Tell us about your grandfather the Nihilist." "Tell us about the bear hunt in your village." "Tell us about the time you escaped from the Germans' train." "Tell us about the comet."

But Dov parried their requests: "These are all things I've already told you, and nothing is more boring than repetition. Let's play some game, instead; or have some contest."

"A wrestling match!" Piotr said. "Who wants to challenge me?"

For a few moments nobody moved; then there was a brief argument between Line and Leonid. Leonid meant to accept the challenge; and Line, for some reason, was trying vigorously to dissuade him. In the end Leonid freed himself; the two adversaries slipped off jackets and boots and were on their guard. They grasped each other by the shoulders, each trying to trip up his opponent; they rolled over several times, then Leonid tried to grab Piotr by the waist and failed. The band's two dogs barked uneasily, snarling, bristling. Besides being stronger than Leonid, Piotr also had the advantage of longer arms. After some confused and not exactly regulation skirmishing, Leonid fell and Piotr was on him at once, pressing his shoulders to the ground. Piotr hailed the audience with his hands upraised, and immediately found Dov standing before him.

"What do you want, Uncle?" Piotr asked; he was almost a full head taller than Dov.

"To wrestle with you," Dov answered, and he was on his guard, but lazily, his hands dangling from his wrists, in the customary attitude of his moments of repose. Piotr waited, puzzled. "Now I'll teach you something," Dov said, and he started in; Piotr stepped back, eyeing him. Dov's movement, in the pale moonlight, couldn't be discerned clearly; Dov was seen extending one hand and one knee, rather lightly, and then Piotr swayed, off balance, and fell on his back. He stood up and shook off the dust: "Where did you learn these moves?" he asked, annoyed. "Did they teach you in the army?" "No," Dov answered. "My father taught me." Gedaleh said that Dov should teach the whole band this way of wrestling, and Dov answered that he'd be glad to, especially with the women. They all laughed, and Dov answered that this was Samoyed wrestling: in the place where he was born various Samoyed families had been deported. "It's the Russians who gave them that name, because the Russians thought they ate human flesh: *Samo-jed* means 'eat oneself,' but they don't like that name. They're fine people, and you can learn many things from them: how to light a fire in the wind, how to take shelter from the blizzard under a pile of faggots. And also how to guide dogsleds."

"That's not likely to be so useful to us," Piotr remarked.

"But this might help," Dov said. From the heavy belt Piotr had set down with his jacket, Dov drew the knife, held its tip with two fingers, waved it for a moment as if taking aim, then flung it at a maple trunk eight or ten meters away. The knife flipped through the air and dug deep into the wood. Others tried, Piotr first of all, amazed and jealous, but nobody succeeded, even when they halved the distance to the tree: at best, the knife hit the tree with its handle or the flat of the blade and fell to the ground. Gedaleh and Mendel didn't even manage to hit the trunk.

"Too bad it's a maple tree and not Dr. Goebbels," said Jozek, who had taken no part in the entertainment or the games. Dov explained that, to kill a man, not just any knife would do; you need special knives, thin but heavy, and well balanced. "You understand, Jozek?" Gedaleh said. "Bear that in mind, the next time you go to market."

Some were already sleeping when Gedaleh took up his violin and began to sing; but he wasn't singing for applause. He sang softly, he who was so loud when he spoke; other Gedalists joined in, some of the chorus's voices were harmonious, others less so, but all had conviction and feeling. Mendel and his friends listened with amazement to the rhythm, which was brisk, almost a march, and the words, which were the following:

> Do you recognize us? We're the sheep of the ghetto,
> Shorn for a thousand years, resigned to outrage.
> We are the tailors, the scribes and the cantors,
> Withered in the shadow of the cross.
> Now we have learned the paths of the forest,
> We have learned to shoot, and we aim straight.
> If I'm not for myself, who will be for me?
> If not this way, how? And if not now, when?
> Our brothers have gone to heaven
> Through the chimneys of Sobibor and Treblinka,
> They have dug themselves a grave in the air.
> Only we few have survived
> For the honor of our submerged people,
> For revenge and to bear witness.
> If I'm not for myself, who will be for me?
> If not this way, how? And if not now, when?

We are the sons of David, the hardheaded sons of Masada.
Each of us carries in his pocket the stone
That shattered the forehead of Goliath.
Brothers, away from this Europe of graves:
Let us climb together towards the land
Where we will be men among men.
    If I'm not for myself, who will be for me?
    If not this way, how? If not now, when?

When they had finished singing, they all wrapped
themselves in their blankets and fell asleep; only the sentries remained awake, having climbed trees at the four
corners of the camp. In the morning Mendel asked Gedaleh, "What were you singing last night? Is that your anthem?"

"You can call it that if you like; but it's not an anthem,
it's only a song."

"Did you write it?"

"The music is mine, but it changes a bit, month after
month, because it's not written down anywhere. But the
words aren't mine. Look: they're written here."

From the inside pocket of his coat, Gedaleh dug out an
oilcloth packet tied with string. He unwrapped it and took
out a folded piece of paper, wrinkled, headed *"13 Juni,
Samstag."* It had been ripped from a diary, and it was all
covered with Yiddish letters, in pencil. Mendel took it,
looked at it carefully, then handed it back to Gedaleh.

"I can hardly read printed letters, and I've forgotten
handwriting completely."

Gedaleh said, "I learned to read it late, in 'forty-two, in
the ghetto at Kossovo: on one occasion it served as a secret
language. At Kossovo Martin Fontasch was with us. By
trade he was a carpenter, and that's how he made his living to the end; but his passion was composing songs. He
did it all by himself, the words and the music, and he was
known throughout Galicia; he accompanied himself on
the guitar; and he used to sing his songs at weddings and
village celebrations; sometimes even in cafés. He was a
peaceful man and he had four children, but he was with

us in the ghetto uprising, he ran off with us and came to the woods, alone, and no longer young; his whole family had been killed. In the spring of last year we were near Novogrudok and there was a bad roundup; half of our people died fighting, Martin was wounded and taken prisoner. The German who searched him found a flute in his pocket: it wasn't so much a flute as a fife, a cheap toy that Martin had made for himself, from an elder twig. Now that German was a flute player: he told Martin that a partisan is hanged and a Jew is shot: he was Jewish and a partisan, and he could choose. But he was also a musician, and since he, the German, was a man who loved music, he would grant Martin a last wish, provided the wish was reasonable.

"Martin asked permission to compose a final song, and the German granted him half an hour's time, gave him this sheet of paper, and locked him in a cell. When the time had passed, he came back, collected the song, and killed him. It was a Russian who told me this story; at the beginning he collaborated with the Germans, then the Germans suspected him of playing a double game, and they locked him into the cell next to Martin's, but he managed to escape, and he stayed a few months with us. It seems the German was proud of this song of Martin's, he showed it to people, like a curiosity, and kept planning to have it translated the first chance he had. But he didn't have time. We were keeping an eye on him, we followed him, spotted him, and one night we went barefoot into the requisitioned izba where he lived. I like justice and I'd have liked to ask him his last wish, but Mottel was pressing me, and so I strangled him in his bed. We found Martin's flute on him, and the song: it didn't bring him luck, but it's like a talisman for us. Here, look at it: down to here the words are what you heard us sing, and these words here at the bottom say: "Written by me, Martin Fontasch, about to die. Saturday 13 June 1943." The last line isn't in Yiddish: it's Hebrew. You know the words: Hear, O Israel, the Lord our God, the Lord is one.

"He had composed many other songs, happy and sad; the most famous was one he wrote many years before the Germans arrived in Poland, at the time of a pogrom: in those days the peasants took charge of pogroms. Almost all Poles know the song, not only Jews, but nobody knows that Martin the carpenter wrote it."

Gedaleh refolded the packet and put it back in his pocket. "That's enough now: these aren't thoughts for every day. They're all right every now and then, but if you live with them you just poison yourself, and you're not a partisan anymore. And bear this in mind: I believe in only three things: vodka, women, and the submachine gun. Once I also believed in reason, but not anymore."

A few days later, Gedaleh decided that the rest period had lasted long enough, and it was time to resume their way: "But this is a free band, and anyone who'd rather stay in Russia can go off: without any weapons, of course. He can wait for the front, or go wherever he likes." Nobody chose to leave the band, and Gedaleh asked Piotr, "Do you know this country?"

"Well enough," Piotr answered.

"How far is the railroad?"

"About a dozen kilometers."

"Fine," Gedaleh said. "We'll cover the next lap by train."

"By train? But all the trains have military escorts," Mendel said.

"Well, we can always try. When you have escorts, you can discuss things." To Gedaleh, Pavel's objection seemed more serious: "What about the horse? Surely you don't plan to abandon him? He's useful, for one thing; he carries half our baggage."

Gedaleh again turned to Piotr: "What trains go by on this line?"

"Freight trains, nearly all of them: sometimes there's some passengers on board, too, black-market people. If the trains are carrying supplies for the Germans, they're guarded; but it's never a big escort: two men on the locomotive and two at the end. Troop trains never go by here."

"What's the nearest station?"

"Kolki, forty kilometers to the south. It's a little station."

"Is there a loading ramp?"

"I don't know; I don't remember."

Dov interrupted: "Why do you want us to take the train, anyway?"

Gedaleh answered impatiently, "Why shouldn't we take it? We've walked more than a thousand kilometers; and the railroad's only a stone's throw away. And besides, I want to enter Polish territory in a way that will make people remember us."

He thought for a moment and added, "Seizing a train in a station is too dangerous. We have to stop it in open country, but then we can't get the horse on to it. All right, we'll take the bulk of the baggage with us: it's only a short distance, after all. You, Pavel, go ahead with the horse and wait for us at Kolki."

Pavel seemed unconvinced. "What if you don't get there?"

"If we don't get there, you come to meet us, with the horse."

"And what if there's no ramp?"

Gedaleh shrugged. "What if . . . what if . . . what if! Only the Germans foresee everything, and that's why they lose wars. If there isn't any, we'll think of something else. We'll decide on the spot: there's bound to be a way. Start moving, Pavel; remember, you're a peasant, and don't show yourself too much in the town. The Germans around these parts requisition horses."

Pavel set off at a trot, but he was still in sight when Thrush fell back into his customary, solemn gait. Gedaleh and his band started walking, and in a little over two hours they reached the railroad. It was a single track, and it bisected the prairie from one horizon to the other, straight as a ray of light.

It is easy to confuse hope with probability. Everyone was expecting the train to come from the north, heading for the Polish border; after several hours' wait they saw, on the contrary, the train arriving from the south. It was a freight train and was traveling slowly. Gedaleh posted some men with guns behind the bushes on either side of the track, then, in his shirt sleeves and unarmed, he stood between the ties, waving a red rag. The train slowed down and stopped, and from the cab they immediately began shooting. Gedaleh darted off in a flash and took cover behind a hazel bush; all the others returned the fire. Mendel, while he also was firing and trying to hit the vents in the locomotive, admired the military preparation of the Gedalists. From what he had seen of their behavior so far, he would have expected them to be foolhardy, as they indeed were; but he hadn't foreseen the economy and the precision of their fire, and the correct technique with which they had stationed themselves. Tailors, scribes and cantors, their song said; but they had learned their new profession quickly and well. The awkward and the frightened men are immediately recognized, because they look for the thickest cover, a boulder or a heavy trunk, which does protect you, true, but it also prevents you from shifting and from shooting without exposing your head. On the contrary, they had all flattened themselves behind overgrown bushes, and were shooting through the leaves, shifting often to confuse the adversary.

The train's escort, too, protected by the steel plating, fired heavily and precisely: there must have been at least four men, and they weren't sparing ammunition. Mendel saw Mottel suddenly leap out and fling himself on the train. In an instant he had scrambled up on to the roof of the last car; up there he was sheltered; and for that matter, they hadn't seen him from the cab. He had a German hand grenade hanging from his belt, the club-shaped kind that explode on schedule, and he was running towards the locomotive from car to car, leaping over the couplings. When he was on the roof of the first car, he was seen ripping the pin of the grenade, waiting a few seconds; then, with the grenade itself, he broke the glass of the cab's sky-light and dropped the grenade inside.

There was an explosion and the shooting stopped. In the cab they found the Germans of the escort, and there were only three of them: one was still alive; Gedaleh finished him off without hesitation. The engineer and the stoker were also dead; too bad, Gedaleh said, they hadn't anything to do with it and would have been useful to us; well, anybody working for the Germans knows he's running risks. He pouted like a child. Mottel's initiative had been brilliant, but it had spoiled his plans.

"Now who'll drive the thing? God only knows how your grenade mucked up the works; and besides, we have to put it in reverse."

"You're stubborn, Chief, and you're never satisfied," Mottel said, since he had been expecting praise. "I make you a present of a train, and you criticize me. Next time you and the others can attack, and I'll sit and smoke my pipe."

Gedaleh didn't listen to him and told Mendel to climb into the cab and see if he could manage to start the engine. Some other men meanwhile were inspecting the train. They came back disappointed: it wasn't carrying valuable stuff, only sacks of cement, lime, and coal. Gedaleh had two roofed cars emptied of the cement, to house the men and the horse: he still hadn't given up the idea of the railway excursion. He was very excited; he issued orders to slash all the sacks with a knife, then he changed his mind and had a good number of them piled up between the tracks, in front of the locomotive. "If we weren't in a hurry we could do a really good job; but even this way, with a bit of rain and a bit of luck, it'll make a nice block." Then he climbed into the cab with Mendel.

"Well? What can you tell me?"

"A locomotive isn't a clock," Mendel answered, irked.

"*Nu,* it's gears all the same, and you haven't given me an answer. A locomotive isn't a clock, and a clockmender isn't a railwayman; and an ox isn't a pig, and a man like me isn't a commander, but he acts as commander the best he can; or rather, he acts as chief bandit." Here Gedaleh laughed, that easy laugh of his that illuminated the air in a moment. Mendel laughed, too.

"Get down and we'll try it."

Gedaleh got down, and Mendel fiddled with the levers. "Watch out, I'm going to give her steam." The smokestack puffed, the buffers creaked, and the train moved backwards a few meters. Everybody shouted, "Hurrah," but Mendel said, "There's pressure still in the boiler, but it won't last long. An engineer isn't enough, we need a stoker, too."

Efficient as they were in fighting, the Gedalists were muddlers in making peaceful choices. Nobody wanted to act as stoker; after a complicated argument, Mendel was given a woman for his assistant, but she was built like a man: Black Rokhele, who was due for a punishment because some days before, in the course of cleaning weapons, she had misplaced the spring of a rifle. She was called Black Rokhele to distinguish her from White Rokhele: her face was dark as a gypsy's, and she was thin and quick. She had very long legs, and her neck was also long, supporting a little triangular face brightened by laughing, slanting eyes. She wore her black hair bound in a knot. She was another veteran of Kossovo, though she was hardly more than twenty. White Rokhele, on the other hand, was a meek, simple creature, who hardly ever spoke; and when she did speak, her voice was so low you had difficulty understanding her. For these reasons nobody knew anything about her, nor did she seem to want to tell anybody anything: she passively followed the progress of the band, obeyed everybody, and never complained. She came from a remote village in Ukrainian Galicia.

Mendel showed Black R. how she should stoke the fire; all the others climbed into the two empty cars and the train moved, pushed instead of drawn. Mendel set the throttle at a very low speed, because from the cab he couldn't see the track. Jozek, with his automatic gun, had positioned himself in the brakeman's compartment in the last car, which was now the first, and he acted as pathfinder; every now and then, both men would stick their heads out and Jozek would signal to Mendel if the path was clear. The stoker laughed as if this were a game for her, and she shoveled coal with childish enthusiasm; soon she was covered with sweat, and really so black, from head to foot, that her eyes and teeth shone like headlights in the darkness. Mendel, on the other hand, wasn't enjoying himself at all. His satisfaction at having tamed this big mechanical beast soon died; the blood on the metal floor made him queasy, he felt nervous proceeding like this, almost blind, and the whole venture seemed to him a gratuitous folly and an extreme imprudence. He couldn't understand what remote purpose Gedaleh might have in mind.

By the time they had gone halfway, he had convinced himself that Gedaleh rarely had remote purposes and preferred to improvise: he leaned out of the car and signaled Mendel to stop. He stopped, and both men got down.

"Listen, watchmender, it occurs to me that it would be a good thing to damage this train as much as we can. What can we do?"

"Here, not a thing," Mendel answered. "If we were proceeding properly, instead of backwards, we could uncouple the cars and block them somehow, but like this, it's another story. Here, the only thing we can do is let down the sides of the open cars; then, with the jolts, all the plaster and coal will be scattered down the embankment."

"What about the cars themselves and the locomotive?"

"We'll think about them later," Mendel said. "When you've had enough."

Gedaleh ignored this prod, sent three men to let down the sides, and the train set off again, gaily sowing its freight on either side. They reached Kolki in the early afternoon, and the cars were almost empty: Pavel was waiting for them with the horse, on the ramp. In the little station there was nobody except the stationmaster, but he saw the gun in Jozek's hands, gave them a kind of military salute, and withdrew. Mendel braked, loaded Pavel and Thrush in an instant, and set off again. Gedaleh was happy, and signaled Mendel to go on, and faster, "To Sarny! To Sarny!" Above the clatter of the engine, from the cars Mendel could hear shouts and singing, and the whinnying of the frightened Thrush.

A little later it was Mendel who took the initiative, stopping the train by a little stream that crossed the uninhabited steppe. Not only to rest and to give Rokhele a chance to wash a bit, but also to alert the others that the water in the tank was about to end. They all set to work, back and forth between train and river with the few receptacles available, some kitchen pots and a bucket found in the locomotive. The operation was drawn out, and Mendel took advantage to listen to Pavel, who was telling what he had seen in Kolki.

"We didn't run any risk at all, me or the horse. Nobody paid any attention to us or spoke to us, and yet I don't believe anybody really took me for a peasant. I didn't see any Germans; there must be some there, because outside the town hall there were propaganda posters, but they don't show themselves in the street. The people are not afraid to talk, or anyway less afraid than before; I went into a tavern, the radio was turned on, and the voice was from Radio Moscow: it said the Russians have recaptured the Crimea, all the German cities are being bombed day and night, in Italy the Allies are at the gates of Rome. Oh, it's a beautiful thing to stroll in the streets of a town, see the balconies with flowerpots, the shop signs, windows with curtains! Look what I brought you: I tore it off a wall. There were others at every corner."

Pavel showed them all a poster, printed in big letters on cheap yellowish paper, in Russian and in Polish. It said: "Don't work for the Germans, don't give them any information. Anybody supplying grain to the Germans will be killed. Reader, we see you. If you tear down this poster, we'll shoot you."

"And you tore it down?" Mottel asked.

"I didn't tear it: I detached it. That's different. I detached it with respect, anybody would have realized I was taking it away to show to somebody; and, in fact, they didn't shoot. You see? It's signed by the Red Star Regiment. They command around here."

"We command, too," Gedaleh interrupted impetuously. "We'll enter Sarny in our way: to make them remember us. Who knows Sarny?"

Jozek knew it, because he had done his military service there in the Polish army: a humble little town, maybe twenty thousand inhabitants. Some factories, a spinning mill, and a shop for repairing rolling stock. The station? Jozek knew it very well, because he had been garrisoned there just before the war broke out; Sarny was the last Polish city before the border, and the Russians had entered without fighting immediately after the opening of hostilities. It was a fairly important station, because the line for Lublin and Warsaw went through it, and also because of the repair shop. There was a big hangar and a revolving platform, used for directing the locomotive towards the repair shop. Gedaleh brightened and said to Mendel: "Your engine will meet a glorious end." Mendel said he hoped the same wouldn't happen to him.

Gedaleh had the train stopped at night, at the entrance to the shunting yard, and told them all to leave the cars. The horse, frightened by the darkness, got out of control: he refused to get down, tried to rear up, whinnied frantically and kicked against the rear wall of the car. They pulled and pushed him, and finally he made up his mind to jump down, but he landed awkwardly, breaking a front leg. Pavel went off without saying a word, and Gedaleh finished off the animal, shooting him in the head. The Sarny station also seemed deserted: nobody reacted to the shot. Gedaleh told Mendel to push the cars onto a siding, and then told Jozek and Pavel to go ahead cautiously, changing the switches in the direction of the platform; when they had done the job, they came back and reported that the deck of the platform was in a transversal position with respect to the arriving track: fine, Gedaleh said. They would send the locomotive crashing into the pit of the platform, the shop would be out of commission for at least a month.

"Aren't you convinced, watchmender? You've grown fond of it, have you? Me, too, a bit. But I don't feel like going any farther, and I don't want to make the Germans a present of it. And I'll tell you something I learned in the woods: the ventures that succeed best are the ones your enemy thinks you're not capable of. Go on, send the cars away, start the engine, then jump down."

Mendel obeyed. The locomotive, unattended, vanished into the darkness, visible only thanks to the sparks that flew from the stack. They all waited, holding their breath; a few minutes later they heard a din of crushed metal plates, a roar of thunder, and a shrill hiss that slowly died away. An alarm siren howled, agitated voices were heard, the Gedalists fled in silence towards the countryside. As they groped their way along, in the blackout darkness, they stumbled over tracks and cables, and in Mendel's head, incongruously, hummed the words of the miracles blessing: "Blessed be Thou, O Lord our God, king of the Universe, who hast made for us a miracle in this place."

This was how the band of Gedaleh marked its entrance into the inhabited world.

7

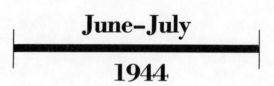

June–July

1944

"I'm sorry for your sake, Pavel, but for a few weeks it would be best for us to keep well away from windows with curtains and balconies and flowerpots, and especially from railroads." This is what Gedaleh had said as he was leading the band to cover in the thickest part of the wood. Nevertheless, three days after they had made camp, Gedaleh put on clothes that were approximately civilian, set down his weapons, told them to wait for him and not to take any initiative, and went off by himself. Those left behind fell to inventing hypotheses, from the most trivial to the most complicated, until Dov told them to stop: "Gedaleh likes to gamble, but he's a good gambler. If he went off without telling us anything, that means he had his own good reasons. Why don't you get busy? In a camp, you can always find work to do."

Several days passed, spent in idleness, worry, and the daily camp chores, which are boring but help time go by. Gedaleh returned on 10 June, quite serene, as if he had made a nice peacetime excursion. He asked for something to eat, lay down and slept for half an hour, woke, stretched, and went off a bit to play the violin. But he was obviously dying to tell his story: he was just waiting for someone to give him an excuse. Bella gave it to him; without having received any special investiture, she considered herself in charge of provisions. When Bella spoke, it was as if she were giving some pecks, stinging but not painful, like a sparrow's.

"You go off without saying a word, pursuing your own thoughts or God knows what, and you leave us here like a bunch of idiots. Our supplies are about to run out, you know."

Gedaleh put down the violin and dug a bundle of banknotes from his pocket: "Here you are, woman. We won't die of hunger yet. Go on, call everybody; we'll hold a meeting. We haven't had one for too long, but we hadn't had any good news for too long, either. Now we have some."

They all collected around Gedaleh, and this is what Gedaleh said: "Don't expect a speech; speeches are not in my line. And don't ask me any questions, at least not for now. I'll tell you what I can tell you, which isn't much but it's important. We're not orphans any more, and we're not stray dogs any more. I talked with somebody, and he knew who we are and where we come from. The locomotive business was useful, more than I thought. I was given some money, and we'll receive more, and maybe also weapons and regular uniforms. I learned that we're not alone: among the bands that have been formed by the Red Army, like Ulybin's, there are spontaneous bands, of peasants, or Ukrainian and Tatar dissidents, bands of bandits, but also other Jewish bands like ours: other Gedalehs and other Gedalists. There isn't much talk about it, because the Russians don't like separatist movements much; but they exist, more or less armed, big and small, stationary and mobile. There are even Russian bands led by Jewish commanders.

"I told them our aims, and they approved: we can go on our way, it's fine with them. We mustn't wait for the front: we're a vanguard, we should precede it. They want us to keep on doing what we've always done: guerrilla, sabotage, harassment, but also something more: we have to advance towards the Polish interior and attack the *Lagers* of war prisoners and Jews, if we can still find any. We have to collect the stragglers and cleanse the country of spies and collaborators. We have to move west. The Russians want us present in the west as Russians; we're interested in being present as Jews, and, for once in our history, the two things aren't contradictory. We have a free hand, we can cross borders, and mete out our own justice."

"Cross all borders?" Line asked.

Gedaleh answered: "I said not to ask questions."

They went on, for days and days, under the sun and under the rain, through the fields and the woods of the sad country of Volhynia. They stayed clear of traveled roads, but they couldn't avoid going through some villages, and in the square of one of these they saw a poster, different from the one Pavel had detached; it was a poster that concerned them closely. It said:

> Whoever kills the Jew Gedaleh Skidler, a dangerous bandit, will receive 2 kilograms of salt. Anyone giving this Headquarters information helpful towards Skidler's capture will receive 1 kilogram of salt. Whoever captures him and delivers him alive will receive 5 kilograms of salt.

Gedaleh slapped his thighs happily, because the photograph printed on the poster wasn't of him: it was the picture of a Ukrainian collaborator well known in the whole district. Gedaleh couldn't leave it: "A fantastic idea. I wish I had thought of it myself. And it would be even better if we were to capture this Gedaleh ourselves." They had to object repeatedly to make him give up this idea and resume the march.

In mid-June it began to pour rain, and the streams were swollen, and it became impossible to ford them. The marshes, too, had become deeper. They spied a windmill, explored it, and discovered it was empty and abandoned. It was empty, all right: there was no flour, not one sack, not a handful, but the acid smell of fermented flour pervaded every cranny of the building, along with the odor of mold and the fungus of wood soaked with rain. Still, the roof was watertight, and the room with the machinery itself was fairly dry; there were broad, sturdy shelves along the walls, meant perhaps to hold sacks of grain. The Gedalists settled in for the night, some on the floor, some on the shelves: in the light of their candles, the place had taken on a picturesque appearance, half stage, half wings. It wasn't comfortable, but there was room for everybody, even lying down, and the drumming of the rain on the wooden roof was merry and cozy.

Isidor, one of the Blizna survivors, had taken possession of a candle and a piece of tin: lying on his stomach, he scraped the floor inch by inch. He was the youngest of the band, not yet seventeen; before joining up with Gedaleh, he had hidden for almost four years, with his father, mother, and a little sister, in a hole dug under the floor of a stable. The peasant, owner of the stable, had extorted from his father all the family's money and valuables, and then reported them to the Polish police. Isidor had been lucky; he was out when the Germans came: every now and then one of the four went out to breathe the clean air of the woods. He was coming back, he hid, and from his hiding place he saw the SS, boys themselves, only a little older than he, clubbing his father, mother, and sister to death. The boys' faces weren't ferocious; on the contrary, they seemed to be having fun. Behind them, Isidor had seen the peasant and his wife, pale as snow. Since then, Isidor hadn't been able to think very logically. He had an absent manner; he was a bit stooped, with long arms and legs; he always carried a knife in his belt, and often he would rave about going back to his village to kill that peasant.

"What are you up to, Isidor? Spring cleaning?" Mottel asked from the height of his shelf. Isidor didn't answer, but went on scraping: every now and then, when he had collected a pinch of white powder, he would put it in his mouth, chew on it, then spit it out.

"Cut that out; you'll get a bellyache," Mottel said. "You're eating more rotten wood than flour." Isidor often got himself into trouble, and they had to keep an eye on him; but he tried to make himself useful, and they were all fond of him. He was obsessed by the idea of hunger; he put anything he could find into his mouth.

"Here, eat this," Black Rokhele said, holding out a handful of gooseberries she had picked in the woods. "Jozek will be back soon; he'll have found something."

Jozek did come back, with scant provisions and scant variety. The local peasants were poor and also suspicious, they had little fondness for the Russians or for the Jews or for the partisans; they had agreed to deal with him only because he had spoken to them in Polish, but they had given him only hard-boiled eggs and bread, demanding an exorbitant price. "There's enough for today and tomorrow; then we'll see," Gedaleh said. "We'll see what strategy to adopt."

The wind had risen, and it was like being in a ship. The building, with colossal wooden beams roughly stripped, creaked and vibrated and rocked. The four blades, stripped of their canvas and broken since God knows when, were set in motion by each gust of wind only to be stopped at once with a dull thud. Their futile effort was transformed into jerks and creaks of the shafts and the gears; the whole building seemed to stretch like a giant slave struggling to break his chains. Only Pavel had managed to fall asleep, and he was lying on his back, mouth agape, snoring.

"Hey, this place is full of worms," Isidor said suddenly, as he was digging a stick between the planks of the floor.

"Leave them alone," Bella said, alarmed. "Eat your bread and go to sleep."

Isidor addressed Bella with a foolish laugh. "Of course, I'll leave them alone. I don't eat worms: they're not kosher."

"Silly, nobody eats worms because they're dirty, not because they're not kosher," said Bella, who was cutting her nails with some scissors. These were the only scissors that the band possessed: Bella insisted that they belonged to her personally, and anybody wishing to use them should ask her personally to borrow them and should absolutely return them. After each nail was cut, she would contemplate the back of her hand with attention and satisfaction, like a painter after a brushstroke.

White Rokhele spoke up, in a faint voice: "Worms are *trayf* precisely because they're dirty. Pigs are dirty, too, and so they're *trayf*. How can anybody not believe in the kashrut? Might as well not be Jews."

"If you ask me," Jozek said, "this is all ancient history. Maybe pigs are dirty, but hares and horses are clean, and yet they're not kosher. Why not?"

"Nobody can know everything," White Rokhele answered, irked. "Maybe in the days of Moses they were dirty, or transmitted some disease."

"That's it. You said it yourself: ancient history. If Moses was here with us, in this mill, he wouldn't think twice about changing the laws. He'd smash the tablets, the way he did that time he got mad about the golden calf, and he'd make new ones. Especially if he had seen the things we have."

"Kosher-schmosher," Mottel said, yawning, exploiting the ingenious Yiddish way of belittling something by repeating the word, distorted: "Kosher-schmosher, if I had a hare, I'd eat it. In fact, tomorrow I'm going to set some traps. When I was a boy, I was a good trapper; I'll have to get back into practice."

Piotr was listening to all this, gaping. He turned to Leonid, who was sitting beside him. "Why can't you eat hare?"

"Don't ask me. I know we shouldn't, but I can't tell you

why not. It's a forbidden animal. It's written in the Torah."

Dov spoke up: "It's forbidden because it doesn't have a cloven hoof."

Isidor said, "Then if my worms had cloven hoofs, they could maybe be eaten?"

Gedaleh had noticed the amazement on Piotr's face.

"Pay no attention, Russian. If you stay with us, you'll have to get used to these questions. All Jews are crazy, but we're a bit crazier than the others. That's why we've been lucky so far; we have the luck of the meshuggener. In fact, now that I think about it: we have an anthem but we don't have a flag. You should make us one, Bella, instead of wasting time on your toilette. A flag with all the colors, and in the center, instead of the sickle or the hammer, or the two-headed eagle, or the star of David, you can put a *meshuggener* with a cap and bells and a butterfly net."

Then he spoke to Piotr again: "For that matter, you've come with us, so you must be a little crazy yourself: there's no other explanation. Russians are crazy or boring, and obviously you belong to the crazy branch. You'll get along fine, even if our laws are a bit complicated. Don't worry, we observe them only when they don't interfere with the *partisanka*. But we enjoy arguing about them. We're good at making distinctions, between the pure and the impure, man and woman, Jew and goy, and we also distinguish between the laws of peace and the laws of war. For example: the law of peace says a man mustn't desire another man's woman . . ."

Piotr, who had stretched out beside Black Rokhele, moved away from her a bit, perhaps unconsciously.

"No, like I say: you needn't worry. Here all the men desire all the women."

"Chief, you never talk seriously," Line interrupted, she who always spoke seriously. Her slightly hoarse contralto voice wasn't loud, but it had the power of being heard over the other voices. "When it comes to the business of other people's women, we have a lot to say."

"We? Who?"

"We women. First of all: why can a woman be one man's, or another man's, when a man can't be a woman's? Does that seem fair to you? For us it isn't fair: we can't accept it. Not any longer. Nowadays women go into exile like men do, they're hanged the same as men, and they shoot better than men. This alone would be enough to show that the Mosaic law is reactionary."

Pavel had waked up; he snickered and said something in a whisper to Piotr. Leonid remained silent, but he was giving Line a worried, sidelong glance. There was a strong gust, rain mixed with hail spattered against the wall; the mill creaked and turned, all of it, like a carousel, on the gigantic axle driven into its buried base. Isidor clung to White Rokhele, who calmed him, stroking his wispy hair.

"Go on, go on, Line," Gedaleh said. "A little wind won't scare you. Tell us what your law is, if it isn't too strict, we'll try to obey it."

"It's not the wind that scares me, it's the rest of you. You're cynical and primitive, you men. Our law is simple: so long as they're not married, men and women can desire one another and make love as much as they want. Love, until marriage, should be free, and actually it already is free, always has been, and there's no law that can imprison it. Even the Bible doesn't say anything different; our fathers weren't any different from us, they made love like us, in those days the same as today."

"In those days more than today," Pavel said, "it's no accident that the Bible begins with a fuck."

". . . but after marriage it's not the same anymore," Line went on, paying no attention to him. "We believe in marriage, because it's a pact, and pacts have to be respected. The wife belongs to the husband, and so the husband belongs to the wife."

"Then we're not going to get married," Gedaleh said. "Right, Bella?"

"You shut up," Bella answered. "Anyway, they all

know you're a dirty pig. And I never asked you to marry me. As a commander you may be all right, but as a husband—better not discuss that."

"Fine," Gedaleh said. "You see? The two of us never disagree. We have time to think it over. First, the war has to end." Then he turned to Leonid, who was huddled up beside Line and grim-looking.

"You, Muscovite? What do you think of your woman's theories?"

"I don't think anything. Leave me alone."

"And I'm not the woman of anybody," Line added.

"What a lot of fuss!" Jozek said from his corner, addressing one of the Slonim men. "Our father Jacob, for example, had four women, and they got along fine together."

Mottel spoke up: "But they weren't the women of other men. Jacob was enjoying his rights, because he had had one by mistake, or rather because of a trick of Laban, and the other two were slaves. He really only had one proper wife: so it was all in order."

"Good for you, Mottel!" Gedaleh said. "I didn't know you were so educated. Did you study in a yeshiva, before you started cutting throats?"

"I studied various things," Mottel replied smugly. "I also studied the Talmud, and you know what the Talmud says, about women? It says that you should never speak to a woman that's not your wife, not even in sign language, not with your hands or your feet or your eyes. You mustn't look at her clothes, even when she isn't wearing them. And listening to a woman sing is like seeing her naked. And it's a grave sin if an engaged couple embrace: the woman is then impure, as if she had her period, and she has to cleanse herself in the ritual bath."

"All this is in the Talmud?" asked Mendel, who hadn't spoken before.

"In the Talmud and other places," Mottel said.

"What's the Talmud?" Piotr asked. "Is it your Gospel?"

"The Talmud is like a soup, with all the things a man

can eat in it," Dov said. "But there's wheat and chaff, fruit and pits, and meat and bones. It isn't very good, but it's nourishing. It's full of mistakes and contradictions, but for that very reason it teaches you how to use your mind, and anyone who's read it all—"

Pavel interrupted him. "I'll explain what the Talmud is to you, with an example. Now listen carefully: Two chimneysweeps fall down the flue of a chimney; one comes out all covered with soot, the other comes out clean: which of the two goes to wash himself?"

Suspecting a trap, Piotr looked around, as if seeking help. Then he plucked up his courage and answered: "The one who's dirty goes to wash."

"Wrong," Pavel said. "The one who's dirty sees the other man's face, and it's clean, so he thinks he's clean, too. Instead, the clean one sees the soot on the other one's face, believes he's dirty himself, and goes to wash. You understand?"

"I understand. That makes sense."

"But wait; I haven't finished the example. Now I'll ask you a second question. Those two chimneysweeps fall a second time down the same flue, and again one is dirty and one isn't. Which one goes to wash?"

"I told you I understood. The clean one goes to wash."

"Wrong," Pavel said mercilessly. "When he washed after the first fall, the clean man saw that the water in the basin didn't get dirty, and the dirty man realized why the clean man had gone to wash. So, this time, the dirty chimneysweep went and washed."

Piotr listened to this, with his mouth open, half in fright and half in curiosity.

"And now the third question. The pair falls down the flue a third time. Which of the two goes to wash?"

"From now on, the dirty one will go and wash."

"Wrong again. Did you ever hear of two men falling down the same flue and one remaining clean while the other got dirty? There, that's what the Talmud is like."

Piotr remained dazed for a few seconds, then he

shrugged, like a dog coming out of the water, laughed shyly, and said: "You made me feel wet behind the ears. Like a recruit who's just arrived in the barracks. Very well, I understand what your Talmud is, but if you give me a second interrogation I'm leaving, I'll go back to Uly-bin. This isn't my kind of thing; I prefer fighting."

"Don't take it to heart, Russian," Gedaleh said. "Pavel didn't mean any harm; he didn't want to make fun of you."

Line spoke up: "He only wanted to make you feel what it's like to be a Jew; I mean, how it feels to have your head made in a certain way, and live among people whose heads are made differently. Yes, now you're the Jew, all alone in the midst of goyim, who laugh at you."

"And you would do well to change your name," Gedaleh said, "because yours is too Christian: instead of Piotr Fomich call yourself Jeremiah or Habakuk or some other unobtrusive name. And learn Yiddish and forget Russian; and maybe get yourself circumcised, if not, sooner or later, we'll make a pogrom." Having said this, Gedaleh yawned luxuriously, blew out the candle, said goodnight to everybody, and retired with Bella. The two or three other candles were also put out. In the darkness, a voice was heard, hoarse with sleep, perhaps one of the Ruzhany men:

"In my village there was a Jew who had eaten a wild-boar sausage. The rabbi reproached him, but he said that the boar was a ruminant, and therefore was kosher. 'Non-sense; boars don't ruminate,' the rabbi said. 'They don't ruminate in general, but this one did. He ruminated in particular: he ruminated like an ox,' the Jew said; and since the boar was gone, the rabbi had to keep quiet."

"In my village," said another voice, "there was a Jew who had himself baptized fourteen times."

"Why? Wasn't once enough?"

"Of course, it was enough; but he liked the ceremony."

Someone was heard hawking and spitting, and then a third voice said, "In my village there was a Jew who got drunk."

"Well, what's so strange about that?" another asked.

"Nothing. I didn't say it was anything strange, but tonight it's strange to tell things that aren't strange, since everybody is telling strange things."

"In my village . . ." Isidor began; a woman's voice interrupted him: "That's enough for now. Sleep; it's late." But Isidor went on: "In my village there was a woman who had seen the devil. His name was Anduschas, he had the shape of a unicorn, and he was playing music."

"What did he play?"

"He played the horn."

"How could he, if it was growing from his forehead?"

"I don't know," Isidor said. "I didn't ask her."

A deep voice, yawning, came from above: "Keep quiet now. It's time to sleep, we've walked a long way. We have to rest. Even the Lord needed six days to create the world, and on the seventh he rested."

Gedaleh answered. "He rested and said: 'Let's hope it works.' "

In the darkness the faint voice of White Rokhele was heard again, as she murmured the evening prayer, "Into Thy hand I entrust my spirit," and the blessing, "Let the Merciful break the yoke that oppresses us, and lead us, heads high, into our land," and then there was silence.

The downpour of the evening had dwindled to a fine, persistent drizzle; and the wind had fallen, too. The skeleton of the old mill no longer groaned, but it crackled softly, as if hundreds of worms were gnawing it, and Mendel, stretched out on the hard planks, couldn't get to sleep. Other confused sounds came from the attic floor, fast and light steps, perhaps of mice or martens, against the ground of breathing and grunting of his sleeping companions. The air was warm, heavy with nocturnal humors and the sharp and sweet odor of pollens, and Mendel felt desire invade him. It was an adolescent's desire, without shape, soft and warm and white: he tried to describe it to himself and failed. Desire for a bed, and a woman's body in the bed; desire to dissolve inside another, a woman, and to be one flesh with her, a double flesh isolated in the world, away from roads, weapons, fears, and memories of the slaughter.

Beside him Sissl was breathing peacefully. Mendel stretched out his hand in the darkness and felt her hip, enfolded in the roughness of the blanket. He pressed, tried to draw her to him, but Sissl resisted, stony in sleep. On the vague screen of his dozing, names and faces pursued one another, present and distant. Sissl, blond and tired. Rivke with her sad black eyes, but Mendel dispelled her at once, he didn't want her, he couldn't think about her. Rivke, Strelka, the grave: go away, Rivke, please. Go back to where you came from, let me live. Mendel tried stubbornly to fall asleep, and he realized that this very effort was the prod that kept him awake. His mind was no longer so confused that it could ignore another face and another name, knocking at its door. A faceless name, the name of Rahab, the harlot of perverse power; the weird information was true: Mendel had only to utter that name, even in his mind, and his flesh tightened. And a nameless face came, a haggard face, young and worn, with great, distant eyes. Mendel started: it wasn't nameless, that face. It had a name, and that name was Line.

He saw her as he had seen her a few hours before, fervent in the debate, with no areas of laziness or doubt, so serious she was almost absurd, vibrating like a taut cable. He flung off the blanket, removed his shoes, and sought her, groping, stumbling over the sleepers' limbs. He had seen where she had gone off to sleep, and he found her easily, under the steps leading to the loft: he touched her hair in the darkness, and his blood had a jolt. Beside Line, Leonid was sleeping, and the two were wrapped in the same blanket; the image of Leonid and that of Sissl for a moment occupied Mendel's consciousness, then went off into the darkness, smaller and smaller, more and more transparent, until they vanished, as the terrible face of Rivke had vanished.

Mendel touched Line's shoulder, then her brow. The girl's hand, small but strong, freed itself from the blanket, found Mendel's arm, and groped up it, exploring it. The hand slipped into the opening of his shirt, then grazed his ill-shaven cheeks; the fingers found the scar on his forehead, followed it, alert and sensitive until it disappeared into his hair. The other hand joined it, and pressed the back of Mendel's head, drawing it down. Mendel helped Line unwrap herself from the blanket without waking Leonid. Together, they climbed to the loft: the steps creaked under their weight, but the noise became mixed with the sound of the wind and the rain.

The loft was cluttered. Touching it, Mendel recognized a hopper, he touched a gear covered with axle grease; he drew his hand back in revulsion and wiped it on the seat of his pants. With his feet he found a free space, and drew Line there; she followed him obediently. They lay down, and Mendel undressed Line, removing her army clothing. The body that emerged was thin and nervous, almost masculine; the belly was flat, arms and thighs were slim and muscular. The knees were square, hard, rough as children's; Mendel's hand greedily searched the two dimples at the sides of the tendon, below the kneecap, then moved up the hip. The breasts, small as they were, felt withered, sad little bags of empty skin beneath which he could feel the ribs. Mendel undressed, and immediately Line clung to him as if to wrestle. Crushed beneath the weight of the male body, Line writhed, a tenacious and resilient adversary, to arouse him and challenge him. It was a language, and even in the red blur of desire, Mendel understood it: I want you but I resist you; I resist you because I want you; I, slim, lie beneath you but am not yours; I am the woman of no one, and by resisting I bind you to me. Mendel felt she was armed though naked, armed like the first time he had glimpsed her in the Novoselki dormitory. Nobody's and everybody's, like Rahab of Jericho: Mendel perceived this and felt stabbed, as at the last moment he tore himself from her. The effort was so lacerating that Mendel sobbed aloud, in the dark silence of the mill.

When the fever had dissolved in the peace of the satisfied body, sweet as a convalescence, Mendel pricked up his ear: the silence wasn't complete, other stifled voices could be heard, difficult to identify. He glided into sleep beside Line, who was already sleeping serenely.

He woke up a little later, at the first light of day, when all the others were still asleep, and he could make out Gedaleh beside Bella, Pavel beside Black Rokhele, and White Rokhele next to Isidor. Line's pale, sharp face rested in the hollow of his arm. Why did I do it? What am I seeking in her? Love and pleasure. No, not only that. I am seeking in her another woman, and this is terrible and unjust. I sought her in Sissl and I didn't find her. I seek the woman who is no more, and I won't find her. And now I am bound to this one: bound by this one, bound by the ivy. Forever, or not forever, I don't know: nothing is forever. And she isn't bound to me: she binds and isn't bound, you should have realized that, Mendel, you're no longer a child, untie yourself while there's still time, this is no time to bind yourself. Untie yourself or you'll come to a bad end: bad like Leonid. He looked around, and Leonid wasn't there. Nothing odd: he could have gone out. He continued fraternally advising himself to free himself of Line, to order it, impose it on himself, and he knew quite well that if another man had spoken to him like that, he, Mendel, the meek clockmender, would have punched his face in. In half an hour everybody was awake, and Leonid wasn't there: his knapsack and his weapon had also disappeared.

Gedaleh grumbled in Polish, urging the devil to deal with Leonid; then he continued in Yiddish: "*Nu*, we're not the Red Army and I'm not Ulybin, and as partisans go he isn't worth much. He's not a man to betray us, but if he stumbles onto the Germans, that's another story. Let's hope he doesn't make any trouble. On his own he won't get far: in three days we'll find him again, you'll see."

"Still, he could have left the automatic rifle behind," Jozek said.

"Yes, that's the bad thing. If he took it with him, then he plans to use it."

Mendel suggested going to hunt for him, Dov added that they could try with the dogs, and Gedaleh said they should do what they could, but without wasting time. Dov led one of the dogs to sniff the blanket Leonid had slept in, then took him outside; the dog listlessly sniffed the ground, raised his nose, and sniffed the air, turned around two or three times; finally he lowered his tail and his ears and pointed his nose towards Dov and Mendel, as if to say: "What do you want from me?"

"Let's be on our way," Gedaleh said. "Get ready to leave. Going to hunt for him is out of the question. If he looks for us, he'll know how to find us." Mendel thought: He's gone to shoot Germans, but maybe he wanted to shoot me.

They resumed their march, between a shining sky and the rain-soaked ground. They skirted a few apparently deserted villages; the column proceeded slowly, led by Jozek, through patches of woods and fields invaded by weeds. The ground was flat, but to the west there was a line of blunted hills. Mendel marched in silence, and didn't feel pleased to be Mendel. In a single night he had betrayed twice, perhaps three times, if Sissl also counted. But Sissl didn't count: there she was, just ahead in the line, walking behind Piotr with her usual, serene gait. And the dead shouldn't be counted, either, they are in their world of the dead, and they almost never leave it. You mustn't let them out of it, it's like when typhus breaks out, you have to reinforce the cordon, keep them locked in their lazaret. The living have the right to defend themselves. But with Leonid it was different. Leonid wasn't dead ... and do you know, now, if he is dead? If you haven't killed him yourself, who were his brother, and when they asked you to account for him, you answered with the insolence of Cain? Perhaps you've taken from him the only thing he had; you've cut the lifeline and he's drowning, or has already drowned. No, you've done worse: you've unhooked the line and you've taken his place. Now you're the one who's being pulled in. By her, the obstinate little girl with the chewed fingernails. Take care what you're doing, Mendel, son of Nachman!

On the morning of the third day of the march, they were at the side of a ravine. It was steep, nasty, marl-rich earth, made slippery by the rain; the opposite slope was also steep, and at the bottom, thirty meters below, it ended in a muddy torrent strangled between the two walks.

"You may be good at making fake dollars, Jozek, but you're not worth much as a guide," Gedaleh said. "We can't get across here. You picked the wrong path."

Jozek had good excuses. There were lots of trails, and after all these years, they couldn't expect him to remember them all. It was the fault of the rain; in dry weather, he was sure of this, it was fairly easy to go down and climb up, and the stream was no more than a trickle that didn't frighten anyone. Anyway, there was no need to retrace their steps. They could go on northwards, following the edge of the ravine; sooner or later they'd find a way across.

They set off again, along faint hints of paths overgrown with brambles. They soon saw that the stream, instead of running north, veered towards a northeast that was almost an east, and Jozek's popularity waned: nobody had ever heard that to go west you had to head east. Gedaleh said this was exactly what Christopher Columbus had done, or rather vice versa, and Bella, worn out, told him to stop clowning. Jozek kept saying there had to be a crossing, not far away; and in fact, around midday they found a well-defined path that ran along the crest. They followed it for half an hour, and they saw that Jozek must have been right: the ravine also turned left, westward, in other words, at an acute angle, and the path, more and more trodden, descended obliquely towards the bottom. In spite of the rain that had fallen a few days before, they could make out cattle tracks: perhaps the path led to a ford, or a bridge, or a watering place. They went down; they saw that beyond the curve the ravine opened out into a flat bed; the stream broke into various branches that flowed slowly over the pebbles. In the brief plain there were the ruins of a stone shed; in the doorway stood six men, and one of them was Leonid. Of the others, four were armed, wearing uniforms of the old Polish army, tattered and faded; the sixth man, unarmed and naked to the waist, was off to one side, sunbathing.

One of the armed men came towards the Gedalists. He slipped off the automatic rifle that he wore over his shoulder, pulling it over his head; he didn't aim it at the newcomers, but he held it lightly, dangling, by the barrel, and said in Polish, "Stop." Gedaleh, who had been born and raised in Poland and who spoke Polish better than Russian, stopped, signaled the line to halt, and said in Russian to Jozek, "See what the *Pan* wants."

The *Pan,* the mister, in other words, understood (and for that matter Gedaleh had done his best to be sure he would understand), and said with cold fury, "I want you to go away. This is our land, and you people have already caused enough trouble."

At the prospect of a quarrel, Gedaleh assumed an ecstatic look that irritated the Pole even more. He said to Jozek: "Tell the gentleman that, if we have caused troubles, it was no fault of ours, or at least without any intention of harming him personally. Ask him if he is referring to the Sarny locomotive, and if that's the case, tell him we won't do it again. Tell him we have a great desire to go on, and we need no encouragement from him. Ask him—"

It emerged that the gentleman understood Russian fairly well, because he didn't wait for Jozek to translate and interrupted Gedaleh violently: "Of course I'm speaking of the locomotive. That's our territory, too, the National Armed Forces, and we were the ones who had to face the Germans' reprisal. But I'm also talking about your man"—and here he indicated Leonid with a con-

temptuous jab of his thumb—"this daredevil fool, this lu-
natic with the red star who goes off by himself to act the
hero, without thinking that—"

This time it was Gedaleh who interrupted, in good Polish, abandoning, abruptly, the game of being interpreted:
"What? What did he do? Where did you capture him?"

"We didn't capture him," the Pole snarled. "We saved
him. And don't go telling this story: because it's the first
time, goddammit, that the NSZ has saved a Jew, and
what's more, a Russian and a Communist, from the Germans' bullets. But he really must be a bit looney: armed,
in broad daylight, not even looking around, he was going
straight towards the Germans' sentry post . . ."

"Which sentry post?"

"The one at the Zielonka power station. He nearly
caused all hell to break loose. To say nothing of the fact
that the Zielonka electricity serves us too. If you want to
sabotage something, go farther away, the devil take you.
And enquire about the political situation. And, most of
all, don't send fools like this one."

"We didn't send him. It was his own idea," Gedaleh
said. "We'll question him and we'll punish him."

"That's what he said, too: that it was his own idea.
We've taken care of questioning him. You surely don't
think we're simple-minded. Or children. Since 'thirty-nine
we've been fighting on two fronts, and we've learned certain tricks. And you've copied from the Nazis: everything
exactly like the time of the Reichstag fire: you pick someone who's simple-minded, you send him off on his own,
and then the reprisal strikes like lightning where it suits
your bunch best."

The Pole stopped to catch his breath. He was tall,
skinny, no longer young, and his gray mustache was shaking with wrath. Gedaleh glanced towards Leonid: he was
sitting on the stone threshold of the barn, his bound hands
resting on his thighs. He was only ten paces away, within
earshot, but he didn't seem to be listening. The Pole observed Jozek with attention: "But he looks like a Jew, too.
We've seen some strange things, all right, but this beats

them all: Jews who wander around Poland, with weapons stolen from the Poles, and pass themselves off as partisans, sons of bitches!"

Gedaleh snapped. With his left hand he snatched the gun from the Pole's hands, and with his right he gave him a violent blow to the ear. The Pole staggered, took a few uncertain steps, but didn't fall. The other three had come up, menacingly, but their leader said something to them, and they withdrew a few paces, still keeping their weapons aimed, however.

"I'm also a Jew, *Panie Kondotierze,*" Gedaleh said in a calm voice. "We didn't steal these weapons, and we know fairly well how to use them. You've been fighting for five years; and we, for three thousand. You, on two fronts; and we, on more fronts than you can count. Be reasonable, Mister Condottiere. We have the same enemy to fight: let's not waste our strength." Then he added, with a polite smile, "Or our insults." Perhaps the Condottiere would have been less accommodating if he hadn't seen himself surrounded by about twenty determined-looking Gedalists. He grumbled some mysterious curse having to do with thunder and cholera, then said gruffly: "We don't want to know anything about your bunch, and we want nothing to do with you. Take back your man. And take that other one, too, who says he's one of yours: we have no use for him."

At a signal from him, his followers grabbed Leonid by the arms, made him stand up, and pushed him towards Gedaleh, who immediately cut the rope that bound his hands. Leonid didn't say a word, didn't raise his eyes from the ground, and stepped into the band of Gedalists standing on the path. The other man the Pole had mentioned, the one who was off to one side sunbathing, came forward spontaneously. He was as tall as Gedaleh, he had a bold, hawk-like nose and a majestic black mustache, but he couldn't have been much over twenty. His body, lithe and muscular, would have been a good model for the statue of an athlete, if it hadn't been for a clubfoot that hindered one leg. He had collected a bundle from the ground and seemed pleased to change masters. It was time to move on. Gedaleh gave the Pole his weapon back and said to him, "Mister Condottiere, I believe we can agree only on one point: we don't want to have anything to do with you, either. Tell us what road we should take."

The Pole replied, "Keep clear of Kovel, Lukow, and the railroad. Don't provoke the Germans in our area, and go to hell."

"Nice character!" Gedaleh said to Mendel when they had started on their way, without showing any residue of anger or any contempt. "A really fantastic type, like a film about Indians. If you ask me, he's got the century wrong."

"Still, you slapped him!"

"I had to. But what's that got to do with it? I admired him, all the same: the way you admire a waterfall or a strange animal. He's stupid, and maybe also dangerous, but he put on quite a show for us."

For that matter, Gedaleh seemed to fall in love with every newcomer, beyond any moral or utilitarian consideration. He circled around Arie, the lame boy, as if he wanted to catch his smell and observe him from every angle. In spite of his handicap, Arie had no trouble following the line; in fact he walked with easy agility, and soon made himself popular by killing a quail with a stone and offering it as a present to White Rokhele. He couldn't speak or understand Yiddish, and he pronounced Russian very oddly: he was Georgian, Arie was, and proud of it. His mother tongue was Georgian, Russian he had studied in school; but his name, of which he was equally proud, was pure Hebrew: Arie means "lion."

Few of the Gedalists had ever met a Georgian Jew before, and Jozek, half joking and half serious, actually dared express doubt about Arie's being Jewish: anyone who doesn't speak Yiddish isn't a Jew, this is almost an axiom, as the proverb goes: *Redest keyn jiddisch, bist nit kejn jid.*

"If you're a Jew, speak to us in Hebrew: say a blessing in Hebrew."

The boy accepted the challenge and recited the blessing of the wine with a Sephardic accent, rotund and solemn, instead of the Ashkenazic, syncopated and fast. Many laughed.

"Ha, you speak Hebrew the way the Christians do!"

"No," Arie replied, nobly offended. "We speak like our father Abraham. You're the ones who speak it wrong."

Arie fitted into the band with surprising speed. He was sturdy and willing and good-naturedly accepted any job; he also accepted that small amount of partisan discipline that the band had retained. Whereas they were all curious about him, he seemed very uncurious about the purposes of the band. "If you're going off to kill Germans, I'll come with you. If you're going to the land of Israel, I'll come with you." He was intelligent, good-humored, proud, and touchy. Proud of many things: of being Georgian (descendant of the Macedons of Alexander, he clarified, though he was unable to prove it in any way), of not being Russian, but at the same time of being Stalin's compatriot; and of his surname, Hazansvili.

"Of course, you even look like him." Mottel laughed. "Not just the mustache, but your name, too."

"Stalin's a great man, and you shouldn't make fun of him. I wish my name did resemble his, but it doesn't. . . . He's a Dzugasvili, which means the son of Dzuga; and I'm only Hazansvili, which means the son of Hazan, the cantor of the synagogue."

He was touchy on the subject of his handicap, and he didn't like it to be mentioned, but in all likelihood it had saved his life: "When I was called up, they declared me unfit for service, and in the village they teased me, because serving as a soldier for us is an honor. But then, in 'forty-two, when they were taking everybody, they mobilized me too, and they sent me to the rear lines behind Minsk, to bake bread in the army bakery. The Germans took me prisoner, but as a civilian worker, and that was my good luck. They didn't notice that I'm Jewish . . ."

"It's all thanks to your mustache, believe me," Jozek

said. "Too bad so few of us thought of that, of growing one."

"My mustache and my height. And also because I said I was a peasant, specializing in grafts."

"You were smart!"

"No, no, that really is my job, me and my father and my grandfather, we've always grafted vines. So they sent me to an agricultural station, to graft trees I'd never seen before. We were left practically free, and in April I ran off. I wanted to join the partisans, and I came upon the ones you met. But I didn't get on well with them, they called me 'Jew' and made me carry loads, like a mule."

Gedaleh liked to make sudden decisions, but in the matter of Leonid he didn't feel up to acting hastily. He called Jozek, Dov, and Mendel off to one side, and he wasn't the usual, everyday Gedaleh: he didn't digress, he weighed what he was saying, and he spoke softly.

"I don't like punishments, giving them or receiving them. That's Prussian stuff; and for people like us they're not much use. But this boy went too far: he took off with weapons, with no orders, no permission, and he did everything he could to get the whole bunch of us into trouble. It was a stroke of luck that the main body of the NSZ troops were far off, otherwise we'd have had a hard time. He acted like a fool, and he made us all look like fools: fools and intruders, muddlers and bunglers. We've never been much loved around here; after this business we'll be loved even less, and we have a long road ahead, and we need the people's support. Or at least a silent neutrality. Leonid must understand these things: we have to make him understand them."

Jozek raised his hand, to ask to speak. "If it was another man, I'd say the best remedy would to beat him up a bit and then make him do self-criticism, like the Russians. But Leonid's a strange character; it's hard to figure out why he does the things he does. You're right, chief: we have to make him understand certain things. Well, if you ask me, at least for the moment that boy isn't capable of understanding anything. Since we've taken him back, he hasn't said a word: not one. He hasn't looked me in the face once, and every time I take him his messtin he pretends to eat and then, the minute I go off, he pours it all away: I've seen him clearly. If we were in peacetime, I know what he would need."

"A doctor?" Gedaleh asked.

"Yes, the lunatics' doctor."

"You two have known him longer," Gedaleh said, to Mendel and Dov, "what do you think?"

Dov spoke first, and this made Mendel happy. "At Novoselki he gave me some trouble because he wasn't punctual on the job. I sent him on a sabotage mission, to test him and to give him a chance to look good in front of the others: he seemed to need that. He brought it off, not badly and not well, with courage and haste: his nerves got the best of him. In my opinion, he's a good boy with a nasty temper, but I don't believe you can judge a man by what he did at Novoselki. Or by what he does here, for that matter."

"I'm not interested in judging him," Gedaleh said. "I'm interested in knowing what we must do with him. What do you say, watchmender?"

Mendel was uneasy. Did Gedaleh know, or had he guessed the real reason for Leonid's suicidal action? If he did, it was childish and dishonest not to speak of it. If he didn't, if he hadn't guessed, Mendel would have preferred not to supply material for his curiosity and for everybody's gossip. It was his private business, after all, wasn't it? His and Line's, a personal matter. He didn't have the heart to make Leonid's position worse, and tell that Leonid had deserted because of a story with a woman: that meant worsening his position. And worsening your own. Yes, of course: worsening mine. He remained vague, feeling privately that he was a liar, as contemptible as a worm:

"We've been together for a year, we met last July in the

Bryansk forests. I agree with Dov: he's a good boy with a difficult temper. He told me his story, his life has never been easy, his suffering began much earlier than ours. In my opinion, punishing him would be cruel and, what's more, useless: he's punishing himself. And I agree with Jozek, too: he would be a man to be treated."

Gedaleh sprang to his feet and began pacing up and down: "You are all fine advisers. Treating him is impossible. Punishing him is a mistake. You might as well come out and say it: your advice is to leave things the way they stand, and let the matter resolve itself. You're like the counselors of Job, to me. All right, for the present we'll leave it at that; I'll see if the girl can give me a more concrete suggestion: she knows him better than you, or at least from a different viewpoint."

So he doesn't know, Mendel thought with relief, ashamed, at the same time, of this relief. But of the talk between Gedaleh and Line Mendel heard no more: either it didn't take place, or (more probably) Line said nothing vital. Gedaleh's ill humor was short-lived; in the days that followed he regained his usual humor, but, as before at Sarny, he vanished again at the beginning of July when the column was encamped near Annopol, not far from the Vistula. He reappeared the next day, with a new velvet jacket, a peasant's straw hat, a bottle of ersatz perfume for Bella, and little presents for the other four women. But he hadn't gone into the city for purchases; after that, various things changed. Precautions increased: again, as in spring, they marched at night, and in the daytime the band made camp, trying to remain inconspicuous, which became less and less easy, because the zone was covered with a thick network of roads and dotted with villages and farmhouses. Gedaleh seemed in a hurry; he demanded long laps, even twenty kilometers in a night, and he was heading in a specific direction, towards Opatow and Kielce. He warned them all to stick with the group and not to talk to any peasants they might encounter: with the local people only those speaking Polish could have dealings, but even they, as little as possible.

Both on the marches and in their rest periods, Leonid's presence had become painful for them all, and especially for Mendel. Mendel had to admit to himself that he was afraid of Leonid: he avoided his vicinity; when they marched in Indian file, he went to the head when Leonid was at the rear, and vice versa. But, as Mendel observed with dismay, Leonid, on the contrary, whether wittingly or not, maneuvered to be near him, still without addressing a word to him. He confined himself to looking at Mendel, with those great black eyes charged with sadness and appeal, as if to afflict him with his presence, not let him forget, and take revenge by this affliction. Or was it perhaps also to keep an eye on him? Perhaps: some of Leonid's actions suggested that he was overcome by suspicion. He would snap his head around, looking over his shoulder. During their rests, which took place in the daytime, and mostly in abandoned peasant huts, he would lie down to sleep, choosing the place nearest the door, and he would sleep little; he would waken with a start, glance around uneasily, peering out of the door or the windows.

One gray, cloudy morning, after a nighttime lap that had wearied them all, Mendel was gathering wood in the forest and saw Leonid at his side, also gathering wood, though nobody had ordered him to. He had grown thin and tense, his eyes glistened. He spoke to Mendel with an air of complicity: "You've caught on, too, haven't you?"

"Caught on to what?"

"That we've been sold out. We can't fool ourselves any more. We've been sold, and he sold us."

"Who?" Mendel asked, dumbfounded.

Leonid lowered his voice. "Him, Gedaleh. But there was nothing else he could do: they were blackmailing him, he was a puppet in their hands." Then he signaled, his forefinger on his lip, to be silent and went back to collecting wood.

Mendel told nobody about the episode, but a few days later, Dov said to him, "That friend of yours has strange ideas. He says Gedaleh is working for the NKVD or some other secret police, I don't know which, and they're black-mailing him, and we're all hostages in their hands."

"He said something of the sort to me," Mendel said. "What should we do?"

"Nothing," Dov said.

Mendel remembered he had once compared Leonid to a watch clogged with dust; but now Leonid reminded him of some other watches that they had brought him to mend: perhaps they had had a blow, the coils of the springs had become tangled, they ran a bit slow, then were wildly fast for a bit, and all of them in the end were broken beyond repair.

The summer was bright and windy, and the Gedalists realized they had entered the land of hunger. Gedaleh's warnings to avoid contacts with the local people proved superfluous, if not ironic. There weren't many people in that countryside: no men, few women, at the doors of the destroyed farms, only old folk and children. They weren't people to be feared; on the contrary, they themselves were branded by fear. A few months before, the partisans of the Polish Interior Army had unleashed an attack on the German garrisons in the zone, while south of Lublin Soviet paratroops cut the German lines of communication that were carrying ammunition and supplies to the front. Other Polish units had blown up bridges and viaducts and had attacked a village from which the Germans had forcibly driven away the peasants in 1942 in order to install settlers from the Thousand-year Reich. German reprisal had been extended through the whole zone and had been ferocious. It hadn't been directed against the bands, virtually impossible to apprehend, who had taken refuge in the forests, but against the civilian population. The Germans had brought in reinforcements from the distant rear; at night they surrounded the Polish villages and set fire to them, or else they deported all the men and women of working age: they gave them half an hour to prepare for the journey, then they loaded them on to their trucks and carried them away. In some towns they had devoted their attention to the children: they deported to Germany those children who looked "Aryan" and killed the others. The villages, which had always been poor, were reduced to heaps of smoking ruins and rubble, but the fields had remained intact, and the ripe rye waited in vain for someone to harvest it.

It was Mottel who had the idea. He had gone to ask for water at an isolated farm, perhaps a kilometer from the village of Zborz, and he had found there only an old woman, lying on the straw in the barn, but there were no more animals in the barn. The old woman could hardly move, she had a broken leg, which nobody had treated. She told Mottel to go to the well and take all the water he wanted, and bring her a little, too. But to bring her also something to eat: anything. She hadn't eaten for three days; every now and then someone in the village remembered her and brought her a slice of bread. And yet in the field out there there was enough rye to feed a big family, but at the first rain it would rot, because there was no one to scythe it.

Mottel told Gedaleh, and Gedaleh decided then and there: "We have to help these people. This is our war too. It's a good opportunity to show them that we come as friends and not as enemies."

Jozek grimaced. "They've never been fond of us around these parts; before the Germans burned their houses, they burned ours. They don't like Jews, and they don't like Russians either, and many of us are both Jews and Russians. They know what happened to the Russian peasants in the 'twenties, and they're afraid of collectivization. Let's help them, but let's watch out, too."

All the others, on the contrary, agreed without reservations: they were tired of destroying, tired of the negative and stupid actions that war forces on people. The most enthusiastic were Piotr and Arie, who were experienced in farming. Mottel had reported that "his" old woman's roof had collapsed, and Piotr said, "I'll fix it. I'm good at mending thatch roofs, it's a job I did at home, and they paid me to do it. But now, to fix the roof of your old woman, I'd give all the rubles they used to give me. If I had them, mind you, because I don't actually have any."

The old woman accepted. Piotr, with the help of Sissl, went to work, and a few days later an old man with a drooping mustache was seen lurking in the area. He pretended to be interested in something else: he straightened stakes, checked the walls of locks of the ditches although they were desperately dry, but from a distance he observed the two at work. One day he introduced himself to Piotr and, in Polish, asked him various questions; Piotr pretended not to understand and went looking for Gedaleh.

"I'm the *Burmistrz,* the mayor of the village," the old man said, with dignity, though he looked like a beggar. "Who are you? Where are you going? What do you want?"

Gedaleh had come to this conversation unarmed, in shirt sleeves, in torn and faded civilian trousers, and with the straw hat he had bought. He spoke Polish without any Yiddish accent, and it would have been difficult for anyone to identify his condition. At first he was cautious. "We're a group of stragglers, men and women. We come from different countries, and we mean you no harm. We're passing through; we're going far off, we don't want to disturb anybody, but we don't want to be disturbed, either. We're tired, but we have strong arms: perhaps we can be useful to you somehow."

"For example?" the mayor asked suspiciously.

"For example, we could harvest the rye before it's spoiled."

"What do you want in exchange?"

"A part of the harvest, whatever seems fair to you; and some water, a roof, and no talk about us."

"How many are there of you?"

"About forty; five of us are women."

"Are you their chief?"

"I am."

"We are fewer than you: not even thirty, even counting the children. Mind you, we've never had any money; we don't have any more livestock, and there aren't even any young women."

"Too bad about the young women," Gedaleh said, laughing, "but that's not the first thing on our minds. I told you: we're content with water, silence, and if possible a roof under which we can sleep for a few nights. We're tired of war and walking, we're homesick for the tasks of peacetime."

"We're tired of war, too," the mayor said; and he immediately added: "But do you know how to reap?"

"We're out of practice, but we can manage."

"At Opatow there's the mill," the mayor said, "and it seems to be working. There are scythes; they left us those. You can begin tomorrow."

All the men of Blizna and Ruzhany went to reap, and with them Arie, Dov, Line, and Black Rokhele, who were joined by Piotr when he had finished fixing the roof: about twenty of them in all. Arie was the most skilled, and he taught all the others how to prop the stooks erect and how to sharpen the scythe first with the hammer and then with the whetstone. Piotr also proved good and able to stand up to the toil. Line amazed everybody: slight as she was, she reaped from dawn to dusk without showing signs of fatigue, and she easily put up with the heat, thirst, and the swarm of horseflies and mosquitoes that had promptly assembled. It wasn't the first time she had done this job: she had done it a thousand years before, near Kiev, on a collective farm where young Zionists prepared for emigration to Palestine, in the remote days when being Zionists and Communists hadn't yet become an absurd contradiction. Dov also worked well, despite the weight of his years and his wounds. For him, too, it was not an entirely new experience: he had harvested the sunflowers when he was confined at Vologda, where the summer days were eighteen hours long and you had to work every one of them.

The others of the band, including Mendel, Leonid, Jozek, and Isidor, scattered through the village to perform the various jobs that the mayor had indicated: there were chicken coops to be restored; more roofs to mend, gardens to hoe. Once the first distrust was overcome, it turned out that there were also potatoes to be dug, and it was these potatoes that acted as cement between the wandering Jews and the desperate Polish peasants, at evening, under the summer stars, when they were all seated in the farmyard, on the packed hard earth still warm from the sun.

8

July–August

1944

While some of the potatoes were being boiled in the pot, and others were baking in the ashes, the mayor looked around, studying the faces of the foreigners in the red light of the fire. Beside him, in the circle, was his wife, broad-faced, with high cheekbones and an impassive expression. She wasn't looking at the Gedalists, but at her husband, as if she feared for him, wanted to protect him, and at the same time prevent him from saying rash things.

"You are Jews," the old man said suddenly, in a calm voice. But his wife spoke rapidly into his ear, and he answered:

"Calm down, Seweryna; you never let me speak."

"This one's Russian," Gedaleh said, pointing to Piotr, "all the rest of us are Jews, Russian and Polish. But how did you recognize us?"

"By your eyes," the mayor said. "There were Jews here among us, too, and they had eyes like yours."

"What are our eyes like?" Mendel asked.

"Uneasy. Like animals being hunted."

"We're not hunted animals any longer," Line said. "Many of us have died fighting. Our enemies are yours, the ones who destroyed your houses."

The mayor was silent for a few minutes, chewing his ration of potatoes, then he said, "Girl, things here with us aren't that simple. In this village, for example, Jews and Poles lived together for I don't know how many centuries, but there was never any friendliness between them. The Poles worked in the fields, the Jews were artisans and merchants, they collected the taxes for the landowners, and in church the priest said they were the ones who had sold Christ and crucified him. We never shed their blood, but when the Germans came in nineteen thirty-nine, and the first thing they did was strip the Jews, and mock them, and hit them, and shut them up in the ghettos, I have to say truly—"

Here Seweryna interrupted again, whispering something into her husband's ear; but he shrugged and went on: "I have to say truly, we were glad, and I myself was glad. We didn't like the Germans either, but we thought they had come to mete out justice, in other words, to take the Jews' money away from them and give it to us."

"Were they so rich then, the Jews of Zborz?" Gedaleh asked.

"Everybody said they were. They were badly dressed, but people said that was because they were tightfisted. And people said other things, too: that the Jews were Bolsheviks and wanted to collectivize the land, like in Russia, and kill all the priests."

"But that doesn't make sense!" Line interrupted. "How could they be rich, stingy, and Bolsheviks?"

"But it does make sense. One Pole said that all the Jews are rich, another Pole said they're all Communists. And yet another Pole said that one Jew is rich and another is a Communist. You see it's not simple? But things became even more complicated afterwards, when the Germans gave guns to the Ukrainians so they could help slaughter the Jews, and instead the Ukrainians fired on us and took away our livestock, and then when the Russian partisans began to disarm and carry off the Polish partisans. About you people I changed my mind later, when I saw with my own eyes what the Germans did to the Jews of Opatow."

"What did they do to them?"

"They pulled them out of the ghetto and shut them all up in the movie theater: even the children and the old people and the dying: more than two thousand people in a theater with five hundred seats. They left them in there for seven days, not giving them anything to eat or drink, and they shot any of us who showed pity and tried to hand something in through the windows; and they also shot some others of us who also took them water, yes, but in exchange wanted the last money they had. Then the Germans opened the doors and ordered them to come out. Only about a hundred came out alive, and they killed them in the square, and they ordered us to bury them all, the ones in the square and the ones still inside the theater. Well, seeing children dead like that made me begin to think that the Jews are people like us, and in the end the Germans would do to us what they had done to them; but if I have to tell you the truth, not everybody has understood that yet. And I'm telling you these things because when a man makes a mistake it's good for him to recognize his mistakes, and also because you've harvested and you've dug the potatoes."

"Mayor," Gedaleh said, "the things you've told us are not new to us, but we have some new things to tell you. Maybe we seem strange to you: you must realize that a live Jew is a strange Jew. You must realize that what you saw at Opatow has happened wherever the Germans have set foot, in Poland, in Russia, in France, in Greece. And I also have to tell you that while the Germans, with their weapons or with hunger, kill one Pole out of five, they don't leave a single Jew living."

"These aren't new things you're telling me. We don't

even have a radio, but news arrives all the same. We know what the Germans have done, and what they're still doing, here and everywhere."

"You don't know everything. There are other things, so horrible you wouldn't believe them: and yet they happen not far from here. The only ones of us who are saved are those who have chosen our way."

"I realized this at once, too. That you people are armed."

"Was it our eyes again?" Gedaleh asked, laughing.

"No, not the eyes; all your jackets have a shiny patch on the left shoulder because of the gunstrap. Please, I beg you by your God, by ours, and by all the saints, don't attack the Germans here. Go farther on, go wherever you like, but don't cause trouble here, otherwise there's no use in your having worked for us. But why don't you hide in the woods and wait for the Russians to get here? They're not all that far away now, maybe they're already at Lublin; when the wind's right you can hear the sound of their artillery."

"Our things are not simple either," said Gedaleh. "We are Jews and we are Russians and we are partisans. As Russians, we would like to wait for the front to come by, and then rest and go back to look for our homes, but our homes don't exist any more, and neither do our families; and if we did go back, maybe nobody would want us, like when you take a wedge out of a log and then the wood closes again. As partisans, our war is different from the one the soldiers fight, and you know that: we don't fight it at the front, but behind the enemy's back. And as Jews, we have a long road ahead of us. What would you do, Mayor, if you were alone, a thousand kilometers from your village, and you knew that your village, and the fields, and your family no longer existed?"

"I'm an old man, and I believe I'd hang myself from a beam. But if I were younger, I'd go to America, the way my brother did, who was braver than I and more far-sighted."

"You're right. Among the Jews, too, there are some who have relatives in America and want to go to them. But nobody in this band has relatives in America; our America is not that distant. We will fight until the end of the war, because we believe that making war is a bad thing, but that killing Nazis is the most just thing that can be done today on the face of the earth; and then we'll go to Palestine, and we'll try to build the house we've lost, and to start living again the way all other people live. That's why we won't stop here and will go on again towards the west: to stay behind the Germans' back and to find the road towards our America."

After finishing the potatoes, Gedalists and peasants had gone off to sleep; in the farmyard only Gedaleh, Mendel, Line, the mayor, and his wife remained. The mayor was staring pensively at the embers; then he said, "What will you go and do in Palestine?"

"We'll farm," Line said, "there the land will be ours."

"You'll go there to be peasants?" the mayor asked. "You are right to go far from here, but you're wrong to be peasants. Being a peasant is hard."

"We'll go there and live the way all other nations live," said Line, who had put her hand on Mendel's arm. Mendel added: "We'll do all the jobs there'll be to do."

"Except collect taxes for landowners," Gedaleh added. The wind had fallen, fireflies could be seen dancing at the edge of the yard, and in the silence of the night it was clear that the mayor had spoken the truth: in the distance, from some unspecified point, perhaps from many points, came the subdued grumble of the front, full of hope and menace. The mayor pulled himself up with an effort and said it was time to go to bed. "I'm glad I met you. I'm glad you harvested for us. I'm glad I talked with you the way a man speaks with friends, but I'm also glad you're going away."

It was easier to maintain contacts and receive news from the rest of the world in the marshes and forests of

Polessia than in the densely populated country through which Gedaleh and his band proceeded in August of 1944. Moving at night and avoiding built-up areas had become a strict rule, but even when they observed these obvious precautions, every road that had to be crossed and, especially, every bridge, represented a danger and a problem. The area was crawling with Germans; no longer with their collaborators, more and more treacherous and disheartened, but with authentic Germans, army and police, in all the towns and villages, and in a frantic traffic along the roads and the railways. The Russians had broken through at Lublin, had crossed the Vistula near Sandomierz, and had established a strong bridgehead on the left bank, and the Germans were preparing a counterattack.

Contacts with the peasants, necessary for revictualing, had been reduced to the indispensable minimum; Gedaleh didn't want any talk, nor for that matter did the peasants, terrified and bewildered, have any wish to talk. In these circumstances, paradoxically, the chief source of information was the newspapers, found rarely in farmhouses, more often salvaged, torn and soiled with garbage, and sometimes boldly bought by Jozek at the kiosks. From the newspapers they learned that the Allies had landed in Normandy and were advancing on Paris; that on 20 July there had been an unsuccessful attempt to assassinate Hitler; that Warsaw had risen up (the *Völkischer Beobachter* played down the event, and spoke of "traitors, subversives, and bandits"). But they also learned other things, and not from the newspapers. Besides Germans, the rear lines teemed with undefined people who, like the Gedalists themselves, were not fond of daylight: they were Poles, Ukrainians, Lithuanians, Tatars of the German auxiliary corps, who had sniffed the wind, deserted, and were now living underground, as black marketeers or bandits; there were partisans from the various Polish formations who had lost contact with their units and had found refuge with the peasants; and further, there were professional smugglers, highway robbers, and spies of the Germans and the Russians disguised as members of all the other mentioned categories. From these people Gedaleh heard confirmation of the rumors he had heard before and had mentioned to the mayor of Zborz: the Germans had dismantled their first slaughter camps, Treblinka, Sobibor, Belzec, Majdanek, Chelmno, but only to replace them with one that took the place of them all, where they exploited the experience gained through the others: Auschwitz, in Upper Silesia. Here they killed and cremated Poles and Russians and prisoners from all over Europe, but especially Jews; and now, one trainload after another, they were slaughtering the Jews of Hungary. From a Ukrainian deserter they learned finally a disturbing piece of news: the bands of Russian partisans, parachuted behind the lines or escaped from the German *Lagers,* were not all behaving in the same way. Some commanders had liberated Jewish labor camps, had saved and protected the survivors found there, and had invited them to join their units. Others, on the contrary, had tried to disband by force groups of Jewish partisans they had encountered in the forests: there had been fighting and some casualties. Other Jews had been disarmed or killed by more or less regular units of Polish partisans.

"They accept us as martyrs: maybe afterwards they'll put up monuments in the ghettos, but as allies they won't accept us," Dov said.

"We'll keep on our way," Gedaleh said. "We'll decide what to do, as the occasion presents itself, moment by moment."

The first moment to decide came soon. Mendel and Dov and Line had sensed that the passing of the Polish border had brought about a profound change in Gedaleh's plans, or rather in the nature of his improvisations. He felt farther away from Russia, and not only physically: more in the open, more autonomous, more threatened, and at the same time freer. In other words, more responsible. Once again, around 20 August, he had gone off on his own, but he had brought back no presents and had made no purchases. Contrary to his habit, which was to arrive at decisions in confused meetings, he immediately drew Dov, Mendel, and Line aside; they had never seen him so tense. He came straight to the point:

"Twenty kilometers from here there's a *Lager*, near Chmielnik. It's not one of the big ones, there are a hundred and twenty prisoners, all Jews except the Kapos. They all work in a nearby factory that produces precision instruments for the air force . . ."

"How do you know these things?"

"I know. Now the front is approaching, the factory will be moved to Germany, and all the prisoners will be killed because they know some secrets. They don't know if they will be killed here or elsewhere: they've sent out a message, they would like to attempt an uprising, if they knew they would have some support. They say there aren't many German guards, ten or twelve."

"Do the prisoners have weapons?"

"They don't mention any, so they don't."

"Let's go have a look," Dov said. "We can't do much, but we can have a look."

"Yes, but not all of us," Gedaleh said. "We would be too visible. This is the first time we've broken up; but here we have to break up. Six of us will go: we'll have to count on the surprise element, if that fails we can't do any good, even if there are thirty of us."

"Can we send an answer?" Line asked.

"We can't. It would be too dangerous, for them, too. We have to go there. We have to leave now."

"The four of us, and who else?" Line asked again; she seemed anxious to burn her bridges.

Gedaleh hesitated: "Not Dov. Dov stays with the main group. We don't have ranks, but practically speaking he's second-in-command. And he's the most experienced one among us."

Dov betrayed no feeling, in words or in the expression on his face, but Mendel knew these weren't the reasons why Gedaleh was leaving him out, and Dov had also understood and was saddened.

"The three of us, with Piotr, Mottel, and Arie," Mendel suggested.

"Not Arie. He's lame and he has no army experience," Gedaleh said.

"But he's good with a knife!"

"Mottel is better. Arie isn't mature yet. I don't want him. I want Leonid."

Mendel and Line, amazed, spoke at the same time: "But Leonid isn't . . . Leonid isn't well. He's not in condition to fight."

"Leonid has to fight. He needs it the way he needs bread and the air he breathes. And we need him: he was a German prisoner, he knows how a *Lager* works. He's a paratrooper, he followed the course, he knows about sabotage and commando raids. And he's brave: he's showed that recently."

"He showed it in a strange way," Line said.

"He only needs to be brought in line and receive clear orders," Gedaleh said, with unusual harshness. "Believe me. At Kossovo we had others like him, and I know what I'm talking about."

With this, he stood up, to signify that the discussion was over. Dov and Line went off; to Mendel, who had stayed behind, Gedaleh said: "You go, too, and get ready, watchmender. I have experience in these matters: for desperate missions you want desperate men."

"Desperate missions shouldn't be carried out," Mendel said, but he went off to get ready, as Gedaleh had ordered. Gedaleh put a hand on his shoulder and gave him a little push, saying: "Ah, Mendel, I know that wisdom of yours. It's the same as mine; but this isn't the right place for it. It applied maybe a hundred years ago; it'll apply in maybe another hundred years, but here it does as much good as last year's snow."

They set off at night. All six were good walkers; they carried nothing except their weapons, and even these were not very heavy: if only they had been. Nevertheless, it took them five or six hours to reach the vicinity of Chmielnik, because none of them knew the area, and because they again had to avoid roads and towns. In the light of dawn, this town seemed sad, blackened by smoke and coal dust, surrounded by a horizon of low hills, piles of coal and of slag, of chimneys and sheds. They lost more time finding the *Lager;* the directions given Gedaleh had been summary, and the countryside seemed dotted with *Lagers,* or rather with barbed-wire enclosures. "One big prison," Line murmured to Mendel, who was walking behind her. She had taken advantage of a moment when Leonid wasn't between the two of them; whether by chance or by calculation, all during that march to the place, Leonid had always found a way to get between Mendel and Line, though never addressing a word to them. He walked rapidly, with a tense, resolute manner.

They found the factory before they found the *Lager;* indeed, it was the factory that put them on the right track. Among those old kilns, distilleries of tar, sheds that covered heaps of wreckage, blackened foundries, it stood out because it was new, big, and clean: they saw from a distance that beside the gate there was a sentry box. The *Lager* couldn't be far away, and in fact they found it three kilometers away, nestled in a bowl of hills. It was different from the other enclosures they had seen before. The fence was double, with a broad space between the two squares of wire; the buildings were camouflaged: there were four of them, not very big, on the four sides of a yard. From the center of the yard rose a column of black smoke. Outside the fences there were two wooden guard towers and a little white house.

"Let's go closer," Gedaleh said: the hilly amphitheater around the *Lager* was covered with woods, and they could approach without danger. They moved down cautiously; they found a rusted barbed-wire barrier, they followed it for a stretch, and saw a plank sentry box. The door was open, and there was no one inside. "Nothing but cigarette butts," said Mottel, who had gone to see. It was easy to cut the wire; the six resumed their descent, but then they stopped, frozen: the wind had shifted, the smoke was coming towards them, and they all caught its odor at the

same time: burned flesh. "It's over. We got here too late,"
Gedaleh said. From the place they had reached they could
make out the details better: the column of smoke rose
from a pile, around which some men were stirring: not
many, perhaps ten.

Mendel let the gun he was holding in his hand slip to
the ground, and he let himself slip down, too, to sit among
the bushes. He felt overwhelmed by a wave of weariness
the like of which he couldn't recall ever having felt before.
The weariness of a thousand years, and with it, nausea,
rage, and horror. Rage hidden and overcome by the horror. Helpless rage, icy, with no more fire from which to
draw warmth and the will to resist. A will not to resist, to
dissolve in smoke: in that smoke. And shame and wonder:
wonder that his companions had remained standing,
weapons in hand, and found the voice to speak among
themselves; but their voices reached him as if from afar,
through the cushion of his nausea.

"They're in a hurry, the bastards," Gedaleh said.
"They've gone. They don't want to leave any traces."

Piotr said, "They can't all of them have gone. Somebody must have stayed behind, to take charge of this job.
And we must kill him." (Piotr is the best, Mendel thought,
hearing his calm voice: the only real soldier. I would like
to be Piotr. Bravo, Piotr.) He felt Line looking at him, and
he stood up.

"There must be six of them left," Leonid said, opening
his mouth for the first time since they had set out.

"Why six?" Gedaleh asked.

"Two towers, and three for each tower, taking shifts on
guard. That's how the Germans do." But Mottel and
Line, who had the best eyes of the lot, said that the situation might be different: they could see clearly from this
distance the little balcony on the top of the towers, and
the machine guns aimed at the *Lager* were no longer there.
Why would a guard remain, without the machine gun?

"They'll be in the house. It only takes one to supervise
the pile," Mottel said.

"Certainly not many can have stayed, to guard a dismantled camp. Tonight we'll attack them, no matter how many they are," Gedaleh said. "We'll see if the work goes on into the night; but I don't think it will. Then we'll decide."

Mendel said, "However we attack them, the first thing they'll do is kill those working at the pile. They are people who mustn't talk."

"It doesn't matter if they die," Line said.

"Why?" Mendel answered, "they're people like us."

"They're not like us any more. They'll never be able to look one another in the eye again. For them it'll be better to be dead."

Gedaleh said to Line that it wasn't up to them to decide the fate of those wretches, and Piotr said that all this was meaningless talk. They listlessly ate the little they had brought with them and settled down to wait for night; at dusk the fire at the pile was put out, but the prisoners weren't transferred to the house.

They spent a few hours stretched out, in a restless waiting that was neither sleep nor rest. Mendel felt a strange relief when Piotr said, "Let's go." A double relief: because the waiting was over, and because the order had come from Piotr. Despite the official blackout, the house and the *Lager* were illuminated by searchlights. Leonid said that the Smolensk camp, from which he had escaped in January of 'forty-three, was illuminated at night: the Germans were more afraid of escapes than of air raids. There was only one sentry, guarding both the house and the camp: he made a figure-eight turn around both, at regular intervals, but sometimes in one direction and sometimes in the other. "Go," Piotr said to Mottel.

Mottel slipped down the hill silently and stationed himself in the shadow, around the corner of the house; the others also moved closer, to within thirty meters. The guard seemed sleepy; he advanced with a slow step until he was almost in front of Mottel, then bent over to tie his shoe and resumed his patrol in the opposite direction. He circled around the *Lager*, vanished behind the house, and didn't reappear. Instead Mottel was seen; he had stepped from his hiding place and was signaling them to advance. They all looked at Gedaleh interrogatively, Gedaleh looked at Piotr, and Piotr also signaled to move down. Piotr advanced first: he had an Italian grenade in his hand, one of those assault bombs that cause more racket than harm, but at that moment this was all the Gedalists had. Piotr approached the house; there were three windows on the ground floor, protected by grilles. Piotr moved to the first, and motioned Gedaleh and Line to go to the other two: he stationed Mendel and Leonid behind a hedge, facing the front door. Then, with the butt of his gun thrust through the bars of the grille, he smashed the window, threw in his grenade, and crouched down; Line and Gedaleh did the same at the other two windows. There were only two explosions: for some reason Gedaleh's grenade hadn't worked. Gedaleh tossed in a second, then he, Line, Piotr, and Mottel ran to take positions behind the hedge surrounding the house: it was a yew hedge, very low, forcing all of them almost to lie down.

For an instant or two, nothing happened; then the crackle of an automatic weapon was heard: somebody was firing in bursts, blindly, along the corridor of the house and out of the door. Mendel flattened himself on the ground, heard the bullets whistling in midair above his head, and out of the corner of his eye he saw Leonid jump to his feet. "Get down," he whispered, trying to restrain him: but Leonid eluded him, jumped over the hedge, fired a round in reply, and plunged, head down, in the direction of the door. From the house came a single, isolated shot, and Leonid fell across the threshold.

Two or three brief volleys then came from the door. Mendel, without standing up, shifted along the hedge; it was clear that the German was firing from the end of the corridor, because the bullets pierced the hedge in a narrow arc. In the position he had taken Mendel was out of range, but the German was also out of the range of his weapon. Mendel still had two hand grenades: he ripped off the safety catch of one and flung it over his head in the direction of the door. The grenade went off just beyond Leonid's body, and the German came out with his hands raised: he was an SS *Scharführer*. He didn't seem wounded, and he looked around with his lips contracted, baring his teeth. "Don't move," Mendel shouted to him in German. "Keep your hands up. You're within range." As he spoke, he saw Line cross the hedge, a ridiculous sight in her out-size army clothing; with a calm tread, showing no sign of haste or nerves, she came up behind the German, opened his holster, took out his ordnance pistol, pocketed it, and joined Mendel.

Gedaleh and Piotr had also stood up. Gedaleh spoke briefly with Piotr, then asked the German, "How many of you are there?"

"Five: four inside, and one outside, on guard."

"What happened to the three left inside?"

"One is dead, for sure. I don't know about the others."

"Let's go see," Gedaleh said to Piotr and Mendel. They left the German guarded by Line and Mottel and went around the house, to look in the windows. "Wait," Piotr said: he slipped off his jacket, tied the sleeves together, to make a bundle the size of a man's head, stuck it on the barrel of his gun and held it to the bars, shouting in a loud voice: "Who goes there?" Nobody answered; there was no sign of life. "All right then," Piotr said. He put his jacket on again and went into the house. From inside they heard his footsteps, then a single pistol shot. Piotr came out again.

"Two were already dead. The third, almost."

Leonid had been shot in the chest, he must have died immediately. The sentry killed by Mottel was lying in a pool of blood, his throat cut. Mottel displayed his famous knife: "If you want to make sure they don't yell, you have to do like this," he said to Mendel with professional gravity, "cut immediately, here under the chin." It was only then that they realized the fighting had been witnessed: about ten human forms had come out of the *Lager* buildings at the racket of the shots and explosions, and now they stood there in silence, watching, behind the barrier of barbed wire. In the glow of the searchlights, they seemed haggard, their gray-and-blue-striped uniforms tattered, their faces black from smoke and unshaven beard. "We must free them, kill the German, and go," Piotr said. Gedaleh nodded his assent. Mottel went towards the fence, but Mendel restrained him. "Wait: it could be electrified." He moved closer and saw that between the stakes and the wire there were no isolators. He wanted to be surer: he looked around, he saw a piece of an iron rod on the ground. He drove it into the earth near the fence, then he pushed one end against the wires with a stick. Nothing happened; Mottel and Piotr, with the butts of their guns, knocked down a stretch of the fence, making a breach. The ten prisoners hesitated about coming out.

"Come out," Gedaleh said. "We've killed them all, except for that one."

"Who are you?" one of them asked, tall and stooped.

"Jewish partisans," Gedaleh answered. He nodded towards the pile and added, "We got here too late. And who are you?"

"You can see for yourself," the tall prisoner replied. "There were a hundred and twenty of us; we worked for the Luftwaffe. They took us out, the ten of us, and killed the others. They took us out to do this job. My name's Goldner: I was an engineer. I come from Berlin." The other prisoners had approached, but they stood behind Goldner and didn't speak.

"What can you tell me about that one over there?" Gedaleh asked, pointing to the German with his hands up.

"Kill him at once. No matter how. Don't let him talk. He was the chief; he was the one who gave orders, and he shot, too, from the turret. He enjoyed doing it. Kill him right away."

"Do you want to kill him?" Gedaleh asked. "No," Goldner answered.

Gedaleh seemed undecided. Then he went to the German, who still had his hands up, as Line and Mottel still had their guns trained on him. Gedaleh quickly patted the man's pockets and his clothes. "You can lower your hands. Give me your identification tag."

The German fiddled with the chain, but he couldn't open the clasp. Piotr stepped up, ripped it from his neck with a yank, and handed it to Gedaleh, who put it in his pocket. Then he said, "We're Jews. I don't know why I'm telling you; it doesn't change much, but we want you to know. I had a friend who wrote songs. You people took him, and you gave him half an hour to write his last. But you? You don't write songs, do you?"

The German shook his head.

"This is the first time I've spoken to one of you," Gedaleh then said. "If we let you go, what would you do?"

The German stood more erect. "Enough of all of this. Do a quick, clean job." Gedaleh took a step back and raised his weapon, then lowered it, and said to Mottel: "The uniform might come in handy. You take care of it." Mottel pushed the German into the house and took care of it, quick and clean.

"Let's go," Gedaleh said, but Line asked, "Aren't we going to leave a signature?" They all looked at her, puzzled; the girl insisted: "We have to say it was us; otherwise it has no meaning."

Piotr was opposed. "It would be foolish, and a pointless risk." Gedaleh and Mendel were uncertain. "Us—who?" Mendel asked, "the six of us, or the whole band? Or all those who—" But Mottel cut the delay short. He ran to the pile, picked up a piece of coal, and wrote on the white stucco of the house, five big Hebrew letters: "VNTNV."

"What did you write?" Piotr asked.

"*V'nosnu.* 'And they will pay back.' You see? You can read it from left to right and from right to left: it means that all can give and all can repay."

"Will they understand?" Piotr then asked.

"They'll understand enough," Mottel answered.

"Come with us," Gedaleh said to Goldner, but there was no conviction in his voice.

"Each of us will choose for himself," Goldner said, "But I won't come. We're not like you; we don't feel right with other people."

The ten conferred for a moment, then told Gedaleh that they were of Goldner's opinion: all except one. They would wait for the Russians, hidden in the woods or in the rubble of the destroyed villages. The one who declared himself ready to come with the Gedalists was a young man from Budapest. He set off with the five, who, though weighted down with new weapons, marched briskly. But after half an hour, the boy collapsed and sat down on a stone. He said he would rather go back with the other nine.

Mendel hadn't dreamed for a long time: he could no longer remember when it had happened last, before the war had broken out, he thought. That night, perhaps because he was exhausted by the tension and the march, he had a strange dream. He was at Strelka, in his little watchmender's shop, which he himself had set up in a cubbyhole of his house: it was cramped, but in the dream it was even more cramped. Mendel couldn't even stretch his elbows to work. Still he was working, he had dozens of clocks in front of him, all stopped and broken, and he was mending one, with his loup in his eye, and with a tiny screwdriver in his hand. Two men had come looking for him, and they ordered him to come with them; Rivke didn't want him to go, she was angry and afraid, but he went with them anyway. They led him down a stairway, or perhaps it was the pit of a mine, and then down a long tunnel: the ceiling was painted black, and there were many clocks hung on the walls. These were running: their tick could be heard, but each of them marked a different time, and some were actually running backwards; for this Mendel felt vaguely responsible. Along the tunnel, towards him, came a man dressed in civilian clothes, with a necktie and a contemptuous manner; he asked Mendel who he was, and Mendel couldn't answer, he didn't remember his name anymore, or where he was born, nothing.

Dov woke him, and he also woke Line, who was sleeping at Mendel's side. As often happens after deep dreams, Mendel had a hard time recognizing where he was; then he remembered, the previous evening the band had taken refuge in the cellars of a bombed-out glass factory: the ceiling was black like the one in his dream. Bella and Sissl had cooked some soup, and they were distributing it. Gedaleh was already awake, and was telling Dov how the mission had gone: ". . . in other words, the best were Piotr and Mottel. And Line, yes, of course. Here's the uniform, with chevrons and all: even ironed."

"Do you think we'll have any use for it?" Dov asked.

"No, that game's too risky. We'll sell it: Jozek will handle that."

Jozek was gulping his soup beside Pavel, Piotr, and White Rokhele. ". . . but it was Saturday," Pavel said. "After sunset on Friday evening, it's already Saturday. And isn't killing on the Sabbath a sin?"

Rokhele was very distressed. "Killing is a sin always."

"Even killing an SS?" Pavel asked, to provoke her.

"Even that. Or maybe not. An SS is like a Philistine, and Samson killed them. He was a hero because he killed the Philistines."

"But maybe he didn't kill them on the Sabbath," Jozek said.

"Well, I just don't know. Why are you tormenting me? My husband would have been able to answer you. He was a rabbi, and the whole bunch of you are ignorant and unbelievers."

"What happened to your husband?" Piotr asked.

"They killed him. He was the first one they killed in our town. They forced him to spit on the Torah, and then they killed him."

"Wasn't it one of the SS who killed him?"

"Of course. He had a skull and bones on his cap."

"There, you see?" Piotr concluded. "If Mottel had killed him first, your husband would still be alive." Rokhele didn't answer; she went off. Piotr looked at Pavel interrogatively, and Pavel raised his arms a bit, then dropped them.

"And nobody talks about him" Mendel said to Line.

"Who?"

"Leonid. Nobody thinks of him any more. Not even Gedaleh; and yet he was the one who wanted Leonid along. Look at them: it's as if yesterday nothing had happened."

The distribution of the soup was over. In one corner of the cellar, Isidor, with Bella's scissors, was trimming the hair and beard of anybody who asked. His customers waited in line, seated on piles of bricks. Last in line was Gedaleh; to pass the time, he had produced his violin, and was scraping out a song, with a light hand so it wouldn't be heard outside. It was a comic song that they all knew, the one about the miraculous rabbi who makes a blind man run, a deaf man see, and a lame man hear, and in the last verse steps fully dressed into the water and emerges miraculously soaked. Isidor, though continuing his work, laughed and hummed with the music; Black Rokhele also sang in a low voice. She had asked Isidor to cut her hair short like Line's, and she was seated under his scissors at that moment.

"Gedaleh has many faces," Line said. "That's why it's hard to understand him; because there isn't just one Gedaleh. He flings everything behind him. Today's Gedaleh flings yesterday's Gedaleh behind him."

"He's flung Leonid behind him, too," Mendel said. "But why did he want Leonid to go on the mission at all costs, instead of Arie? Ever since yesterday I've been asking myself that."

"Maybe he meant well. He wanted to give Leonid a chance and thought that fighting would do him good, help him find himself again. Or he wanted to put him to the test."

"I think it was something else," Mendel said. "I think

that Gedaleh didn't know he wanted it, but it was something else he wanted. At the bottom of his consciousness he wanted to be rid of him. Before we set out, he almost told me."

"What did he tell you?"

"That for desperate missions you want desperate men."

Line was silent, gnawing her nails; then she asked: "Did Gedaleh know why Leonid was desperate?"

Mendel was also silent for a long time, then said, "I don't know if he knew. Probably he did; he must have guessed. Gedaleh finds out things by sniffing the air; he doesn't need evidence and doesn't have to ask questions." He had sat down on a block of rubble, and with his heel he was making drawings on the packed earth floor. Then he added: "It wasn't the German who killed Leonid, and not Gedaleh, either."

"Who then?"

"The two of us."

Line said, "Let's go and sing with the others."

Another three or four had collected around Gedaleh, and to the sound of the violin they sang other jolly songs, of weddings and of the tavern. Piotr tried to follow the rhythm and to imitate the harsh Yiddish aspiration, and he laughed like a child.

"I don't feel like singing," Mendel said. "I don't feel like anything. I don't know who Gedaleh is anymore, I don't know what I want or where I am, and perhaps I don't even know who I am anymore. Last night I dreamed somebody was asking me that, and I didn't know the answer."

"You mustn't take dreams too seriously," Line said curtly. At that moment, along the cone of rubble that descended from outside into the cellar, Izu, the Gorin' fisherman, came running down; he was on lookout duty.

"Are you all crazy? Or are you drunk? You can hear everything up above; are you really trying to call the police down on us?"

Gedaleh apologized, like a schoolboy caught in some mischief, and put his violin away. "Come here, everybody," he said. "We have two or three things to decide. In June I said to you that we aren't orphans or stray dogs anymore. I can confirm what I said; but we're changing masters, or, if you prefer, we're changing fathers. We're part of a huge family, fighting the Germans, from Norway to Greece. In this family there's some disagreement: there's much arguing about what's to be done after Hitler's hanged, where the borders will be, who gets the land and who gets the factories. In this family there's Josif Vissarionovich, yes, Arie's cousin. Maybe he's the first-born son, but he doesn't get along with Churchill on the question of what color to paint Poland; Stalin wants red; Churchill has another color in mind, and the Poles yet another: that is, they have maybe five or six different colors among them. Not all the Poles are like those clowns of the NSZ; they're good partisans, fighting the Germans, but they don't trust the Russians, and they don't trust us.

"We are few, and weak. The Russians aren't much interested anymore in what we do, now that we've crossed the border. They let us go on our way; but this way is exactly what we have to talk about."

"I'm not Stalin's cousin," Arie said, irritated. "We're just fellow countrymen. And for me there's only one way: shoot the Germans, as long as there are any left, and then go to the land of Israel and plant trees."

"I believe we all agree on that point," Gedaleh said. "Don't you, Dov? Well, I'm sorry; we'll talk about it later. What I wanted to tell you now is that we have support, or at least a compass, an arrow pointing out the way to us. In these woods we're not alone. There are men that everybody respects: the ones who fought in the ghettos, like us, in Warsaw, Vilna, in the Ninth Fort of Kovno, and those who had the strength to rebel against the Nazis at Treblinka and Sobibor. They're not scattered any more: they're organized into the ZOB, the Jewish Combat Organization, the first that has the courage to call itself that,

before the whole world, since Titus destroyed the Temple.
They're respected, but neither rich nor numerous; and the
fact that they're respected doesn't mean they're strong:
they have no forts or planes or cannons. They have few
weapons and little money, but with the little they have,
they've already helped us and they'll help us more. We'll
go on being independent, because we've earned our independence, but we'll pay attention to their suggestions.
The most important is this: our way goes through Italy.
When the front has passed us, if we're still alive, and if
we're still a band, we'll try to get to Italy, because Italy's
like a springboard. But that isn't to say our way will be
easy."

"When Hitler's dead, all ways will be easy," Jozek said.

"They'll be easier than now, but still not all that easy.
The English will hinder us as much as they can, because
they don't want trouble with the Arabs in Palestine; but
the Russians will help us, because in Palestine there are
the English, and Stalin is trying to weaken them every
possible way because he envies them their empire. Already
ships are leaving Italy illegally for the land of Israel; some
make it, others don't, and it isn't the Germans that stop
them: it's the English."

"And what if somebody tries to stop us?" Line asked.

"That's the point," Gedaleh said. "Nobody can say
when and how the war will end, but it could be that we'll
still need our weapons. It may be that this band, and
other bands like us, will have to keep on with the war
when all the rest of the world is at peace. That's why God
singled us out among all peoples, as our rabbis tell us.
That's what I had to say to you. Did you want to say
something, Dov? I've finished: speak up."

Dov was brief: "Passing the front in the midst of the
war is impossible, especially for a man alone; but if it were
possible, I would have done it already. I'll stay with the
rest of you as long as I can be useful, but when the Russians overtake us, I'll go with them. I was born in Siberia,
and I'll go back to Siberia; there the war hasn't arrived,

and my house will still be standing. Maybe I'll still have the strength to work, but I don't feel like fighting any more. And the Siberians don't say 'Jew' to you, and they don't force you to cry, 'Long live Stalin.' "

"You will do as you like, Dov," Gedaleh said. "Hitler's still alive, it's early to make certain decisions. And you're still useful to us. What do you want, Piotr?"

Piotr, to whom Gedaleh had entrusted the commando action against the *Lager,* and who had carried it out with intelligence and courage, stood up like a schoolboy being questioned; they all laughed, then he sat down again, and said, "I only wanted to know if in this land of Israel where you want to go, they'll take me, too."

"Of course they'll take you," Mottel said. "I'll give you a recommendation, and you won't have to change your name or get yourself circumcised. Gedaleh was joking, that night at the mill."

Pavel's great voice was heard: "You listen to me, Russian: the name doesn't matter, but get yourself circumcised. Take advantage of the opportunity. It isn't so much a question of the covenant with God: it's rather like apple trees. If they're pruned at the right moment, they grow up nice and straight and bear more apples." Black Rokhele let out a long, nervous laugh; Bella stood up, her face all red, and declared that she hadn't walked all these kilometers and run all these risks to hear this kind of talk. Piotr looked around, intimidated and bewildered.

Line spoke, grave, as always: "Of course they'll take you, even without Mottel's recommendation. But tell me something: why do you want to come?"

"Well," Piotr began, more embarrassed than ever, "there are lots of reasons . . ." He held up his hand, with the little finger extended, as the Russians do when they begin to count. "First of all . . ."

"First of all?" Dov encouraged him.

"First of all, I'm a believer," Piotr said, with the relief of someone who has found a good reason.

"Got, schenk mir an oysred," Mottel quoted, in Yiddish.

They all burst out laughing, and Piotr looked around, crossly.

"What did you say?" he asked Mottel.

"It's a saying of ours. It means: God, send me a good excuse. You surely don't want to persuade us you want to stay with us because you believe in Christ. You're a partisan and a Communist, and you don't look as if you believe in Christ all that much; and besides, we don't believe in Christ, and not all of us even believe in God."

Piotr the believer cursed fervently in Russian and went on: "You are all good at complicating things. Well, I don't know how to explain it to you, but that's how it is. I want to stay with you because I believe in Christ, and you can all go hang, with your quibbles." He stood up with an offended look, and strode towards the exit, as if he wanted to go away, but then he turned back: "And I have another ten reasons for staying with this bunch of fools. Because I want to see the world. Because I quarreled with Ulybin. Because I'm a deserter, and if they catch me again, I'll come to a nasty end. Because I've screwed your whore-mothers, and because . . ." At this point Dov was seen, running towards Piotr as if he wanted to attack him; but instead he embraced him, and the two men exchanged strong blows on the back with their fists.

9

September 1944–
January 1945

The front had stopped and summer was ending. The Polish earth, exhausted by five years of war and pitiless occupation, seemed to have returned to primordial Chaos. Warsaw had been destroyed: no longer just the ghetto, this time, but the entire city, and with it, the seed of a free and harmonious Poland. As the Poles had allowed the ghetto uprising in the spring of 1943 to die out, so now the Russians had allowed the rebellion of Warsaw to die, as it was prepared and directed by the Polish government in exile in London; let the Germans see to punishing the hotheads, on this occasion as on the previous one. And the Germans saw to it; routed by now on all the war fronts, they were victorious, on the contrary, on the internal fronts, in their daily war against the partisans and the helpless peoples.

From the capital swarms of refugees spread all through the country, without bread and without shelter, terrified by the German reprisals and their roundups. The Germans hungered not only for revenge, but also for manpower: peasants and city-dwellers, men and women, old and young, children, hastily rounded up on all sides, had been put to work at once, with spade and pick, to dig antitank trenches in the earth that was waiting to be plowed. Faithful to the Nazi destructive genius, squads of German troops dismantled and carried away anything that might have been useful to the advancing Red Army: tracks, cables, rolling stock; and trams, wood, iron, whole factories. The Polish partisans of the Interior Army, the old guard, who had fought the Germans since their 1939 blitz, the others who had chosen the life of the forests out of love for their lacerated country or out of fear of deportation, to the last escapees from dying Warsaw, continued fighting with desperate tenacity.

Gedaleh's band proceeded in slow stages, alternating their marches with cautious harassment actions. Gedaleh obtained money and ammunition fairly easily, but it became increasingly harder to trade the money for food. The virtually abandoned fields produced next to nothing, and what little the peasants possessed was periodically sacked by the requisitions of the Germans and by those, no less feared, of genuine partisans and of bandits who declared themselves partisans.

At the beginning of October, two of the Slonim men, who had gone ahead to spy out the land, brought back the news that on a siding at the Tunel station a freight train was standing, and probably it transported provisions. The train was long, so long that the last cars were inside the tunnel that gave the village its name; it was guarded only by some "blues," the Polish police. Gedaleh had the band make camp at about a kilometer away, beside the railroad line, and that night he went to the station with Mendel, Mottel, and Arie. There were only two blues, one far off at the head of the train, and the other at the tail; but the latter wasn't inside the tunnel. He stood at its mouth, where he couldn't see the last cars. Gedaleh told the other three to wait for him in silence, and he vanished into the darkness. He returned a few minutes later.

"No, Mottel, this time we don't need your handiwork. A bit of cash did the trick. Go, hurry back to Dov, and bring four strong men."

Mottel left, and returned in twenty minutes with Pavel and three others: eight men in all, nine, counting the blue finally, who helped them uncouple the last car. He had seen it loaded: it contained potatoes and forage turnips and was destined for the German command in Cracow. When the car was uncoupled, all nine put their shoulders to it and pushed, but the car wouldn't budge an inch. They tried again, as Gedaleh gave the order in a low voice, so their efforts would be simultaneous, but still nothing happened. "Wait," the blue whispered, and went off.

"Did you put a spell on him?" Mendel asked, with wonder.

"No," Gedaleh said. "Besides the money, I promised him some potatoes for his family, and I suggested he come with us. He lives here in the vicinity."

The Pole kept them waiting. Uneasily Gedaleh's eight men watched out for his return, in the bluish light of the blackout headlamps. Opposite the station a field was visible: on the ground lay some unfamiliar, roundish forms. Mottel, his curiosity aroused, went to see: they were pumpkins, nothing interesting or dangerous. The Pole came back silently, holding in his hand an instrument he called "the slipper." It was a long lever ending in a steel sole, wedge-shaped; when the lever was pressed, the sole rose a few millimeters. "It's used for pushing cars, in fact," he explained. "They have them in all the freight stations. You just have to budge them, then they move on their own." He bound the slipper with a rag so it wouldn't make any noise, thrust it under one of the wheels, and lowered the lever. The wagon budged, imperceptibly, then stopped.

"Good," Gedaleh murmured. "How long is the tunnel?"

"Six hundred meters. A little farther on, there's an intersection; to one side there's a sidetrack that crosses the woods and leads to an abandoned foundry. You'd do best to send the car on to the sidetrack: you can unload it and nobody will see you. Shall we go?"

But Gedaleh had something in mind. He sent four men to collect a dozen pumpkins, and he had them set in the pylons that supported the overhead power line that ran the train, one pumpkin to each pylon.

"What are they for?" Mendel asked.

"Nothing," Gedaleh said. "They're there to make the Germans wonder why they're there. We've wasted maybe two minutes; they're methodical, they'll waste a lot more."

The blue told them all to stand ready, and he resumed working with the slipper: "There. Now, push." The car moved again and went on, silent and very slow. "It'll go better afterwards," the Pole said. "The sideline is downhill." Gedaleh sent Arie on ahead, to alert the band that the car was on its way: they were to come towards it, along the siding, and be ready to unload.

"But there's ten tons!" Mottel said. "How will we manage to unload it all?"

Gedaleh didn't seem worried. "Somebody will help us. We'll only keep a part, and we'll give the rest to the peasants."

They came out of the tunnel and found themselves in a fog bank, through which the first daylight was filtering. From the fog they saw human forms emerge, six, twelve, more still: too many for the vanguard of the band. A strong voice shouted in Polish: "*Stoj!*": a dozen armed men, in uniform, were blocking the line. Exploiting the moment's surprise, the blue darted off and vanished into the fog; Gedaleh and the others did their best to restrain the course of the car, which still proceeded for another ten meters, until Mottel climbed into the cab and applied the hand brake. The same voice as before repeated "*Stoj!*", underlining the command with a brief volley of automatic fire, and then added: "*Ręce do gory!* Hands up!"

Gedaleh obeyed, and, after him, all the others: they were armed only with pistols and knives and had left their automatic arms with the main body of the band: there could be no thought of putting up any resistance.

A young man stepped forward, slim, with a serious look, regular features: he was wearing steel-rimmed eyeglasses. "Who's your leader?"

"I am," Gedaleh answered.

"Who are you? Where are you taking that car?"

"We're Jewish partisans; some Russian, some Polish. We come from far away. We've taken the car from the Germans."

"You'll have to prove that you're partisans. Anyway, we're in control of this zone."

"Who are you?"

"*Armia Krajowa*, the Polish Internal Army. Come with us. If you try to escape, we'll shoot."

"Lieutenant, we'll come with you and we won't run away; but in a little while the Germans will be here. Isn't it a pity to leave them a carload of potatoes?"

"The Germans won't come here. Not right away, at least. They're afraid of us. They attack us if they find us isolated, but they won't come into the woods. We'll take the car into the woods. What were you going to do with the potatoes?"

"Keep some for ourselves, and distribute the rest to the peasants."

"For the moment we'll take charge of them. Go on, keep pushing," Edek, the lieutenant, said; but he sent six of his men to help and to accelerate the progress of the car. During the march he fell in beside Gedaleh and asked further, "How many of you are there?"

"You can see for yourself: there're eight of us."

"That's not true," Edek said. "You were seen, some days ago, while you were on the march, and there are far more of you. You don't have to tell me lies; we have nothing against you, provided you don't trouble us. There are Jews in our force, too."

"There are thirty-eight of us," Gedaleh said. "About thirty are armed and able to fight. There are five women."

"Don't the women fight?"

"One woman fights, and one man—no, two—don't fight."

"Why?"

"One is too young and isn't very bright. The other is too old and was wounded."

Even if Gedaleh insisted on lying it would have been useless: the car's progress was silent, the fog had thickened, and the majority of the Gedalists, confidently advancing to meet Gedaleh, found themselves within sight of Edek's vanguard before they could try to hide. The Polish partisans (there were about a hundred) surrounded them and had them go on, with their arms and baggage; Gedaleh explained to Dov what had happened.

After an hour's walk they found themselves in the heart of the wood: Edek ordered them to halt: their quarters were not far. He sent a messenger, and quickly the unloading of the car was organized. Jews and Poles worked with a will, one sack per man, going back and forth between the car and the camp. The empty car was pushed to the abandoned factory, the sacks piled up in the camp storeroom, and all the Gedalists shut up in one of the half-buried wooden barracks that served as the base for Edek's unit. The Polish partisans were well armed, efficient, cold, and correct. They offered food to the Jews, but after that busy night, they wanted to sleep instead. The main body of the Polish platoon went out, armed, first thing in the morning; only some guards remained in the barracks, and the Gedalists were left in peace, the women on army cots, the men on clean straw. But "temporarily" they had to hand over their weapons, which were inventoried and stacked in another shed.

Edek and his men came back towards evening, and rations were distributed: a cereal soup, tins of beer, and tins of meat with labels in English.

"You're rich people," Dov said, with awe.

"This is stuff that comes by parachute," Edek said. "The Americans drop it but it comes from England; our government in London sends it. The Americans are always in a hurry and they drop the stuff hit-or-miss: they come from Brindisi, in Italy, and this is the limit of their range. They arrive, drop, and go off, so half the stuff ends up in the hands of the Germans; but there's always enough for us, because by now there aren't many of us left."

"Have a lot of your men been killed?" Mendel asked.

"Killed and missing, and others have got tired and gone home."

"Why do they go home? Aren't they afraid the Germans will deport them?"

"They're afraid, but they go off all the same. They don't know why we're fighting anymore, or for whom."

"And who are you fighting for, you personally?" Gedaleh asked.

"For Poland, for the freedom of Poland. But it's a desperate war. It's hard to fight like this."

"But Poland will be free, the Germans will leave, they've already lost, they're falling back on every front."

Through the eyeglasses, Edek trained his gaze on the three men talking with him: Dov, Mendel, and Gedaleh. He was considerably younger than they, but he seemed burdened by a weight that the others didn't know.

"Where are you going?" he asked finally.

"We're going a long way," Gedaleh answered. "We want to fight the Germans until the end of the war, and—who knows?—maybe even afterwards. Then we'll try to go away. We want to go to Palestine; in Europe there's no place for us anymore. Hitler's won the war against the Jews, and even his pupils have done a good job. Everybody has learned his gospel: Russians, Lithuanians, Croats, Slovaks." Gedaleh hesitated, then added, "Your people have also learned it; or perhaps you already knew it before. Tell me, Lieutenant: are we your guests or your prisoners?"

"Give me time," Edek answered, "soon I'll be able to give you a reply. But I wanted to tell you, in the meantime, that the pumpkins were a good idea."

"How do you know about the pumpkins?"

"We have friends everywhere around here. We also have friends among the railroad men, and they tell us that so far the Germans of the garrison haven't dared touch the pumpkins. They've blocked the line and have brought in a team of mine detectors from Cracow. They're more worried about the pumpkins than about the car you stole."

He opened two packs of Lucky Strikes and offered the cigarettes to everybody, to the admiring wonder of the Gedalists; then he went on: "You mustn't be unjust, even if some Poles have been unjust to you. Not all of us have been your enemies."

"Not all, but many," Gedaleh said.

Edek sighed. "Poland's a sad country. It's a country that has always been unhappy, crushed by neighbors that were too powerful. It's hard to be unhappy and not hate, and we've hated everybody for all the centuries of our servitude and our partition. We've hated the Russians, the Germans, the Czechs, the Lithuanians, and the Ukrainians; we've hated your people, too, because you had scattered over our country but didn't want to become like us, dissolve in us, and we didn't understand you. We began to understand you when you rose up in Warsaw. You showed us the way; you taught us that even in desperation, people can fight."

"But it was late by then," Gedaleh said. "We were all dead."

"It was late. But now you are richer than we are: you know where to go. You have a destination and a hope."

"Why shouldn't you Poles hope, too?" Dov asked. "The war will end, and we'll build a new world, without slavery and without injustice."

Edek said: "The war will never end. From this war, another war will be born, and there will always be war. The

Americans and the Russians will never be friends, and Poland has no friends, even if the Allies now are helping us. The Russians would prefer for us not to exist, never to have been created. The Germans, when they invaded us in nineteen thirty-nine, immediately deported and killed our professors, writers, and priests; but the Russians, advancing from their border, did the same, and what's more, they handed over to the Gestapo any Polish Communists who hadn't taken refuge in Russia. They didn't want Poland to have a soul, neither side did; they didn't want it when they were allies; and they don't want it now, either, when they are enemies. The Russians were glad that the Warsaw uprising failed and that the Germans exterminated the rebels: while we were dying, they were waiting on the other bank of the river."

Dov spoke up: "Lieutenant, I'm Russian. A Jew, but Russian, and many of us were born in Russia, and that tall boy you see over there is a Russian Christian who is following our way. This one"—and he pointed to Mendel—"and many others who are dead were soldiers in the Red Army: I was, too. Before beginning our journey, we fought as Russians first and as Jews second: as Russians for the Russians. It's the Russians who are liberating Europe. They are paying with their blood, they died by the millions, and the things you are saying seem unfair to me. I myself, who was tired and wounded, was treated in Kiev, and then the Russians brought me back to my companions."

"The Russians will drive the Nazis out of our country," Edek said, "but then they won't go away. You mustn't confuse wishes with reality; Stalin's Russia is the czar's Russia: it wants a Russian Poland, not a Polish Poland. That's why our war is desperate: we have to defend ourselves and the people from the Nazis, but we also have to look over our shoulder, because the advancing Russians don't want to hear of any *Armia Krajowa*. When they find us, they stick us into their units, here and there; if we refuse, they disarm us and deport us to Siberia."

"And why do you refuse?" Dov asked.

"Because we're Poles. Because we want to show the world we still exist. If necessary, we'll show it by dying."

Mendel looked at Dov, and Dov returned the look. Both had remembered the sentence Dov had shouted at Mendel at Novoselki, in the midst of the fighting: we're fighting for three lines in the history books. Mendel told the story to Edek, and Edek answered: "It's stupid to be enemies."

Several days went by during which Edek tried in vain to establish contact with his superiors and get instructions about what was to be done. The Poles had a radio transmitter, modern and powerful, but they used it very little: after the fall of Warsaw, the *Armia Krajowa* was in a critical state, more for reasons of morale than for any material reason; contacts were destroyed, one after the other, and many of the leaders were dead or were being held by the Russians. Finally a messenger came back, and Edek, with a wan smile, said to Gedaleh, "Everything's all right. You're guests, not prisoners; and soon you'll become allies, if you want."

Edek was a medical student, twenty-three years old. He had barely enrolled in the first year, at Cracow, in 1939, when the Germans called an assembly of the entire academic body. Some teachers had got a whiff of the deceit and hadn't turned up; all the others had immediately been deported to Sachsenhausen. "Then all of us, professors and students, began to organize a secret university, because we didn't want Polish culture to die. In the same way, during those years we had a government, a church, and an army, all secret: all of Poland was living underground. I studied, and at the same time I worked in an underground printing shop; but even to study I had to go into hiding. Hitler and Himmler had decided that for the Poles four years of elementary school would be enough, they only had to learn how to count to five hundred and sign their name; it was pointless for them to learn really to read and write; in fact, it was harmful. So my schoolmates and I studied anatomy and physiology out of books, never seeing a microscope, not even from a distance, never dissecting a corpse, never visiting a hospital ward. But in Warsaw, in August, I was there, too, I saw more sick and wounded and dead than an army doctor has seen by the end of his career."

"Not bad," Gedaleh said to him, "you had the practical part before the theoretical. We learn to walk and to talk by practice, isn't that right? Peace will come, and you'll become a famous doctor, I'm sure of that." The undiscriminating friendliness that Gedaleh displayed towards all human beings seemed multiplied by ten in the case of Edek. Mendel asked him why, and Gedaleh answered that he didn't know. But then he thought again: "Maybe it's the novelty. It's been a long time since I came across anybody with a necktie and a pen in his breast pocket. There weren't any like that in the forest."

"But Edek doesn't wear a tie!"

"In spirit, he does. Everything is as if he did."

They spent the long evenings of rain and waiting in conversation, smoking; sometimes Gedaleh also played the violin. But in the Poles' camp there was no drinking: Edek was a human and reasonable commander, but on some matters he was strict, and he had a number of little fixations. After a brawl that had been caused some months earlier by a drunken hanger-on, Edek had forbidden alcohol, and he insisted on this veto with a puritan's severity. He had asked Gedaleh to do the same with his men, so they wouldn't set a bad example, and Gedaleh had reluctantly agreed. Edek was also afraid of dogs. He wanted nothing to do with the two poor Gedalist dogs, the ones who had led the band among the mines of Turov and who knew the Gedalists individually. Edek hit on the excuse that the dogs might reveal the position of the camp by barking at night, and in spite of Gedaleh's protest he had them sold in a nearby village.

Edek was reserved and asked few questions, but he, too,

was curious about the Gedalists, and especially about Gedaleh and his past.

"Eh, who knows what a great violinist I would have become!" Gedaleh said, laughing. "My father was very serious about it: the violin, he used to say, doesn't take up much room, whatever happens you can take it with you everywhere; and talent takes up even less room and there's no duty on it. You can tour the world, give concerts, and make money; and maybe even become an American, like Jascha Heifetz. I liked playing, but not studying; instead of going to my music lessons I would run off to go ice skating in the winter or swimming in the summer. My father was a little merchant, in 'twenty-three he went bankrupt, so he began to drink, and he died when I was only twelve. We didn't have any money, and my mother put me in a shop; I was clerk in a shoestore, but I went on playing, just to console myself, after I had spent the whole day with the customers' feet in my hands. I used to write poems, too: sad, and not very good. I would dedicate them to the lady customers who had pretty feet; but then I lost all of them.

"Playing has always kept me company. I would play instead of think; in fact, I must say that thinking has never been my strong suit: I mean thinking seriously, arriving at conclusions from premises. Playing was my way of thinking; and even now, when I'm in a different line of work, well, my best ideas come to me when I play the violin."

"The idea of the pumpkins, for example?" Edek asked.

"No, no," Gedaleh answered modestly. "I got the idea of the pumpkins when I was looking at the pumpkins."

"And how did you get this idea of taking up your new line of work?"

"It came to me from heaven: a nun brought it to me." As he was speaking, Gedaleh took up his violin; and without actually playing it, he stroked the strings with the bow, drawing idle and subdued notes from it. "Yes, a nun. When the Germans came to Bialystok, my mother managed to get herself taken in by a convent. At the beginning

I was against being shut in; I was going with a girl, I slept every night in a different place. I must say: by that time I was already twenty-four, but I lived as if I were asleep, from day to day, the way an animal would. I didn't realize anything, the danger or my duty.

"Then the Germans sealed the Jews into the ghetto. My mother sent word that the convent would take me, too, so I went. My mother was Russian; a strong woman, she knew how to take command, and I liked having her command me. No, I didn't have to dress as a nun; the nuns hid me under a stairway. They didn't try to baptize me, they housed us out of compassion, with no ulterior purpose, and at risk to themselves. They brought me food, and I was getting along fine in the convent: I wasn't a warrior, I was a twenty-four-year-old child good for selling shoes and playing the violin. I would have waited under the stairs till the end of the war: the war was other people's business, the Germans' and the Russians'; it was like a hurricane, when a hurricane comes, sensible people look for shelter.

"The nun who brought me food was young and good humored, the way nuns are good humored. One day, it was March of 'forty-three, along with my bread she handed me a note: it came from the ghetto, it was written in Yiddish, was signed by a friend of mine, and it said: Come join us, your place is here. It said that the Germans had begun deporting the children and the sick from the ghetto to Treblinka, and soon they would wipe out everybody, and it was time to prepare some resistance. While I was reading, the nun was looking at me with a very serious expression, and I realized that she knew what was written there. Then she asked me if there was any answer: I told her I would think about it; and the next day I asked her how she got the note. She answered that in the ghetto there were a number of baptized Jews, and the sisters had been given permission to take medicines to them. I told her I was ready to go, and she said I should wait till night. She came before matins and told me to follow her; she led me to a storeroom, carrying a lantern in her hand. She gave it to me to hold and said, "Turn your back, Panie." I heard her habit rustling and some profane thoughts cme to me; then she allowed me to turn around; and she gave me two pistols. She gave me the contacts to get into the ghetto and wished me good luck. In the ghetto the armed young men were few, but determined: they had learned how a gun was made from an encyclopedia, and they learned to shoot on the spot. We fought together for eight days; there were two hundred of us. Nearly all died. Five others and I opened the road as far as Kossovo and we joined up with the rebels in the ghetto there."

The group around Edek and Gedaleh had gradually been increasing. Not only the Poles, but also a number of the Jews had listened to that story that not all of them knew. When Gedaleh had finished, Edek uncrossed his legs, sat erect on the stool, smoothed his hair, pulled at his trousers and asked stiffly, "What are your political opinions?"

Gedaleh drew from the violin the equivalent of a burst of laughter. "Speckled and spotted and brown, like the sheep of Laban!" He looked around: at the table, in the harsh light of the carbide lamp, mixed with the broad, blond faces of the Poles, he pointed out to the lieutenant the Caucasian mustache of Arie; the white, well-combed mane of Dov; Jozek, with his sly eyes; Line, fragile and taut; Mendel, with the weary, haggard face; Pavel, half shaman and half gladiator; the savage faces of the men of Ruzhany and Blizna; Isidor and the two Rokheles, asleep on their feet. "As you see, we're assorted goods."

Then he picked up his violin and continued: "All joking aside, Lieutenant, I understand the reason for your question, but I feel some embarrassment in answering it. We're not orthodox, we're not regular, we're not bound by oath. None of us has much time to meditate and clarify his ideas; each of us has a grim past behind him, different for each. Those of us who were born in Russia sucked communism with their mother's milk: yes, their mothers, and their fathers made Bolsheviks of them, because the October Revolution had emancipated the Jews, made them citizens with full rights. In their way they've remained Communists, but none of us loves Stalin anymore, not since he signed the pact with Hitler; and for that matter Stalin has never loved us much.

"As for me, and the others who were born in Poland, our ideas vary, but we have something in common, we and the Russian Jews. All of us, some more and some less, some sooner and some later, have felt like foreigners in our own country. We've all wanted a different homeland, where we won't feel like intruders or be pointed at as outsiders; but none of us has ever thought of fencing off a field and saying, 'This land is mine.' We don't want to become landowners: we want to make fertile the sterile land of Palestine, plant orange trees and olive trees in the desert and make it fruitful. We don't want Stalin's kolkhozes: we want communities where all are free and equal, without force and without violence, where you can work during the day and, in the evening, play the violin; where there's no money, but everybody does what work he can and is given what he needs. It sounds like a dream, but it isn't: this world has already been created by our brothers, more farsighted and courageous than us, who emigrated down there before Europe became a *Lager*.

"In this sense you could call us Socialists, but we didn't become partisans because of our political beliefs. We're fighting to save ourselves from the Germans, to get revenge, to clear the way for ourselves; but most of all—and excuse the solemn word—for dignity. And finally I have to say this to you: many of this bunch had never enjoyed the taste of freedom, and they learned it here, in the forests, in the marshes and in danger, along with adventure and fraternity."

"And you're one of them, isn't that right?"

"I'm one of them, and I don't regret anything, not even the friends I've seen die. If I hadn't found this job, maybe I would have remained a child: now I'd be a twenty-seven-year-old child, and at the end of the war, if I were saved, I would have started writing poems again and selling shoes."

"Or you would have become a famous violinist."

"That's difficult," Gedaleh said. "A child doesn't become a violinist. Or if he does, he remains a child-violinist."

Edek, who was twenty-three, looked gravely at Gedaleh, who was twenty-seven. "Are you sure you haven't remained a bit of a child?"

Gedaleh set down the violin. "Not always. Only when I want. Not here."

"Who do you take orders from?" Edek asked further.

"We're an autonomous group, but we follow the suggestions of the Jewish Combat Organization, when and where we manage to maintain contact, and their instructions are these: destroy German lines of communication, kill the Nazis responsible for the slaughter, move westwards, and avoid contacts with the Russians, because though they've helped us so far, that doesn't mean they'll want to help us in the future."

Edek said: "That suits us, too."

The war seemed far away. For several weeks it had rained uninterruptedly, and the Poles' camp was besieged by mud; but also at the front it seemed that operations were suspended. The rumble of artillery could no longer be heard, even the hum of planes was heard rarely: unknown planes, unreal, perhaps friendly, perhaps hostile, inaccessible in their secret routes above the clouds. There had been no more drops, and food was beginning to grow scarce.

At the beginning of November, the rain let up, and a little later Edek received a radioed message. It was a request for help, urgent, from headquarters in the Mountains of the Holy Cross, eighty kilometers to the northeast; an *Armia Krajowa* company had been surrounded by the Wehrmacht, and their situation was desperate. Edek's men were to set out at once to lend a hand. He ordered seventy of his platoon to prepare themselves; and as Gedaleh, a long year before, had invited Dov to a dire hunting party, now Edek invited Gedaleh and his band to take part in the expedition. Gedaleh accepted at once, but not gladly: it was the first time that his men and he were asked to face the Germans in the open; not to harass an isolated garrison, as in Lyuban in April, but to fight against the German infantry and artillery, with all their experience and organization: and yet even at Lyuban the Jews had been killed by the dozen. On the other hand, this time they weren't alone: Edek's Poles were resolute, expert, well armed, and driven by a hatred of the Germans that surpassed even the Jews' hatred of them.

Gedaleh chose twenty of his people, and the mixed platoon set off. The fields were soaked with rain. Edek was in a hurry, and he chose the most direct route, against every partisan orthodoxy: they marched along the railroad, in threes, on the wooden ties from sunset to dawn, and even past dawn. No patrols protecting the flanks of the column, no rear guard: a vanguard of only six men, which included Mendel, as well as Edek himself. Mendel was amazed at the temerity of the behavior, but Edek reassured him: he knew this country, the peasants wouldn't turn them in, they were favorable to the partisans and anyone who wasn't favorable feared their reprisals.

On November 16th they came within sight of Kielce: at Kielce there was a German barracks full of Ukrainian auxiliaries, and Edek was forced to give the city a wide berth, losing valuable time. Just beyond it, they encountered the first rolling country: grim, wooded hills, striped by bands of fog, which drifted slowly in the wind, shredding at the tops of the firs. According to the information Edek had received, the battlefield should be close, in the valley between Gorno and Bieliny, but they found no trace of battle. Edek ordered them all to rest for a few hours, until first light.

At first light the fog had thickened. Some isolated shots

were heard, brief volleys of machine-gun fire, then silence, and in the silence the voice of a loudspeaker. It was faint; it came from a distance, probably from the other side of the encirclement. They could hardly make it out; the words came in patches, at the whim of the wind: they were Polish words, the Germans were urging the Poles to surrender. Then the shooting was resumed, weak and scattered: Edek gave orders to advance.

Halfway up the slope, they positioned themselves behind the bushes and trees and opened fire in the direction where they presumed the Germans were. It was a blind battle; the fog was so thick that, strictly speaking, it would have been superfluous to take cover, but precisely because of this veil that surrounded them and limited visibility to about twenty meters, the feeling of danger was all the more acute: the offensive could come from any side. The Germans' reaction was angry, but brief, and ill coordinated: a heavy machine gun opened fire, then a second, both to the left of Edek's deployment. Mendel saw bark ripped off the trees in front of him, sought cover, and fired his submachine gun in the direction the volley seemed to have come from. Edek ordered a second round, longer: perhaps he wanted to give the Germans the impression that the unit that had arrived was stronger, but it was a waste of bullets. A few minutes later outgoing artillery rounds were heard; these, too, distant and to the left, and a little later the incoming shells: they fell at random, before and behind; these were closer, one fell not far from Mendel, but it burrowed into the soft earth, without exploding; another landed to his right; Mendel saw the flash through the curtain of fog. He ran there and found Marian, Edek's second-in-command, on the spot: the shell had cut down a little tree, and two dead Poles lay in the turned earth. "They're not firing from above," Marian said, "they're on the Gorno road. There can't be that many of them."

The shelling stopped abruptly, there were no more shots, and around ten they heard a muffled hum of engines.

"They're going off!" Marian said.

"Maybe they think we're stronger than we are," Mendel answered.

"I don't believe so. But they don't like the fog either." The hum of the German vehicles became fainter, until it died away. Edek ordered them to advance in silence. From tree to tree, the men began climbing up, encountering no resistance and no sign of life. A bit higher, the trees thinned out, then disappeared: the fog, too, had lifted, and the battlefield became visible. The top of the hill was a bare heath, furrowed by traces of paths and by a single dirt road that led to a massive building, perhaps an old fortress. The ground was full of bodies, some already cold and stiff, many mutilated or torn by horrible wounds. Not all were Poles of the *Armia Krajowa*: one compact group, which must have held out to the end, was made up of Russian partisans; others, at the edges of the field, belonged to the Wehrmacht.

"They're all dead. I can't understand who they were asking to surrender," Gedaleh said: without realizing it, he was speaking in a low voice, as if they were in church.

"I don't know," Edek answered. "Perhaps the shots we heard coming were fired by the last who remained."

Mendel said, "The fog was very thick before, and they were asking the dead to surrender."

"Maybe," Marian said, "the loudspeaker's words were on a record: the Germans have done that before."

They explored the ground, examining the bodies one by one: someone might perhaps be still alive. No one was alive; some showed the sign of the coup de grace at their temple or nape. Even inside the fort there were only dead men, Russians and Poles, mostly shut up inside the tower, which had been shattered by an artillery shell. They noticed that some of the corpses were extremely thin. Why?

"Then the rumor is true," Marian said.

"What rumor?" Mendel asked.

"That on the Mountains of the Holy Cross there was a prison, and the Germans starved the prisoners to death." In fact, in the cellars of the fort they found corridors and cells, whose wooden doors had been stove in. Mendel found words scrawled on a wall with charcoal, and he called Edek to decipher them.

"They are verses by a poet of ours," Edek said. "They say:

> Mary, don't give birth to Poland,
> Unless you want to see your son
> Nailed to a cross the moment he's born."

"When did he write these words, this poet?" Gedaleh asked.

"I don't know. But for my country, any century would have done."

Mendel was silent, and he felt himself filled with confused, boundless thoughts. Not only us. The sea of grief has no shores, no bottom; no one can sound its depths. Here they are, the Poles, the fanatics of the cross, those who knifed our fathers and who invaded Russia to stifle the Revolution. And Edek, too, is Polish. And now they are dying like us, with us. They've paid: aren't you pleased? No, I'm not pleased, the debt hasn't been reduced, it's grown, nobody will ever be able to pay it now. I wish that nobody would die anymore. Not even the Germans? I don't know. I'll think about it afterwards, when it's all over. Maybe killing Germans is like when a surgeon performs an operation: cutting off an arm is horrible, but it has to be done and it is done. Let the war end, Lord, in whom I don't believe. If you exist, make the war end. Quickly and everywhere. Hitler is already defeated; these dead are no use to anybody any more.

Beside him, standing as he was, in the heather stained with blood and soaked with rain, Edek, his face ashen, was looking at him.

"Are you praying, Jew?" he asked, but on Edek's lips the word *Jew* had no venom. Why? Because everybody is somebody else's Jew, because the Poles are the Jews of the Germans and the Russians. Because Edek is a gentle man who has learned to fight; he has chosen as I did and he's my brother, even if he's a Pole and is educated, and I am a village Russian and a Jewish watchmender.

Mendel didn't answer Edek's question, and Edek went on: "You should. I should, too, and I can't anymore. I don't believe it does any good, for me or for the others. Maybe you'll live and I'll die, and then tell what you have seen on the Mountains of the Holy Cross. Try to understand, tell, and try to make others understand. These men who died with us are Russians, but the Russians are also the ones who tear the guns from our hands. Tell it, you who still await the Messiah: maybe he will come for you, but for the Poles he came in vain."

It really seemed that Edek was answering the questions that Mendel was asking himself, that he read in the depths of Mendel's brain, in that secret bed where thoughts are born. But it isn't so strange, Mendel thought; two good clocks mark the same hour, even if they are of different make. They only have to start together.

Edek and Gedaleh called the roll; four of the Poles were missing, and one of the Jews, Jozek the counterfeiter. He hadn't died a counterfeiter's death. They found him at the bottom of a gully, his belly ripped open: perhaps he had called at length and nobody had heard him. Bury the dead? "All or none," said Edek, "and all is impossible. We'll just collect the papers and the tags, from those who have them." Many young boys were without documents; and Edek and Marian recognized them as members of the Polish Peasant Battalions. They went back to the camp in silence, their heads bowed, like a defeated army. There was no hurry now, and they proceeded in open order, at night, through fields and woods. In the Sobkow wood they realized they had lost their bearings: the only compass the platoon possessed had remained in the pocket of Zbigniew, one of the dead Poles: nobody had remembered to salvage it. Reluctantly, Edek decided to wait till dawn, and then follow one of the trails to some village; they would ask directions of the peasants. But in the foggy dawn, among the roots of an ash tree, Arie found a half-frozen bird, and it, he said, would show them the way. Arie picked the bird up, warmed it holding it under his shirt against his chest, handed it some breadcrumbs he had softened with saliva, and when the bird had perked up, he let it fly away. The bird vanished into the fog in a clearly defined direction, without hesitation. "Is that south?" Marian asked. "No," Arie answered, "it was a starling, and starlings, when winter comes, fly to the west." "I'd like to be a starling," Mottel said. They reached the camp without any mistakes, and Arie gained prestige.

Weeks of inertia and tension followed. The cold had begun, and the frost had hardened the mud, and all the roads, large and small, had filled with German convoys heading for the front or returning towards the rear of the lines. Motorized artillery units went by, Tiger tanks already camouflaged in white, in expectation of the snow, German troops in armored trucks, Ukrainian auxiliaries in wagons or on foot. There were military police or Gestapo offices in all the villages, and the partisans' contacts had become more difficult. German patrols stopped all young men and sent them to dig tank traps, make embankments and trenches: scouts, men and women, moved only at night. The only communication route between Edek's unit and the outside world was the radio, but the radio was silent, or broadcast disturbing, contradictory news.

Radio London was triumphant and sarcastic. It assumed the Germans and the Japanese were defeated, but at the same time it admitted that the Germans had attacked in strength in the Ardennes. Where was the Ardennes? Is it going to start all over again, with the Germans spreading out in France? The German Radio was triumphant too; the Führer was invincible, the real war was only just beginning, the great Reich possessed new, secret, total weapons against which there was no defense.

Christmas went by; and New Year's, 1945. In the Polish

camp uncertainty and dejection, the partisans' two great
enemies, were increasing. Edek felt abandoned: he received no orders or information; he no longer knew who
there was around him. Some of his men had vanished;
they had gone off, just like that, in silence, with their
weapons or without. Inside the camp, too, discipline had
relaxed; quarrels sprang up and often degenerated into
brawling. For the moment, there wasn't any friction between Poles and Jews, but hints and sidelong glances indicated it was imminent. Despite Edek's orders, vodka
had reappeared, first hidden, then in broad daylight. Lice
had also spread: a bad sign: combatting them wasn't easy,
there was no powder, no medicines, and Edek didn't know
what measures to take. Marian, sanguine and taurine,
formerly top sergeant in the Polish army, held a public
demonstration: he kindled a little wood fire inside one of
the barracks, on a sheet of metal, and showed how to hang
your clothes at a certain distance from the flames: the lice
explode without harming the cloth. But it was a vicious
circle: lice are born from demoralization, and they create
further demoralization.

Line separated from Mendel. It was sad, like all part-
ings, but it didn't surprise anyone: it had been in the air
for a long time, ever since the attack on the Chmielnik
Lager. Mendel suffered, but his suffering was gray and
slack, without the stab of despair. Line had never been his,
except in the flesh, nor had Mendel been hers. They had
sated themselves with each other, often, in pleasure and
rage, but they had spoken little, and almost always their
talk had been impeded by incomprehension or discord.
Line never had doubts, and couldn't put up with Mendel's doubts: when they surfaced (and they surfaced always at the moment of fatigue and of truth, when their
bodies were detached from each other), Line turned
harsh, and Mendel was afraid of her. He was also, ob-
scurely, ashamed of himself, and it's difficult to love a
woman who inspires shame and fear in you. In confusion,
vaguely, Mendel felt that Line was right. No, it was not
that she was right; she lived in rightness, on the side of the

right. A partisan, Jew or Russian or Pole, a combatant must be like Line, not like Mendel. He mustn't doubt: your doubt turns up in the sight of the gun, and it spoils your aim worse than fear. That was it: Line killed Leonid and doesn't suffer. She would kill me, too, if I were skinless the way he was: if I didn't have a callused hide on me, an armor. Not gleaming and resonant, but opaque and resistant; blows strike me, but are blunted. They dent but don't wound. And yet Line reawakened his desire, and Mendel was wounded when he learned that Line was Marian's woman. Wounded, and at the same time, offended, and maliciously content and hypocritically indignant. So she was a *shiksa*, who goes with everyone, even with Poles. Shame, Mendel, this isn't why you became a partisan. A Pole is as good as you are; in fact, better than you, since Line prefers Marian. Rivke wouldn't have done it. True, she wouldn't have done it, but Rivke doesn't exist anymore, Rivke is in Strelka under a meter of lime and a meter of earth, Rivke is not of this world. She belonged to order, to the world of the right things done at the right time: she cooked and kept the house clean, because in those days men and women lived in a house. She kept accounts, including mine, and encouraged me when I needed it: she gave me courage even on the day the war broke out and I left for the front. She didn't wash that much, modern girls in Strelka washed more than she did, she bathed once a month, as is written, but we were one flesh. She was a *ballebusteh*: a queen of the house. She commanded, and I wasn't aware of it.

With a slothful eye, Mendel watched other bonds form in the camp, distracted and ephemeral. Sissl and Arie: fine, good for them, in gaiety and health; let's hope that he doesn't beat her, the Georgians beat their wives, and Arie is more Georgian than Jew. They have solid bones, and not only their bones: they will make handsome babies, good *chalutzim*, good settlers for the land of Israel, if we ever get there. Let's hope that no Pole looks too close at Sissl, because Arie is fast with his knife.

Black Rokhele and Piotr. This, too, was fine: it had been ripening for quite a while. Among the Poles, Piotr was even more isolated than the Jews, and a woman is the best remedy for loneliness. Or even half a woman: the situation wasn't clear, and for that matter Mendel didn't feel like investigating, but it seemed that Black R. also had Mietek, the radio operator, tailing after her. Too bad for Edek; more than all the others, Edek would have needed a woman, some company, someone to share his suffering: but Edek, on the contrary, tried to isolate himself, to dig a hollow, to build a wall between himself and the world.

Bella and Gedaleh: about this couple nobody had a word to say. They had been a couple forever, an incredibly steady couple, though the reason wasn't clear. Gedaleh, so free in words and deeds, so unpredictable, seemed bound to Bella by a now firm anchorage, like a ship tied up at the dock. Bella was not beautiful, she seemed considerably older than Gedaleh, she didn't fight, she took part in the band's daily jobs lazily, reluctantly, criticizing the others (especially the women), rightly or wrongly. She carried with her incongruous remnants of her previous, bourgeois life, of which no one knew anything; awkward leftovers, encumbering even physically, habits that all had given up and that Bella had no intention of giving up. It often happened, almost ritually, that Gedaleh would get carried away by an idea, a plan, or even simply a farfetched, lighthearted story, and Bella would bring him back to earth again with a flat, trite remark. Then Gedaleh would address her with simulated irritation, as if the two were play-acting: "Bella, why do you clip my wings?" After almost eight months of living together, and after so many shared experiences, Mendel never stopped wondering what kept Gedaleh bound to Bella: for that matter, Gedaleh was hard to interpret not only in this respect, and his actions were impossible to predict. Perhaps Gedaleh knew he had no brakes, and he needed to find some outside himself; perhaps he felt beside him, embodied in Bella, the virtues and joys of peacetime: security, common sense, economy, convenience. Modest, faded joys, but everyone, consciously or not, regretted them and hoped to find them again, at the end of the slaughter and the way.

Gedaleh was restless, but he hadn't given in to the backwash that, beginning with the Poles, had swept with it to a greater or lesser degree also the Gedalists. He reminded Mendel of the starling that Arie had found: like that bird, he was impatient to resume his way. He roamed around the camp, he tormented the radio operator, he argued with Edek, with Dov, with Line, with Mendel himself. He still played the violin, but no longer with abandon: according to the moment, with ennui or with frenzy.

White Rokhele was neither restless nor disheartened. She was no longer alone: ever since the band had found refuge in the Polish camp, it was unusual to come upon her separated from Isidor. At the beginning no one was amazed; Isidor tended to get into trouble, or at least to behave foolishly, and it seemed only natural that White R. should act a bit as his mama. Before, Sissl had looked after Isidor, and in fact, between the two women a hint of rivalry had arisen, but now Sissl had other things on her mind. As for White R. herself, she seemed to need someone who needed her. She kept her eyes on the boy, made sure he dressed up warmly and washed regularly, and when necessary she scolded him, with maternal authority.

Now, since the beginning of December, both the couple and the relationship between them had undergone a change, hard to define but clear to all. Isidor spoke less and better; he no longer raved of impossible vendettas, no longer carried the knife in his belt, and instead had asked Edek and Gedaleh to let him take part in target practice. His gaze had become more alert, he tried to make himself useful, his stride had become quicker and more confident; and even his shoulders seemed to have broadened slightly. He asked questions: few, but not futile or childish. As for Rokhele, she seemed at once more mature and more youthful. Or rather, whereas, before, she had no age, now she did; it was surprising, cheering to see her return, day by day, to her age of twenty-six, till then repressed by shyness and mourning. She no longer kept her eyes on the ground, and all realized that her eyes were beautiful: big, brown, affectionate. Elegant she wasn't, to be sure (none of the five women was), but she was no longer a shapeless bundle; she could be seen, in the lantern light, using her needle to alter the army clothes that for months she had worn without paying attention, now making them suit her size. Now, White R. also had hair, legs, a bosom, a body. When you came upon the couple together, among the camp buildings, Isidor no longer walked behind White Rokhele, but at her side; taller than she, he bent his head very slightly in the woman's direction, as if to protect her.

One evening when Isidor was on duty cleaning up, White R. called Mendel aside: she wanted to speak to him in confidence.

"What is it, Rokhele? What can I do for you?" Mendel asked.

"You must marry us," White R. said, blushing.

Mendel opened his mouth, then shut it, and said, "What are you thinking of? I'm not a rabbi, or even a mayor; you don't have any papers, you could even be married already. And Isidor is only seventeen. And does this seem to you a time to get married?"

White R. said: "I know very well that this isn't the regulation. I know there are difficulties. But age doesn't count: a man can marry at the age of thirteen, the Talmud says so. And I'm a widow, as everybody knows."

Mendel couldn't find any words. "It's nonsense, a *narishkeit*! A whim, and tomorrow you'll get over it. And why did you come to me particularly? On top of everything else, I'm not even a devout Jew. It makes no sense: it's as if you asked me to fly or cast a spell."

"I've come to you because you're a just man, and because I'm living in sin."

"If you're living in sin, there's nothing I can do about it: that's something that concerns the two of you. And besides, in my opinion sins aren't what you two are doing, they're something else, they're what the Germans are doing. And whether or not I'm so just remains to be seen."

Rokhele wouldn't give up. "It's like when people are on a ship or an island: if there's no rabbi, anybody can perform the marriage. If he's a just man, that's better; but anybody is good enough to do it. In fact, he must do it. It's a *mitzvah*."

Mendel drew on memories that had been dormant for centuries: "For a marriage to be valid you need the *ketubah*, the contract: you must pledge yourself to give Isidor a dowry; and he has to guarantee that he can support you. Support you? Him? Isidor? Does that seem serious to you?"

"The *ketubah* is a formality, but marriage is something serious; and Isidor and I love each other."

"Let me think it over at least till tomorrow. This is a business that doesn't cost me any effort or money, but it seems a fraud to me: it's as if you said to me: Dear Mendel, deceive me. You understand me? And if I do what you ask, I'm the one commiting the sin. Couldn't you wait till the war ends? You'd find a rabbi, and you could do the thing properly. I wouldn't even know what words to say: they have to be said in Hebrew, don't they? I've forgotten my Hebrew, and if I get it wrong, you'll believe you're a bride and instead you'll remain single."

"I'll dictate the words to you, and it doesn't matter if they're in Hebrew or not: any language will do, the Lord understands them all."

"I don't believe in the Lord," Mendel said.

"That doesn't matter. It's enough for Isidor and me to believe in him."

"Well, I just don't understand why you're in such a hurry."

White R. said: "I'm pregnant."

The next day Mendel reported the conversation to Gedaleh. He expected the chief to burst out laughing, but Gedaleh, very grave, answered that Mendel had to accept, of course. "I must tell you: I have something to do with this. Isidor had never been with a woman. He told me some time ago, one day when I was teasing him a bit: it was the day of the windmill. I saw that he was suffering; he told me he'd never had the courage. He was only thirteen when he had to hide under the barn, he was there four years, then you know what happened. 'He has to be helped,' I thought; in a sense it seemed to me a *mitzvah*, and in another sense the experiment made me curious. So I talked about it with Rokhele, who had also been left alone, and I suggested she look after him. And she looked after him. But I never believed the business would proceed so quickly and turn out so well."

"Are you sure it's turned out well?" Mendel asked.

"I don't know, but I think so. To me it seems a good sign; even if they're a couple of nebbishes. Or rather, precisely because they're two nebbishes."

Somewhat ashamed of himself, Mendel married Isidor and White Rokhele as best he could.

10

January–February

1945

It was a good sign. The Gedalists, and some Poles who had asked to be invited, celebrated the wedding, with little food but much merriment. Gedaleh, naturally, played the violin, which should never be absent even at the humblest weddings. He had a vast and varied repertory, which ranged from Kreutzer to the most trivial little songs. It was already well into the evening, and Gedaleh was playing and singing the "Song of the Foolish Boy"; the others were accompanying him in low voices. Gedaleh didn't necessarily mean to refer to Isidor; or if he did, it wasn't a nasty reference, but an innocent, if somewhat coarse, joke, the kind that is customary at weddings. Maybe the song just came into his head, through an association of ideas, but for that matter it's so popular that if you don't sing it at a wedding it's not really a party. The song, too, is foolish, but at the same time it is tinged with a strange tenderness, like a dazed and timid dream that has blossomed in the warmth of a little wooden house, beside the great tile stove, under the smoke-blackened beams of the ceiling; and above the ceiling you picture a dark and snowy sky, where perhaps a great silver fish is swimming, a bride dressed in white veils, and an upside down green billy goat.

The foolish boy of the song, the *narische bucher,* is one who can't make up his mind: all through the night he thinks and thinks again about which girl to choose, because he is a respectful fool, and he knows that by choosing one, he will humiliate all the others. How the choice is made isn't told, but then, to the *meidele* the boy asks (all night long?) absurd and pathetic questions: who is the king who has no country? what water doesn't wash away sand? what is faster than a mouse and higher than a house? And finally, what can burn without a flame, and what can weep without tears? These riddles aren't gratuitous, they have a reason: they are the tortuous way the boy had chosen in order to declare himself, and the clever girl has realized this.

"Foolish boy," she answers him melodiously, "the king who has no country is the king of cards, and the water that has no sand is the water of tears. Faster than a mouse is a cat, and higher than a house is its chimney. And love can burn without flame, and a heart can weep without tears." This inconclusive skirmishing ends badly: while the boy is still tormenting himself, whether this is really the girl of his heart, another youth brutally comes and takes her away from him.

It was a holiday for everyone, Poles and Jews: a truce, a relief of their tension and waiting. Even the austere Edek beat time on his messtin with his knuckles, and the Poles, though they understood no Yiddish, joined in the almost meaningless refrain:

Tumbala-tumbala-tumbalalaika,
Tumbala-tumbala-tumbalalaika,
Tumbalaika, schpil balalaika,
Tumbalaika, frailich sol sain!

Others stamped their feet on the floor or pounded on the table; the closest ones gave the bridal pair friendly nudges in the ribs and asked them lewd questions. Isidor and Rokhele, glistening with sweat and flushed with emotion, looked around, embarrassed.

First a few, then all of them succumbed to the hypnotic rhythm of the song and began to dance; holding hands, in a circle, smiling obliviously, nodding from side to side and raising their heads, stamping their feet in cadence: *frailich sol sain*, let happiness reign! Even the white-haired Dov, even the bride and groom, even the overconfident Line, even the Slonim weavers with their clumsy movements, even Mottel the throat-cutter. Let happiness reign! In no time, the little space among the benches and the walls of the barrack was full of dance and festivity.

All of a sudden the earth shook and they all stopped. It wasn't an earthquake, it was a round of heavy artillery; a moment later they heard squadrons of planes filling the sky with their racket. There was a great turmoil; they all rushed for their weapons, but neither Gedaleh nor Edek knew what orders to give. Then Marian was heard shouting: "Don't go outside! Stay under cover!" The walls of the barracks, made of solid logs, could, in fact, offer a certain protection. The explosions became more frequent, deafening; Mendel listened carefully; his experience in the artillery told him that the outgoing rounds were to the east and the shells were exploding to the west, near Zarnowiec; they went howling over their heads. So it was a Russian attack, no doubt about that: a large-scale attack, maybe the definitive one. Over all the racket Dov's voice was heard: "It's the front! It's the front moving past!" At that same moment Bogdan came into the shed, the Pole who was on guard outside. He was pushing ahead of him a man covered with mud, unshaven, bundled up in a long, tattered coat. "You find out who this character is!" he said to Edek and Marian; but the two paid no attention to him, they were having an agitated quarrel between themselves, and with other Poles standing around them. Bogdan repeated his request; then, out of patience, he turned to go back to his post, but Edek recalled him: "No, you stay in here, too; we have to decide." Bogdan turned to the Gedalist group: "You people deal with this one; he must be one of yours. He's unarmed."

The man was looking around, dazed, confused by the explosions and the excited voices, dazzled by the carbide lamps. Mottel asked him, "Who are you? Where do you come from?" At the sound of the Yiddish words, he started, amazed; he didn't answer, but asked in his turn, "Jews? Jews here?" He seemed a trapped animal. His eyes sought the door, Mendel stopped him with a gesture; and he drew back in a jerk of defense: "Let me go! What do you want from me?" In the barracks they had to shout to make themselves heard; nevertheless, Mendel finally figured out that the man, whose name was Schmulek, had been stopped by the guard as he was running past the sentry post: in the darkness, he had been taken for a German. At the same time, he realized that the Poles were discussing whether to wait on the spot for the Red Army or to disperse.

When Schmulek understood that the Jews were not prisoners of the Poles, nor the Poles of the Jews, and that nobody wanted to arrest him or harm him, he exploded with speech: they should all follow him, quickly, at once. He had escaped a bomb by a miracle, he had remained buried by the loose dirt. As if to confirm his words, there was another deafening explosion, very close: the door of the barracks caved in, then was sucked outside by the blast. The lights went out, and the din became deafening: now the shells were falling thickly, far and near, and the walls of the barracks were creaking, threatening to shatter. It wasn't clear whether the bombs came from planes or the artillery. Everybody went outside in disorder, into the freezing air illuminated by the flashes: with the authority of his terror, Schmulek shouted that they should follow him, he had a shelter, nearby, secure. He grabbed, at random, Bella by one arm and dragged her off, in jerks; Mendel and some others followed them, more than a dozen, perhaps; the others scattered in the woods.

Schmulek darted along, bent over, from tree to tree, and the others came behind him in Indian file, holding hands like the blind. Some trees were ablaze. Mendel caught up with Schmulek and shouted into his ear, "Where are you taking us?", but the other man just kept on running. He led them to a bunker of logs, half underground; next to it was a well. Schmulek climbed over the edge, went down until only his head was sticking out, then said: "Come, this is how you get in." In the reddish glow of the fires, Mendel and the others also climbed down. Inside the well, rusted iron hooks were set into the wall. About two or three meters down, a hole opened in the wall; they groped their way inside and found themselves in a slightly descending passage; farther on, there was a hollow dug out of the clayey earth, its ceiling supported by stakes. Here Schmulek was waiting for them, out of breath, a lighted torch in his hand. "I live here," he said to Mendel.

Mendel looked around. There were Dov, Bella, Mottel, Line, Piotr; Gedaleh wasn't there, but there were six or seven of the survivors from Ruzany and Blizna, and four Poles he didn't know. Down here, the roar of the explosions was muffled; the air was damp and smelled of the earth. In the walls some niches had been dug, and there you could see vague objects, rolled-up blankets, pots, pans. A bench ran along one wall; on the floor of packed earth there were boughs and straw. "Sit down," Schmulek said. "How long have you been here?" Dov asked. "Three years," he answered.

Line spoke. "Are you alone?"

"I'm alone. Before, there was my nephew, a boy. He went out to look for food and never came back. But six months ago there were twelve of us, last year there were forty, and two years ago, more than a hundred."

"All in here?" Line asked, incredulous and horrified.

"Look down there," Schmulek said, raising his torch. "The passage continues, forks, and there are other caves. There are also two other exits, inside two oaks hollowed by lightning. We lived badly, but we were alive. If we could have stayed underground all the time, they wouldn't have found us, and only the ones who caught spotted fever would have died. But we had to go out, to find food, and then they shot us."

"The Germans?"

"Everybody. Germans, Hungarians, Ukrainians. Sometimes also the Poles, though we were all Polish. We had escaped from the ghettos around here. There was never any telling: sometimes they would let us by, sometimes they would shoot us like rabbits, and other times they even gave us food. The last who came weren't partisans: they were bandits, they only had knives. They came by surprise. They cut the survivors' bellies open and took away what we had."

"How did you save yourself?"

"By chance," Schmulek said. "In civilian life I was a horse dealer, I went around the villages in this zone, I knew all the trails in the woods. Several times I acted as guide for the partisans. In September I guided a group of Russian soldiers who had escaped from a German *Lager;* they wanted to go up in the Mountains of the Holy Cross, and I led them out of the forest. That's when the bandits came and slaughtered everyone. The boy was also outside by chance."

"We found those Russian soldiers," Mendel said. "They were surrounded by the Germans; they're all dead. But now the war's about to end."

"I don't care whether the war ends. When the war ends, there won't be any Jews left in Poland. I don't care about anything anymore. What I care is that you people had the courage to take up guns; and I didn't have that courage."

"That doesn't mean anything," Mendel said. "You made yourself useful in a different way. Fighting isn't a job for older people."

"How old do you think I am?"

"Fifty," Dov ventured, though he thought seventy.

"I'm thirty-six," Schmulek said.

Outside, the battle continued; in Schmulek's den only a dull rumble arrived, broken at times by louder explosions that shook the ground and were heard not so much with the ears but with the whole body. Nevertheless, halfway into the night, they were all asleep, though they knew these hours were decisive: anxiety itself and their waiting had worn them out.

Mendel found himself awake late in the morning, and he realized that he had been wakened by the silence. The earth no longer shook; there was no sound except for the heavy respiration of the sleepers. The darkness was absolute. He groped at his sides; to his left, he recognized the thin body of Bella, to his right the rough cloth and cartridge belt of a Pole. It could be only a respite; or else the Russians could have drawn back, and this refuge could be in no-man's land. But then his ear, sharpened by the silence, caught an improbable, childish sound, not heard for years. Bells: yes, those were bells, a faint tolling, delicate, filtered through the earth that buried them; a toy music box playing festively, and it meant that the war was over.

He was about to wake up his companions, but he restrained himself: later, there was time, now he had something else to do. What? His accounts, he had to do his accounts. He felt as if he had escaped a raging storm at sea, and had landed on a deserted and unknown land. Not ready, not prepared, empty; calm and unwound, the way an unwound watch is calm. Calm and not happy, calmly unhappy. Swollen with memories: Leonid, the Uzbek, the Venya band, rivers and woods and marshes, the battle of the monastery, Ulybin, the return of Dov. The little girl of Valuets with her goats, Line, Sissl. Mendel the womanless. He saw again, beyond his eyelids, Rivke's sharpened face, with the eyes sealed, the hair twisted like snakes. Rivke underground like us. She's the one who snatches away the other women from around me, like blowing the chaff from the grain. *Ballebusteh* still: who said that the dead have no more power?

Crammed with memories, and at once filled with forgetting: his memories, even recent ones, were faded, they had hazy outlines, they overlapped in this effort of his, as if someone were making drawings on the blackboard, then only half erasing them, before making new ones on top of the old. Perhaps this is how a man remembers his life when he is a hundred, or how the patriarchs, who were nine hundred, remembered. Perhaps memory is like a bucket; if you want to cram into it more fruit than it will hold, the fruit is crushed.

The bells meanwhile went on ringing, no telling where: in some village the peasants must have been celebrating; for them the Nazi nightmare was over, the worst was over. I should celebrate, too, and ring my bells, Mendel thought, clinging to sleep to prevent it from leaving him. Our war, too, is over, the time of dying and killing is over, and yet I am not happy, and I wish my sleep would never end. Our war is over, and we are sealed in a dirt cave, and we have to go out and start walking again. This is the house of Schmulek, who has no house, who has lost everything, even himself. Where is my house? It is in no place. It's in the knapsack I carry on my back, it's in the shot-down Heinkel, it's at Novoselki, it's in the camp of Turov and in Edek's camp, it's beyond the sea, in fairy-tale land, where milk and honey flow. A man enters his house and hangs up his clothes and his memories; where do you hang your memories, Mendel, son of Nachman?

One by one, they all woke up and all asked questions, but nobody could answer. The front had gone by, there was no doubt of it: now what was to be done? Wait some more, as Schmulek urged them to? Go out to meet the Russians? Look for food? Send somebody up first to spy out the situation?

Dov offered to go; he was well suited, he spoke Russian, was wearing a Russian uniform, with Russian papers: he was Russian, in other words, more in order than Piotr. He started up the passage, but came back immediately: they would have to wait, someone was lowering a bucket into the well. The bucket rose, full; Dov could go out, and he found himself in the midst of a platoon of soldiers, stripped to the waist, joyously washing in the water they had poured into a drinking trough. On the ground there were a few inches of snow, trampled and half-melted by the night's fires. Not far off, some other soldiers had lighted a fire and were drying out their clothes. They received Dov with good-natured indifference:

"Hey, Uncle! Where did you pop up from? What regiment are you?"

"We almost pulled you up in the bucket!"

"I'll tell you where he comes from: he got drunk and fell in."

"Or else they threw him in. Say, Uncle: did the Germans throw you into the well? Or did you go down to take shelter?"

"You see strange things in this country," a Mongol soldier said pensively. "Yesterday, in the midst of the fighting, I saw a hare: instead of running off, he sat there, spellbound. And the day before I saw a beautiful girl in a barrel . . ."

"What was she doing in the barrel?"

"Nothing. She was hidden there."

"And what did you do?"

"Nothing; I said to her: Good morning, *panienka*, sorry to bother you; and I closed the lid again."

"Either you're a liar or a fool, Afanasij; you roast a hare, and with a girl, you make love."

"Well, all I wanted to say is that this is a strange country. Yesterday, the hare. The day before, the girl. And now a soldier with white hair comes out of the well. Come here, soldier: if you're not a ghost, have a drop of vodka; and if you're a ghost, go back where you came from."

The corporal of the platoon came over to Dov, touched him, and said, "But you're not even wet!"

"There's a passage in the well," Dov said. "I'll explain it to you."

The corporal said, "Come with me to headquarters. You can explain everything there."

Half an hour later Dov and the corporal came back, with a lieutenant who was wearing the NKVD band on his arm; seeing him, the soldiers stopped their chatter and resumed washing. The lieutenant told Dov to go back down in the well and have everybody who was hidden there come out. They came out one by one, into the white light of the sky that threatened more snow, to the silent amazement of the Russians. The lieutenant ordered two soldiers to get dressed and collect the weapons, and he had the group escorted along the road in the opposite direction, retracing the way they had come in the night, guided by Schmulek; he led them, in other words, back to the barracks of the Polish camp. Here they found Edek and Marian and almost all their men; there was also Gedaleh with the Gedalists who hadn't followed Schmulek. Both the Poles and the Jews were disarmed, and the shed where they were shut up was guarded by two Russian sentries.

All that day nothing happened. At noon two soldiers came, bringing bread and sausage for everybody; at evening came a pot with a steaming soup of millet and meat. There were more than a hundred prisoners, and they were cramped in the building; they complained to the sentries, the corporal came and divided them into two groups, one per barrack, so the guard had to be doubled. Neither the corporal nor the soldier showed any hostility; some seemed curious, others annoyed, and others looked as if they wanted to apologize.

The Poles were restless, and humiliated at having had to turn in their weapons.

"Cheer up, Edek," Gedaleh said. "The worst is over. No matter what happens, these Russians won't treat us the way the Germans did. You can see: you can talk things over with them." Edek didn't answer.

In the morning a can of ersatz coffee arrived, and a little later the lieutenant came, accompanied by a clerk. He seemed in a bad humor, and he was brisk. He transcribed the vital statistics of them all in a schoolboy's copybook, and he had them all show him their hands, palms and backs, which he examined carefully. When he had finished, he divided the confined party into three groups.

The first group was made up of the majority of the Poles.

"You are soldiers, and you will continue to be soldiers. You will be given uniforms and arms, and will be absorbed into the Red Army." There were comments, murmuring, some protests; the sentries lowered the barrels of their guns, and the protests died out.

"You will be useful to us in another way," he said, turning to the second group. This was very small: it included Edek with half a dozen former students and clerks.

"I'm the commander of this unit," Edek said, pale as snow.

"There is no unit any more and no commander," the lieutenant said. "*The Armia Krajowa* has been disbanded."

"Disbanded by whom? Disbanded by you people!"

"No, no, it was disbanded on its own; it no longer had any reason to exist. We are liberating Poland. Haven't you heard the radio? No, not ours: Radio London. For three days they've been broadcasting a message from your commander in chief. He greets you, thanks you, and says that your war is over."

"Where will you send us?" Edek then asked.

"I don't know, and it's not my concern. I have orders only to send you to area HQ; there you will be given all the information you wish."

The third group comprised the Gedalists plus Schmulek; or, in other words, all the Jews plus Piotr. Mendel hadn't noticed before, but he noticed now that Piotr had taken off his tattered partisan uniform, the one he had seen Piotr wear since the Turov camp. He was tall and slim like Gedaleh, and he was wearing the civilian clothes that Gedaleh had flaunted after the Sarny coup.

"As for you others," the lieutenant said, "for the present there are no orders. You're not civilians, and you're not soldiers, either. And you're not prisoners of war. You're men and women, and you have no papers."

"Comrade lieutenant, we're partisans," Gedaleh said. "Partisans belong to partisan units. Nobody has ever heard of Jewish partisans: that's something new. You don't belong to any category. For the present, you stay here. I've asked for instructions. You will receive the same treatment as our soldiers. Then we'll see."

Gedaleh's band, having returned after more than three months to its original pure composition, experienced days of inertia and suspicion. Toward the end of January, from the little window of the shed they saw the Poles of the second group go off through the snow that was falling heavily. For the occasion, the lieutenant had had the doors barred; Gedaleh's band had to be satisfied with waving goodbye to Edek from inside the window. Climbing into the truck, Edek waved his hand towards them; the vehicle set off with a jolt, and Sissl burst into tears.

Unlike the others, Dov, Mendel, Arie, and Piotr had belonged to the Red Army and would have had no difficulty in clarifying their position. Piotr had no doubts.

"They didn't make any distinctions, and that suits me fine. It's obvious that for the moment the NKVD is interested only in the Poles; Stalin doesn't want Polish partisans in his way."

"They've taken you for a Jew!" Gedaleh said, amused. "For that matter, you've earned it."

"I don't know. The lieutenant asked me two or three questions; he saw I was answering in Russian, and that was enough for him."

"Hm," Gedaleh said. "If you ask me, your case isn't closed yet."

"It is for me," Piotr answered. "I'm staying with you."

Dov had no doubts, either, but in the opposite direction. He hadn't changed his decision; on the contrary, it had been strengthened by the most recent adventures; he was tired of fighting and roaming, tired of the uncertainties of the precarious life; he wanted to go home, since he had a home. A home far away, untouched by the war, in a country whose distance in time and space had made it legendary: the land of tigers and bears, where they were all like him, stubborn and simple. In that land, which Dov never tired of describing, the winter sky was violet and green: the aurora borealis shimmered there, and when he was a boy the terrible comet had exploded nearby. Mutoraj, with its four thousand inhabitants, deportees, Nihilists and Samoyeds, was a village unique in the world.

Dove went off in silence, sad without despair. He reported to the Russian command, stated his army position and his record; at their request he wrote out in a neat hand a report on the circumstances under which he had been taken from Turov, treated at the Kiev hospital, and taken back to the partisan zone; then he waited. Two weeks later he took his leave of them all, and made a dignifed exit.

As for Mendel and Arie, they conjured up no problems for themselves on this score, and the Russians made no problems for them either. The front had rapidly moved on, westwards; the NKVD lieutenant didn't show up again, and the guard around the barracks became more and more relaxed until it disappeared completely. Gedaleh's band, complete, was transferred at the beginning of February to a schoolhouse in the town of Wolbrom, not far away, and here it was left to its own devices: the Russian garrison, which for that matter consisted only of an elderly captain and a few soldiers, paid no attention to them, except to bring them supplies from the quartermaster stores: potatoes, turnips, barley, meat, salt. The bread arrived already baked, from a requisitioned bakery; but the cooking operations had to be performed on the spot, and there was no equipment in the school, nor had the Russians supplied any. Gedaleh filled out a proper requisition, the captain promised, and nothing arrived. "We'll go into the city and get ourselves what we need," Gedaleh said.

The enterprise proved easier than they had foreseen. The little city was deserted and sinister: it must have been bombed, and then looted several times, but always in haste. In the half-destroyed houses, in the cellars, the attics, in the air raid shelters, they found everything. Not only pots and pans, but also chairs, quilts, mattresses, furniture of every description. More furnishings appeared every day in the market that had spontaneously sprung up in the main square. Piles of half-smashed furniture were sold for firewood; there was a great supply and prices were low. Soon the school was transformed into an inhabitable shelter, though hardly cozy; but there were no stoves, in the rooms or in the vicinity, and the soup had to be cooked on fires out in the open, in the courtyard, next to the sandy pit for the long jump. In compensation, in one of the classrooms, the Gedalists set up a regal nuptial bed for White Rokhele and Isidor, surmounted by a canopy they had run up from army blankets.

The Russian captain was a melancholy, weary man. Gedaleh and Mendel went several times to talk with him, to get from him some information about the intentions of the Russian authorities as far as they were concerned. The man was polite, absent, and evasive; he knew nothing, nobody knew anything, the war wasn't over, they would have to wait till the end of the war. In the war he had lost two sons, and he had had no news of his wife, in Leningrad. Gedaleh and his men had food to eat, they were warm; they should wait, as everybody was waiting. He, too, was waiting. Maybe the war wouldn't end all that soon; nobody could say. Maybe it would go on: who could know? Against Japan, against America. Permit to leave? He couldn't issue permits; that was another department; and for that matter, where would they go? In what direction? There were bands of Polish rebels and Germans in circulation: on all the roads, the Russians had set up checkpoints. They were not to try to leave the city: they wouldn't get far, the checkpoints had orders to shoot on sight. He himself avoided moving about, except on duty; it wouldn't be the first time that Soviet soldiers had fired on one another.

But Gedaleh had little patience with being shut up. To

him, and not only to him, this way of life seemed empty, humiliating, and ridiculous. Men and women took turns cooking and cleaning, and yet avalanches of free time remained; paradoxically, with a city around them, a roof over their heads, and a table at which they ate, they felt an undefined malaise, which was homesickness for the forest and the open road. They felt useless, alien: no longer at war, not yet at peace. Despite the captain's warnings, they went out often, in little groups.

At Wolbrom, the war was over, but it continued, furiously, not very far away. Through the city, and on the dirt road around it, ceaselessly day and night, Soviet army units went by, heading for the Silesian front. During the day it seemed not so much a modern army going by but a horde, a migration: men of every race, Viking giants and squat Lapps, tanned Caucasians and pale Siberians, on foot, on horseback, in trucks, tractors, great ox-drawn wagons, some even riding camels. There were soldiers and civilians, women dressed in every possible way; sheep, cows, mules, and horses: at evening the squads stopped where they were, set up their tents, slaughtered the animals, and cooked the meat on makeshift fires. These improvised camps were teeming with children, bundled in too-big army clothing; some wore pistols and knives in their belts, all had the red star sewn on their enormous fur hats. Who were they? Where did they come from? Mendel and his companions stopped to question them: they spoke Russian, Ukrainian, Polish, even Yiddish; others refused to speak. They were uneasy and wild, war orphans. The Red Army, in its advance through the devastated lands, had collected them by the thousands, amidst the rubble of the cities, lost in the fields and woods, hungry and vagabond. The Soviets hadn't had the time to settle them in the rear or the vehicles to transfer them farther back: and so they were dragged along, everybody's children, soldiers themselves, also in search of loot. They wandered around the fires; some of the soldiers gave them bread, soup, and meat; others, annoyed, drove them off.

Surprisingly different were the troops that crossed the

city in the hours of darkness. Mendel, who retained the searing memory of units surrounded and cut to pieces in the great annihilating battles of 'forty-one and 'forty-two, could hardly believe his eyes. Here, this was the new Red Army that had broken the spine of Germany: different, unrecognizable. A mighty machine, ordered, modern, that filed almost soundless along the main street of the blacked-out city. Gigantic tanks mounted on trailers with rubber tires; self-propelled cannons never seen or dreamed of before; the legendary Katyushas, covered by tarpaulins that concealed their features. Mingled with the artillery and the armored units there were also marching companies, on foot, in closed order, singing. Theirs were not warlike songs, but rather melancholy and subdued; they didn't express thirst for war, as the German songs did, but the mourning accumulated during four years of massacre.

Mendel, artilleryman Mendel, witnessed this passage with his spirit shaken. In spite of everything, in spite of the disastrous and culpable defeat that had forced him underground, despite the contempt and the wrongs he had suffered in other days, despite Ulybin, this was, nevertheless, the army whose worn, faded uniform he was wearing yet. A *krasnoarmeetz:* so he was still a soldier, even if he was a Jew, even if was heading for another country. Those soldiers who marched by, singing, mild in peace and indomitable in war, those soldiers built like Piotr, were his comrades. He felt his chest swell in a flood of conflicting emotions: pride, remorse, resentment, respect, gratitude. But one day he heard groans coming from a cellar; he went down there with Piotr, and he saw ten soldiers of the Waffen SS lying on their stomachs, half-naked: some were pulling themselves along with their arms, all had a bleeding slash halfway down their backs. "That's what the Siberians do," Piotr said, "when they find them, they don't kill them, but they cut the marrow out of their spine." They climbed back up to the street, and Piotr added: "I wouldn't want to be a German. No, no, these next months, I really wouldn't want to be a Berliner."

One morning they woke up and found on the facade of

the school a swastika painted with tar; under it was written: "NSZ—Death to the Bolshevik Jews." A little later, from the window of the second floor, they saw three or four youths down in the street, talking among themselves and looking up. That same evening, while they were seated, eating, the window pane was shattered, and, between the legs of the table, a bottle fell, with a burning fuse. Piotr was quickest: in a flash he grabbed the bottle, which hadn't broken, and flung it back into the street. There was a thud, and on the pavement a burning puddle formed, which went on burning for a long time: the smoky flame rose all the way to their window. Gedaleh said, "We have to get some arms and go."

Finding arms, too, was easier than they had expected: in different ways, Schmulek and Pavel took care of it. In his cave there were weapons, Schmulek said: not many, but in good condition, buried under the hard earth. He asked Gedaleh for someone to come with him; they went out at sunset and came back at dawn with various pistols, hand grenades, ammunition, and a submachine gun. After Jozek's death, Pavel had succeeded him as quartermaster, and he reported that buying weapons at the market was easier than buying butter and tobacco. Everybody was offering them, in broad daylight; the Russians themselves, both passing soldiers and the civilians following the troops, sold German sidearms found in warehouses or on the battlefields; other stuff was sold nonchalantly by Poles in the militia that the Russians had hastily established. Many of these Poles, the moment they had signed up, deserted with their weapons to join bands that were preparing for guerrilla fighting; others sold or bartered the weapons at the market. Within a few days the Gedalists found themselves possessors of numerous knives and a dozen ill-assorted firearms. It wasn't much, but it would suffice to keep off the Polish rightist terrorists.

At the end of February the Russian captain summoned Gedaleh and held him for more than an hour, talking.

"He offered me cigarettes and drink," Gedaleh reported to his companions. "He isn't as absentminded as he seems, and if you ask me, he's been prompted. He's heard about the Molotov, he says these are difficult times, and he's worried about us. And that they aren't able to guarantee our safety, and that we would be wise to protect ourselves on our own: in other words he knows about the weapons and its all right with him for us to have them. It's only natural; he must be about as fond of the NSZ as we are. He kept saying this is a bad place. He said that the other time, too, but then he said it was dangerous to leave the city; and instead, today, he asked me why we're staying here. 'You could move on ahead, the front is far off by now: farther ahead, towards the Allies . . .' I told him we would like to go to Italy, and from there we would try to get to Palestine, and he said we had the right idea, England is going to have to leave Palestine, and also Egypt and India: the colonial empires have their days numbered. And Palestine is where we must go, to build our state. He told me he has many Jewish friends and has even read Herzl's book: but I don't believe this is true, or else he didn't read it carefully, because he said to me that, basically, Herzl was also a Russian, whereas really he was Hungarian. But I didn't contradict him. In other words, the captain is a man who knows a thing or two: it's convenient for the Russians if we bother the English, and for us it's time to leave. But no official permits: on that subject he immediately backed away."

"We'll go away without permits," Line said, shrugging. "When did we ever have permits?"

Bella's nasal voice was heard: "Those NSZ people are Fascists and cowards, but there's one thing that we agree with them and the Russians about: they want to send us away, and we want to go."

Pavel had got into the habit of leaving the school early in the morning, then not showing up again until evening. In the space of a few days the atmosphere in Wolbrom had changed: now, the tide of troops flowing towards Ger-

many was overwhelmed by the tide in the opposite direction, of soldiers coming back from the front. Some were
on leave, but the majority were wounded or mutilated
soldiers, leaning on makeshift crutches, seated on the piles
of rubble that flanked the roads, with the pale, beardless
faces of adolescents. From his exploratory rounds Pavel
never came back empty-handed: on the black market by
now anything could be found. He brought coffee, pow-
dered milk, soap and razor blades, powders for puddings,
vitamins, treasures that the Gedalists hadn't seen for six
years or had never known before. One day he brought
with him a lanky, sandy-haired character, who spoke no
Russian or Polish or German, and only a few words of
Yiddish: Pavel had found him on the ruins of the Wolbrom synagogue, chanting the morning prayers; he was a
Jewish soldier from Chicago that the Germans had taken
prisoner in Normandy and that the Red Army had liberated. They celebrated together, but the American was
no good at expressing himself and even less good at drinking; after the vodka had gone around the first time, he
ended up under the table, he slept until noon the next
day, and then went off without saying good-bye to anyone. Along the roads wandered ex-prisoners of every country and every race, and swarms of prostitutes.

On February 25th Pavel came home with five pairs of
silk stockings, and there was great, excited talk: the
women quickly tried them on, but they were a size that
could just do for Sissl and Black Rokhele; for the other
Rokhele, Line, and Bella they were too big. Pavel silenced
the chatter: "That's all right. No matter. Tomorrow I'll
exchange them or I'll bring some more. I have something
else to tell you. I've found a truck!"

"Did you buy it?" Isidor asked.

No, he hadn't bought it. It emerged that behind the
railroad station the Russians had set up a yard for junk
and discarded material, and you could find everything
there. Pavel wasn't knowledgeable, somebody had to go
there with him tomorrow. Who knew about trucks? Who
knew how to drive them? The band had covered more

than a thousand kilometers on foot: wasn't it time now for them to travel by truck?

"It'll have to be paid for," Mottel said.

"I don't think so," Pavel said. "The yard isn't fenced in; there's only a ditch around it, and only one guard. The important thing is to act fast: there are lots of people coming and going, this morning I saw two kids taking away a motorcycle. Who's coming with me tomorrow morning?"

They would all have liked to go, for the diversion if nothing else. Line and Arie declared they had driven tractors; Piotr and Mendel were licensed army drivers, and further, in his village, Mendel had had occasion to repair tractors and trucks. Gedaleh, with an unusual abuse of authority, said he would go because he was the commander, but the most insistent was Isidor, who could advance no claim at all. He wanted to go with Pavel at all costs: for vehicles, for all vehicles, he had a selfless and childish passion, and he said that he would learn to drive the truck in a moment.

Mendel went, and he saw that Pavel hadn't exaggerated: in the junkyard there really was everything, not only wrecks. The Russians, supplied by the Allies with war material of every kind, didn't split hairs: as soon as a machine or a vehicle began to give them some touble, they discarded it and collected a new one. More damaged material arrived daily from the war zone, on trucks or by rail; nobody examined it or checked it, it was flung into the yard and left there to rust. In the lugubrious metallic graveyard the curious, the experts wandered around, and packs of kids played hide-and-seek.

There were trucks: of every brand and in every state of preservation. Mendel's attention focused on a line of Italian trucks; they were three-ton Lancia 3RO's, and they looked like new: maybe they came from some German depot. While Pavel was trying to distract the guard, offering him tobacco and chewing gum, Mendel took a closer look at the vehicles. They actually had the keys in the dashboard and seemed ready to go; Mendel tried the ignition, but nothing happened. The reason was soon clear:

the trucks had no batteries, and never had had any; the lugs of the electric system were still covered with grease. When Pavel came back, Mendel said to him, "Go back to your man and keep him occupied. I'm going to look around for a charged battery."

"But what'll I tell him?"

"Invent something; tell him about when you were an actor."

While Pavel was straining his memory and his imagination to amuse the guard without arousing his suspicions, Mendel began methodically exploring the other vehicles. Soon he found what he was looking for, a Russian truck of the same capacity as the Lancias, in relatively good condition: it must have arrived a short time before. He raised the hood and touched the poles of the battery with the blade of his knife. There was a crackle and a blue flash: the battery was charged. He went back to the school with Pavel, the hours passed slowly; it seemed that night would never come.

When it was dark, they collected their weapons and went back to the junkyard. There was no sign of the guard: either he was sleeping nearby or had calmly gone back to the barracks. Instead, among the dark outlines of the vehicles and the wreckage, swarmed a furtive population: like termites, they dismantled or demolished anything that might prove useful or salable: seats, cables, tires, auxiliary motors. Some were siphoning off the fuel from the tanks; Pavel borrowed a tube, did the same, and poured some gas into the tank of the first 3RO in the line. Then Mendel took out the good battery and, with Pavel's help, dragged it to the truck. He remounted it, connected it, they climbed into the cab, and Mendel turned the key. He groped for the headlights switch, and the lights came on. "And there was light," he thought to himself. He turned them off and started the engine. It started smoothly and responded obediently to the gas pedal. Perfect.

"We're all set!" Pavel whispered.

"We'll see about that," Mendel answered. "I've fixed several of these animals, but I've never driven one."

"Didn't you say you had a license?"

"Yes, I have it, all right," Mendel muttered. "In those days they passed them out to everybody. The Germans were at Borodino and Kaluga. Six half-hour lessons, and you were on your way. But then I've only driven cars and tractors; and at night it's a different matter. Now shut up, please."

"Just one more thing," Pavel said. "Don't drive out the gate. There's a sentry box there, and there could also be somebody around. And now I'll shut up."

Frowning, as intent as a surgeon, Mendel pressed the clutch in, shifted into gear, and raised his foot: the truck started off with a wild jerk. He turned the headlights on again, and, gunning the engine, he headed very slowly towards the end of the yard, along a cleared passage.

"You needn't hope I'm going to shift gears. I'll shift tomorrow. For the present we proceed like this."

The truck proceeded to the ditch, dipped forward, and aimed majestically towards the sky. "We're out," Pavel said, breathing in the rainy air: he realized that for perhaps a full minute he hadn't taken a breath. A voice behind them shouted: "*Stoj!* Halt!" Pavel leaned out of the window and fired a brief volley into the air, more out of high spirits than for intimidation. When they reached the road, Mendel summoned all his courage and shifted into second: the roar of the engine dropped a bit, and the speed increased slightly. Nobody followed them, and they reached the school in a few minutes.

Gedaleh, also armed, was waiting for them in the street. He hugged Mendel, laughing and reciting the blessing of miracles. Mendel, his forehead beaded with sweat in spite of the cold, answered him, "The other blessing would be better, the one for escape from danger. We mustn't waste time; we're leaving right now."

Wakened abruptly, the Gedalists brought down baggage and arms and crammed into the back of the truck.

Mendel started the engine again. "Towards Zawiercie!" Gedaleh shouted at him, having taken the seat at his side in the cab. Following the signs that the Russians had set up at the crossroads, Mendel left the city and found himself on a side road full of potholes and puddles. Gradually, scraping the gears quite a few times, he learned to shift into high, and they picked up a fair speed. The jolts also increased, but nobody complained. He climbed a hill and started the descent: the brakes worked and he felt reassured, but the tension of driving was undoing him.

"I can't take much more of this. Who'll spell me?"

"We'll see!" Gedaleh shouted, over the racket of the motor and the metal. "Just think about getting away from the town."

Halfway down the hill they came to a roadblock, an unstripped log resting on two gasoline cans at the sides of the road.

"Now what do I do?"

"Don't stop! Accelerate!"

The log flew off like a straw, and they heard bursts of automatic fire; from the back somebody returned the fire with scattered shots. The truck went on its way in the night, and Gedaleh shouted, laughing, "If not this way, how? And if now now, when?"

11

February–July

1945

They were comfortable up front, but the men and women crammed into the back, along with the first air of freedom, were breathing the icy winds of the night: they were numb from the cold and the discomfort and aching from the jolts. Some complained, but Gedaleh paid no attention.

"How much gas do we have?" he asked Mendel.

"Hard to say. Maybe enough for another thirty-forty kilometers, no more than that."

They made a stop at dawn, on a side road. At the edges a mass of wreckage was piled up, incredible both in its variety and its quantity: the only wealth that war produces. Shattered and overturned, there were trucks, armored cars, half-tracks, boats and pontoons used for bridging rivers. There was a German cook truck, intact: it would have been valuable, but they had no more room. Too bad.

"We have to find gas," Gedaleh said, "otherwise our excursion is soon over. Spread out, open the tanks, see if they're empty." Isidor had the most luck; he found an upright armored car, without wheels, but with its tank almost full.

"Will it be the right kind?" Mottel asked.

"The only thing is to try it," Mendel said. "But in wartime engines get used to anything."

"Like us," Black Rokhele said, sighing and stretching like a cat.

Gedaleh was impatient to get the truck off the road: in daylight it was too visible, and he wasn't sure that the theft and their running the roadblock hadn't been reported. He paced up and down nervously: "Hurry up with the tranfusion!" But it wasn't simple, there was no rubber tube: nobody had one. Somebody suggested overturning the armored car, but Isidor said: "I'll do it." Before anyone could stop him, he grabbed a jerrican, whipped out a Luger that had been issued him, and fired at the bottom of the tank. A spurt of yellowish gasoline came out.

"What if it had exploded?" Pavel asked, with retrospective fear.

"It didn't explode," Isidor said.

The sky was growing light, and from the south a distant thunder of artillery could be heard: the road to the west was free, the Germans had fallen back even beyond Legnica (but Breslau, besieged, was still holding out); instead, all along the Czechoslovakian border, the fighting had never stopped. Driving by night and hiding the truck in the daytime, they traveled for several days. Mendel got tired of driving, but nobody, not Piotr or Arie or Line, showed much enthusiasm about relieving him. Isidor, on the other hand, was asking for nothing better; he had fallen more in love with the truck than with Rokhele, and he spent all his free hours cleaning the mud and dust off it, and he never missed a chance to stick his nose under the hood. Mendel gave him a couple of driving lessons, and he learned with incredible speed, after which it was impossible to wrench him loose from the wheel. He was an excellent driver, and everybody—Mendel, most of all—was pleased.

Nobody knew the area; at every crossroads Isidor slowed down and asked Gedaleh, "Where do we go?" Gedaleh conferred with Schmulek, then decided by instinct. Almost by chance they reached Rawicz, on the border between Great Poland and Silesia: when they had hidden the truck in some woods they entered, in little groups, the town, the first they had encountered on their way that hadn't been destroyed by the war. Life was not yet back to normal, but some shops were open, newspapers were on sale at the station kiosk, brightly colored posters announced a romantic film that was being shown in the only theater. In the main street, a lady in furs and high heels was leading a dog on a leash, so tiny it seemed like a cat. The Gedalists felt dirty, wild, and shy, but there were many refugees, and nobody paid any attention to them. Gedaleh invited Bella, White R. and Isidor into a café for some coffee; they accepted, but they seemed to be seated on pins. Schmulek wouldn't come into the city; he volunteered to stay in the truck with three other men, to guard it and the weapons.

They bought various humble wonders for which they had long felt a need or a desire: stockings, toothbrushes, underwear, pans. Pavel, though he read Polish with difficulty, found in a stall an old illustrated edition of *Les Misérables*. He had to give it to Bella, who asked to borrow it, but Piotr made Bella give it to him on some pretext. Piotr didn't keep the book long, either: not only was he totally unable to understand Polish, but he couldn't even make out the letters. The volume, in the days that followed, went from hand to hand, and in the end was considered collective property.

They all had a great yen to go to the movies, Gedaleh perhaps most of all, but he had read in the papers that the Americans had crossed the Rhine at Remagen and had taken Cologne. "We'll go meet them: with them we'll be safer. It's time to move on." Reluctantly they tore themselves away from the lures of the city; at Rawicz, the refugees, from whatever part of the world they came, had an easy life. In the streets there were English soldiers walking about, and Americans, Australians, New Zealanders, all former prisoners of war; and also French, Yugoslavs, Italians, who had worked (voluntarily or not) in the German factories. The people were kind and hospitable with them all, also with Gedaleh and his Jews, who blended into the varicolored background.

They set off late in the evening in the direction of Glogau; they stopped and rested for a few hours on a little road among the fields. Wrapped in their blankets, they stayed in the back of the truck, which by now was their home. A little before dawn they set off again. Just after a curve the truck's headlights framed another vehicle, stopped, headed towards them, and Isidor was forced to put on the brakes. "Turn! Drive into the fields!" Gedaleh shouted at him, but it was too late. A squad of armed Russian soldiers had surrounded the truck: they were all forced to get out. Those Russians were in a very bad humor, because their truck had become stuck in the mud: its tires were so threadbare that they got no traction on the snow. The corporal was furious. He was covering the driver with insults, and when he got his hands on the Gedalists he poured out all his wrath on them. He asked: "Where are you going?"

"To Glogau," Gedaleh answered.

"No Glogau. Come on, all of you out: lend us a hand. Don't you understand? Get moving, you parasites, you do-nothings, you damned foreigners!"

Speaking in Yiddish, Gedaleh said rapidly, "Hide the weapons under the blankets. And obey without making any fuss." Then, to Pavel and Mendel: "You two speak, in Russian. Poles, be quiet."

In the interlocking beams of the headlights of the two vehicles a frightful confusion ensued. Fifty men, all the Russians plus all the Gedalists, literally couldn't find room around the stuck vehicle, but the corporal, with insults and curses, drove back into the scrimmage anyone who drew aside. All attempts were useless: the rescuers' boots slipped in the mud, and anyway, the truck was so heavy that it could never be got going again simply by pushing.

Mendel said to Gedaleh, "Shall we offer to tow it out? Our tires are new."

"Try. Maybe he'll calm down and let us go."

"Comrade Corporal," Mendel said, "if you have a stout rope or a chain we can try to pull you out."

The Russian looked at him as if a horse had talked. Mendel had to repeat his offer, after which the corporal immediately resumed insulting his men because they hadn't had the idea first. There was a rope, in fact there was a steel cable, strong but a bit short. The maneuver succeeded; Gedaleh's truck, in the first light of dawn, set out in reverse, slowly towing the Russians' vehicle, nose to nose: the road was too narrow for the Lancia to try to turn around, and driving into the fields meant getting stuck almost certainly. Isidor, forced to drive with his body half thrust out of the window, succeeded in a praiseworthy fashion, but the corporal, instead of showing gratitude, continued cursing and shouting: "Faster, faster!"

Finally, after about a kilometer, the side road arrived at the highway of the province. They stopped, and Mendel got down to unhook the tow cable. From the cab, Gedaleh said to him:

"Say good-bye to them and wish them a good journey: be as polite as possible, so they won't get the idea of searching us."

"And what if they do get the idea?"

"We'll let them do it. Surely you don't want to start fighting the Russians. We'll see what happens and what lies we must tell them."

What happened was bad, and prompt; and there was no chance to tell lies. The minute he was on the ground, and without saying a word, the corporal signaled to his men, who again surrounded the truck. They made the whole band get out, and they searched the back, immediately finding the weapons hidden under the blankets: but not the pistols and knives that the Gedalists were carrying on them. There was no use protesting and pleading; the corporal wouldn't listen to reason, he divided them, heavily guarded, between the two trucks, put one of his men at the wheel of the Lancia, and gave the signal to leave.

"Where are you taking us?" Pavel ventured to ask.

"Didn't you want to go to Glogau?" the corporal answered. "Well, we're taking you there. You should be pleased." All the way to Glogau he kept his mouth shut and answered none of their questions.

Glogau, dominated by a gloomy fortress, was the first German city the band had encountered. It was (and is) a mining center, and to them it seemed squalid, black with lignite dust, surrounded by dozens of pits, each of which the Germans had transformed into a little *Lager*. The Russians had occupied Glogau only a few weeks before; they hadn't changed its appearance or its purpose, but in the lignite pits, instead of the slave laborers of the Nazi *Lagers*, now German prisoners of war went down, transferred in a few hours from the front to the mine. In the miniature *Lagers* the Russians jumbled together all the stragglers or suspect people that the Red Army came upon in the zone.

With the Gedalists they didn't go into detail. It was all over in five minutes: they didn't search them, didn't even question them: the Lancia vanished, and for the first time the fighters of Kossovo, Lyuban, and Novoselki knew the humiliating siege of barbed wire. The enclosure to which they had been assigned contained already about fifty internees, Polish Jews, German, French, Dutch, and Greek Jews that the Russians had liberated from the *Lager* at Gross-Rosen. The buildings were heated, the Russians supplied food irregularly but always abundantly, the front was moving away, and the days were now rapidly growing longer, but these former prisoners wouldn't emerge from their isolation. They spoke little and in whispers, and they rarely raised their eyes from the ground. The Gedalists tried in vain to establish contact with them: once their primary needs were satisfied, they seemed to have no further desires or interests or curiosity. They asked no questions, and when questioned, they didn't answer. There were also women: they were still wearing the striped dress, the wooden clogs on their feet, and their hair had just begun to grow again. At the end of the second night, Mendel came out of the barracks to go to the latrine. The moment he stepped across the threshold he bumped into a human body and felt it swaying, inert; it was still warm, hanging from the beams of the ceiling. This act was repeated in the next days, like a silent obsession.

Schmulek parted from the Gedalists and joined the ex-prisoners. Instead, little by little, first Sissl, then the other women of the band, and finally all the Gedalists managed to overcome the resistance of one of the women of the *Lager*. Her name was Francine, and she came from Paris, but a long way round: she had been deported first to Auschwitz, from there to a little *Lager* near Broslau, and finally, when the Russians were close, and when the Germans had evacuated all the *Lagers* of the area, forcing the prisoners on an insane march towards a new prison, she had managed to escape. Francine was a doctor, but in the *Lager* she hadn't been able to practice her profession because she didn't know German well; still, she had picked up enough to be able to tell what she had seen. She had been lucky: every living Jew was a lucky person. But she had been lucky in other ways, too: she still had her hair, since she was a doctor they hadn't cut it off; the Germans have very precise rules.

Francine declared herself a Jew, but she didn't resemble any Jew the Gedalists had ever encountered. On the contrary, they wouldn't even have believed it, if they hadn't thought that there's nothing to be gained by declaring yourself a Jew when you aren't one. She didn't speak Yiddish, didn't understand it, and told them that when she was in Paris she didn't even know what language it was:

she had vaguely heard it mentioned, she thought it was a kind of corrupt Hebrew. She was thirty-seven; she had never married, she had lived first with one man, then with another; she was a pediatrician, she liked her work, she had an office right in the center of Paris, and in her day she had taken wonderful vacations, Mediterranean cruises, trips to Italy and Spain, skiing and ice skating in the Dolomites. To be sure, she had been in Auschwitz, but she preferred to talk about other things, about her life before. Francine was tall and slim, her hair was reddish brown, her face was stern, haggard.

Her meeting with Gedaleh's band was full of reciprocal amazements. Yes, in the *Lager* she had come to know the Jewish women of eastern Europe, but they weren't like the five women of the band. She had never loved her companions, she had felt they were foreign, a hundred times more distant than her French Christian women friends. She had felt irritation and compassion for their passivity, their ignorance, the dumb resignation with which they went to the gas . . .

To the gas? The expression was new. Francine had to explain, and she did it with a few words, not looking into the faces of the Jewish combatants who were questioning her, almost like judges. To the gas, yes, of course: how could they fail to know about it? By the thousands, the millions: she didn't know how many, but the women of the *Lager* melted around her, day after day. At Auschwitz dying was the rule; living was the exception. She was an exception, in fact: every living Jew was lucky. And what about her? How had she survived?

"I don't know," she said. Even Francine, like Schmulek, like Edek, when she spoke of death, lowered her voice. "I don't know: I met a French woman who was a doctor in the infirmary, she helped me, she gave me food, for a little while she had me work there as a nurse. But that wouldn't have been enough; many women ate more than I did and they died all the same, they let themselves go under. I held out: I don't know why; perhaps because I loved life more than they did, or because I believed life had a meaning. It's strange: it was easier to believe that back there than it is here. In the *Lager* nobody killed himself. There wasn't time, there were other things to think about, bread, boils. Here there's time, and people kill themselves. Also out of shame."

"What shame?" Line asked. "You're ashamed when you're guilty of something, and they aren't guilty of anything."

"Ashamed of not being dead," Francine said. "I feel it, too. It's stupid, but I feel it. It's hard to explain. It's the impression that the others died in your place, that you're alive gratis, thanks to a privilege you haven't earned, a trick you've played on the dead. Being alive isn't a crime, but we feel it like a crime."

Gedaleh couldn't keep away from Francine, Bella was jealous, and Gedaleh paid no attention to Bella's jealousy.

"Yes, yes," Bella said, "he always acts like this, it's natural with him. Foreign women interest him; he always runs after the latest one he's met."

To the questions of Gedaleh and the others, Francine replied with nervous volubility. She had been a nurse, yes; she felt compassion for the sick women, but sometimes she hit them. Not to hurt them, only to defend herself, she didn't know how to explain, to defend herself from their demands, their lamentations. She knew about the gas, all the old prisoners knew, but she didn't tell the newcomers, it wouldn't have done any good. Run away? Madness: where to? And how could she, who spoke German badly and no Polish?

"Come with us," Sissl said to her, "now it's all over; you'll be our doctor."

"And in a few months a baby will be born, too. My son," Isidor added.

"I'm not like the rest of you," Francine answered, "I'm going back to France; it's my country." She saw the novel in Bella's hands, she read "Victor Hugo," and she seized on it with a cry of joy. "Oh! a French book!", but she immediately saw the Polish title, undecipherable, and she handed the volume back to Bella, who resumed reading it with cold ostentation. For a few days Pavel did his best to court Francine, with the charm of a bear; but she laughed at his French, picked up by ear in cabarets, and Pavel retired without any fuss, indeed with some grumbled boasts: "She wasn't my type, I made that clear to her. Too refined, too delicate: a bit meshuggeh, probably the effect of the troubles she's had, but all she thinks of is eating. I saw her myself, she collects all the crumbs she can find and puts them in her pocket. And she bathes too much, anyway."

Time, in the Glogau camp, passed strangely. The days were empty, but all the same, they trickled by, long and boring. In memory they flattened out, became short, and were all mixed together, one with another. The weeks passed, the Russians were absentminded, often also drunk, but they gave no passes to go out. Inside the fence there was a constant bustle: prisoners arrived, of every nationality and condition; others were released on the basis of inscrutable criteria. The Greeks left, then the French, and Francine with them; the Poles and the Germans remained. The camp commander was kind, but he shrugged: he knew nothing, it didn't depend on him, he just carried out the orders he received from the High Command. Kind, but firm; in fact, the war was won, but they were still fighting, and not far away: around Breslau, and also in the Western Sudeten mountains. Orders were strict: nobody was to clutter the roads.

"Just be patient for a few more days, and don't ask for things we can't grant you. And don't try to escape: that's a favor I ask of you."

Kind, firm, and curious. He called Gedaleh into his office, then all the others, one by one. He had lost his left hand, and on his chest he wore a silver medal and a bronze one; he looked about forty, thin and bald, dark-skinned; he had thick, black eyebrows, he spoke in a calm and educated voice, and he seemed very intelligent.

"If you ask me, Captain Smirnov hasn't been called

Smirnov for very long," Gedaleh declared, coming back from his questioning.

"What do you mean?" asked Mottel, who hadn't yet been called.

"I mean that he's managed to have his name changed. I mean he's a Jew, but he doesn't want it known. You see for yourselves, when your turns come. But be careful."

"What should we say, or not say?" Line asked.

"Say as little as possible. That we're Jews, that's obvious. That we were armed—we can't deny that. If he asks, admit that we were partisans, it's always better than passing for bandits. Insist on the fact that we fought against the Germans: say where and when. Not a word about Edek and about our contacts with the Jewish Combat Organization. Not a word about the truck, either, if possible, because we went a bit far there. If worse comes to worst, say that we found it broken down and we fixed it. It's best to be vague about everything else: where we're going and where we come from. Anybody who was in the Red Army keep it to himself; especially you, Piotr: make up a story that will hold water. But I don't think he belongs to the police; he's just curious on his own, and we interest him."

Mendel's turn came at the end of April, when the birches were already budding and the insistent rain had washed the dark lignite dust off the roofs of the barracks. The war news was triumphal: Bratislava and Vienna had fallen, the troops of the First Ukrainian Front were already fighting on the outskirts of Berlin. Also on the western front Germany was in its death throes, the Americans were in Nuremberg, the French in Stuttgart and Berchtesgaden, the English at the Elbe. In Italy, the Allies had reached the Po, and in Genoa, Milan, Turin, the partisans had driven out the Nazis even before the liberation troops had arrived.

Captain Smirnov was elegant in his well-pressed uniform, he spoke Russian without any accent, and he kept Mendel for almost two hours, offering him Irish whisky and Cuban cigars. The fairy tale that Mendel had made up about himself, rather implausible for that matter, proved superfluous: Smirnov knew a great deal about him, and not only his first name, patronymic, and surname. He knew where and when he had been listed as missing, he knew what had happened at Novoselki and Turov. Instead he asked him many questions about the meeting with the band of Venjamin. Who had informed him? Ulybin himself? Polina Gelman? The two messengers in the plane? Mendel was unable to figure it out.

"So it was this Venjamin who didn't want you people? And why not?"

Mendel remained vague: "I don't know. I couldn't say: a partisan chief has to be suspicious, and there were all sorts of people roaming around those woods. Or perhaps he didn't consider us suited to join his band; we didn't know that zone . . ."

"Mendel Nachmanovich, or rather Mendel ben Nachman," Smirnov said, underlining the Jewish patronymic, "with me, you can speak. I would like to convince you that I'm not an inquisitor, even if I collect information and ask questions. No, I would like to write your story, so it isn't lost. I would like to write the stories of all of you, of the Jewish soldiers of the Red Army, who made your choice, and who remained Russians and Jews even when the Russians informed them, whether with words or deeds, that a decision had to be made, a man couldn't be both. I don't know if I'll succeed, and if I write this book, I don't know if I'll be able to publish it: times can change, perhaps for the better, perhaps for the worse."

Mendel remained silent, dazed, torn between respect and suspicion. Out of old habit, he distrusted anyone who showed benevolence and asked questions.

Smirnov went on: "You don't trust me, and I can't say you're wrong. I know the things you know; I, too, trust few people, and I often force myself to resist the temptation to confide. Think it over: but there's one thing I want to say to you: I admire you and your companions, and I also envy you a little."

"You envy us? We're not to be envied. We haven't had an easy way. Why do you envy us?"

"Because your choice wasn't imposed on you. Because you invented your destiny."

"Comrade Captain," Mendel said, "the war isn't over, and we don't know that this war may not give birth to another. Maybe it's early to write our story."

"I know." Smirnov said, "I know what partisan warfare is. I know also that a partisan may happen to have done, seen, or said things that he mustn't tell about. But I also know that what you learned in the marshes and the forest mustn't be lost; and it isn't enough for it to survive in a book."

Smirnov had uttered these last words, separating each syllable and looking straight into Mendel's eyes.

"What do you mean?" Mendel asked.

"I know where you are going, and I know your war isn't over. It will begin again, in a few years, I couldn't say when, and no longer against the Germans. Not for Russia, but with the help of Russia. There will be a need for people like you, for example; you could teach others the things you've learned on the Kursk front, at Novoselki, at Turov and perhaps elsewhere, too. Think about it, artilleryman: think also about that."

Mendel felt as if an eagle had clutched him and borne him high into the sky.

"Comrade Captain," he said, "this war isn't yet finished and you're already talking to me about another. We're tired people, we've done and undergone many things, and many of us have died."

"I can't say you're wrong. And if you were to tell me you want to start being a watchmender again, I couldn't say you were wrong about that, either. Still, think about it."

The captain poured whisky for Mendel and for himself, raised his glass, and said "*L'khayim!*" Mendel jerked his head up: this expression is the Hebrew equivalent of "Your health!" and is said, in fact, when you drink; but it has a deeper meaning, because literally it means "To

Life!" Few Russians know it, and as a rule they pronounce it wrong; but Smirnov had got the harsh aspirated *kh* sound just right.

In the days that followed, Smirnov called all the Gedalists for a talk, one by one, some more than once. With all of them he was extremely polite, but about him and about his real identity endless arguments sprang up. A converted Jew, a disguised Jew, a Jew who pretends he's a Christian, or a Christian who pretends he's a Jew. A historian. A busybody. Many considered him ambiguous, at the very least; others came right out and said he was an NKVD agent, only a bit more clever than the norm; but the majority of the Gedalists, including Mendel and Gedaleh himself, trusted him and narrated the band's exploits and their personal stories, because, as the saying goes, "*Ibergekumene tsores iz gut tsu dertseyln*"; it's good to tell your past troubles. The proverb holds true in all the languages of the world, but in Yiddish it sounds particularly appropriate.

In the tumultuous and memorable days that ended the Second World War on the European fronts, at the beginning of May 1945, the Russian command responsible for the constellation of little camps in Glogau vanished as if by magic. At night, with no farewells, no good-byes, they all went away, including Captain Smirnov: no one knew whether they had been transferred or demobilized or simply absorbed by the collective frenzy of the Red Army, drunk with victory. There were no more guards, the gates were open, the stores looted; but nailed to the outside door of their barracks, the Gedalists found a hastily scrawled note:

> We have to leave. Dig behind the kitchen chimney; there's a present for you. We don't need it any more. Good luck.
> Smirnov

Behind the kitchen they found some hand grenades, three pistols, a German machine pistol, a little supply of ammunition, an army map of Saxony and Bavaria, and a little roll of eight hundred dollars. Gedaleh's band set off once again: no longer at night, no longer by furtive paths or in desert and wild country, but over the roads of Germany once prosperous and haughty and now devastated, between two hedges of sealed faces, marked by their new impotence, which gave new nourishment to their old hatred. "First rule: keep together," Gedaleh said: they proceeded mostly on foot, occasionally asking a lift from Soviet army vehicles, but only if they had room for all. White Rokhele was now in her seventh month of pregnancy: Gedaleh gave only her permission to ride in an occasional horse-drawn wagon, but then the whole band was deployed as escort.

Against the indifferent background of the springtime countryside, those roads were swarming with a divided humanity, distressed and rejoicing. German citizens, on foot or in wagons, were reentering their shattered cities, blind with fatigue; on other wagons the peasants flowed in, to feed the black market. In contrast, Soviet soldiers, on bicycles, motorcycles, in army vehicles, and requisitioned cars drove madly in both directions, singing, playing music, shooting into the air. The Gedalists were nearly run down by a Dodge truck on which two grand pianos had been loaded: two uniformed officers were playing, in unison, with gravity and commitment, the *1812 Overture* of Tchaikowsky, while the driver wove among the wagons with brusque swerves, pressing the siren at full volume, heedless of the pedestrians in his way. Former prisoners of every nationality moved in groups or isolated, men and women, civilians in tattered everyday clothes, Allied soldiers in the khaki uniforms with the big letters "KG" on their back: all were on their way home or in search of some place to rest.

Towards the end of May the band camped at the gates of the village of Neuhaus, not far from Dresden. Ever since they had advanced into German land, they had realized that it was almost impossible to buy food in the larger cities, half-destroyed, half-empty, and starving. Pavel,

Black Rokhele, and two other men on a foraging mission knocked at the door of a farmhouse two or three times; nobody answered. "Shall we go inside?" Pavel suggested. The shutters on the windows had been freshly painted, with brightly colored paint. They gave way at once, but beyond them there was no glass: a compact wall of rein-forced concrete, and inside where the window should have been, a funnel-shaped end of an air vent. It wasn't a farmhouse, but a camouflaged bunker, now abandoned and empty.

But the village was teeming with people. It was girdled by walls, and through the gates women and old men en-tered and left, looking furtive and ravenous, dragging carts with food or bric-a-brac. At either side of the main gate stood two guards, grim-faced, in civilian clothes, evi-dently unarmed. "What do you want?" they asked the four, whom they had recognized as foreigners.

"To buy food," Pavel answered, in his best German. One of the guards nodded that they could enter.

The village was intact. The little cobbled streets were still lined with picturesque facades, brightly colored, criss-crossed by exposed beams painted black. The setting was peaceful, but the human presence was disturbing. The streets were crammed with people walking in all direc-tions, apparently without goal or purpose: old people, children, the maimed. No able-bodied men were to be seen. Even the windows were filled with frightened, suspi-cious faces.

"It seems a ghetto," Rokhele said, who had been at Kossovo.

"It is," Pavel said. "These must be refugees from Dres-den. Now it's their turn." They had spoken in Yiddish, and perhaps in too-loud voices, because one heavyset woman, wearing a pair of men's boots, turned to the old man with her and said, in a tone meant to be overheard: "Here they are again, more shameless than before." Then, directly addressing the four Jews, she added, "This isn't your place."

"Where is it, then?" Pavel asked, in good faith.

"Behind barbed wire," the woman answered.

Impetuously, Pavel grabbed her by the lapels of her overcoat, but he immediately let go of her because out of the corner of his eye he had seen that a crowd was gathering around them. At the same moment he heard a sharp report over his head, and at his side Rokhele staggered and fell prone. The people around them vanished in an instant; even the windows emptied. Pavel knelt beside the girl: she was breathing, but her limbs were limp, inert. She wasn't bleeding, he couldn't see any wounds. "She's fainted. Let's take her away," he said to the other two.

At the camp, Sissl and Mendel examined her more closely. There was a wound, almost invisible, hidden beneath her thick black hair: a neat hole just above the left temple; there was no exit hole, the bullet had remained in her skull. Her eyes were closed; Sissl raised the lids and saw the white of the sclera, the irises were turned upwards, hidden in the sockets. Rokhele was breathing more and more faintly, irregularly, and she had no pulse. While she lived, nobody dared speak, as if for fear of snapping that thread of breath; at evening the girl was dead. Gedaleh said, "Let's go, with all our weapons."

They went off at night, all of them; at the camp only Bella and Sissl remained, to dig the grave, and White R. to recite the prayer of the dead over the body of her black companion. The weapons were few, but the Gedalists' rage drove them as a storm drives a ship: a woman, twenty years old, not even a combatant, a woman who had survived the ghetto and Treblinka, now killed in peacetime, treacherously, for no reason, by a German hand. A woman unarmed, hardworking, lighthearted, and carefree, the one who accepted everything and never complained, the only one who didn't know the paralysis of despair, Mendel's stoker, Piotr's woman. Piotr was the most enraged, and also the most lucid.

"To the Rathaus," he said curtly. "The ones who count will be there." Rapid and silent, they reached the gate of the village; there were no guards now, they burst running into the deserted streets, while to Mendel's mind distant images returned, faded and importunate, images that block you instead of driving you. Simon and Levi who avenge with blood the Schechemites' insult to their sister Dinah. Had that revenge been just? Does a just revenge exist? It doesn't exist, but you're a man, and vengeance cries out in your blood, and then you run and destroy and kill. Like them, like the Germans.

They surrounded the Rathaus. Piotr was right: in Neuhaus there was still no electricity, the streets were dark, and so were most of the windows, but those on the second floor of the city hall were faintly illuminated. Piotr had asked for and been given the automatic pistol given them by Smirnov; from the shadows where he had hidden, with two single shots, he killed the two men on guard outside the entrance. "Hurry, now!" he cried. He ran to the door and tried furiously to break it open, first with the butt of his pistol, then with his shoulders. It was heavy and it resisted, and already excited voices could be heard inside. Arie and Mendel moved away from the facade and, simultaneously, each threw a hand grenade against the lighted windows; fragments of glass rained down in the street, three very long seconds went by, then they heard the two explosions: all the windows of the floor caved in and vomited out pieces of wood and papers. Meanwhile Mottel was trying in vain to help Piotr open the door. "Wait!" he shouted: he climbed in a flash to the ground-floor window, smashed the glass with a blow of his hip, and jumped inside. A few seconds later they heard him fire three, four shots with his pistol, and then the lock of the door was immediately opened from the inside. "All of you stay out here," Piotr ordered four of the Ruzany men, "and don't let anyone escape." He and all the others rushed up the stairs, stepping over the body of an old man lying across the steps. In the council chamber were four men with their arms raised; two others were dead, and the seventh was moaning in a corner, weakly writhing. "Who is the *Burger-*

meister?" Gedaleh cried; but Piotr had already pressed the automatic trigger and mowed them all down.

No one had intervened, no one had escaped, and the four men put on guard hadn't seen anyone approach. In the cellars of the Rathaus the Gedalists found bread, ham, and lard, and they came back to the camp laden and unharmed, but Gedaleh said, "We've got to get away from here. Bury Black R., strike the tents, and we're off: the Americans are thirty kilometers away."

They walked in the night, with haste, and remorse for the easy vendetta, and relief because it was all over. White R. marched bravely, assisted in turns by the others, so she wouldn't remain behind. Mendel found himself marching at the head of the column, between Line and Gedaleh.

"Did you count them?" Line asked.

"Ten," Gedaleh answered. "Two at the door, one Mottel killed on the stairs, seven in the big room."

"Ten against one," Mendel said. "We did what they did: ten hostages for one German killed."

"You're counting wrong," Line said. "The ten of Neuhaus don't go on Rokhele's account. They go on the account of the millions of Auschwitz. Remember what the Frenchwoman told you."

Mendel said, "Blood isn't paid for with blood. Blood is paid for with justice. Whoever shot Black R. was an animal, and I don't want to become an animal. If the Germans killed with gas, must we kill all the Germans with gas? If the Germans killed ten for one, and we do the same as they, we'll become like them, and there will never be peace again."

Gedaleh intervened: "Maybe you're right, Mendel. But then how do you explain the fact that now I feel better?"

Mendel looked inside himself, then admitted, "Yes, I feel better, too, but this doesn't prove anything. In Neuhaus they were refugees from Dresden. Smirnov told about it: in Dresden a hundred and forty thousand Germands died in a single night. That night, in Dresden there was a fire that melted the cast iron of the street lamps."

"We weren't the ones who bombed Dresden," Line said.

"That's enough of this," Mendel said. "It was our last battle. Let's walk. Let's get to the Americans."

"We'll go see what they look like," said Gedaleh, who didn't seem too concerned by the problems that were worrying Mendel. "The war is over: it's hard to understand, we'll understand it little by little; but it's over. Tomorrow day will break, and we won't have to shoot anymore or hide. It's spring, and we have food to eat, and all the roads are open. We're going to look for a place in the world where he can be born in peace."

"He? Who?" Line asked.

"The baby. Our son, the son of two innocents."

They ventured into the no-man's land with mixed feelings. They were uncertain and hesitant, they felt freshly cleansed, like blank pages, children again. Adult, wild children, who had grown up in hardship, isolation, in camps and warfare, unprepared at the threshold of the West and of peace. There, under their boots, patched and repatched twenty times, was the soil of the enemy, the exterminator, Germany-Deutschland-Dajclamd-Niemcy: a tidy countryside, untouched by the war. But wait: this is only the appearance, the real Germany is in the cities, the Germany glimpsed at Glogau and Neuhaus, that of Dresden, Berlin, and Hamburg, whose stories they had listened to with horror. That is the real Germany, that had been drunk on blood and had been made to pay; a prostrate body, mortally wounded, already rotting. Naked. Along with the barbaric joy of revenge, they felt a new disgust; they felt indiscreet and shameless, like one who uncovers a forbidden nakedness.

At either side of the road they saw houses with the windows barred, like spent eyes, or eyes refusing to see; other houses were covered with roofs of straw, still others were roofless, or the roof was charred. Lopped spires, playing fields where weeds were already growing. In the towns, piles of rubble on which there were signs reading: "Don't trample: human bodies"; long lines outside the few open shops, and citizens busy erasing and chipping away the symbols of the past, those eagles and hooked crosses that were to have lasted a thousand years. From the balconies strange red flags flapped: they still bore the shadow of the black swastika that had been unstitched in great haste; but soon, as they progressed on their way, the red flags became rarer and finally vanished. Gedaleh said to Mendel, "If your enemy falls, don't rejoice; but don't help him to his feet."

The line of demarcation between the two armies was not yet consolidated. On the morning of the second day of walking they found themselves in a gentle countryside, green and brown, hilly, dotted with farms and little houses; in the fields the peasants were already at work. "Americans?" The peasants shrugged with distrust and nodded vaguely to the west. "Russians?" No Russians; no Russians here.

They found themselves in the midst of the Americans without being aware of the passage. The first patrols they came upon glanced without interest at the Gedalists' tattered caravan: in Germany there was nothing but refugees; these Americans had seen worse. Only at Scheibenberg a patrol stopped them and escorted them to the local HQ. The little office, set up on the ground floor of a requisitioned villa, was swarming with people, almost all Germans, evacuated from the bombed cities or fleeing before the Red Army. The men of the band left their baggage (their arms hidden in the baggage) in the safekeeping of Mottel and stood in an orderly line.

"You speak for us all," Gedaleh said to Pavel.

Pavel was intimidated: "I don't speak English. I pretend to, but I just know a few words, the way actors do, and parrots."

"That doesn't matter; he'll question you in German. You answer in bad German, say we're Italians and we're going to Italy."

"He won't believe me; we don't look like Italians."

"Try it. If it works, fine; if it doesn't work, we'll see. We're not risking much. Hitler's gone now."

The American seated behind the desk was sweating, in his shirt sleeves, bored, and he questioned Pavel in surprisingly good German, so that Pavel had a hard time inventing a language that sounded credible for an Italian. Luckily the American seemed completely indifferent to what Pavel was saying, to how he said it, to the band, to its composition, its intentions, its past and its future. After a few moments he said to Pavel, "Please, be more concise." After another minute, he interrupted him, told him to wait outside the house, with his companions. Pavel came out, all the others put their packs on their backs, and they left Scheibenberg with heads high.

Gedaleh said: "This doesn't mean that all the Americans are so distracted, and we don't know what agreements the Russians and the Americans have made. To be on the safe side, anybody wearing a Soviet uniform or chevrons or carrying any in the pack, had better get rid of them. If they were to ship us back, it wouldn't be very funny."

By now they were no longer in any hurry. They continued westwards in easy stages, stopping to rest often, in scenery that was always new, idyllic, and tragic. Frequently they were passed by American army units, motorized or on foot, marching towards the heart of Germany; or they would encounter endless columns of German war prisoners escorted by American soldiers, white or black, with their automatic rifles idly slung over a shoulder. At the Chemnitz station, on a siding, there was a freight train of fifty cars standing, headed towards the line of demarcation; it contained all the machinery of a paper mill, including supplies, enormous rolls of paper just produced, and the office furniture. Guarding the train there was only one soldier, very young and blond, in Soviet uniform, sprawled on a sofa, jammed in the midst of the machinery. Piotr greeted him in Russian, and the soldier explained that the paper plant was going to Russia, he didn't know where: it was a present from the Americans to the Russians, because all the Russian factories were *kaput*.

The soldier asked Piotr no questions. A little farther on there was a bombed-out factory, perhaps a mechanics shop; a team of prisoners of war was shoveling the rubble, under the surveillance of American officers and experts. They weren't working as diggers, but rather as archeologists: with the tips of their spades, often with their bare hands: and at every metal finding, the Americans would bend over, alert, to examine it, tag it, and carefully put it aside.

Rokhele never complained, but she was tired, and her condition worried everyone. She had a hard time walking: her ankles became more swollen every day; she had to give up wearing her boots, and awkwardly cut the uppers of the shoes that Mottel had procured for her, then finally she was reduced to walking in slippers. For short stretches they carried her on a litter, but it was clear that some solution had to be found. In mid-June they reached Plauen, on the Berlin-Munich-Brenner railway line, and Gedaleh sent Pavel and Mottel to study the situation. The situation was confused; trains went by irregularly, with unpredictable schedules, packed beyond any reasonable limit. The Gedalists camped in the waiting room, which had taken on the appearance of a public dormitory. In their reserve fund there was no longer enough money to pay the whole band's way to the Brenner, as Gedaleh would have liked; money also had to be spent on a gynecological examination of White R., who was put in a hospital and came out enthusiastic at the cleanliness and order she had found there; she was healthy, a normal pregnancy, she was just a bit tired. She could walk, yes, but not too much. In the meanwhile, most of the members of the band roamed around the city, like tourists, but also looking for some barter that would bring in money. "We can get rid of our heavy clothes, because we're heading south and towards summer," Gedaleh said. "The cooking things only if you get a good price. Not the weapons, not at any price."

None of the Gedalists had any experience of city life; only Leonid had had that, and many missed him. At

Plauen they were intimidated and surprised by the contradictions: through the streets still cluttered with rubble the milkman made his rounds with his little cart and bugle, prompt, every morning at the same hour. Coffee and meat commanded wild prices; but silver was cheap. For a few marks Mottel bought a fine camera already loaded; they formed a group, some standing, others crouched in the front row, all with their weapons clearly in sight. Nobody wanted to miss being in the picture, so they had to ask a passerby to snap them, against the background of crumbled houses. The trains were working badly, but the Reisebüro, the only travel office in the city, was working well: the telephone line had been restored, and they knew more than the station people did. Nevertheless, Gedaleh never went very far from the station. He was often noticed in the company of one of the railwaymen, a worker; Gedaleh was generous with him, bought him beer at the tavern, and one day they were seen together, off to one side in a little garden of the station: Gedaleh was playing the violin and the German, the flute, both serious and intent. Without giving any explanation, Gedaleh insisted that nobody stray: maybe they would be leaving soon, they should all be within a few minutes' call.

Instead they spent several more weeks in the station, in an atmosphere of laziness and unfocused waiting. It was hot; in the station a Red Cross bureau was working, and every day it handed out soup to anyone asking for it: refugees and stragglers of every race and nationality trickled in and out constantly. Some of the citizens of Plauen established cautious relations with the encamped Gedalists: the Germans were curious but asked no questions. Dialogue was impeded by the linguistic friction; anyone who speaks Yiddish can understand German fairly well, and vice versa, and further, nearly all the Gedalists could manage to speak some German, more or less correctly, and with a stronger or less strong Yiddish accent, but the two languages, historically sisters, appear to their respective speakers each as the parody of the other, just as to us humans, monkeys seem our caricatures (as we surely seem to them). Perhaps this fact has something to do with the Germans' ancient resentment of the Ashkenazic Jews, considered the corrupters of High German. But other, deeper factors intervened to block reciprocal comprehension. To the Germans, these Jewish foreigners, so different from the local bourgeois Jews who had, with discipline, allowed themselves to be rounded up and slaughtered, seemed suspect: too quick, too energetic, dirty, tattered, proud, unpredictable, primitive, too "Russian." The Jews found it impossible, and at the same time necessary, to distinguish the headhunters they had eluded and on whom they had taken passionate revenge from these shy, reserved old people, these blond, polite children who looked in at the station doors as if through the bars of the zoo. They aren't the ones, no; but it's their fathers, their teachers, their sons, themselves yesterday and tomorrow. How to resolve the puzzle? It can't be solved. Leave: as soon as possible. This land, too, is searing under our feet, this neat, trim town, loving order, this sweet and bland air of full summer also scorches. Leave, leave: we haven't come from the depths of Polessia in order to go to sleep in the Wartesaal of Plauen-am-Elster, and to while away our waiting with group snapshots and the Red Cross soup. But on July 20th suddenly the signal came, in the heart of the night, to fulfill their collective, unexpressed wish. Gedaleh rushed into the waiting room, among the sleepers:

"Everybody on your feet, now, packs on your back. Follow me, but keep quiet. We're leaving in fifteen minutes." In the confusion that followed there was a flurry of questions and hasty explanations: all were to follow him, not far, along the siding. His friend the flautist, the worker, had performed the miracle. There it was, practically new, good as new, the coach that would take them to Italy: bought, yes; bought for a few dollars, not all that legally; a damaged car, recently repaired, still to be tested: organized, in other words. Organized? Yes, that's what you say, that's what they said in the ghettos, in the *Lagers*, in all of Nazi Europe; a thing you procure illegally is called organized. And the train would soon arrive; the station bell was already ringing.

They were all ready in a moment, but Pavel was missing. Gedaleh cursed in Polish (because there are no curses in Yiddish) and sent one of the followers running to look for him; he was found, not far off, with a German prostitute, and brought back to the station while he was still buttoning up his trousers. He was also cursing, in Russian, but he made no objections. They all climbed into the car, making no noise.

"Who's going to couple it to the train?" Mendel asked.

"He will, Ludwig. He promised me. If necessary, we'll also lend him a hand."

"How did you manage to make such a friend of him?"

"With the violin. Like that character, in ancient times, who tamed tigers with his lyre. Not that Ludwig's a tiger: he's kind and full of talent, it was a pleasure playing with him; and to do us this favor he asked for very little."

"He's still a German, though," Pavel grumbled.

"Well, so what? He didn't go to war; he's always worked on the railroad, he plays the flute, and in 'thirty-three he didn't vote for Hitler. Do you know what you would have done if you'd been born in Germany, from purebred father and mother, and if they had taught you in school all those *bubkes* of theirs about blood and soil?"

The women, in a corner of the car, were preparing a pallet for White R., with straw and blankets. Bella turned to Gedaleh and said: "Tell the truth, though: you've always been fond of trains. I believe that if it hadn't been for that business of the nun in Bialystok, you wouldn't have become a violinist but a railroad man."

Gedaleh laughed happily and said it was the absolute truth, he did like trains and all vehicles. "But this time the game was profitable, we're going to Italy in a car all our own, in style. Only heads of state travel like this!"

"*Nu*," Isidor said, pensively, "you're still young enough.

Now that the war is over there's no use for partisans. Why shouldn't you be a railroad man? I'd like it myself, down there in the land of Israel."

At that moment they heard a clang of wheels, they saw the glare of a headlight on the tracks, and a long freight train entered the station. It braked, with a shriek, stood still for half an hour, then maneuvered slowly: perched on the buffers of the last car, a man waved his lantern in greeting: it was Ludwig. The train backed up very slowly, there was an impact, then the scrape of the couplings was heard. The train set off again, drawing the Gedalists towards the Alps, in their private car.

12

July–August

1945

They had never traveled like this: not on foot but in a car hooked up to a train; not in the cold, exposed to shooting, not hungry, not straggling. Papers in order, no, not yet, and God knows when they would be; but on the side of the car was a sign with its itinerary: München-Innsbruck-Brenner-Verona. Ludwig had thought of everything. "Leave the car as little as possible," Gedaleh said, "the less we show our faces, the less likely somebody will have the idea of checking up."

Nobody checked up; along that whole line, and on the majority of European railroads, there was still plenty of other work to do: repairing tracks, removing rubble, putting the signals back into operation. The train traveled slowly, almost entirely at night; during the day it remained endlessly on sidings, roasting in the sun to allow other trains, with precedence, to go by. The passenger trains were few: these were convoys of freight cars carrying human beings, but packed in like freight; the hundreds of thousands of Italians, men and women, soldiers and civilians, employees and slaves, who had worked in the factories and the camps of the destroyed Third Reich. Mingled with them, less noisy, less numerous, anxious to avoid notice, other passengers were traveling, Germans swarming from occupied Germany to elude the Allies' justice; SS men; functionaries of the Gestapo and the party. Paradoxically, for them, as for the transient Jews, Italy was the land of least resistance, the best jumping-off place for more hospitable countries: South America, Syria, Egypt. Openly or in disguise, with documents or without, this varicolored tide headed south, towards the Brenner: the Brenner had become the narrow neck of a vast funnel. Through the Brenner you gained Italy, the land of the mild climate and notorious, open illegality; the affectionate mafioso land whose double reputation had reached even Norway and the Ukraine and the sealed ghettos of eastern Europe; the land of evaded prohibitions and anarchic forbearance, where every foreigner is welcomed like a brother.

When the train stopped in stations, they kept the doors shut, but they opened them when the train was moving, and during the frequent stops in open country. Sitting on the floor, his legs hanging down, Mendel witnessed the solemn unfolding of the landscape: the fertile fields, the lakes, the woods, the farms and towns of the Upper Palatinate, then of Bavaria. Neither he nor any of his companions had ever inhabited a land so rich and civilized. Behind them, as if dotted by their countless footsteps, stretched the trail of their march, endless, as in a tormented dream, through marshes, fords, forests filled with ambush, snow, rivers, death suffered and inflicted. He felt tired and alien. Alone, now; without women, without destination, without homeland. Without friends? No, he couldn't say that; the companions remained, and would remain: they filled his emptiness. He didn't care where the train pulled him; he had fulfilled, he had done what he

316 If Not Now, When?

had to do, not easily, not always willingly, but he had done it. That was over, finished. The war was over, and what does an artilleryman do in peacetime? What is he capable of being? A watchmender? Who knows? Perhaps never again. Shooting stiffens the fingers, makes them insensitive, and the eyes become used to looking into the distance, through the sight. From the promised land he received no summons; perhaps there, too, he would have to march and fight. Very well, it's my destiny, I accept it, but it doesn't warm my heart. It's a duty, and you do it, like when I killed the Ukrainian in the auxiliary police. Duty isn't a wealth. Neither is the future. They, yes. They are my riches; they remain to me. All of them: with their roughness and their faults, even those who have offended me, and those I have offended. The women, too, Sissl, whom I stupidly left, and Line, who knows what she wants, who wants them all, and who left me; even Bella, who is tiresome and slow-witted, even White Rokhele with her bold belly, ripening like a fruit.

He looked at his sides and behind him. There was Piotr, innocent as a baby and awesome in battle, crazy like all respectable Russians. Would you give your life for Piotr? Yes, I would, without hesitating: as anyone who knows he's making a good trade doesn't hesitate. On the face of the earth he is better off than I am. He is coming into Italy with us, lighthearted and confident like a child getting on to a carousel. He chose to fight with us and for us like the knights of old, because he's generous, because he believes in that Christ we don't believe in; and yet the priest must have told him too that we were the ones who nailed Christ to the cross.

There is Gedaleh. It's funny he should be named Gedaleh; the Biblical Gedaliah was a good-for-nothing. Nebuchadnezzar the Chaldean had appointed him governor of Judah, of the few Jews left in Judah after the exile: then, as now, like the governors Hitler appointed. He was a collaborator, in other words. And he had been killed by Ishmael, a partisan, a man like us. If we're right, Ishmael was right, and he did well to kill that Gedaliah. . . . What stupid thoughts! A man isn't responsible for the name he bears: I'm called the Consoler and I don't console anybody, not even myself. Anyway, Gedaleh should really have a different name; Jubal, for example, the one who invented the flute and the guitar; or Jabal, his brother, who was the first to roam the world and live in a tent; or Tubalcain, the third brother, who taught everyone how to work brass and iron. They were all sons of Lamech. Lamech had been a mysterious avenger, nobody knows any more what the offense was that he avenged. Lamech at Ljuban, Lamech at Chmielnik, Lamech at Neuhaus. Perhaps Lamech had also been a jolly avenger, like Gedaleh; in the evening, in the tent, after the vendetta, he played the flute with his sons. I don't understand Gedaleh, I couldn't predict any of his acts or his decisions, but Gedaleh is my brother.

And Line? What could he say of Line? She's not my sister: she's much more and much less, she's a mother-wife-daughter-friend-enemy-rival-teacher. She was flesh of my flesh, I entered inside her, a thousand years ago, on a windy night inside a windmill, when the war was still on, and the world was young; and each of us was an angel holding a sword. She isn't lighthearted, but she is sure, and I am neither lighthearted nor sure, and I'm a thousand years old and I carry the world on my back. There she is beside me, she isn't looking at me: she's staring at this German landscape, and she always knows precisely what must be done. A thousand years ago, in the marshes I also knew, and now she knows still, and I no longer know. She doesn't look at me but I look at her, and I feel pleasure in looking at her, and unrest, and laceration; and coveting my neighbor's woman. Line, Emmeline, Rahab: the holy sinner of Jericho. Whose woman? Everyone's, which is like saying no one's; she forms ties and she doesn't. I don't care whose woman, but when I see her body again in memory, when I sense it under her clothing, I feel lacerated, and I would like to start again, and I know it can't be done, and for that very reason I am lacerated. But I would feel lacerated in any case, even without Line, even without Sissl. Even without Rivke? No, Mendel, that you don't know, that you can't say. Without Rivke you'd be a different man, thinking God knows how: a non-Mendel. Without Rivke, without the shadow of Rivke, you would be ready for the future. Ready to live, to grow like a seed: there are seeds that sprout in all lands, also in the land of Israel, and Line is a seed of that kind, and so are all the others. They come out of the water, and they shake themselves like dogs, and they dry away their memories. They have no scars. Come now, how can you say that? They have scars, but they don't talk about them; perhaps each of them, at this moment, is thinking the way you are.

The train had passed Innsbruck, and was toilsomely climbing towards the Brenner and the Italian border. Gedaleh, seated in a corner of the car, his back against the wooden wall, was playing in his fashion, softly, absently. He was playing a zigeuner tune, or Jewish, or Russian: people mutually alien often touch one another in their music, they exchange music, through music they get to know one another, not to be suspicious. A humble tune, heard a hundred times, commonplace, cheaply nostalgic; and then, suddenly, the rhythm turned fast; and the tune, accelerated in this way, became something else: lively, new, noble, filled with hope. A dancing, happy rhythm that invited you to follow it, swaying your head and clapping your hands; and many of the band, with straggly beards, skin baked by the sun, bodies hardened by their toil and their war, followed it like that, enjoying the racket, oblivious and wild. The traps were over, the war was over, the way, the blood and ice; the *satan* of Berlin was dead, the world was empty and vacant, to be re-created, repopulated, like after the Flood. As they climbed, in their jolly climb towards the pass: the climb, the *alia*, this was the word for the road when you are coming out of exile, out of the depths, and you climb towards the light. The rhythm of the violin also climbed, more and more rapidly, became wild, orgiastic. Two of the Gedalists, then four, then ten, cut loose in the car, dancing in pairs, in groups, shoulder to shoulder, stamping the heels of their boots on the resonant flooring. Gedaleh, too, had risen to his feet, and was dancing as he played, spinning around, lifting his knees high.

All of a sudden a sharp click was heard, and the violin fell silent. Gedaleh held the bow still in midair; the violin had snapped. "*Fidl kaput!*" Pavel snickered; others also laughed, but Gedaleh didn't laugh. He looked at the veteran violin; the instrument that had saved his life at Luninets, and perhaps also other times, unnoticed, keeping him afloat above boredom and despair; the violin wounded in battle, pierced by the bullets meant for him, that he had decorated with the Hungarian's bronze medal. "It's nothing: we'll have it mended," White Rokhele said, but she was wrong. Perhaps the sun and the elements had weakened the wood, or perhaps Gedaleh himself had forced it too far in the witches' sabbath he had been playing: in any case, the damage was beyond repair. The bridge had sunk, breaking the delicately convex belly of the instrument and penetrating it; the strings dangled, loose and ignoble. There was nothing to be done. Gedaleh held his arm out of the door, opened his fingers, and the violin fell on the gravel of the railroad with a funereal sound.

The train reached the Brenner at noon on 25 July 1945. During the stops at the preceding stations Gedaleh had never neglected to close the doors, but now he seemed to have forgotten: and yet it was important, this was a border station, there would almost certainly be a check. Line dealt with it, even before the train stopped; she made those sitting in the opening get up, slid the two leaves shut, bound them on the inside with bits of wire, and told everybody to keep quiet. On the platforms there was at first a certain amount of bustle, but then there was silence outside; too, and the hours began to pass and their impatience began to grow. The heat grew, too, in the closed car, motionless under the sun. The Gedalists, thirty-five people packed into a few square meters, felt once more trapped. Whispers were heard:

"Are we already in Italy? Have we passed the border barrier?"

"Maybe they've uncoupled the car."

"No, no, we would have heard the noise."

"Open up, let's get out and see."

"Let's all get out and continue on foot."

But Line ordered silence; on the deserted platform they heard footsteps and voices. Pavel peeked through the crack of the door: "Soldiers. They look English."

The voices approached: there were four or five people, and they stopped to talk, right beneath this car. Pavel pricked up his ears:

"But they aren't speaking English," he said, in a whisper. Then somebody tapped twice on the door with his knuckles, and asked an incomprehensible question. But Line understood, pushed through the crush, and answered. She answered in Hebrew: not in the liturgical, embalmed Hebrew of the synagogues, which all had ears trained to hear; but in the flowing, living Hebrew that has always been spoken in Palestine and that, of them all, only Line understood and spoke: she had learned it from the Zionists in Kiev, before the sky closed over, before the deluge. Line opened the door.

On the platform there were four young men in neat, well-pressed khaki uniforms. They wore comical, broad shorts, low shoes, wool stockings to their knees; on their heads they had a black beret with British insignia, but on their short-sleeved shirts a six-pointed star was sewn, the shield of David. English Jews? English disguised as Jews? For the Gedalists, the star on your chest was a sign of slavery, it was the brand imposed by the Nazis on the Jews in the concentration camps. The puzzled Jews on the train and the calm Jews on the platform faced one another in silence for a few moments. Then one of them spoke, a stocky young man with very fair skin, a rosy, jolly face. In Hebrew he asked: "Who knows Hebrew?"

"Only me," Line answered. "The others speak Yiddish, Russian; and Polish."

"Then let's speak Yiddish," the boy said, but he spoke it with effort and with frequent hesitations. His three companions showed signs of understanding, but they didn't speak it. "You mustn't be afraid of us. We belong to the Palestinian Brigade, we come from the land of Israel, but we belong to the British Army. We've fought our way up through Italy, along with the English, the Americans, the Poles, the Moroccans, the Indians. Where do you come from?"

It wasn't an easy question; they answered in confusion, all of them more or less: they came from Polessia, from Bialystok, from Kossovo, from the ghettos, from the marshes, from the Caucasus, from the Red Army. The young man, whose companions called him Chaim, made the gesture of one calming things down. "You speak, girl," he said. Line, before speaking, had a whispered conference with Gedaleh and Mendel: tell them everything? tell the truth? These are strange soldiers: Jews, but with British uniform. Who do they take orders from? London? or Tel Aviv? Could they be trusted? Gedaleh seemed hesitant, or rather, indifferent: "You decide," he said, "stick to generalities." Mendel said: "What gives them the right to question us? Wait before answering, and try to question them. Then we'll see what line to take."

Chaim was waiting. He smiled, then laughed openly: "The wise man hears one word and understands seven: I told you, this uniform is British, but the war's over now, and we act on our own initiative. We're not here to block your way: on the contrary. We, and all our company, are moving around Germany, Hungary and Poland: we're looking for Jews who have survived the *Lagers*, the ones who were hidden, the sick, the children."

"And what do you do with them?"

"We help them, we treat them, we collect them, and we

escort them here, to Italy. My squad was in Cracow two weeks ago; tomorrow it will be at Mauthausen and Gusen, and the day after tomorrow in Vienna."

"And do the English know what you're doing?"

Chaim shrugged.

"There are wise men among them, too, who understand and let us do what we want. There are also some fools, who don't notice anything. And there are sticklers; they're the biggest trouble, the ones who get in the way. But we weren't born yesterday, and we know how to deal with them, too. Where do you all want to go?"

"To the land of Israel, but we're tired and we have no money, and that woman is going to give birth soon," Line said.

"Are you armed?"

Caught off guard, Line said no, but in such an unconvincing tone that Chaim had to laugh once again. "*Nu*, I told you we weren't born yesterday. Do you think that, with the job we've been doing for the past three months, we can't tell a veteran from a refugee, and a refugee from a partisan? It's written all over you what you are: and why should you be ashamed of it?"

Mottel spoke up: "Nobody's ashamed, but we're keeping our arms."

"We surely won't take them away from you. I told you: we're only passing through here. But you should be reasonable. A bit below the pass there's our brigade HQ: I don't know if they'll handle you, but the most sensible thing would be for you to present yourselves there and turn the weapons over to them. Farther below, at Bolzano, there's the British command, and they will surely check you. So better to hand the stuff over to us than have it requisitioned by them; am I right?"

Pavel said, "You have your experience, but we also have ours. And our experience is that weapons are always handy. In war and in peace, in Russia and in Poland, in Germany and in Italy. Two months ago, when the war was over, the Germans killed a girl, one of us, and we avenged her; how would we have managed if we hadn't had our weapons? And in Poland, under the Russians, the Polish Fascists threw a bomb at our feet."

Chaim said, "Let's not behave like enemies: we're not enemies. Come down from that car, let's go sit on the grass. They've detached the locomotive; your train won't leave for at least two hours. You see: there's something important to discuss." They all got out of the train and sat in a circle on the grass, in the resin-scented air, under a sky swept clear by a high wind. "We call this a *kum-sitz*, a come-and-sit-down," Chaim said, then he went on: "It's the story of the lion and the fox. You come from a terrible world. We know it very little: from the stories of our fathers, and from what we've seen on our missions; but we know that each of you is alive through some miracle, and we know you've left Gehenna behind you. You and we have fought the same enemy, but in two different ways. You had to do it on your own: you had to invent everything, defense, arms, allies, strategy. We were luckier: we were trained, organized, part of a big army. We didn't have enemies at our sides, but only facing us; we didn't have to conquer our weapons, they were issued to us, and we were taught to use them. We have had hard battles, but behind us there were the rear lines, kitchens, infirmaries, and a country that hailed us as liberators. In this country your weapons will be of no use to you anymore."

"Why won't they be of use to us?" Mottel asked. "And how is this country different from other countries? We're foreigners here, the same as everywhere else; in fact we're more foreign here than in Russia or Poland, and a foreigner is an enemy."

"Italy is an odd country," Chaim said. "It takes a long time to understand the Italians, and not even we, who've come all the way up Italy, from Brindisi to the Alps, have yet managed to understand it clearly; but one thing is certain, in Italy foreigners aren't enemies. You'd think the Italians are more enemies to one another than to foreigners: it's strange, but it's true. Maybe this comes from the fact that the Italians don't like laws, and since Mussolini's laws, also his policy and his propaganda, condemned foreigners, for this very reason the Italians helped them. The Italians don't like laws: in fact, they like disobeying them: it's their game, like the Russians' game is chess. They like to cheat; they dislike being cheated, but only up to a point: when someone cheats them, they think: look how smart he is, smarter than me. And they don't plan their vengeance, but at most another game, to get their own back. Like chess, in fact."

"Then they'll cheat us, too," Line said.

"That's probable, but it's the only risk you run. That's why I said your weapons won't be of use. But at this point I must tell you the strangest thing of all: the Italians have proved to be the friends of all foreigners, but they haven't been as friendly with any as with the Palestine Brigade."

"Maybe they didn't realize you were Jews," Mendel said.

"Of course, they realized, and for that matter we made no secret of it. They helped us not in spite of the fact we're Jews, but *because* of it. They also helped their own Jews; when the Germans occupied Italy, they made every effort they could to capture the Italian Jews, but they caught and killed only a fifth. All the others found refuge in Christians' houses, and not only the Italian Jews, but many foreign Jews who had sought refuge in Italy."

"Maybe this happened because the Italians are good Christians," Mendel ventured again.

"That may be, too," Chaim said, scratching his brow, "but I'm not sure of it. Even as Christians, the Italians are odd. They go to Mass, but they curse. They ask favors of the Madonna and the saints, but they don't seem to believe much in God. They know the Ten Commandments by heart, but at most they observe two or three. I believe they help those in need because they're good people, who have suffered a lot, and who know that those who suffer should be helped."

"The Poles have also suffered a lot, but . . ."

"I don't know what to say to you: there could be a

dozen reasons, all good and all bad. But there's one thing you should know: Italian Jews are as odd as the Catholics. They don't speak Yiddish, in fact they don't even know what Yiddish is. They only speak Italian; or rather, the Jews of Rome speak Roman, the Jews of Venice speak Venetian, and so on. They dress like everybody else, they have the same face as everybody else . . ."

"Then how can they be told from the Christians when they walk along the street?"

"They can't: that's the point. Isn't that an unusual country? For that matter, there aren't very many of them; the Christians don't give them any thought, and they themselves don't think much about being Jews. In Italy there's never been a pogrom, not even when the Roman Church told the Christians to despise the Jews and accused them all of being usurers, not even when Mussolini decreed the racial laws, not even when northern Italy was occupied by the Germans: nobody in Italy knows what a pogrom is, they don't even know what the word means. It's an oasis, this country. Italian Jews were Fascists when all the Italians were Fascists and applauded Mussolini; and when the Germans came, some escaped to Switzerland, some became partisans, but the majority remained hidden in the city or the countryside; and very few were discovered or reported, even though the Germans promised a lot of money to anyone who collaborated. There, this is the country you're entering: a country of good people, who don't much like war, who like confusing issues; and since, to get to Palestine, we have to cheat the English, this is really the ideal place: it's like a dock just in the right place, as if it had been put there specially for us."

Crouched or lying on the grass of the Brenner, the Gedalists didn't much relish the idea of handing over their arms to anybody or for whatever reason; but to the four men from Palestine, wearing the uniform of the Allies and apparently so sure of what they were saying, they didn't dare display their disagreement. They remained silent for a bit, then they began debating among themselves in whispers. Chaim and his three companions showed no signs of impatience; they went off a few steps and began strolling on the grass. They came back a few minutes later, and Chaim asked, "Who's your leader?"

Gedaleh raised his hand. "I suppose I am. I'm the one who led the band, for better or worse, from White Russia to here; but you see, we don't have ranks, we never have had. I've almost never needed to give orders. I would suggest something, or sometimes another person would, and we would discuss it and come to an agreement; but most of the time we found we already agreed, without discussing. We lived and fought like that, for eighteen months, and we walked for two thousand kilometers. I was their leader because I invented things, because I had the ideas and thought of the solutions; but why should we have a leader now, when the war is over and we're entering a peaceful country?"

Chaim turned to his companions and said something to them in Hebrew; they answered, showing no scorn or impatience in their faces, but rather forbearance and respect. Chaim said, "I understand you, or think I do. You're strange birds, too, stranger than the Italians; but everybody seems strange to somebody else: that's the way things are, and the war stirs everything up. Well, as far as your leader is concerned, do as you please: elect one or confirm him (and he pointed to Gedaleh, who waved the notion aside), or do without one. But the weapons are another matter. We understand you well, but the English and the Americans won't understand you at all. They're fed up with partisans; partisans were convenient as long as there was fighting, but now nobody wants to hear them even mentioned. The allies actually wanted to retire them, the Italian partisans, this past winter, even before the war ended; and now, they're given all the medals and diplomas anybody could want, but no weapons. If they find one with a weapon on him, or in his house, they put him in jail. So you can imagine how they'll feel about foreign partisans, especially coming from Russia. So you should be reasonable and hand over the arms to us; we'll know what to do with them. In other words, keep whatever you can hide on you, and give the rest to us. All right?"

Gedaleh hesitated a moment, then he shrugged, and said crossly, "Well, my dear companions, we're back to law and order now." He climbed into the car, then came down with Smirnov's machine pistol and a few other weapons. The four soldiers didn't act strict, asked nothing else, and piled everything into the jeep they had parked nearby.

"Good. Now what's to become of us?" Gedaleh asked, when they had come back.

"It's a simple business," Chaim said. "Now that you're disarmed, or almost, you're no longer so strange. You've become DPs."

"What have we become?" Line asked suspiciously. "What's a DP?"

"A DP is a 'displaced person': a refugee, a straggler, a homeless person."

"We're not DPs," Line said. "We had a homeland, and it's not our fault if we don't have one anymore; and we'll build ourselves another one. It lies before us, not behind. We've met lots of stragglers along our way, and they weren't like us. We're not DPs, we're partisans, and not in name only. We've built our future with our own hands."

"Calm down, girl," Chaim said. "This isn't the moment to fuss about definitions; you mustn't give words too much weight. You all have to be flexible, instead. Here, now, there are the Allies; sooner or later you'll run into the military police. They're not like the Nazis, but they're a nuisance, and they'll shut you up God knows where and God knows till when. They'll give you food and drink, but you'll be caged, perhaps until the war with Japan is over, and provided, too, that in the meanwhile a war between Americans and Russians hasn't broken out. They won't ask you so many questions; for them a partisan is a Communist, and if he comes from the East he's a Communist twice over: have I made myself clear? In other words, the fraternity of arms is over. Would you like to end up in a camp, now, of all times?"

The Gedalists answered this question with a confused muttering, in which Chaim could make out a few shreds of words.

"Go underground? Don't even think about it: Italy isn't like the countries you've come from, especially northern Italy. It's as populated as a chicken yard. Thee are no forests, or marshes either, and you don't know the land. The peasants wouldn't understand you, they would take you for bandits, and you'd end up becoming bandits. Be flexible: turn yourselves in."

"Where? How? To who?" Gedaleh asked.

"Try to get to Milan without attracting too much attention, and in Milan go to this address."

He wrote a few words on a slip of paper and gave it to Gedaleh, then added, "If we ever meet again, you'll tell me I gave you good advice. Now get back into your train; they're hooking up the locomotive."

When they climbed down from the car in the Central Station of Milan, under the high roof of glass and steel peppered by bombs, they thought another war had broken out. There were people camped everywhere, between the tracks, on the platforms, on the big staircases leading down to the square, on the escalators (out of order), and in the square itself. There were Italians wearing rags, coming back to their country, foreigners in rags waiting to leave for God knows where; there were Allied soldiers, with white skin or black, in their elegant uniforms, and Italian civilians, well dressed, with suitcases and rucksacks, leaving for their vacations. In the square in front of the ugly stone facade a few trams were circulating and a few rare automobiles; there were flowerbeds that had been transformed into victory gardens, then looted and abandoned, and now overgrown with weeds. Tents had been set up, in front of which wretched-looking women were cooking on makeshift fires. Other women pressed around the drinking fountains with cans, pots, and improvised receptacles. On every side there were buildings maimed by bombs.

Only Pavel knew a few words of Italian, learned in the days when he traveled around Europe as an actor. He showed the address to a passerby, who looked at him suspiciously and answered, with irritation, "No longer exists!" What no longer existed? Was the address wrong? Or had the building collapsed? The conversation was painful, hindered by reciprocal incomprehension: "Fascio, fascism, fascisti: nothing, finished," the passerby kept repeating. Pavel finally understood that this address had been an important Fascist headquarters, which now no longer existed: however, the Milanese explained as best he could the way to get there. They would have to walk three kilometers: what were three kilometers? A laughable distance. They set off, shy and curious; never, in all their very long march, had they felt so foreign.

It was early afternoon. They proceeded in an untidy file, careful not to lose sight of Pavel, who was marching at the head; but often they held him back so they could take a look around. Blackened ruins alternated with tall, intact, pretentious buildings; many shops were open, the windows crammed with tempting goods under the incomprehensible signs. Only around the station were there ragged people; the passersby they encountered in the downtown streets were well dressed and cordially answered their questions, trying to understand and to make themselves understood. Via Unione? Straight ahead, another two kilometers. One kilometer. Duomo. Duomo? *Capeesh?* Piazza del Duomo, then straight on. In front of the bulk of the Duomo, pockmarked by the shelling, they stopped, suspicious, dirty, and intimidated, laden with their sun-faded bundles; furtively, Piotr blessed himself with three fingers joined, Russian-style.

In via Unione they found again an atmosphere that was more familiar to them. The Assistance Center was teeming with refugees, Poles, Russians, Czechs, Hungarians; al-

most all of them spoke Yiddish; all of them needed everything, and the confusion was extreme. There were men,
women, and children encamped in the corridors, families
that had built themselves shelters with sheets of plywood
or strung-up blankets. All along the halls and behind the
windows there were women of every age, busy, breathless,
perspiring, tireless. None of them understood Yiddish
and only a few, German; improvised interpreters yelled
in an effort to establish order and discipline. The air was
torrid, with odors of latrine and kitchen. An arrow and
a sign, written in Yiddish, indicated the window the newcomers should report to; they got in line and waited patiently.

The line moved slowly, and Mendel was pondering
shapeless and contradictory thoughts. He, too, had never
been so foreign: Russian in Italy, Hebrew facing the
Duomo, village watchmender in a big city, partisan in
peacetime; foreigner in language and in spirit, foreigner
alienated by years of savage life. And yet, never before, in
none of the hundred places they had crossed, had he
breathed the air he was breathing here. Foreigner, but accepted, and not only by the kind ladies of the Assistance
Center. Not tolerated, accepted; in the faces of the Italians
they had spoken to, from the Brenner on, there was sometimes a flash of distrust or slyness, but never that murky
shadow that separates you from the Russian or the Pole
when he recognizes you as a Jew. In this country they are
all like Piotr; perhaps less brave, or more sly, or only older.
Sly the way old people are, who have seen a lot.

Mendel and Pavel presented themselves at the window
side by side; behind the window there was a lady of about
thirty, in a neatly pressed white blouse, tiny, pretty, polite,
with brown hair fresh from the hairdresser's. She was per-
fumed, and beside the wave of her perfume, Mendel perceived uneasily the heavy, goatish odor of Pavel's sweating
body. The lady understood German and spoke it fairly
well: there were no great difficulties of understanding, but
Pavel made a point of speaking Italian, thus complicating

instead of simplifying the situation. Name, once again: age, where from, nationality. Three or four of them answered at the same time, and there was some confusion. The lady realized they were a group, and showing no signs of impatience, she asked Pavel to answer for all of them: she addressed him formally, as *Sie*, and this, too, was pleasant, embarrassing, and had never happened before. It really was an assistance center: they were trying to assist, to be helpful, not to get rid of them or to shut them up in a box of barbed wire.

The lady wrote and wrote; thirty-five names are a lot, and the list was growing longer. Exotic first names and surnames, bristling with consonants; she had to stop, check, ask for a word to be repeated, the spelling. There, done. The lady leaned from the window to look at them. A group, a strange group; refugees different from usual, different from the human flotsam that for days and days had been filing past her in that office. Dirty and tired, but erect: different in their eyes, in their speech, their behavior.

"Have you always been together?" she asked Pavel, in German.

Pavel didn't miss this opportunity to cut a figure. He summoned up all the shreds of Italian he had collected years before in his travels, picked up backstage, in cheap hotels and brothels. He swelled his chest.

"*Gruppo*, lovely signora. Group. *Sempre* together. Russia, Polandia. March. Forest, river, snow. Dead Germans. Many. We *partizani*, all of us, *porca miseria*. No DP. We, war, *partizanka*. All soldiers, *madosha*. Women, too."

The lovely signora was puzzled. She asked the Gedalists please to step aside and wait, and she picked up the telephone. She spoke at length, in an excited voice, but covering her mouth with her hand to avoid being overheard. In the end, she told Pavel to be patient: they would have to spend another night camping, here in the corridors, too, as best they could. But the next day she would find a better arrangement for them. Wash up? It wasn't easy. There were no baths, not even any showers; the buildings had been reactivated only recently. But there was water, lavatories, soap, and even three or four towels. Not many for all these people, of course, but what was to be done? It wasn't her fault, or her colleagues'; they were all doing their best, even making personal contributions. In her words and in her face Mendel read reverence, pity, solidarity, and alarm.

"Where are you sending us?" he asked her, in his best German.

The lady smiled beautifully, and with her hand she made a complicated and allusive gesture that Mendel didn't understand.

"We're not sending you to the refugee camp, but to another place more suitable for you."

In fact, the next morning two trucks came to load them up; the signora reassured them, they wouldn't be going far, to a farm on the outskirts of Milan, half an hour's trip at most; they would get along well there, better than in the city, more comfortable, more relaxed. . . . So she'll be more relaxed, Mendel thought. He asked her how she happened to speak German: are there many Italians who speak it? Very few, the lady answered, but she was a German teacher; yes, she had taught it in a school, until Hitler came and she escaped to Switzerland. Switzerland is forty kilometers from Milan. She had been interned in Switzerland with her husband and her little boy; it wasn't bad there; she had come back to Milan only a few weeks ago. She watched the spectacle of the Gedalists climbing into the trucks with their gypsy baggage; she said she would be in touch with them, then said good-bye, and went back into the office.

The farm had been damaged during the last days of the war, then patched up again. They found about fifty Polish and Hungarian refugees there, but the rooms were spacious, enough for at least two or three hundred people, and well equipped with cots and bunks. They looked around: no, no sentries, no barbed wire, for the first time. It wasn't a house, but almost; no restrictions, if you want to come in, come in; if you want to go, go. Food at the proper times, water, sunshine, grass, a bed: practically a hotel, what more do you want? But you always want something more: nothing is ever as beautiful as you expect; but then nothing is ever as ugly as you expect, either, Mendel thought, recalling the days of industrious fervor at Novoselki, in the midst of the fog and the swamps, and the oblivious intoxication of the battles.

There was a second registration at a second window: a thin, brisk young man, who spoke Yiddish well but came from Tel Aviv. He signed them in without too much paperwork, but when he came to Bella and White Rokhele he stopped: no, no, not them, they have to go back to Milan, they're not suited to farm work; especially this woman here: what are they up to in via Unione, have they gone crazy? What's come over them, sending a pregnant woman here to us? Line intervened, Gedaleh, Pavel, and Isidor, who shouted loudest of all: we won't split up, we're not refugees, we're a band, united. If White R. goes to Milan, then all of us go to Milan. The young man made a strange face, but he didn't insist.

But he had to insist the next day. There was some work to be done, an urgent job: the Gedalists realized that this was a strange farm, where farm work counted little, and instead there was a great traffic of merchandise. There were crates of food and medicines, but some were too heavy for you to believe what was printed on them, in English. The young man said everybody had to lend a hand to load the crates onto the trucks. Three or four of the Ruzany men grumbled that they hadn't cleared themselves a path, fighting, from Byelorussia into Italy, to become porters, and one even muttered, "Kapo." Zvi, the young manager of the farm, didn't heed the insult, shrugged, and said: "When your ship comes, this stuff will be useful for you, too." And then, with the help of two Hungarian boys, he fell to loading the crates himself with a will. Then all of them stopped complaining and went to work.

At the farm there was a great movement of people, too: refugees of every age came and went, so it was difficult to pursue acquaintances. All the Gedalists soon realized that certain of the residents were permanent: they avoided attracting attention, but they must have performed some essential function. Two, in particular, aroused Mendel's interest. They were about thirty, athletic, agile; they spoke little, and between themselves they spoke Russian. Often they went out into the farmyard with a team of young men, carrying sickles, pitchforks, and rakes, and they vanished towards the river. They would come back only at evening; from the wood that flanked the river at times isolated shots were heard.

"Who are those two?" Mendel asked Zvi.

"Instructors. They're from the Red Army: smart boys. If any of you . . ."

"We'll talk about it another time," Mendel said, without committing himself. "We've just arrived; give us time to breathe. And anyway, I don't believe our bunch has much to learn."

"*Nu*, I didn't mean that. On the contrary, I meant that you have a lot to teach," Zvi said, underlining his words. Mendel remembered the proposal that Smirnov had made him at the Glogau camp, and that he hadn't accepted because of his weariness. No, he felt no regret. In all conscience, no. We have done our part, me and all the others. Not now, in any case; we're still catching our breath, we haven't yet learned to breathe the air of this country.

After a couple of days a letter arrived at the camp from Milan: it was written in German, addressed to Herrn Pavel Yurevich Levinski, signed by Signora Adele S.; it gave off the same perfume as the pretty lady in via Unione, and it carried an invitation for tea, Sunday afternoon, at five, in her house in via Monforte. The invitation wasn't limited to Pavel, but said vaguely, "You and some of your friends"; not too many, in other words, not the whole band: only reasonable. This stirred up a great excitement, and the band was divided into three factions: those who wanted to go to the tea party, those who didn't want to go at any price, and the uncertain and indifferent. Pavel himself wanted to go, and so did Bella, Gedaleh, Line, and a good number of the others, impelled by various motives. Pavel, because he considered himself indispensable as interpreter, and because it was his name on the envelope; Bella and Gedaleh out of curiosity; Line for ideological reasons, namely because she was the only one in the band who had had a Zionist education; and the others because they hoped to find something good to eat. Piotr and Arie didn't want to go out of shyness and because they didn't understand German; White R. because for several days she'd been having abdominal pains; Isidor didn't want to be separated from her; and Mottel, because he said the signora's *goyische* ways made him ill at ease, and he didn't see himself in a drawing room.

So Pavel, Bella, Line, Gedaleh, and Mendel went. Mendel, to tell the truth, was among the uncertain, but the other four insisted that he come: it was a unique opportunity to see how the Italians live, they would enjoy themselves, have fun, they would have a chance to hear useful news; but above all, whether he liked it or not, he was the key man of the band, the one who represented them best and had taken part in all their ventures; and hadn't he belonged to the Red Army? Certainly for the Italians this would be important, or at least interesting.

They put on their best clothes. Line, who owned nothing but the clumsy army clothing she had worn since Novoselki, said she would go to the party just as she was: "If I put on something else, it would be like wearing a disguise. Like I was telling a lie. If they want me, they have to take me as I am."

But they all tried to convince her to dress a bit better, especially Bella and Zvi. From the farm's storerooms Zvi produced a white silk blouse, a pleated ivory cotton skirt, a leather belt, a pair of nylon stockings and some cork-soled sandals. Line let herself be convinced and she withdrew, carrying the trousseau; a few minutes later, from the dressing room, a totally unfamiliar creature sprang forth, like a butterfly from the cocoon. Almost unrecognizable: tinier than the Line they all knew, younger, almost a child, clumsy in the skirt, since she had worn none for years, and in the high orthopedic sandals; but her dark, steady eyes, widely set, and the thin, straight snub nose, had remained the same, and so had the tense pallor of her cheeks, that sun and wind were unable to tan. The film of nylon lent grace to her slender legs and ankles; Bella grazed them with one hand, as if to make sure they weren't bare.

In the living room of Signora S. there were many guests, all Italian. Some were dressed elegantly, others in threadbare clothes: still others wore Allied uniforms. Only two or three understood Russian, and none spoke Yiddish, so the conversation immediately became complicated. The five of the band, as if to defend themselves against attack, tried to stick together, but this succeeded only for a few minutes: soon each of them found himself isolated, surrounded by curious guests and subjected to a hail of questions, melodious and incomprehensible. Pavel and the signora were kept busy translating, but with scant results; the supply was too inferior to the demand. Through a gap between two backs, Mendel glimpsed Line, assailed by five or six elegant ladies. "Like animals in the zoo," the girl murmured to him in Yiddish.

"Fierce animals," Mendel answered. "If they knew everything we've done, they'd be scared of us."

The hostess was anxious. They were hers, those five: a *trouvaille*, a discovery of hers, and she claimed her monopoly. Every word spoken by them belonged to her, should not be lost; she went to great lengths to pursue them through the press of her guests, making them repeat to her the remarks she hadn't heard. But she was anxious also for another reason: she was a refined, properly educated lady, and certain things that the five were telling offended her

ears. Pavel and Gedaleh, especially, had no reticence. One
knows, these things exist, they happened, war is no joke,
and even less of a joke the war that these poor people had
fought; but in a living room, really, in her living room. . . .
Yes, feats of valor were all right, reprisals against the Germans, sabotage, marches in the snow; but they needn't
talk about lice, and the way they bound their feet, and the
people hanged in the latrines. . . . She almost regretted
having invited them: chiefly because of Pavel, who unfortunately knew a few words of Italian, but, for some unknown reason, seemed to have a distinct preference for
curses and dirty words. She couldn't deceive herself: her
friends would have a good laugh and would tell the story
all over Milan. After half an hour she took refuge on a corner sofa, beside Bella, who seemed less rough, spoke little,
and ate chocolates, admiring the pictures on the walls.
Every now and then the signora glanced at the grandfather clock; her husband was late. If only he would hurry
up and get there! He would help her hold the reins of the
party, so that every guest, exotic or local, would receive his
due and not transgress.

Signor S. arrived a little before six and apologized to
everybody: his train had left Lugano on time, but he had
been held up at the border for the usual checks. He kissed
his wife and apologized to her, too. He was stout, cordial,
noisy, bald, with a crown of blondish hair around the
back of his head. He also spoke German, but hit-or-miss,
without grammar; he had picked it up in his travels. He
was in business; he went abroad often. He found himself
facing Mendel and immediately began describing his
business as if he had always known him, the way people
do when they have great self-esteem and little interest in
the person they are addressing. How uncomfortable travel
was, how hard it was to reestablish contacts. . . . Mendel
thought of the way they had traveled and of trading salt
for the Uzbek's rabbit; but he said nothing. The other
man finally broke off: "But you must be thirsty. Come,
come with me!"

He grasped Mendel's wrist and pulled him to the refreshments table. Mendel, dazed, went along: he was feeling an intense sensation of unreality, as in the dreams you dream when your stomach's too full. He took advantage of the moment when S. was raising a glass to his mouth and found the courage to ask him the questions that had been buzzing in his head since the beginning of the party. Who were all these people? Were he and his wife really Jews? Was this house theirs? Hadn't the Germans come here too, to Milan? How had they saved themselves, and all the beautiful things he could see around him? Were all Italian Jews rich like them? Or all the Italians? Did they all have beautiful houses like this?

His host looked at him with a strange expression, as if Mendel's questions were stupid or inopportune; and he answered patiently, as if talking with a not very bright child. Why, of course, they were Jews, anybody with the name S. was Jewish. Their guests, no, not all of them; but was it that important? They were friends, that's all, nice people, wanting to know them, who have come from far away. And the house was his: why not? He had made good money, before the war, and even during the first years of the war, until the Nazis came. Afterwards, they had requisitioned the house and installed a high Fascist official in it, but he, S., the moment he got back from Switzerland, had moved a few pawns and had got the Fascist out. No, no, not everybody had a house like his: neither Christians nor Jews. Not everybody, but many: Milan is a rich city. Rich and generous, many Jews had remained in the city, hidden or with faked documents; their neighbors and friends that they met pretended not to know them, but secretly brought them food.

The two were interrupted by a big man with a light, youthful voice, who neither spoke nor understood German, but acted extremely friendly with Mendel. He asked to be introduced: S. made the introduction, mispronouncing the name of Mendel, and he said to Mendel, "This is Signor Longo, the lawyer." The lawyer proved more tactful than their host; he listened in respectful silence to the story that Mendel told, in an abridged form, and that the host translated sentence by sentence, and in the end he said to him, "These friends of yours must be tired: they need rest. Ask them if they would like to be my guests at Varazze. There's room in my villa, and perhaps they have never seen the sea!"

The invitation caught Mendel by surprise. He hesitated, stalled for time, then tried to reach his companions and consult them. He wouldn't have accepted, himself; he felt distant, different, unpleasant, wild; he felt he carried on him the sepulchral smell of Schmulek's cave. Still, if the others said yes, he would agree. Bella, Line, and Gedaleh also tended to refuse: they invented vague excuses, the fact was that they were intimidated, they didn't feel up to the role being thrust on them. Pavel, on the other hand, would have liked to accept, but not alone; so he fell in with the majority opinion, and they all thanked and declined, happy that their awkward words were being translated into the harmonious Italian of Signora S. "All the same, I wouldn't have minded seeing the sea," Bella murmured to Gedaleh.

Their hostess exploited the moment when the five were together and introduced them to another friend, a tall and bony young man with an energetic look, who was wearing shirt and trousers of a military cut, but without insignia or chevrons. "This is Francesco, a colleague of yours," she said, with a sly smile; Francesco, on the contrary, remained serious. "He was also a partisan," the signora went on. "In maltellina, in the Alps, in these mountains you see down there, in other words. A young man with nerve: too bad he's a Communist."

With the signora interpreting, the conversation proceeded with difficulty, contorted; but when Francesco learned that Mendel had belonged to the Red Army, he came over and embraced him: "From the day Germany attacked you, I never doubted for a moment that Germany would be defeated. You tell him, Adele. Tell him that we fought, too, but if the Soviet Union hadn't held out, it would have been the end of Europe." The signora translated as best she could, and added, on her own; "He's a dear boy, but hardheaded, and he has strange ideas. If it was up to him, he wouldn't think twice: dictatorship of the proletariat, the land to the peasants, the factories to the workers, and that would be that. At most, for us, for his friends, a little job at the local soviet."

Francesco only half understood and didn't go into it; still grave, he made her say that his party had been the backbone of the Resistance and the true voice of the Italian people; then he had her ask Mendel why he and his friends were leaving their country. Mendel was embarrassed. He had some vague ideas about what had happened in Italy during the war, he was amazed that the signora said so openly that her friend was a Communist: was it a joke perhaps? And was she also joking when she referred to her fear of communism? Or was she really afraid of it? And if she was, was she right to be afraid? But now he had to answer this Francesco's question. How to explain to him that being a Jew in Russia or Poland wasn't like being a Jew in Switzerland or in Milan, in via Monforte? He would have liked to tell the young man their whole story. He confined himself to saying that he and his companions had nothing against Stalin; on the contrary, they were grateful to him for having destroyed Hitler; but their homes had also been destroyed, they had the void behind them, and they were hoping to find a home in Palestine. The signora translated, and Mendel had the impression that the translation was longer than the text; Francesco looked unconvinced, and went off. To Mendel, the faces of the Italians weren't clear, either; their expressions, their grimaces: he was unable to read them, or was afraid he read them wrong. Francesco. A partisan, a fellow fighter. How long did you fight, Francesco? Sixteen months, eighteen: after Venjamin's radio on the shore of the Dnepr announced that Mussolini was in prison, after Dov learned that Italy had surrendered. How far did you walk, Francesco? How many friends did you lose? Where is your home? In Milan, perhaps, or on these mountains whose name I can't say; but you have a home, a home you fought for, as well as for your ideas. A home, a land beneath your feet, a sky above your head that is yours and always the same. A mother and a father; a girl or a wife. You have someone and something that makes you want to live. If I spoke your language I could try to explain to you.

Behind him, Signora Adele talked with Line: ". . . but now they are the ones who help us most. The arms come from them, through Czechoslovakia. It's the Italian Communist party that declares the strikes; when the English try to stop a refugee ship, all the workers in the port go out on strike, and the English have to let it sail . . ."

Mendel felt disoriented: in a living room filled with beautiful things and polite people; and he felt also like a pawn in a gigantic, cruel game. Perhaps always, always a pawn, and he had been a missing person, since he had met Leonid: you think you're making a decision and instead you are following the destiny someone else has already written. Who? Stalin, or Roosevelt, or the Lord of Hosts. He turned to Gedaleh: "Let's go, Gedaleh. Let's say goodbye. This isn't our place."

"What?" Gedaleh asked, amazed: perhaps he was afraid he hadn't understood, or was following another train of thought. At that moment the phone rang in the corner where Bella was sitting, and the signora went to answer it. A little later she put down the receiver and said to Mendel, "It's Zvi, at the farm. Your friend, the one you call White, isn't well. They had to bring her into town. She's in a hospital, not far from here."

They reached the maternity hospital, all five of them, packed into the car of Longo the lawyer. It was a private hospital, neat and clean, but many of the windowpanes had been replaced with plywood panels, and strips of paper were glued across the others. Rokhele was in a room with three other women; she was pale, calm, and moaning faintly: perhaps they had given her a sedative. In the corridor, outside the door of the room, there was Isidor, nervous and frowning, along with Izu, the one who went fishing barehanded, and three others from Blizna, the roughest in the band. Isidor paced up and down, and had a pistol thrust into his belt. Two of his companions were sitting on the floor and seemed drunk; the other two talked among themselves at the window. Mendel could see through the worn leather of their boots the bulge of their knives. On the windowsill there was a bottle of red wine and two peasant loaves.

"How is she?" Bella whispered to Isidor.

Without lowering his voice, Isidor replied, "She's not well. It hurts. She was yelling, before. Now they gave her an injection." At the end of the corridor two nuns peeked in, exchanged a few words, and promptly disappeared.

"Come away; she's in good hands," Mendel said, "what are you all doing here?"

"I'm not moving," Isidor said. The other four said nothing: they simply gave Mendel and the rest a hostile look.

"You're not helping, and you're getting in the way," Line said.

"I'm not moving," Isidor repeated. "I stay here; I don't trust them."

The five went off to one side. "What are we going to do?" Gedaleh asked.

"There are too many of us here," Mendel said. "I'll stay and see what happens; I'll try to calm them down. You go back to the farm: the lawyer is waiting below. If things look bad, I'll telephone you."

"I'm staying, too," Line said, unexpectedly. "A woman can be useful." Gedaleh, Bella, and Pavel went off; Line and Mendel sat in the armchairs in the waiting room. Through the half-open door they could keep an eye on the five men camping in the corridor.

"Is Isidor drunk, too?" Line asked.

"He doesn't seem drunk to me," Mendel answered. "He's acting up because he's afraid."

"Afraid about the birth. For Rokhele?"

"Yes, but maybe not only for that. He's a boy, and he needs to feel important. Gedaleh was wrong to let him drive the truck."

Line, in her unfamiliar feminine clothng, seemed also changed on the inside. She answered softly, "When was that? In February, wasn't it? There was still snow."

"It was the beginning of March, when we left Wolbrom; yes, it must have been just at the beginning of March."

"It's hard to keep memories straight, isn't it? Doesn't it happen to you, too?"

Mendel nodded, without speaking. A nurse came and said something to them in Italian; Line and Mendel didn't understand, the nurse shrugged and went off. Line entered Rokhele's room and came out again at once. "She's sleeping," Line said. "She seems calm, but her pulse is fast."

"Maybe that's how it is with all women in childbirth."

"I don't know," Line answered. She was silent, then went on: "We're not made right. Does it seem right to you that a man should become a father at the age of seventeen?"

"Maybe it's never right to become a father," Mendel said.

"Shut up, Mendel. Don't think those thoughts. Tonight a baby must be born."

"Do you think our thoughts can touch him? Make him be born different?"

"Who knows?" Line said. "A newborn baby is such a delicate thing! Where was he conceived?"

Mendel made a mental calculation. "When we were with Edek, near Tunel. In November. Will he be a Polish baby? Or Ukrainian, like Rokhele? Or Italian?"

"*Narische bucher, vos darst du fregen?*" Line said, laughing, and quoting the song that had marked the passage of the front: "Foolish boy, why must you ask?" Strangely, Mendel was not in the least offended at being called that: on the contrary, he was moved. This new Line was no longer Rahab, but the pitying, clever *meidele* of the song.

"Why must you ask?" Line repeated, putting her hand on Mendel's forearm. "A baby's a baby; he becomes something else only later. Why are you worrying? Anyway, he's not even our child."

"True. He's not even our child."

"We were also born," Line said abruptly. Mendel questioned her with a look, and Line tried to clarify her thought: "Born, expelled. Russia conceived us, nourished us, made us grow in her darkness, as in a womb; then she had labor pains, contractions, and threw us out; and now here we are, naked and new, like babies just born. Isn't it the same for you?"

"Narische meidele, vos darst du fregen?" Mendel rebutted, feeling on his lips an affectionate smile and a light veil over his eyes.

There was movement in the corridor, footsteps, whispers. Mendel stood up and went to peer in at the door: White R. was breathing heavily and moaning at intervals. All of a sudden she writhed and cried out, twice, three times. The four Blizna men sprang to their feet, bellicose and sleepy; Isidor knelt beside the bed, then strode out into the corridor. He came back a minute later, dragging a nun and the doctor on duty after him. All three were frightened, for different reasons. Isidor was shouting in Yiddish, "This woman must not die, Doctor, you understand me? She's my wife, we've come all the way here from Russia, we fought, we marched. And the baby is my son, he has to be born. He mustn't die, you understand? God help you if the woman or the baby dies: we're partisans. Go on, doctor, do what you have to do, and be careful about it."

Line went over to Isidor, to calm him and reassure him, but Isidor, who kept his hand on the grip of the pistol stuck into his belt, pushed her violently away. The doctor didn't understand Yiddish, but he understood the meaning of a pistol in the hand of a terrified boy; he spoke rapidly with the nun, then he took a step towards the telephone at the corner of the corridor, but Isidor blocked his path. Then the doctor and the nun took the litter, on rollers, that was nearby and shifted White R. on to it, and she continued screaming; they headed for the delivery room. Isidor signaled to his friends and followed. Mendel and Line followed Isidor.

Isidor didn't dare force his way into the delivery room. The seven sat down outside the door, as the hours began to go by. Several times Mendel tried to calm Isidor and make him hand over the pistol. He would even have tried to tear it away from him, if he hadn't seen the other four at his back. He didn't achieve anything. Isidor was facing him, without listening: first arrogant, then completely concentrated on the muffled sounds that came from the room.

Sitting beside Line, Mendel looked at her knees that protruded beneath the skirt. He was seeing them for the first time: never before, except with his clairvoyant fingers, trembling with desire, in the darkness of their pallets, different every night, or through the dull fabric of her trousers. Don't give way. Don't give way to her. Don't start again, be wise, hold out. You wouldn't live a life at her side, she isn't a woman for a lifetime, and you're not yet thirty. At thirty life can begin again. Like a book, when you've finished the first volume. Begin again from where? From here, from today, from this Milanese dawn that is breaking beyond the frosted glass: from this morning. This is a good place to start living. Perhaps you should have done as they did, they were right, the two nebbishes; they didn't act like you with Line, they closed their eyes and abandoned themselves, and the man's seed was not spilled, and a woman conceived.

A nun went by pushing a trolley. Line, tired and dozing, stirred and said, "It's been a long time since I spent a night awake."

"It's been a long time since we spent a night together," Mendel answered. No, I wouldn't live a lifetime with

Line, but I can't leave her, and I don't want to leave her. I will carry her inside me always, even if we are separated, as I was separated from Rivke.

They could hear the city waking, the trams shrieking, the shutters of the shops being pulled up. A nurse came from the delivery room, then the doctor himself came out and went back in a moment later. Isidor, no longer arrogant but supplicating, asked questions that were understood despite the language: the doctor made reassuring gestures, showed his wristwatch: in two hours, an hour. They heard repeated cries, a motor hum, then silence. Finally, in broad daylight, a nurse came out with a happy face, carrying a bundle. "A boy, a boy." She was laughing. Nobody understood; she looked around, found the hairy Izu at hand, and gave his beard a tug. "Male—like him!"

They all stood up. Mendel and Line hugged Isidor, whose eyes, reddened from lack of sleep, had become shiny. The doctor also came out, slapped Isidor on the shoulder, and started down the corridor, but he encountered a colleague coming with an unfolded newspaper and stopped to discuss things with him. Around the two, other doctors gathered, nuns, nurses. Mendel also went over and managed to see that the newspaper, consisting of a single sheet, bore a very big headline, whose meaning he couldn't understand. That newspaper bore the date of Tuesday 7 August 1945 and carried the news of the first atomic bomb, dropped on Hiroshima.

AUTHOR'S NOTE

THIS BOOK WAS BORN from things told me many years ago by a friend of mine, who in the summer of 1945, in Milan, had worked as a volunteer at the assistance center described in the final chapter. At that time, along with a great tide of repatriated Italians and refugees, some bands similar to the one I have aimed to portray really did arrive in Italy: men and women whom years of suffering had hardened but not humiliated, survivors of a civilization (almost unknown in Italy) that Nazism had destroyed to its roots. Exhausted, these survivors still were aware of their dignity.

My purpose has not been to write a true story, but rather to reconstruct the itinerary, invented but plausible, of one of these bands. For the most part, the events I depict really did take place, even if not always on the sites and dates I have given them. It is true that Jewish partisans fought the Germans, almost always in desperate conditions, sometimes as members of more or less regular bands under the Russians or the Poles, and at other times in units composed entirely of Jews. There were wandering bands like Venjamin's, which, depending on the situation, accepted or rejected (and sometimes disarmed or killed) the Jewish fighters. It is true that groups of Jews, amounting to a total of ten or fifteen thousand people, survived for a long time, some of them until the end of the war, in fortified camps like the one I have arbitrarily situated in Novoselki, or even (incredible as it may seem) in catacombs like the one where I have placed Schmulek. Actions of harassment, such as sabotaging railroads and misdirecting parachute drops, are amply documented in the literature on partisan warfare in eastern Europe.

With the sole exception of Polina, the girl pilot, all the characters are imaginary. In particular, the figure of Martin Fontasch is imaginary; but it is true that many Jewish poet-singers, famous and obscure, in cities and in remote villages, were killed as this Martin is, and not only in the years 1939–1945, and not only by the Nazis. So the song of the "Gedalists" is also invented, but its refrain, which is also the title of this book, was prompted by some words I found in the *Pirké Avoth* (*The Maxims of the Fathers*), a collection of sayings of famous rabbis, edited in the second century A.D. and a part of the Talmud. In the first chapter, verse thirteen, it says: "He (Rabbi Hillel) also said: 'If I am not for myself, who will be for me? And even if I think of myself, what am I? And if not now, when?' " Naturally, the interpretation of this saying that I attribute to the characters is not the Orthodox one.

Since I had to reconstruct a period, a setting, and a language that I myself knew only marginally, I relied considerably on documents, and many books proved valuable for reference. I list the main ones:

Ainsztein R. *Jewish Resistance in Nazi-Occupied Eastern Europe*. London: P. Elek, 1974.
Armstrong, J. A. *Soviet Partisans in World War II*. Madison: The University of Wisconsin Press, 1964.

Artuso, A. *Solo in un deserto di ghiaccio.* Torino: Tipografia Bogliani, 1980.

Ayalti, H. J. *Yiddish Proverbs.* New York: Schocken Books, 1963.

Eliav A., *Tra il martello e la falce.* Roma: Barulli, 1970.

Elkins, M. *Forged in Fury.* New York: Ballantine Books, 1971.

Kaganovic, M. *Di milkhomeh fun di Jiddische Partisaner in Mizrach-Europe.* Buenos Aires: Union Central Israelita Polaca, 1956.

Kamenetsky, J. *Hitler's Occupation of Ukraine.* Milwaukee: Marquette University Press, 1956.

Karol, K. S. *La Polonia da Pilsudski a Gomulka.* Bari: Laterza, 1959.

Kovpak, S. A., *Les Partisans Soviétiques.* Paris: La jeune Parque, 1945.

Landmann, S. *Jüdische Witze.* München: DTV, 1963.

Litvinoff, B. *La lunga strada per Gerusalemme.* Milano: Il Saggiatore, 1968.

Minerbi, S. *Raffaele Cantoni.* Roma: Carucci, 1978.

Pinkus, O. *A Choice of Masks.* Englewood Cliffs, N.J.: Prentice-Hall, 1969.

Sereni, A. *I clandestini del mare.* Milano: Mursia, 1973.

Sorrentino, L. *Isba e Steppa.* Milano: Mondadori, 1947.

Vaccarino, G. *Storia della Resistenza in Europa 1938–1945.* Vol. 1. Milano: Feltrinelli, 1981.

I thank these authors, as I thank all those who encouraged me with their views, and whose criticisms were my guide. I owe a special debt of thanks to Emilio Vita Finzi, who narrated to me the kernel of the story and without whom the book would not have been written; and to Giorgio Vaccarino, who followed my work affectionately and placed his remarkable archive at my disposal.